PRIZE STORIES 1986

The O. Henry Awards

PRIZE STORIES 1986

The O. Henry Awards

EDITED AND WITH
AN INTRODUCTION
BY WILLIAM ABRAHAMS

Anchor Books

ANCHOR PRESS/DOUBLEDAY
Garden City, New York
1986

Library of Congress Catalog in Publication Data

Prize stories. 1947–
Garden City, N. Y., Doubleday.

v. 22 cm.

Annual.
The O. Henry awards.
None published 1952–53.
Continues: O. Henry memorial award prize stories.
Key title: Prize stories, ISSN 0079-5453.

1. Short stories, American—Collected works.
PZ1.O11 813'.01'08—dc19 21-9372
MARC-S
Library of Congress [8402r83]rev4

ISBN 9780385231565(pbk)

PRINTED IN THE UNITED STATES OF AMERICA

146718297

CONTENTS

PUBLISHER'S NOTE

This volume is the sixty-sixth in the O. Henry Memorial Award series.

In 1918, the Society of Arts and Sciences met to vote upon a monument to the master of the short story, O. Henry. They decided that this memorial should be in the form of two prizes for the best short stories published by American authors in American magazines during the year 1919. From this beginning, the memorial developed into an annual anthology of outstanding short stories by American authors, published, with the exception of the years 1952 and 1953, by Doubleday & Company, Inc.

Blanche Colton Williams, one of the founders of the awards, was editor from 1919 to 1932; Harry Hansen from 1933 to 1940; Herschel Brickell from 1941 to 1951. The annual collection did not appear in 1952 and 1953, when the continuity of the series was interrupted by the death of Herschel Brickell. Paul Engle was editor from 1954 to 1959 with Hanson Martin coeditor in the years 1954 to 1960; Mary Stegner in 1960; Richard Poirier from 1961 to 1966, with assistance from and coeditorship with William Abrahams from 1964 to 1966. William Abrahams became editor of the series in 1967.

In 1970 Doubleday published under Mr. Abrahams' editorship *Fifty Years of the American Short Story,* and in 1981, *Prize Stories of the Seventies.* Both are collections of stories selected from this series.

The stories chosen for this volume were published in the period from the summer of 1984 to the summer of 1985. A list of the magazines consulted appears at the back of the book. The choice of stories and the selection of prize winners are exclusively the responsibility of the editor. Biographical material is based on information provided by the contributors and obtained from standard works of reference.

her that night as she tried to sleep, then became lost in the many other questions that presented themselves well into the dawn.

Why, for instance, did Ivan no longer like her? And how could you live with someone for over a decade and "love" them, and then, as soon as you were no longer married, you didn't even like them?

Her marriage had been wonderful, she felt. Only the divorce was horrible.

The most horrible thing of all was losing Ivan's friendship and comradely support, which he yanked out of her reach with a vengeance that sent her reeling. Two weeks after the divorce became final, when she was in the hospital for surgery that only after the fact proved to have been minor, he neither called nor sent a note. Sheila, now his wife, wouldn't have liked it, he later (years later) explained.

The next day all the children were in school, and Barbara stood behind Aunt Lily's chair combing and braiding her long silver hair. Rosa sat on the couch looking at them. Raymyna busily vacuumed the bedroom floors, popping in occasionally to bring the mail or a glass of water. She was getting married in a couple of weeks and would be moving out to start her own family. Rosa had of course not said anything when she heard this, but her inner response was surprise. She could not easily comprehend anyone getting married, now that she no longer was, but it was impossible for her to feel happy at the prospect of yet another poor black woman marrying God knows who and starting a family. She would have thought Raymyna would have already had enough.

But who was she to talk. Miss Cynical. She had married. And enjoyed it. She had had a child, and adored it.

In the afternoon her aunt and Raymyna took them sight-seeing. As she understood matters from the local newspapers, all the water she saw—whether canal, river, or ocean—was polluted beyond recall, so that it was hard even to look at it, much less to look at it admiringly. She could only gaze at it in sympathy. The beach she also found pitiable. In their attempt to hog it away from the poor, the black, and the local in general, the beachfront "developers" had erected massive boxlike hotels that blocked the view of the water for all except those rich enough to pay for rooms on the beach side of the hotels. Through the cracks between hotels Rosa saw the mostly elderly sun worshipers walking along what seemed to be a pebbly, eroded beach, stretching out their poor white necks to the sun.

Of course they cruised through Little Havana, which stretched for miles. Rosa looked at the new Cuban immigrants with interest. *Gusa-*

nos, Fidel called them, "worms." She was startled to see that already they seemed as a group to live better and to have more material goods than the black people. Like many Americans who supported the Cuban revolution, she found the Cubans who left Cuba somewhat less noble than the ones who stayed. Clearly the ones who left were the ones with money. Hardly anyone in Cuba could afford the houses, the cars, the clothes, the television sets, and the lawn mowers she saw.

At dinner she tried to explain why and how she had missed her grandfather's funeral. The telegram had come the evening before she left for Cyprus. As she had left her stoop the next morning she had felt herself heading in the wrong direction. But she could not stop herself. It had taken all her meager energy to plan the trip to Cyprus, with a friend who claimed it was beautiful, and she simply could not think to change her plans. Nor could she, still bearing the wounds of her separation from Ivan, face her family.

Barbara and Aunt Lily listened to her patiently. It didn't surprise her that neither knew where Cyprus was, or what its politics and history were. She told them about the man whose son was killed and how he seemed to hate his "worthless" daughter for being alive.

"Women are not valued in their culture," she explained. "In fact, the Greeks, the Turks, and the Cypriots have this one thing in common, though they fight over everything else. The father kept saying, 'A man should have many sons.' His wife flinched guiltily when he said it."

"After Ma died, I went and got my father," Aunt Lily was saying. "And I told him, 'No smoking and drinking in my house.' "

But her grandfather had always smoked. He smoked a pipe. Rosa had liked the smell of it.

"And no card playing and no noise and no complaining, because I don't want to hear it."

Others of Rosa's brothers and sister had come to see him. She had been afraid to. In the pictures she saw, he always looked happy. When he was not dead-tired or drunk, happy was how he'd looked. A deeply silent man, with those odd peaceful eyes. She did not know, and she was confident her aunt didn't, what he really thought about anything. So he had stopped smoking, her aunt thought, but Rosa's brothers had always slipped him tobacco. He had stopped drinking. That was possible. Even before his wife, Rosa's grandmother, had died, he had given up liquor. Or, as he said, it had given him up. So, no noise. Little company. No complaining. But he wasn't the complaining type, was he? He liked best of all, Rosa thought, to be left alone. And he liked baseball. She felt he had liked her too. She hoped he did. But never did he say so. And he was so stingy! In her whole life he'd only given her fifteen cents. On the other hand, he'd financed her sister Barbara's trade-school education, which her father, his son, had refused to do.

Was that what she had held against him on the flight toward the Middle East? There was no excuse, she'd known it all the time. She needed to be back there, to say goodbye to the spiritcase. For wasn't she beginning to understand the appearance of his spiritcase as her own spirit struggled and suffered?

That night, massaging Barbara's thin shoulders before turning in, she looked into her own face reflected in the bureau mirror. She was beginning to have the look her grandfather had when he was very, very tired. The look he got just before something broke in him and he went on a mind-killing drunk. It was there in her eyes. So clearly. The look of abandonment. Of having no support. Of loneliness so severe every minute was a chant against self-destruction.

She massaged Barbara, but she knew her touch was that of a stranger. At what point, she wondered, did you lose connection with the people you loved? And she remembered going to visit Barbara when she was in college and Barbara lived a short bus ride away. And she was present when Barbara's husband beat her and called her names and once he had locked both of them out of the house overnight. And her sister called the police and they seemed nice to Rosa, so recently up from the South, but in fact they were bored and cynical as they listened to Barbara's familiar complaint. Rosa was embarrassed and couldn't believe anything so sordid could be happening to them, so respected was their family in the small town they were from. But, in any event, Barbara continued to live with her husband many more years. Rosa was so hurt and angry she wanted to kill, but most of all, she was disappointed in Barbara, who threw herself into the inevitable weekend battles with passionately vulgar language Rosa had never heard any woman, not to mention her gentle sister, use before. Her sister's spirit seemed polluted to her, so much so that the sister she had known as a child seemed gone altogether.

Was disappointment, then, the hardest thing to bear? Or was it the consciousness of being powerless to change things, to help? And certainly she had been very conscious of that. As her brother-in-law punched out her sister, Rosa had almost felt the blows on her body. But she had not flung herself between them wielding a butcher knife, as she had done once when Barbara was being attacked by their father, another raving madman.

Barbara had wanted to go to their brother's grammar-school graduation. Their father had insisted that she go to the funeral of an elderly church mother instead. Barbara had tried to refuse. But *crack,* he had slapped her across the face. She was sixteen, plump, and lovely. Rosa adored her. She ran immediately to get the knife, but she was so small no one seemed to notice her, wedging herself between them. But had she been larger and stronger she might have killed him, for even as a child she was serious in all she did—and then what would her life, the life of a murderer, have been like?

Thinking of that day now, she wept. At her love, at her sister's anguish.

Barbara had been forced to go to the funeral, the print of her father's fingers hidden by powder and rouge. Rosa had been little and weak, and she did not understand what was going on anyway between her father and her sister. To her, her father acted like he was jealous. And in college later, after such a long struggle to get there, how could she stab her brother-in-law to death without killing her future, herself? And so she had lain on her narrow foldaway cot in the tiny kitchen in the stuffy apartment over the Laundromat and had listened to the cries and whispers, the pummelings, the screams and pleas. And then, still awake, she listened to the sibilant sounds of "making up," harder to bear and to understand than the fights.

She had not killed for her sister. (And one would have had to kill the mindless drunken brutalizing husband; a blow to the head might only have made him more angry.) Her guilt had soon clouded over the love, and around Barbara she retreated into a silence that she now realized was very like her grandfather's. The sign in him of disappointment hinged to powerlessness. A thoughtful black man in the racist early-twentieth-century South, he probably could have told her a thing or two about the squeaking of the hinge. But had he? No. He'd only complained about his wife, and so convincingly that for a time Rosa, like everyone else in the family, lost respect for her grandmother. It seemed her problem was that she was not mentally quick; and because she stayed with him even as he said this, Rosa and her relatives were quick to agree. Yet there was nowhere else she could have gone. Perhaps her grandfather had found the house in which they lived, but she, her grandmother, had made it a home. Once the grandmother died, the house seemed empty, though he remained behind until Aunt Lily had moved him into her house in Miami.

The day before Rosa and Barbara were to fly back north, Aunt Lily was handing out the remaining odds and ends of their grandfather's things. Barbara got the trunk, that magic repository of tobacco and candy when they were children. Rosa received a small shaving mirror with a gilt lion on its back. There were several of the large, white "twenty-five-cent hanskers" her grandfather had used. The granddaughters received half a dozen each. That left only her grandfather's hats. One brown and one gray: old, worn, none-too-clean fedoras. Rosa knew Barbara was far too fastidious to want them. She placed one on her head. She loved how she looked—she looked like him—in it.

It was killing her, how much she loved him. And he'd been so mean to her grandmother, and so stingy too. Once he had locked her grandmother out of the house because she had bought herself a penny stick of candy from the grocery money. But this was a story her parents told her, from a time before Rosa was born.

By the time she knew him he was mostly beautiful. Peaceful, mystical almost, in his silences and calm, and she realized he was imprinted on her heart just that way. It really did not seem fair.

To check her tears, she turned to Aunt Lily.

"Tell me what my father was like as a boy," she said.

Her aunt looked at her, she felt, with hatred.

"You should have asked him when he was alive."

Rosa looked about for Barbara, who had disappeared into the bathroom. By now she was weeping openly. Her aunt looking at her impassively.

"I don't want to find myself in anything you write. And you can just leave your daddy alone, too."

She could not remember whether she'd ever asked her father about his life. But surely she had, since she knew quite a lot. She turned and walked into the bathroom, forgetful that she was thirty-five, her sister forty-one, and that you can only walk in on your sister in the toilet if you are both children. But it didn't matter. Barbara had always been accessible, always protective. Rosa remembered one afternoon when she was five or six, she and Barbara and a cousin of theirs about Barbara's age set out on an errand. They were walking silently down the dusty road when a large car driven by a white man nearly ran them down. His car sent up billows of dust from the dirt road that stung their eyes and stained their clothes. Instinctively Rosa had picked up a fistful of sand from the road and thrown it after him. He stopped the car, backed it up furiously, and slammed on the brakes, getting out next to them, three black, barefoot girls who looked at him as only they could. Was he a human being? Or a devil? At any rate, he had seen Rosa throw the sand, he said, and he wanted the older girls to warn her against doing such things, "for the little nigger's own good."

Rosa would have admitted throwing the sand. After all, the man had seen her.

But "she didn't throw no sand," said Barbara, quietly, striking a heavy, womanish pose with both hands on her hips.

"She did so," said the man, his face red from heat and anger.

"She didn't," said Barbara.

The cousin simply stared at the man. After all, what was a small handful of sand compared to the billows of sand with which he'd covered them?

Cursing, the man stomped into his car, and drove off.

For a long time it had seemed to Rosa that only black people were always in danger. But there was also the sense that her big sister would know how to help them out of it.

But now, as her sister sat on the commode, Rosa saw a look on her face that she had never seen before, and she realized her sister had heard what Aunt Lily said. It was a look that said she'd got the reply she deserved. For wasn't she always snooping about the family's business and turning things about in her writing in ways that made the family shudder? There was no talking to her as you talked to regular people. The minute you opened your mouth a meter went on. Rosa could read all this on her sister's face. She didn't need to speak. And it was a lonely feeling that she had. For Barbara was right. Aunt Lily, too. And she could no more stop the meter running than she could stop her breath. An odd look across the room fifteen years ago still held the power to make her wonder about it, try to "decipher" or at least understand it. This was her curse: never to be able to forget, truly, but only to appear to forget. And then to record what she could not forget.

Suddenly, in her loneliness, she laughed.

"He was a recorder with his eyes," she said, under her breath. For it seemed to her she'd penetrated her grandfather's serenity, his frequent silences. The meter had ticked in him, too; he, too, was all attentiveness. But for him that had had to be enough. She'd rarely seen him with a pencil in his hand; she thought he'd only had one or two years of school. She imagined him "writing" stories during his long silences merely by thinking them, not embarrassing other people with them, as she did.

She had been obsessed by this old man whom she so definitely resembled. And now, perhaps, she knew why.

We were kindred spirits, she thought, as she sat, one old dusty fedora on her head, the other in her lap, on the plane home. But in a lot of ways, before I knew him, he was a jerk.

She thought of Ivan. For it was something both of them had said often about their relationship: that though he was white and she was black, they were in fact kindred spirits. And she had thought so, until the divorce, after which his spirit became as unfathomable to her as her grandfather's would have been before she knew him. But perhaps Ivan, too, was simply acting like a jerk?

She felt, as she munched the dry crackers and cheese the pert stewardess brought, in the very wreckage of her life. She had not really looked at Barbara since that moment in the toilet, when it became clear to her how her sister really perceived her. She knew she would not see Aunt Lily again and that if Aunt Lily died before she herself did, she would not go to her funeral. Nor would she ever, ever write about her. She took a huge swallow of ginger ale and tried to drown out the incessant ticking of the meter.

She stroked the soft felt of her grandfather's hat, thought of how peculiarly the human brain grows, from an almost invisible seed, and how, in this respect, it was rather similar to understanding, a process it engendered. She looked into her grandfather's shaving mirror and her eyes told her she could bear very little more. She felt herself begin to slide into the long silence in which such thoughts would be her sole companions. Maybe she would even find happiness there.

But then, just when she was almost gone, Barbara put on their grandfather's other hat and reached for her hand.

PET MILK

STUART DYBEK

Stuart Dybek is the author of a book of poetry, *Brass Knuckles,* and a collection of stories, *Childhood and Other Neighborhoods,* which has won numerous prizes. He has had both NEA and Guggenheim fellowships, and was the recipient of the Nelson Algren Award for 1985. He was joint first prize winner of the 1985 O. Henry Award. Originally from Chicago, he is currently teaching creative writing at Western Michigan University.

Today I've been drinking instant coffee and Pet Milk, and watching it snow. It's not that I enjoy the taste especially, but I like the way Pet Milk swirls in the coffee. Actually, my favorite thing about Pet Milk is what the can opener does to the top of the can. The can is unmistakable—compact, seamless-looking, its very shape suggesting that it could condense milk without any trouble. The can opener bites in neatly, and the thick liquid spills from the triangular gouge with a different look and viscosity. Pet Milk isn't *real* milk. The color's off, to start with. There's almost something of the past about it, like old ivory. My grandmother always drank it in her coffee. When friends dropped over and sat around the kitchen table, my grandma would ask, "Do you take cream and sugar?" Pet Milk was the cream.

There was a yellowed plastic radio on her kitchen table, usually tuned to the polka station, though sometimes she'd miss it by half a notch and get the Greek station instead, or even the Spanish or the Ukranian. In Chicago, where we lived, all the incompatible states of Europe were pressed together down at the staticky right end of the dial. She didn't seem to notice, as long as she wasn't hearing English. The radio, turned low, played constantly. Its top was warped and turning amber on the side where the tubes were. I remember the sound of it on winter afternoons after school, as I sat by her table watching the Pet Milk swirl and cloud in the steaming coffee, and noticing, outside her window, the sky doing the same thing above the railroad yard across the street.

And I remember, much later, seeing the same swirling sky in tiny liqueur glasses containing a drink called a King Alphonse: the crème de cacao rising like smoke in repeated explosions, blooming in kaleidoscopic clouds through the layer of heavy cream. This was in the Pilsen, a little Czech restaurant where my girlfriend, Kate, and I would go sometimes in the evening. It was the first year out of college for both of us, and we had astonished ourselves by finding real jobs—no more waitressing or pumping gas, the way we'd done in school. I was investigating credit references at a bank, and she was doing something slightly above the rank of typist for Hornblower & Weeks, the investment firm. My bank showed training films that emphasized the importance of suitable dress, good grooming, and personal neatness, even for employees like me, who worked at the switchboard in the basement. Her firm issued directives on appropriate attire—skirts, for instance, should cover the knees. She had lovely knees.

Kate and I would sometimes meet after work at the Pilsen, dressed in our proper business clothes and still feeling both a little self-conscious and glamorous, as if we were impostors wearing disguises. The place had small round oak tables, and we'd sit in a corner under a painting called "The Street Musicians of Prague" and trade future plans as if they were escape routes. She talked of going to grad school in Europe; I wanted to apply to the Peace Corps. Our plans for the future made us laugh and feel close, but those same plans somehow made anything more than temporary between us seem impossible. It was the first time I'd ever had the feeling of missing someone I was still with.

The waiters in the Pilsen wore short black jackets over long white aprons. They were old men from the Old Country. We went there often enough to have our own special waiter, Rudi, after a while. Rudi boned our trout and seasoned our salads, and at the end of the meal he'd bring the bottle of crème de cacao from the bar, along with two little glasses and a small pitcher of heavy cream, and make us each a King Alphonse right at our table. We'd watch as he'd fill the glasses halfway up with the syrupy brown liqueur, then carefully attempt to float a layer of cream on top. If he failed to float the cream, we'd get that one free.

"Who was King Alphonse anyway, Rudi?" I sometimes asked, trying to break his concentration, and if that didn't work I nudged the table with my foot so the glass would jiggle imperceptibly just as he was floating the cream. We'd usually get one on the house. Rudi knew what

I was doing. In fact, serving the King Alphonses had been his idea, and he had also suggested the trick of jarring the table. I think it pleased him, though he seemed concerned about the way I'd stare into the liqueur glass, watching the patterns.

"It's not a microscope," he said. "Drink."

He liked us, and we tipped extra. It felt good to be there and to be able to pay for a meal.

Kate and I met at the Pilsen for supper on my twenty-second birthday. It was May, and unseasonably hot. I'd opened my tie. Even before looking at the dinner menu, we ordered a bottle of Mumm's and a dozen oysters apiece. Rudi made a sly remark when he brought the oysters on platters of ice. They were freshly opened and smelled of the sea. I'd heard people joke about oysters' being aphrodisiac but never considered it anything but a myth—the kind of idea they still had in the Old Country.

We squeezed on lemon, added dabs of horseradish, slid the oysters into our mouths, and then rinsed the shells with champagne and drank the salty, cold juice. There was a beefy-looking couple eating schnitzel at the next table, and they stared at us with the repugnance that public oyster-eaters in the Midwest often encounter. We laughed and grandly sipped it all down. I was already half tipsy from drinking too fast, and starting to feel filled with a euphoric, aching energy. Kate raised a brimming oyster shell to me in a toast: "To the Peace Corps!"

"To Europe!" I replied, and we clunked shells.

She touched her wineglass to mine and whispered, "Happy birthday," and then suddenly leaned across the table and kissed me.

When she sat down again, she was flushed. I caught the reflection of her face in the glass-covered "The Street Musicians of Prague" above our table. I always loved seeing her in mirrors and windows. The reflections of her beauty startled me. I had told her that once, and she seemed to fend off the compliment, saying, "That's because you've learned what to look for," as if it were a secret I'd stumbled upon. But, this time, seeing her reflection hovering ghostlike upon an imaginary Prague was like seeing a future from which she had vanished. I knew I'd never meet anyone more beautiful to me.

We killed the champagne and sat twining fingers across the table. I was sweating. I could feel the warmth of her through her skirt under the table and I touched her leg. We still hadn't ordered dinner. I left money on the table and we steered each other out a little unsteadily.

"Rudi will understand," I said.

The street was blinding bright. A reddish sun angled just above the rims of the tallest buildings. I took my suit coat off and flipped it over my shoulder. We stopped in the doorway of a store to kiss.

"Let's go somewhere," she said.

My roommate would already be home at my place, which was closer. Kate lived up north, in Evanston. It seemed a long way away.

We cut down a side street, past a fire station, to a small park, but its gate was locked. I pressed close to her against the tall iron fence. We could smell the lilacs from a bush just inside the fence, and when I jumped for an overhanging branch my shirtsleeve hooked on a fence spike and tore, and petals rained down on us as the bush sprang from my hand.

We walked to the subway. The evening rush was winding down; we must have caught the last express heading toward Evanston. Once the train climbed from the tunnel to the elevated tracks, it wouldn't stop until the end of the line, on Howard. There weren't any seats together, so we stood swaying at the front of the car, beside the empty conductor's compartment. We wedged inside, and I clicked the door shut.

The train rocked and jounced, clattering north. We were kissing, trying to catch the rhythm of the ride with our bodies. The sun bronzed the windows on our side of the train. I lifted her skirt over her knees, hiked it higher so the sun shone off her thighs, and bunched it around her waist. She wouldn't stop kissing, and she was moving her hips to pin us to each jolt of the train.

We were speeding past scorched brick walls, gray windows, back porches outlined in sun, roofs and treetops—the landscape of the "L" I'd memorized from subway windows over a lifetime of rides: the podiatrist's foot sign past Fullerton; the bright pennants of Wrigley Field, at Addison; ancient hotels with "Transients Welcome" signs on their flaking back walls; peeling and graffiti-smudged billboards; the old cemetery just before Wilson Avenue. Even without looking, I knew almost exactly where we were. Within the compartment, the sound of our quick breathing was louder than the clatter of tracks. I was trying to slow down, to make it all last, and when she covered my mouth with her hand I turned my face to the window and looked out.

The train was braking a little from express speed, as it did each time it passed a local station. I could see blurred faces on the long wooden platform watching us pass—businessmen glancing up from folded newspapers, women clutching purses and shopping bags. I could see the expression on each face, momentarily arrested, as we flashed by. A high-school kid in shirtsleeves, maybe sixteen, with books tucked under one arm and a cigarette in his mouth, caught sight of us, and in the instant before he disappeared he grinned and started to wave. Then he was gone, and I turned from the window, back to Kate, forgetting everything—the passing stations, the glowing late sky, even the sense of missing her—but that arrested wave stayed with me. It was as if I were standing on that platform, with my schoolbooks and a smoke, on one of those endlessly accumulated afternoons after school when I stood almost outside of time simply waiting for a train, and I thought how much I'd have loved seeing someone like us streaming by.

CRAZY LADIES

GREG JOHNSON

Greg Johnson grew up in Tyler, Texas, and attended Southern Methodist University in Dallas and Emory University in Atlanta, where he earned a PhD in English in 1979. He has published more than thirty short stories in such magazines as *The Virginia Quarterly Review, The Ontario Review, Prairie Schooner,* and *Kansas Quarterly.* He has also published criticism, poetry, and more than one hundred book reviews. His first book, *Emily Dickinson: Perception and the Poet's Quest,* was published by University of Alabama Press in 1985.

Every Southern town had one, and ours was no exception. One year, my sister and I had an after-school routine that included watching the Mouseketeers on TV, holding court in the neighborhood treehouse we'd built, along with several other kids, in a vacant lot down the street, and finally, as dusk began and we knew our mother would soon be calling us to supper, visiting the big ramshackle house where the crazy lady lived. Often she'd be eating her own supper of tuna fish and bean salad, sitting silently across from her bachelor son, John Ray, who was about the same age as our parents. Becky would slither along through the hydrangea bushes, then scrunch down so I could stand on her shoulders and get my eyes and forehead—just barely—over the sill of the Longworths' dining room window. After a few minutes I'd get down and serve as a footstool for Becky. More often than not we dissolved into a laughter so uncontrollable that we had to race back through the bushes, snapping branches as we went, and then dart around the corner of the house to avoid being caught by John Ray, who sometimes heard us and would jump up from the table, then come fuming out the back door. He never did catch us, and to my knowledge was never quick enough even to discover who we were. Naturally his mother didn't know, and didn't care. But there came a time—that summer afternoon, the year Becky was thirteen and I was eleven—when the crazy lady took her obscene revenge.

For me, that entire summer was puzzling. Our father, the town druggist, had begun keeping unusual hours. We could no longer count on his kindly, slump-shouldered presence at the dinner table, and when he did join us there was a crackling energy in him, a playfulness toward Becky and me that he'd never shown when we were younger. And while our father, a balding and slightly overweight man in his forties, had taken on this sudden, nervous gaiety, our mother underwent an alarming change of her own. Her normally delicate features, framed by fine, wavy auburn hair, had paled to the point of haggardness. There was a new brusqueness in her manner—she scrubbed the house with a grim ferocity, she made loud clattering noises when she worked in the kitchen—and also a certain inattention toward her children, a tendency to focus elsewhere when she talked to us, or to fall into sudden reveries. This bothered me more than it did Becky, for it seemed that even she was changing. In the fall she'd be starting junior high, and she'd begun calling me "Little Brother" (with a slight wrinkling of her nose) and spending long hours alone in her bedroom. All through childhood we'd been inseparable, and Becky had always been called a tomboy by the neighborhood kids, even by our parents; but now she'd started curling her hair and painting her stubby nails, gingerly paging through movie magazines while they dried. What was wrong with everyone? I wanted to ask—but when you're eleven, of course, you can't translate your puzzlement into words. For a long while I stayed bewildered, feeling that the others had received a new set of instructions on how to live, but had forgotten to pass them along to me.

One humid afternoon in August, the telephone rang; from the living room, we could hear our mother snatch up the kitchen extension.

"What?" she said loudly, irritated. "Slow down, Mother, I can't make out—"

At that point she called to us to turn down the TV; from my place on the floor I reached quickly and switched the volume completely off, earning a little groan from Becky. She sat crosslegged on the couch with a towel wrapped tightly around her head, like a turban. We'd been watching *American Bandstand.*

"*You* turn it up," I said, with the same defiant smirk she'd begun using on me.

"Hush," Becky whispered, leaning forward. "I think something's wrong with Grandma."

We sat quietly, listening. Our mother's voice had become shrill, incredulous.

"Why did you let her in?" she cried. "You know she's not supposed to—"

A long silence. Whenever our mother was interrupted, Becky and I exchanged a puzzled look.

"Listen, just call John Ray down at the bank. The operator, Mother —she'll give you the number. Oh, I know you're nervous, but— Yes, you can if you try. Call John Ray, then go back in the living room and be nice to her. Give her something to eat. Or some coffee."

Silently, Becky mouthed the words to me: *the crazy lady.*

I nodded, straining to hear our mother's voice. She sounded weary.

"All right, I'll call Bert," she said, sighing. "We'll get there as soon as we can."

When she stopped talking, Becky and I raced into the kitchen.

"What is it, Mama?" Becky asked, excited. "Is it—"

"It's Mrs. Longworth," Mother said. Absent-mindedly, she fiddled with my shirt collar, then looked over at Becky. "She's gotten out of the house again, and somehow ended up in your grandmother's living room." Briefly, she laughed. She shook her head. "Anyway, I've got to call your father. We'll meet him over there."

But what had the crazy lady done? we asked. *Why was Grandma so frightened? Why were we all going over there?* Mother ignored our questions. Calmly she dialed the pharmacy, setting her jaw as though preparing to do something distasteful.

Within five minutes we were in the car, making the two-mile drive to Grandma Howell's. Dad was already there when we arrived, but he hadn't gone inside.

"Well, what's going on?" Mother asked him. She sounded angry, as if Dad were to blame for all this.

He looked sheepish, apprehensive. He always perspired heavily, and I noticed the film covering his balding forehead, the large damp circles at his armpits. He wore the pale blue, regulation shirt, with *Denson Pharmacy—Bert Denson, Mgr.* stitched above the pocket, but he'd removed his little black bow tie and opened his collar.

"I just got here," Dad said, helplessly. "I was waiting for you."

Mother made a little *tsk*ing noise, then turned in her precise, determined way and climbed the small grassy hill up to Grandma's porch. Dad followed, looking depressed, and Becky and I scampered alongside, performing our typical duet of questions. *Do you know what's wrong?* Becky asked him. *Why did you wait for us?* I asked. *Is Mother mad at you?* Becky asked. *Are you scared of the crazy lady?* I asked. *Scared to go inside?*

I asked this, of course, because *I* was scared.

Dad only had time to say, uneasily, that Grandma's St. Augustine was getting high again, and I'd have to mow it next Saturday. It was just his way of stalling; he'd begun evading a lot of our questions lately.

The front door was already open, and as we mounted the porch steps I could see Grandma Howell's dim outline from just inside the screen. Then the screen opened and I heard her say, vaguely, "Why, it's Kathy and Bert, and the kids. . . ." From inside the room I heard a high, twittering sound, like the cries of a bird.

In the summertime Grandma Howell kept all the shades drawn in her living room; she had an attic fan, and the room was always wonderfully cool. It was furnished modestly, decorated with colorful doilies Grandma knitted for the backs of chairs and the sofa, and with dozens of little knick-knacks—gifts from her grandchildren, mostly—set along the mantel of the small fireplace and cluttering the little, spindly-leg tables, and with several uninspired, studiously executed paintings (still-lifes, mostly) done by my grandfather, who had died several years before I was born. A typical grandmother's house, I suppose, and through the years it had represented to us kids a sanctuary, a place of quiet wonder and privilege, where we were fed ginger cookies and Kool-Aid, and where Grandma regaled us with stories of her childhood down in Mobile, where her family had been among the most prominent citizens, or of her courtship by that rapscallion, Jacob Howell, who'd brought her northward (that is, to our town—which skirted the northern edge of Alabama) and kept her there. Grandma liked to roll her china-blue eyes, picturing herself as a victim of kidnapping or worse; through the years she refined and elaborated her act to rouse both herself and us to helpless laughter, ending the story by insisting tongue-in-cheek that she'd met, and adjusted to, a fate worse than death. (Grandfather Howell was a postal clerk, later the postmaster, and by all accounts a gentle, kind, rather whimsical figure in the town; it was always clear that Grandma had adored him.) Now, at sixty-one, she looked twenty years younger, the blue eyes still clear as dawn, her figure neat, trim, and erect, her only grandmotherly affectation being the silvery blue hair she wore in a small and tidy bun. On that day I decided she'd always seemed brave, too, even valorous in her quiet, bustling self-sufficiency, for that afternoon I saw in her eyes for the first time a look of unmitigated fear.

"Yes, come in, come in," she said, still in that vague, airy way, obviously trying to pretend that our visit was a surprise. Then she turned back to the room's dim interior—her head moving stiffly, I thought, as if her neck ached—and said in a polite, tense, hostessy voice: "Why look, Mrs. Longworth, it's my daughter and her family. We were just talking about them."

Grandma Howell nodded, as though agreeing with herself, or encouraging Mrs. Longworth's agreement. The twittering birdlike sound came again.

By now we were all inside, standing awkwardly near the screen. Slowly, our eyes adjusted. On the opposite side of the room, and in the far corner of Grandma's dainty, pale blue sofa, sat Mrs. Longworth: a tiny, white-haired woman in a pink dress, a brilliant green shawl, and soiled white sneakers, one of whose laces had come untied. The five of us stared, not feeling our rudeness, I suppose, because for the moment Mrs. Longworth seemed unaware of our presence. She kept brushing wispy strands of the bone-white hair from her forehead, though it immediately fell back again; and she would pat her knees briskly with open palms, as if coaxing some invisible child to her lap. It was the first time I had encountered the crazy lady up close, and my wide-eyed scrutiny confirmed certain rumors that had circulated in the town for years—that she wore boys' sneakers, for instance, along with white athletic socks; that her tongue often protruded from her mouth, like a communicant's (as it did now, quivering with a sort of nervous expectancy); and that, most distasteful of all, the woman was unbelievably dirty. Even from across the dimmed room I detected a rank, animal odor, and there was a dark smear—it looked like grease—along one of her fragile cheekbones. The palms and even the backs of her hands were filthy, the tiny nails crusted with grime. Like me, the rest of my family had been stunned into silence at the very sight of her; it was only when her tongue popped back inside her mouth, and she cocked her head to begin that eerie, high-pitched trilling once again, that my mother jerked awake and abruptly stepped forward.

"Mrs. Longworth?" she said loudly, trying to compete with the woman's shrill birdsong. "We haven't met before, but I'm—"

She gave it up. Mrs. Longworth's head moved delicately as she trilled, cocking from side to side as if adjudging the intricate nuances of her melody—which was no melody at all, of course, but only a high, sweet, patternless frenzy of singing. (For it was clear that Mrs. Longworth thought she was singing; her face and eyes, which she still had not turned to us, had the vapid, self-satisfied look of the amateur performer.) She would stop when she was ready to stop. My mother stepped back, then drew Grandma closer. They began a whispered conference.

"How did she get in?" my mother said hoarsely. "Why did you—"

"It happened so fast," Grandma interrupted. Her face had puckered, in an uncharacteristic look of chagrin. "I was outside, watering the shrubs, and suddenly there she was, standing in the grass. Right away I knew who she was, but she looked so—so frail and helpless, just standing there. Then she asked for a glass of iced tea. She asked in a real sweet way, and it was so hot out, and she didn't *act* crazy. But once we got inside. . . ."

Grandma's voice trailed away. I saw that her hands were shaking.

"You *know* what happened the last time she got loose," Mother said. She was almost hissing. "Wandered down to the courthouse and started screeching all kinds of things, crazy things, and then started taking off her clothes! In broad daylight! It took four men to restrain her before John Ray finally got there."

Becky whispered, excitedly, "But doesn't he keep her locked up? At school the girls all say—"

"Yes, yes," Mother said impatiently, with a little shushing motion of her hand. "But she manages to get out, somehow. I've never understood why John Ray can't hire someone to stay with her in the daytime, or else have her committed. My Lord," she said, whirling back upon Grandma, "just imagine what could have happened. People like her can get violent, you know."

"Ssh. Kathy, please," Grandma said anxiously. She glanced back at the crazy lady, who had continued trilling to herself, though more softly now. "She isn't like that, really. I don't think she'd hurt anyone. In fact, if you'd heard what she told me—"

"Mother, the woman's crazy!" my mother whispered, hard put to keep her voice down. "You can't pay any attention to what she says."

"What was it?" Becky asked, and though I was afraid to say anything, I seconded her question by vigorously nodding my head.

"Hush up," Mother said, giving a light, warning slap to Becky's shoulder blade, "or I'll send you both outside."

Now my father spoke up. "Listen, Kathy," he said, "we ought to just call John Ray down at the bank. He'll come get her, and that'll be that."

"I've a mind to call the police," Mother said, and I looked at her curiously. She had sounded hurt.

"She hasn't done anything," Dad said gently. "And anyway, it's none of our business."

Grandma pressed her hands together, as if to stop their shaking. "Oh, if you'd heard what she told me, once I brought her inside. I gave her the iced tea, and a little saucer of butter cookies, and for a while she sat there on the sofa, with me right beside her, and she just talked in the sweetest way. Said she was just out for a walk this afternoon, but hadn't realized how hot it was. She said the tea was delicious, and asked what kind I bought. Hers always turned cloudy, she said. And I'd started thinking to myself, This woman isn't crazy at all. She dresses peculiar, yes, and she should bathe more often, but people have just been spreading ugly gossip all these years, exaggerating everything. Anyway, I gave her more tea, and tried to be nice to her. She kept looking around the room, saying how pretty it was. She noticed Jacob's pictures, and couldn't believe he'd done such beautiful work. She asked if I still missed him, like she missed Mr. Longworth, and if I ever got lonesome, or frightened. . . . And it was then that she changed, so suddenly that I couldn't believe my ears. She started talking about John Ray, and saying the most horrible things, but all in that same sweet voice, as if she was just talking about the weather. Oh, Kathy, she said John Ray wanted—wanted to kill her, that he was going to take her into the attic and chop her into little pieces. She said he beats her, and sometimes won't let her eat for days on end, but by then she'd started using her husband's name—you know, mixing the names up. One minute she'd be saying Carl, the next she was back to John Ray. And pretty soon she was just spouting gibberish, and she'd started that crazy singing of hers. She said did I want to hear a song, and that's when I came to phone you. I didn't know what to do—I didn't—"

Tears had filled her eyes. Mother reached out, taking both her hands. "Never mind, you were just being kind to her," she said. "Bert's right, of course—we'll just call John Ray, and that'll be that."

Grandma couldn't speak, but her blue eyes had fixed on my mother's with a frightened, guilty look. It was then that Mrs. Longworth's eerie trilling stopped, and we heard, from the sofa: "Bert's right, of course, we'll just call John Ray. And that'll be that." The voice was sly, insinuating—it had the mocking, faintly malicious tone of a mynah bird.

I looked at Dad. His face had reddened, his mouth had fallen partway open.

"Would you like more tea?" Grandma asked, in a sweet overdone voice. She inclined her head, graciously, though it was clear she couldn't bring herself to take another step toward Mrs. Longworth. But the crazy lady didn't seem to mind. She cocked her head, and at the very moment I feared she would resume her weird singing, she said in a casual, matter-of-fact way, "No thanks, Paulina. I like the tea, but it isn't sweet enough." And she smiled, rather balefully; her teeth looked small and greenish.

Grandma began, "I could add more sugar—"

"Do you have Kool-Aid?" Mrs. Longworth asked. "That's my favorite drink, but my son won't let me have it."

"Yes, I think so," Grandma said, uncertainly. "I'll go and look."

"Red, please," Mrs. Longworth said. "Red's the best."

Grandma hurried back to the kitchen, leaving the rest of us to stare awkwardly at the old woman, while she looked frankly back at us. She had a childlike directness, but her eyes glittered, too, with the wry omniscience of the aged. Particularly when she looked down at Becky and me, her glance seemed full of mischief, as though she were exercising her right to a second childhood. And there was something in her glance that I could only feel as love, born of some intuitive sympathy. Young as I was, I remember sharing Grandma's thought: This woman isn't crazy at all.

For the moment, her attention had fixed on Becky. She held out a dirty, clawlike hand, as though to draw my sister closer by some invisible string.

"You're a pretty girl," she said, in the tone one uses for very young children. "Such pretty hair, and those cute freckles. . . . I used to have freckles, when I was young. *I* was a pretty girl." She shook her head, as though hard put to say how pretty. "And I had nice dresses, cotton and gingham, all trimmed in lace. I'll bet you like pretty dresses. Your little nose is turned up, just like mine was."

Becky looked spellbound; her face had paled. "Thank you—thank you very much—" she stammered.

"Would you like to have some of the dresses I wore?" the old woman asked. "They're up in the attic, in a special trunk. We'll steal the key from John Ray. The dresses are safe, no bloodstains and none of them ripped. You could wear them to church, or when the young men come calling." She raised one finger of the still-outstretched hand. "But you'd have to bring them back. You couldn't steal them. We'll sneak them back late one night, when John Ray's asleep."

Becky tried to smile. I could see how scared she was; and I stood there hoping Mrs. Longworth wouldn't turn to me. Somehow I felt safer, being a boy.

"I—I don't know— It's real nice of you—" Becky couldn't put her words together.

"And you still have pretty clothes," my mother said suddenly, stepping forward. "That's a lovely shawl, Mrs. Longworth."

The crazy lady glanced down; she pulled the shawl tighter around her shoulders, as though she'd suddenly felt a chill.

"I had a cashmere shawl, pale gray," she said, "that my husband gave me. It was before John Ray was even born. Mr. Longworth went up to Memphis, and afterward he showered me with presents. An opal ring, too. And a set of hair combs. I was a pretty woman, you know. I still wear shawls, but it's not the same. This one's green."

She spoke in a circular, monotonous rhythm, as though reminiscing to herself, as though she'd spoken these words a thousand times. It was a kind of sing-song. I thought again of her birdlike trilling.

"Well, it's very pretty," Mother said.

"It's *too* green," the crazy lady said, "but I think it hurts John Ray's eyes. He has weak eyes, you know. When he goes blind, I won't have to wear it."

Grandma came in from the kitchen, carrying a tray with six glasses and a large pitcher of Kool-Aid.

"It's raspberry, Mrs. Longworth," she said as she put the tray on the coffee table. Her hands still shook, and the glasses clattered together. "I hope you like it."

She poured a glass and held it out; Mrs. Longworth grasped it quickly, then took several long gulps. She closed her eyes in bliss. "Oooh!" she cried. "Isn't that good!"

Grandma maintained her brave smile. "Kathy, would you and Bert like—"

"No, Mother. We can't stay long, and Bert has a phone call to make. Don't you, Bert?"

"Yes—right," Dad said awkwardly.

"How about you kids?" Grandma said. She was trying gamely to make all of this appear normal; then, perhaps, it would somehow *be* normal. That was always Grandma's way. But, much as I loved her, I was afraid to join in anything the crazy lady was doing. Like Becky, I stiffly shook my head.

Mrs. Longworth emptied her glass, then held it out to Grandma. "More, please," she said. While Grandma poured, she said (again in that matter-of-fact way): "You might not believe it, but I don't get good Kool-Aid like this. John Ray says it rots my teeth and my brain. I can drink water, or coffee without sugar." She made a face. "And if I don't drink it, John Ray gets mad. Now Carl, he never got mad. But my son is going to cut me with a long knife one of these days, and hide the pieces in the attic, all in separate trunks. When it starts to smell, he'll throw the trunks in the river."

She took the second glass of Kool-Aid that Grandma shakily handed her. Then she sighed, loudly, as if the details of her gruesome demise had become rather tiresome. "My son works in a bank," she said, "and his teeth are big and strong. So he can have sugar. If I try to sneak some, he pinches my arms, or hits me with a newspaper. That hurts, because he rolls it up first and makes me watch. The pinches hurt, too, but not always. He works in a bank, and so he knows all about locks and trunks and vaults. He has a map, so he can find the river when he needs it. I should be able to have red Kool-Aid, and to sing. I used to sing for Carl, and sometimes I sang to John Ray when he was a baby. Now, he's tired of taking care of me. He says, Don't I have a life to live? Don't I?" Again she spoke like a mynah bird, pitching her voice very low. "That's what he says, and that's why he wants to cut me into pieces, and why I have all these bruises on my arms. You want to see them? It's not fair, because my singing is pretty. Carl said I had a prettier voice than Jenny Lind, and he heard her in person when he was a boy. He's dead, though. You want to hear me sing?"

She stopped abruptly, her eyes widened. She waited.

"Would you like some more Kool-Aid?" Grandma asked, helplessly.

"Bert, you and Jamie go back into the kitchen. We'll wait out here with Mrs. Longworth." My mother gestured to her ear, as if holding an invisible telephone.

Dad said, "Come on, sport," and I joined him gladly. I glimpsed Becky's look of envy and longing as we escaped into the dining room, and finally back into Grandma's tiny kitchen.

"What's wrong with her? Why does she say those things?" I asked breathlessly, while Dad fiddled with the slender phone directory. I tugged at his arm, like a much smaller child; my heart was racing. I wore only a T-shirt and short pants, and I remember shifting my weight back and forth, my bare feet unpleasantly chilled by the kitchen linoleum.

"Just simmer down, son," he said, tousling my hair in an absent-minded way. Frowning, he moved his eyes down a column of small print. "Ah, here it is. First National." And he began to dial.

I didn't understand it, but I was on the verge of tears—angry tears. When Dad finished talking with John Ray, his eyes stopped to read the little chalkboard hanging by the phone. "I can't believe it," he said, shaking his head. "It's still there."

Grudgingly, I followed his gaze to the chalkboard, and for the hundredth time read its message, in that antique, elaborate hand: *Paulie, Don't forget Gouda cheese for dinner tonight. I'll be hungry at six o'clock sharp. (Ha ha) Jacob.* If Grandma was out when my grandfather came home for lunch, he would leave her a note on the chalkboard. But he hadn't lived to eat that Gouda cheese—he was stricken at four that afternoon, and died a short while later—and Grandma had insisted that his last message would never be erased. Mother disapproved, saying it was morbid, and more than once I'd seen Grandma's eyes fill with tears as they skimmed across the words yet another time. But she could be stubborn, and the message stayed.

"You'd know it was still there," I said, sniffling, "if you ever came with us to visit Grandma. But you're always gone."

The resentment in my voice surprised us both. My father's clear brown eyes flashed in an instant from anger, to guilt, to sorrow. He shook his head; the gesture had become familiar lately, almost a tic.

"Well, Jamie," he said slowly, licking his lips. "I guess it's time we had a little talk."

And for five or ten minutes he did talk, not quite looking at me, his voice filled with a melancholy dreaminess. He told me how complicated the grown-up world was, and how men and women sometimes hurt each other without wanting to; how they sometimes fell "out of love," without being able to control what was happening. He knew it must sound crazy, but he hoped that someday I would understand. Things were always changing, he said softly, and that was the hardest thing in the world for people to accept. Even my mother hadn't accepted it, not yet; but he hoped that she would, eventually. He hoped she wouldn't make it even harder for all of us.

The speech was commonplace enough, though startling to my young ears. As he spoke I kept thinking of Mrs. Longworth, and how she'd talked of her husband who had died, and how everything changed after that. I felt the cold, sickish beating of my heart inside my slender ribcage.

"But will Mother turn crazy, like Mrs. Longworth?" I asked, imagining myself, in a moment of terrified wonder, turning mean like John Ray. "Is it always the ladies who go crazy?"

Dad looked stymied; nor did I know myself what the question meant. I wouldn't even recall it until decades later, visiting my sister Becky in the hospital, where she was recuperating from a barbiturate overdose after the disappearance of her third husband. It would come back to me, in a boy's timid, faraway voice, like the echo of a terrible prophecy, a family curse. After a moment, though, my father reacted as though I'd said something amusing. Again, he tousled my hair; he smiled wearily.

"No, son," he said gently. "It's not always the ladies. You shouldn't let Mrs. Longworth get to you."

"But she said—"

"She's a crazy old lady, Jamie. She has nothing to do with us—don't pay any attention to what she says."

Hands stuffed in my pockets, one foot rubbing the toe of the other, I stood looking up at him. There were questions I wanted to ask, but I couldn't put them into words; and I somehow knew that he didn't have the answers.

"Now," Dad said, with a false heartiness, "why don't we—"

It was then that the kitchen door swung open, and there was my mother; she looked back and forth between Dad and me, as though she didn't recognize us.

"Honey? What is it?" Dad said, panicked.

"We—we couldn't stop her," Mother began, wildly. "She took off the shawl, then started unbuttoning her dress, that filthy dress—"

Dad crossed to her; he gripped her firmly by the upper arms.

"Calm down, Kathy. Now tell me what happened."

My mother was trembling. She said, haltingly, "Mrs. Longworth, she —she said she would show us, prove to us how cruel John Ray was. Before we could say anything, she started undressing. She undid the dress, then slipped it down to her waist. We—we just stared at her. We couldn't believe it. There were bruises, Bert, all over her arms and chest. Big purplish bruises, and welts. . . . And she said, *John Ray did this*, in that little singing voice of hers—"

Dad had already released her arms. He went to the phone and dialed again. For a moment my mother's eyes locked onto mine. I'd never seen her lose her composure before, yet for some reason I was filled with a remarkable calm. From that moment forward, everything was changed between us.

"Oh God," she whispered, grief-stricken. "How I wish Becky hadn't seen."

Dad hung up the phone, then led us back into the living room; he kept one arm draped lightly around Mother's shoulder. John Ray had arrived, and sat on the sofa beside Mrs. Longworth. Her dress and shawl were in place, so it was hard for me to envision the scene my mother had described. Mrs. Longworth sat staring blankly forward, as if her mind had wandered to some distant place. John Ray held one of her hands, and sat talking amiably to Grandma. He was a big-chested man, almost entirely bald, and had teeth that were enormous, white, and perfectly straight. He smiled constantly. He was telling Grandma about all the times his mother had been "naughty," wandering into a department store, or a funeral parlor, or a private home. He hoped she hadn't been too much trouble. He hoped we understood that she meant no harm; that for years she hadn't had the slightest idea what she was doing or saying.

A small, terrible smile had frozen onto Grandma's face. She stood near the front door, her arm around Becky, who looked pale and dazed.

"She—she wasn't any trouble," my mother gasped.

"Oh no, none at all," said Grandma.

There were a few moments of silence, during which the five of us stared at the Longworths, John Ray giving back his imperturbable smile and Mrs. Longworth seeming lost in the corridors of her madness, her mouth slightly ajar, her hand resting limply inside her son's. I tried to picture John Ray beating her, or shouting his threats of a gruesome death. I decided it could not be true.

When the police arrived, neither John Ray nor his mother protested. The officer spoke to Mrs. Longworth by name, and returned a few pleasantries to the smiling John Ray. As he followed them out the door, the officer gave a knowing, barely perceptible look to my father, who nodded in acknowledgment, then turned his attention back to us.

"Well," he said, jovially, "why don't we all go out for an ice cream sundae?"

Beyond that, I can't remember clearly. I don't believe that anyone, including myself, ever talked about the incident again; there was a tacit assumption between Becky and me that we would not resume our spying on the Longworths, but they continued to be tormented by other kids we knew. I remember feeling, for years afterward, that life had become disappointingly routine. Evidently the police hadn't charged John Ray: he was still working at First National by the time I left home for college. Nor had anything untoward happened to Mrs. Longworth: one night, about three years after wandering into our lives, she died peacefully in her sleep. It was whispered around town that John Ray was wild with grief.

By then, the tensions between my parents had all but vanished; my father's unexplained absences had stopped, my mother no longer seemed angry or depressed. Grandma stayed absorbed in her garden, her knitting, her memories. Becky had plunged headlong into her adolescent social career, and with great effort had attained her obsessive goal: popularity. It seemed that I alone had changed. Violence had failed to erupt, and I became uneasy, tense, and vaguely suspicious. If I could have forseen what would happen to my sister, I would not have been surprised. Like her, I left the South as soon as I was old enough, relocating in a big, overpopulated city where violence is commonplace. Although I often worry about Becky, and Mother, and even Grandma, I know there is no reason to feel guilty, just as there is no logic to the dream I've had, recurrently, for more than twenty years: a dream in which I open a door to find the three of them perched on a sofa, cocking their heads from side to side, trilling their songs of madness and despair.

THE COMEDIAN

JOHN L'HEUREUX

John L'Heureux, from South Hadley, Massachusetts, directs the writing program at Stanford University, where he is Lane Professor of Humanities. His fiction has appeared in *The Atlantic, Esquire, Harper's, The New Yorker,* and many quarterlies; he is the author of eleven books of poetry and fiction. Godine will publish his new novel, *Lies,* later this year.

Corinne hasn't planned to have a baby. She is thirty-eight and happy and she wants to get on with it. She is a stand-up comedian with a husband, her second, and with no thought of a child, and what she wants out of life now is a lot of laughs. To give them, and especially to get them. And here she is, by accident, pregnant.

The doctor sees her chagrin and is surprised, because he thinks of her as a competent and sturdy woman. But that's how things are these days and so he suggests an abortion. Corinne says she'll let him know; she has to do some thinking. A baby.

"That's great," Russ says. "If you want it, I mean. I want it. I mean, I want it if you do. It's up to you, though. You know what I mean?"

And so they decide that, of course, they will have the baby, of course they want the baby, the baby is just exactly what they need.

In the bathroom mirror that night, Russ looks through his eyes into his cranium for a long time. Finally he sees his mind. As he watches, it knots like a fist. And he continues to watch, glad, as that fist beats the new baby flat and thin, a dead slick silverfish.

Mother. Mother and baby. A little baby. A big baby. Bouncing babies. At once Corinne sees twenty babies, twenty pink basketball babies, bouncing down the court and then up into the air and—whoosh—they swish neatly through the net. Babies.

Baby is its own excuse for being. Or is it? Well, Corinne was a Catholic right up until the end of her first marriage, so she thinks maybe it is. One thing is sure: the only subject you can't make a good joke about is abortion.

Yes, they will have the baby. Yes, she will be the Mother. Yes.

But the next morning, while Russ is at work, Corinne turns off the television and sits on the edge of the couch. She squeezes her thighs together, tight; she contracts her stomach; she arches her back. This is no joke. This is the real thing. By an act of the will, she is going to expel this baby, this invader, this insidious little murderer. She pushes and pushes and nothing happens. She pushes again, hard. And once more she pushes. Finally she gives up and lies back against the sofa, resting.

After a while she puts her hand on her belly, and as she does so, she is astonished to hear singing.

It is the baby. It has a soft reedy voice and it sings slightly off-key. Corinne listens to the words: "Some of these days, you'll miss me, honey. . . ."

Corinne faints then, and it is quite some time before she wakes up.

When she wakes, she opens her eyes only a slit and looks carefully from left to right. She sits on the couch, vigilant, listening, but she hears nothing. After a while she says three Hail Marys and an Act of Contrition, and then, confused and a little embarrassed, she does the laundry.

She does not tell Russ about this.

Well, it's a time of strain, Corinne tells herself, even though in California there isn't supposed to be any strain. Just surfing and tans and divorce and a lot of interfacing. No strain and no babies.

Corinne thinks for a second about interfacing babies, but forces the thought from her mind and goes back to thinking about her act. Sometimes she does a very funny set on interfacing, but only if the audience is middle-aged. The younger ones don't seem to know that interfacing is laughable. Come to think of it, *nobody* laughs much in California. Everybody smiles, but who laughs?

Laughs: that's something she can use. She does Garbo's laugh: "I am so hap-py." What was that movie? "I am so hap-py." She does the Garbo laugh again. Not bad. Who else laughs? Joe E. Brown. The Wicked Witch of the West. Who was she? Somebody Hamilton. Will anybody remember these people? Ruth Buzzi? Goldie Hawn? Yes, that great giggle. Of course, the best giggle is Burt Reynolds's. High and fey. Why does he do that? Is he sending up his own image?

Corinne is thinking of images, Burt Reynolds's and Tom Selleck's, when she hears singing: "Cal-i-for-nia, here I come, Right back where I started from. . . ." Corinne stops pacing and stands in the doorway to the kitchen—as if I'm waiting for the earthquake, she thinks. But there is no earthquake; there is only the thin sweet voice, singing.

Corinne leans against the doorframe and listens. She closes her eyes. At once it is Easter, and she is a child again at Sacred Heart Grammar School, and the thirty-five members of the children's choir, earnest and angelic, look out at her from where they stand, massed about the altar. They wear red cassocks and white surplices, starched, and they seem to have descended from heaven for this one occasion. Their voices are pure, high, untouched by adolescence or by pain; and, with a conviction born of absolute innocence, they sing to God and to Corinne, "Cal-i-for-nia, here I come."

Corinne leans against the doorframe and listens truly now. Imagination aside, drama aside—she listens. It is a single voice she hears, thin and reedy. So, she did not imagine it the first time. It is true. The baby sings.

That night, when Russ comes home, he takes his shower, and they settle in with their first martini and everything is cozy.

Corinne asks him about his day, and he tells her. It was a lousy day. Russ started his own construction company a year ago just as the bottom fell out of the building business, and now there are no jobs to speak of. Just renovation stuff. Clean-up after fires. Sometimes Victorian restorations down in the gay district. But that's about it. So whatever comes his way is bound to be lousy. Corinne knows this, but she asks how his day was anyhow, and he tells her. This is Russ's second marriage, though, so he knows not to go too far with a lousy day. Who needs it?

"But I've got you, babe," he says, and pulls her toward him, and kisses her.

"We've got each other," Corinne says, and kisses him back. "And the baby," she says.

He holds her close then, so that she can't see his face. She makes big eyes like an actor in a bad comedy—she doesn't know why; she just always sees the absurd in everything. After a while they pull away, smiling, secret, and sip their martinis.

"Do you know something?" she says. "Can I tell you something?"

"What?" he says. "Tell me."

"You won't laugh?"

"No," he says, laughing. "I'm sorry. No, I won't laugh."

"Okay," she says. "Here goes."

There is a long silence, and then he says, "Well?"

"It sings."

"It sings?"

"The baby. The fetus. It sings."

Russ is stalled, but only for a second. Then he says, "Plain chant? Or rock-and-roll?" He begins to laugh, and he laughs so hard that he chokes and sloshes martini onto the couch. "You're wonderful," he says. "You're really a funny, funny girl. Woman." He laughs some more. "Is that for your act? I love it."

"I'm serious," she says. "I mean it."

"Well, it's great," he says. "They'll love it."

Corinne puts her hand on her stomach and thinks she has never been so alone in her life. She looks at Russ, with his big square jaw and all those white teeth and his green eyes so trusting and innocent, and she realizes for one second how corrupt she is, how lost, how deserving of a baby who sings; and then she pulls herself together because real life has to go on.

"Let's eat out," she says. "Spaghetti. It's cheap." She kisses him gently on his left eyelid, on his right. She gazes into his eyes and smiles, so that he will not guess she is thinking: Who is this man? Who am I?

Corinne has a job, Fridays and Saturdays for the next three weeks—at the Ironworks. It's not The Comedy Shop, but it's a legitimate gig, and the money is good. Moreover, it will give her something to think about besides whether or not she should go through with the abortion. She and Russ have put that on hold.

She is well into her third month, but she isn't showing yet, so she figures she can handle the three weekends easily. She wishes, in a way, that she were showing. As it is, she only looks . . . She searches for the word, but not for long. The word is *fat.* She looks fat.

She could do fat-girl jokes, but she hates jokes that put down women. And she hates jokes that are blue. Jokes that ridicule husbands. Jokes that ridicule the joker's looks. Jokes about nationalities. Jokes that play into audience prejudice. Jokes about the terrible small town you came from. Jokes about how poor you were, how ugly, how unpopular. Phyllis Diller jokes. Joan Rivers jokes. Jokes about small boobs, wrinkles, sexual inadequacy. Why is she in this business? she wonders. She hates jokes.

She thinks she hears herself praying: Please, please.

What should she do at the Ironworks? What should she do about the baby? What should she do?

The baby is the only one who's decided what to do. The baby sings. Its voice is filling out nicely and it has enlarged its repertoire considerably. It sings a lot of classical melodies Corinne thinks she remembers from somewhere, churchy stuff, but it also favors golden oldies from the forties and fifties, with a few real old-timers thrown in when they seem appropriate. Once, right at the beginning, for instance, after Corinne and Russ had quarreled, Corinne locked herself in the bathroom to sulk and after a while was surprised, and then grateful, to hear the baby crooning, "Oh, my man, I love him so." It struck Corinne a day or so later that this could be a baby that would sell out for *any* one-liner . . . if indeed she decided to have the baby . . . and so she was relieved when the baby turned to more classical pieces.

The baby sings only now and then, and it sings better at some times than at others, but Corinne is convinced it sings best on weekend evenings when she is preparing for her gig. Before she leaves home, Corinne always has a long hot soak in the tub. She lies in the suds with her little orange bath pillow at her head and, as she runs through the night's possibilities, preparing ad libs, heckler put-downs, segues, the baby sings to her.

There is some connection, she is sure, between her work and the baby's singing, but she can't guess what it is. It doesn't matter. She loves this: just she and the baby, together, in song.

Thank you, thank you, she prays.

The Ironworks gig goes extremely well. It is a young crowd, mostly, and so Corinne sticks to her young jokes: life in California, diets, dating, school. The audience laughs, and Russ says she is better than ever, but at the end of the three weeks the manager tells her, "You got it, honey. You got all the moves. You really make them laugh, you know? But they laugh from here only"—he taps his head—"not from the gut. You gotta get gut. You know? Like feeling."

So now the gig is over and Corinne lies in her tub trying to think of gut. She's gotta get gut, she's gotta get feeling. Has she ever *felt?* Well, she feels for Russ; she loves him. She felt for Alan, that bastard; well, maybe he wasn't so bad; maybe he just wasn't ready for marriage, any more than she was. Maybe it's California; maybe nobody *can* feel in California.

Enough about feeling, already. Deliberately, she puts feeling out of her mind, and calls up babies instead. A happy baby, she thinks, and at once the bathroom is crowded with laughing babies, each one roaring and carrying on like Ed McMahon. A fat baby, and she sees a Shelley Winters baby, an Elizabeth Taylor baby, an Orson Welles baby. An active baby: a mile of trampolines and babies doing quadruple somersaults, backflips, high dives. A healthy baby: babies lifting weights, swimming the Channel. Babies.

But abortion is the issue, not babies. Should she have it, or not?

At once she sees a bloody mess, a crushed-looking thing, half animal, half human. Its hands open and close. She gasps. "No," she says aloud, and shakes her head to get rid of the awful picture. "No," and she covers her face.

Gradually she realizes that she has been listening to humming, and now the humming turns to song—"It ain't necessarily so," sung in a good clear mezzo.

Her eyes hurt and she has a headache. In fact, her eyes hurt all the time.

Corinne has finally convinced Russ that she hears the baby singing. Actually, he is convinced that Corinne is halfway around the bend with worry, and he is surprised, when he thinks about it, to find that he loves her anyway, crazy or not. He tells her that as much as he hates the idea, maybe she ought to think about having an abortion.

"I've actually gotten to like the singing," she says.

"Corinne," he says.

"It's the things I see that scare me to death."

"What things? What do you see?"

At once she sees a little crimson baby. It has been squashed into a mason jar. The tiny eyes almost disappear into the puffed cheeks, the cheeks into the neck, the neck into the torso. It is a pickled baby, ancient, preserved.

"Tell me," he says.

"Nothing," she says. "It's just that my eyes hurt."

It's getting late for an abortion, the doctor says, but she can still have one safely.

He's known her for twenty years, all through the first marriage and now through this one, and he's puzzled that a funny and sensible girl like Corinne should be having such a tough time with pregnancy. He had recommended abortion right from the start, because she didn't seem to want the baby and because she was almost forty, but he hadn't really expected her to take him up on it. Looking at her now, though, it is clear to him that she'll never make it. She'll be wacko—if not during the pregnancy, then sure as hell afterward.

So what does she think? What does Russ think?

Well, first, she explains in her new, sort of wandering way, there's something else she wants to ask about; not really important, she supposes, but just something, well, kind of different she probably should mention. It's the old problem of the baby . . . well, um, singing.

"Singing?"

"Singing?" he asks again.

"And humming," Corinne says.

They sit in silence for a minute, the doctor trying to decide whether or not this is a joke. She's got this great poker face. She really is a good comic. So after a while he laughs, and then when she laughs, he knows he's done the right thing. But what a crazy sense of humor!

"You're terrific," he says. "Anything else? How's Russ? How was the Ironworks job?"

"My eyes hurt," she says. "I have headaches."

And so they discuss her vision for a while, and stand-up comedy, and she makes him laugh. And that's that.

At the door he says to her, "Have an abortion, Corinne. Now, before it's too late."

They have just made love and now Russ puts off the light and they lie together in the dark, his hand on her belly.

"Listen," he says. "I want to say something. I've been thinking about what the doctor said, about an abortion. I hate it, I hate the whole idea, but you know, we've got to think of you. And I think this baby is too much for you, I think maybe that's why you've been having those headaches and stuff. Don't you think?"

Corinne puts her hand on his hand and says nothing. After a long while Russ speaks again, into the darkness.

"I've been a lousy father. Two sons I never see. Beth took them back when they were, what, four and two, I guess. Back east. I never see them. The stepfather's good to them, though; he's a good father. I thought maybe I'd have another chance at it, do it right this time, like the marriage. Besides, the business isn't always going to be this bad, you know; I'll get jobs; I'll get money. We could afford it, you know? A son. A daughter. It would be nice. But what I mean is, we've got to take other things into consideration, we've got to consider your health. You're not strong enough, I guess. I always think of you as strong, because you do those gigs and you're funny and all, but I mean, you're almost forty, and the doctor thinks that maybe an abortion is the way to go, and what do I know? I don't know. The singing. The headaches. I don't know."

Russ looks into the dark, seeing nothing.

"I worry about you, you want to know the truth? I do. Corinne?"

Corinne lies beside him, listening to him, refusing to listen to the baby, who all this time has been singing. Russ is as alone as she is, even more alone. She is dumbfounded. She is speechless with love. If he were a whirlpool, she thinks, she would fling herself into it. If he were . . . but he is who he is, and she loves only him, and she makes her decision.

"Corinne?" There is fear in his voice now.

"You think I'm losing my mind," she says.

Silence.

"Yes."

More silence.

"Well, I'm not. Headaches are a normal part of lots of pregnancies, the doctor said, and the singing doesn't mean anything at all. He explained what was really going on, why I thought I heard it sing. You see," Corinne says, improvising freely now, making it all up, for him, her gift to him, "you see, when you get somebody as high-strung as me and you add pregnancy right at the time I'm about to make it big as a stand-up, then the pressures get to be so much that sometimes the imagination can take over, the doctor said, and when you tune in to the normal sounds of your body, you hear them really loud, as if they were amplified by a three-thousand-watt PA system, and it can sound like singing. See?"

Russ says nothing.

"So you see, it all makes sense, really. You don't have to worry about me."

"Come on," Russ says. "Do you mean to tell me you never heard the baby singing?"

"Well, I heard it, sort of. You know? It was really all in my mind. I mean, the *sound* was in my body physiologically, but my hearing it as *singing* was just . . ."

"Just your imagination."

Corinne does not answer.

"Well?"

"Right," she says, making the total gift. "It was just my imagination."

And the baby—who has not stopped singing all this time, love songs mostly—stops singing now, and does not sing again until the day scheduled for the abortion.

The baby has not sung in three weeks. It is Corinne's fifth month now, and at last they have been able to do an amniocentesis. The news is bad. One of the baby's chromosomes does not match up to anything in hers, anything in Russ's. What this means, they tell her, is that the baby is not normal. It will be deformed in some way; in what way, they have no idea.

Corinne and Russ decide on abortion.

They talk very little about their decision now that they have made it. In fact, they talk very little about anything. Corinne's face grows daily more haggard, and Corinne avoids Russ's eyes. She is silent much of the time, thinking. The baby is silent all the time.

The abortion will be by hypertonic saline injection, a simple procedure, complicated only by the fact that Corinne has waited so long. She has been given a booklet to read and she has listened to a tape, and so she knows about the injection of the saline solution, she knows about the contractions that will begin slowly and then get more and more frequent, and she knows about the dangers of infection and excessive bleeding.

She knows moreover that it will be a formed fetus she will expel.

Russ has come with her to the hospital and is outside in the waiting room. Corinne thinks of him, of how she loves him, of how their lives will be better, safer, without this baby who sings. This deformed baby. Who sings. If only she could hear the singing once more, just once.

Corinne lies on the table with her legs in the thigh rests, and one of the nurses drapes the examining sheet over and around her. The other nurse, or someone—Corinne is getting confused; her eyesight seems fuzzy—takes her pulse and her blood pressure. She feels someone washing her, the careful hands, the warm fluid. So, it is beginning.

Corinne closes her eyes and tries to make her mind a blank. Dark, she thinks. Dark. She squeezes her eyes tight against the light, she wants to remain in this cool darkness forever, she wants to cease being. And then, amazingly, the dark does close in on her. Though she opens her eyes, she sees nothing. She can remain this way forever if she wills it. The dark is cool to the touch, and it is comforting somehow; it invites her in. She can lean into it, give herself up to it, and be safe, alone, forever.

She tries to sit up. She will enter this dark. She will do it. Please, please, she hears herself say. And then all at once she thinks of Russ and the baby, and instead of surrendering to the dark, she pushes it away.

With one sweep of her hand she pushes the sheet from her and flings it to the floor. She pulls her legs from the thigh rests and manages to sit up, blinded still, but fighting.

"Here now," a nurse says, caught off guard, unsure what to do. "Hold on now. It's all right. It's fine."

"Easy now. Easy," the doctor says, thinking Yes, here it is, what else is new.

Together the nurses and the doctor make an effort to stop her, but they are too late, because by this time Corinne has fought free of any restraints. She is off the examining couch and, naked, huddles in the corner of the small room.

"No," she shouts. "I want the baby. I want the baby." And later, when she has stopped shouting, when she has stopped crying, still she clutches her knees to her chest and whispers over and over, "I want the baby."

So there is no abortion after all.

By the time she is discharged, Corinne's vision has returned, dimly. Moreover, though she tells nobody, she has heard humming, and once or twice a whole line of music. The baby has begun to sing again.

Corinne has more offers than she wants: The Hungry I, the Purple Onion, The Comedy Shop. Suddenly everybody decides it's time to take a look at her, but she is in no shape to be looked at, so she signs for two weeks at My Uncle's Bureau and lets it go at that.

She is only marginally pretty now, she is six months pregnant, and she is carrying a deformed child. Furthermore, she can see very little, and what she does see, she often sees double.

Her humor, therefore, is spare and grim, but audiences love it. She begins slow: "When I was a girl, I always wanted to look like Elizabeth Taylor," she says, and glances down at her swollen belly. Two beats. "And now I do." They laugh with her, and applaud. Now she can quicken the pace, sharpen the humor. They follow her; they are completely captivated.

She has found some new way of holding her body—tipping her head, thrusting out her belly—and instead of putting off her audience, or embarrassing them, it charms them. The laughter is *with* her, the applause *for* her. She could do anything out there and get away with it. And she knows it. They simply love her.

In her dressing room after the show she tells herself that somehow, magically, she's learned to work from the heart instead of just from the head. She's got gut. She's got feeling. But she knows it's something more than that.

By the end of the two weeks she is convinced that the successful new element in her act is the baby. This deformed baby, this abnormal baby she has tried to kill. And what interests her most is that she no longer cares about success as a stand-up.

Corinne falls asleep that night to the sound of the baby's crooning. She is trying to pray, Please, please, but with Russ's snoring and the baby's lullaby, they all get mixed up together in her mind—God, Russ, the baby—and she forgets to whom she is praying or why. She sleeps.

The baby sings all the time now. It starts first thing in the morning with a nice soft piece by Telemann or Brahms; there are assorted lullabyes at bedtime; and throughout the day it is bop, opera, ragtime, blues, a little rock-and-roll, big-band stuff—the baby never tires.

Corinne tells no one about this, not even Russ.

She and Russ talk about almost everything now: their love for each other, their hopes for the baby, their plans. They have lots of plans. Russ has assured Corinne that whatever happens, he's ready for it. Corinne is his whole life, and no matter how badly the baby is deformed, they'll manage. They'll do the right thing. They'll survive.

They talk about almost everything, but they do not talk about the baby's singing.

For Corinne the singing is secret, mysterious. It contains some revelation, of course, but she does not want to know what that revelation might be.

The singing is somehow tied up with her work; but more than that, with her life. It is part of her fate. It is inescapable. And she is perfectly content to wait.

Corinne has been in labor for three hours, and the baby has been singing the whole time. The doctor has administered a mild anesthetic and a nurse remains at bedside, but the birth does not seem imminent, and so for Corinne it is a period of pain and waiting. And for the baby, singing.

"These lights are so strong," Corinne says, or thinks she says. "The lights are blinding."

The nurse looks at her for a moment and then goes back to the letter she is writing.

"Please," Corinne says, "thank you."

She is unconscious, she supposes; she is imagining the lights. Or perhaps the lights are indeed bright and she sees them as they really are *because* she is unconscious. Or perhaps her sight has come back, as strong as it used to be. Whatever the case, she doesn't want to think about it now. Besides, for some reason or other, even though the lights are blinding, they are not blinding her. They do not even bother her. It is as if light is her natural element.

"Thank you," she says. To someone.

The singing is wonderful, a cappella things Corinne recognizes as Brahms, Mozart, Bach. The baby's voice can assume any dimension it wants now, swelling from a single thin note to choir volume; it can take on the tone and resonance of musical instruments, violin, viola, flute; it can become all sounds; it enchants.

The contractions are more frequent; even unconscious, Corinne can tell that. Good. Soon the waiting will be over and she will have her wonderful baby, her perfect baby. But at once she realizes hers will not be a perfect baby; it will be deformed. "Please," she says, "please," as if prayer can keep Russ from being told—as he will be soon after the birth—that his baby has been born dumb. Russ, who has never understood comedians.

But now the singing has begun to swell in volume. It is as if the baby has become a full choir, with many voices, with great strength.

The baby will be fine, however it is, she thinks. She thinks of Russ, worried half to death. She is no longer worried. She accepts what will be.

The contractions are very frequent now and the light is much brighter. She knows the doctor has come into the room, because she hears his voice. There is another nurse too. And soon there will be the baby.

The light is so bright that she can see none of them. She can see into the light, it is true; she can see the soft fleecy nimbus flowing beyond the light, but she can see nothing in the room.

The singing. The singing and the light. It is Palestrina she hears, in polyphony, each voice lambent. The light envelops her, catches her up from this table where the doctor bends over her and where already can be seen the shimmering yellow hair of the baby. The light lifts her, and the singing lifts her, and she says, "Yes," she says, "Thank you."

She accepts what will be. She accepts what is.

The room is filled with singing and with light, and the singing is transformed into light, more light, more lucency, and still she says, "Yes," until she cannot bear it, and she reaches up and tears the light aside. And sees.

OFFERINGS

JOYCE R. KORNBLATT

Joyce Reiser Kornblatt was born in Boston in 1944. She is the author of *Nothing to Do with Love*, a book of stories; *White Water*, a novel; and the forthcoming fictional memoir *Breaking Bread*. She teaches at the University of Maryland.

On Sunday mornings, my mother tells me, my grandfather went to the Quincy Street pool and swam in the nude. My grandmother held this against him. It was not her sole complaint. Against her husband, she had two categories of grievances: bad habits and failures. Swimming in the nude was a bad habit, as were sleepwalking and cluttering. To the latter two, Pa took exception. He did not sleepwalk, he said; he needed solitude, and the middle of the night was the only time he could have it. He said the only walking he did was from the bedroom to the kitchen where he sat at the table, drank a cup of Postum, and studied the moon and the constellations. He told her that what she called clutter, he considered supplies: wood scraps, newspapers, string, jars, cracker boxes. Didn't he make his baby girls alphabet blocks from pieces of pine left over from the trestle table he built? Didn't he use the cracker boxes to start seedlings for the garden he grew each summer on the front porch of their second-floor flat in Boston, redwood planters brimming with marigolds and pansies, morning glories climbing the string trellises he strung between the porch posts? Didn't he wind up using all those newspapers to cover the broadloom when he painted the parlor's twelve-foot-high walls? No matter. Sleepwalking was sleepwalking. Clutter was clutter. My grandmother had recorded them under *bad habits*, and there were no erasures in *her* emotional ledger.

In the *failures* column, she entered "lack of ambition." My grandfather was the storekeeper, but his wife was the one in the family who kept the accounts.

His business was second-hand clothing. "Rags," my grandmother said. "Who can make a living from rags?"

"We do all right," Pa said. "We get along."

She wanted jewelry. She wanted to buy three yards of silk and take it to the dressmaker who would turn it into a tunic with stylish padded shoulders and bound buttonholes and a tassled sash. She wanted to buy her shoes in Filene's Shoe Salon on the third floor instead of in the bargain basement where everything smelled musty and looked dull, even the patent leather, as if a fine rain of dust fell constantly on the discounted merchandise.

She wanted a piano, too. A baby grand. In Lithuania, she'd had a baby grand, and lessons once a week from Malke Weiss, who had trained at the conservatory at Minsk and claimed to have once met Stokowski.

"Did I come to America to lose everything I had?" my grandmother wailed.

"You came like we all did," her husband said. "To save your life."

Sundays, as soon as the weather warmed, my grandfather headed for the beach. He took his youngest daughter, my mother, with him. Nantasket, Wellfleet, Revere. Once they took the ferry to Martha's Vineyard, came home in the moonlight, and my grandfather "turned to silver," my mother says, "like a sculpture of a famous man."

In sleep, a bride in Pittsburgh, my mother returned to the ocean. Pa swung her over the waves. Their laughter rolled in again from that horizon line where memories bob like daring swimmers, like sailboats out too far for safety—rolled in to break beautifully and ferociously on the clean sand whose warmth she felt again in the landlocked rooms she lived in now, pieces of cardboard wedged against the cold in gaps between windows and frames. She would wake with the taste of salt in her mouth, her cheeks stiff with salt, her eyes red from its sting. "Nightmares," she lied to my father as he tried to console her. "Such terrible dreams."

They had lived in Pittsburgh for two years, but she was not used to it at all. My grandfather wrote her letters in his graceful hand: "Is it true you pay double for life insurance there? Are all the fish in the rivers dead?" The fish were not dead, but she hated the acrid smell from the mills, the furniture thick with soot, the mill whistles whining like wolves. Raised there, my father knew all the tricks for living in that sullied place, and he tried to teach them to her.

"It hurts to breathe," she would complain.

"Breathe like this, through your nose," he would tell her, a hand over his mouth as he demonstrated.

"The clothes get dirty as soon as I hang them on the line."

"Hang them in the bathtub," he would say, and one night came home with a drying rack for his wife to set in the claw-footed tub.

"In the middle of the day it's dark!" she would cry.

He would turn on all the lights in the apartment. "Now see? Who needs sunshine when you got Edison?"

"The ocean," she would weep. "I miss the beach."

And he would take her for walks around the municipal reservoir, the filtration plant's machinery churning in their ears.

It was 1943. My mother was three months pregnant with me, her ankles already swollen, her small breasts ballooning, the dark mother-line descending from her navel like the plunge of an anchor dropped into the sea. "I don't recognize myself," she said. "I don't know who I am."

"Don't talk foolish," my father said. "You're my wife."

In December, he was drafted. They had known he would be, but my parents were not people for whom the abstract future held much currency. She handed him the letter that had arrived that morning. He read in a quavering voice, as if the news were unexpected: "Greetings."

"I can't stay here alone," she said.

"You can stay with Lena," he said. His aunt and uncle lived two buildings down. "They have the extra room since Sammy joined."

"I'll go home," she said, reminding him of her heart's geography.

They packed up all their personal belongings. As each item disappeared into a container, it seemed to my mother that her young marriage itself was being dismantled, undone: a steamer trunk of clothing, towels, muslin sheets; a carton of chipped dishes, service for four—the "Silver Rose" pattern she'd found at the thrift shop where she'd also discovered the gilt-framed Rembrandt reproduction (for only a dollar) that she'd bought my father for his twenty-eighth birthday.

Years before, a high-school teacher had noticed my father's talent and provided him with the sketching pads his parents could not afford. For three years, my father had spent all his spare time filling the pages with drawings of bridges and birds and horse-drawn ice wagons plodding up slick cobblestoned hills. When he'd begun to love art more than anything else, knowing it would keep him poor forever (he had read that painters starved, turned to absinthe and cocaine, were always being evicted from their wretched quarters in the worst sections of Paris and New York), knowing this hobby could turn into an addiction, he threw his pencils away and hid the pads in the back of his closet. Years later I discovered them in a cardboard carton on which he'd printed "Art Work." I praised the fine detail, the subtle composition, the purity of line. "So what," he said. "Once upon a time, I had a knack. Now I'm just another working stiff."

Stiff was accurate: in the produce yards, he'd arrive at 4 A.M. to begin unloading the crates of fruits and vegetables the farmers brought in their pickup trucks, then reloading the goods into the vans of merchants who came to haggle with the farmers over the day's offerings. For my father, the pay was meager but dependable. In the beginning, he dreamed of a produce store someday, "being my own man," tried to see his years in the yards as "training in the business." To his new wife, who had come to Pittsburgh one summer to visit a cousin and been pursued by my father from bumper cars to ferris wheel to merry-go-round in a local amusement park, he brought gifts: bagfuls of bruised tomatoes, scarred peppers, lettuce going brown, dented apples, overripe bananas—bounty salvaged from the trash bin.

My mother made stews and soups, applesauce, banana bread. She grew proud of her domestic resourcefulness, resentful that it was required. What she wanted from him was one perfect melon, exotically sweet. If only once he had splurged, she might have forgiven him his common sense.

A year after my mother's wedding and departure from Boston, my grandfather sent her a present: a lace collar, brand new, from the upper levels of Filene's. Never mind that he had never given his own wife such a fine offering. He had no rival for his wife, no need for a canny courtship that struck the precisely right note between lament and aplomb. What he arrived at was a rather irresistible dignity that was, in fact, his actual nature.

Sometimes during those first two years of her marriage, my mother would catch my father staring at Rembrandt's portrait of the aristocrat in the plumed helmet, and my father looked chastened to her, as if rebuked by the elegance of the headpiece, the privileged angle of the head, as if my father suspected that my mother might have bought him this particular print for reasons not entirely testimonial. When my father talked about "making ends meet," was he talking less about money than his own cloven self?

She took down the Rembrandt from its place in the room that served as both parlor and bedroom. French doors camouflaged the bed that folded up into the wall, hidden away like dreams and sex. She took down the shirred organdy curtains she'd made from two yards she'd discovered in the remnant box at Woolworth's. In newspaper, she wrapped the photographs she'd kept on the bureau and placed them in a canvas satchel: her parents, two immigrants "keeping an eye" on their American daughter.

My grandfather was waiting for her at the station. It was snowing. The glittering flakes stuck to his thin white hair, to the shoulders and sleeves of his old tweed overcoat, even to the tops of his age-stained hands. As the train steamed into his view, my mother tells me, he lifted his arms in greeting, and the platform lights transformed them into shining wings. A crown seemed to shimmer on his head.

I called him "Pa" as my mother did, and he never objected. His was the thumb I grasped from my crib. His was the cheek against whose stubble my own softness was revealed to me. His arm was a raft I floated on inside the bathroom sink where he bathed me. "He was getting you ready for swimming," my mother says. "To be happy in the water." I took my first steps toward him, his voice speaking my name. He was the goal toward which I aspired, the reward of his hug sharpening my instinctive ambition.

When he left the house for the store, I spent the hours of his absence mimicking him. I reinvented his presence by wearing his shoes, my tiny feet lost in the leather boats in which I sailed back and forth across the floor. I stood at the parlor window as he did, watching the street, observing the birds that nested in the maple, my hands clasped behind my back, my forehead pressed to the glass so that my breath clouded the pane. I chanted some loose imitation of the prayers he intoned when he woke and before he went to sleep, my body swaying like his, my eyes closed to this world. In the kitchen, I pulled newspapers from his stack beside the icebox, spread them open on the linoleum, pretended to lose myself as he did in the words I could not yet read; still, the print felt alive to me, the letters moved like tiny animals beneath my finger. Later I would come to understand that he was the man from whom I learned transcendence; but in those early years, before I needed words to justify devotion, I simply did what Pa did. I loved him. When he came home at the end of the day, I sat on the seat he made of his ankles, I grasped his hands, I rode the ship his body became, and we shouted together like sea gulls swooping down from the sky to the beach, up again, up, into the unpeopled heights.

By the time my father came home from the service, I was already my grandfather's child. My mother seemed to will the taxi into view—that was how deeply she concentrated on the corner around which it turned. It cruised down the block of one-time Victorian mansions converted now into rental units with dumbwaiters boarded up, closets for fancy wardrobes made over into bathrooms, and clotheslines strung across the yards in which wealthy families lolled once, or played croquet, or convalesced. My mother had bought me my first pair of Mary Janes and anklets edged with lace. She had dressed me in starched organdy and secured a pink bow in my wispy curls. My mother and grandparents were dressed up in their best clothes as well, their faces serious, anxious, as if they doubted that my father was truly returning or feared what his return implied. We waited in the front yard on that cool October afternoon, the sun's light thinned out, bleached, falling almost like a crust of ice on the leafless branches of the sycamores and elms. On that kind of day—as much the end of something as the beginning—we could have been a rich family of another time, awaiting a hearse or wedding coach, grieving or celebrating, it would have been hard to decipher which.

The stranger, my father, climbed out of the cab. He wore his Navy whites, and looked like the uniformed man in the photograph on my mother's dresser. She had taken me to the picture every evening before bed, as other children are led through prayers, or read to, or taught little rhymes with which they can console themselves in the dark. "This is your daddy," she would say, taking my hand and laying it against the glass. Was I supposed to feel my father's face coming to life against my palm? I did not understand her ritual and had not known what was expected of me. Nor did I now.

"That's your daddy," my mother said. Her voice broke. She ran down the front walk and embraced the stranger. He kissed her on her mouth. Daddy? I held onto Pa's leg, my face pressed against the familiar gabardine; his hand cupped my head, a proprietary gesture.

My father kissed my grandmother, shook Pa's hand, then hugged him with one arm. The other arm cradled a box bound by a thick red ribbon and an oversized bow; he'd left his duffle bag at the curb. Even as he greeted my grandfather, my father's eyes fixed on me. Tears clustered in his lashes and his gaze seemed to require of me a reciprocal intensity. Now he knelt down to my level. He held out the present to me. He said my name. He knew me. Later I would learn that he had kept my picture taped to the bottom of the bunk above his, so that when he went to sleep at night and when he woke in the morning, the first thing he saw was not a Betty Grable pinup, or even a photograph of his wife, but me—an infant on a blanket spread out on the grass in Franklin Park.

I said nothing. He was a stranger. I turned my face back into the fabric of my grandfather's trouser leg, and he allowed me the refuge. "Give your daddy a kiss," my mother instructed, but Pa kept his hand on my head, his claim to me clear.

Against such odds my father rose and took my mother's hand. They mounted the porch steps, his gift for me still unaccepted, the transaction unaccomplished.

Pa and I followed.

My grandmother trailed us all, sighing. Perhaps one of her many ailments—she would be dead by winter—had flared up, or this homecoming had disappointed her, or she was sad because in a few hours it would be time to take off her good dress and who could say when another occasion for wearing it might arise.

Nana died in January, three months after my father's return. My mother tells me her parents' marriage "wasn't good." She tells me anecdotes that support that interpretation. By the time I was born, Nana was a woman who stayed in bed, rising only to complain about something for which no remedy existed: the war, the weather, the passing of time. She was too absorbed with her ailments, her deprivations, her husband's lack of drive to offer her daughter or her grandchild much notice. "Did I come to America to lose everything I had?" Nor did our presence bring her solace. She was inconsolable, which I have come to learn is a clinical term, a disease. Perhaps it was chronic unhappiness that killed her, that rendered her less than alive to me even before she died. My sense of her remains abstract and vague, as much as my memories of Pa are concrete, sensuous, embodied. But did they have feelings for each other that my mother failed to recognize? In spite of the bickering, the criticism, the silences, the averted eyes, did they love each other?

For weeks after her death in the hospital, where she'd faded away like a dimming lightbulb or a radio signal growing weaker until at last it leaves the range of human reach, Pa walked the rooms of our flat not so much searching for his wife as assuring himself of her disappearance. A dozen times a day he spoke her name, silence answered, he nodded. He held her shawl in his arms, the one she'd wrapped around her bulk regardless of the season or the temperature in the house, and the near weightlessness of the garment testified: *she is gone.* He sat on her side of their bed and studied the emptiness, the sheer negation suggested by the space where she had lain. One day I found him there, the fingers of one hand tracing the opened palm of the other. "This is Lithuania," he said, stroking the map of his own flesh. "Your nana came from . . . right here." He stared at the spot until it transformed itself into a peopled town, a world I could not see. Even after he went back to the store, resumed his life, took up again his newspapers, his gardening, his grandchild—still some crucial part of him remained where I found him that day, with the young girl he had married in a town that no longer existed on any map—the Nazis had leveled the place, obliterated it—save the one in his mind.

My mother's grieving took a different form: a series of illnesses that seemed like a speeded-up version of Nana's life. In a single month, my mother contracted bronchitis, middle ear infection, "stomach trouble," water on the knee. It was left to my father, at the time without a job, to care for me. He took me to the park and I would not play: I froze at the top of the slide until he let me climb backwards down the ladder; I dug my toes into the ground to stop the swing he pushed; I let the ball he threw me sail beyond me into the prickly bushes. He cooked meals I left on my plate. He filled the tub for my bath and I drained it. Finally, he withdrew from the effort, and I blamed him for this, too, though I knew I would resist all his appeals, all his suggestions. I knew what he refused to admit: Nana had died to make room for him.

In one way or another I was losing everyone. Pa was divided now between past and present, my mother always ill, Nana dead. I had even been evicted from the room I had shared with my mother. When my father had returned, I was moved to a corner of the parlor. A junior bed, a maple chest, a floor lamp, a small trunk that held my toys: these were the furnishings in the area that came to be considered my "room" as surely as if walls had risen around it, a door hinged to the invisible frame. I was learning the ways in which adults could impose on children realities for which no evidence existed: "This is your father, this is your room, there is no reason in the world for you to be so unhappy." In the room my parents now occupied, the door closed "for privacy," I listened easily to every word of their arguments.

"It's time to make plans to go home," he said.

"He won't come," she said, referring to Pa, meaning herself.

"Then he'll live with your sister." Aunt Joan and her family had a bungalow in Revere, four blocks from the ocean.

"He can't get to his store from Revere," she said. "He'll be lost."

"I'm lost here."

He drove a milk truck for a few months; he worked as a letter-sorter for the post office; he sold Uncle Herb's Vitamin Tonic door-to-door. "In the yards," he said, "I'm established. I know my way around. I know the people."

After Nana died, she said, "Pa needs you, he needs an assistant. He wants you to have the position."

"He needs me like a hole in the head. There aren't enough customers for him to wait on himself."

"He means for you to have it after him."

"I don't want it. When will you hear what I'm telling you?"

I heard.

My mother told me, "We have to break up the house." I was five years old. When she had used those words weeks before to describe this day that had now arrived with no greater signal than the low whine of the moving van which had taken its place outside—when my mother had first said, "We are going to have to break up the house"—I had imagined terrible destruction. Windows would shatter, floors would buckle and splinter, ceilings and walls would cave in on themselves. At night, forcing myself to prepare for the day of terror, I could nearly smell the crumbling plaster, almost feel the night air whip through the shell of the dying house.

My mother had worked out all the details of the plan. The furniture would be sold to our landlord, Mr. Pinsky, who would disperse the pieces to furnished flats he rented out all over the city. My grandfather's store would be liquidated, and he would go to live with Aunt Joan *(I know that,* I thought; *I heard you plotting).* My mother and I would leave Boston on the night train to join my father in Pittsburgh where he had been waiting for months for us to "make the move already." As she made these decisions, finally, after months of tortured refusals and procrastinations, I imagine my mother was stunned by how simply, how logically, how inevitably the plan took form: as if each decision were a spoke on a wheel to which she had been bound without knowing it, on whose momentum she would travel the rest of her life, as surely as the night train would bear her and her child into the darkness.

I had gone with Pa to the store on his last day. I loved to visit there, dressing up in shabby costumes, listening to my grandfather converse in Yiddish with neighbors who came looking for a good winter jacket, a serviceable pair of woolen trousers. Now the old coats and suits and battered hats were gone from the racks and shelves. I helped him soap the windows. He swept the floor, pushing the broom heavily across the worn oak planks. Our voices sounded hollow, lost in the emptiness. In a cardboard carton, we collected the last pieces of litter and together we dragged the box to the curb. He padlocked the front door, and on the tarnished doorknob he hung the For Rent sign with which the landlord had entrusted him. He took my hand. Without looking back a single time, we walked home.

"You're seventy years old," my mother had told him that evening. "You deserve a retirement."

"Like Jonah deserved a whale."

"You won't make this a little bit easy for me?"

"You want I should show you how I really feel? You want I should jump off the roof right now?"

While the movers worked, I sat on a crate and watched them carry out piece after piece of the household I loved. They worked slowly, grunting under their burdens. It was July, hot, the air dead with heat, and the movers' faces gleamed with sweat. When they took off their shirts, their brown-skinned bodies looked like a piano's polished wood, each man a carved African idol, an ebony warrior. I had seen pictures of them in National Geographic, tribal icons discovered in the tombs of long-buried chieftains. Perhaps my grandparents' lamps and chairs and dressers and beds were offerings of some sort. Perhaps the huge van that rested out front like a giant coffin on wheels was a repository for treasures promised a thousand years ago to an undying spirit. That was no more strange than my mother's explanation: "Just because people love each other doesn't mean they stay together." Why not, I asked. "The world has its reasons," my mother said, as if the planet itself had a brain, and a heart. She shook her head mournfully. Her chin shuddered. "Don't think I understand it better than you do. I don't."

Pa did not jump off a roof. His suicide was more subtle, carried out in stages over the course of a year, kindly in that it allowed for other interpretations: hardening of the arteries, senility, geriatric diseases for which no names had yet been invented, but that surely could account for his decline. "He was old," my mother tells me. "You wouldn't realize. For you, he always had energy. But he was an old man."

First he stopped talking. Aunt Joan called from Revere: "I can't get him to say a word," she told my mother. "You try."

My mother coaxed and demanded. She pleaded. In the apartment we lived in now, the flowers and yards of my life in Boston abandoned for brick and alleys and hallways thick with strangers, I was emptying the dollhouse my father had bought me of all its fragile furniture. I stashed the pieces under my bed. I undressed the family of tiny dolls who were meant to live in the once-intact household and assigned each member, alone and naked, to a different barren room. My mother called me from the kitchen. I came to the doorway. "It's Pa," she said, as if I hadn't listened to her entire half of the conversation. She thrust the receiver at me. "He wants to talk to you."

But I knew that could not be true. I had heard her say, "This is a crazy thing you're doing, Pa, refusing to speak."

Well, crazy or not, he had chosen it, as he had not chosen anything else that had happened to him in the last year. I would not take the phone. I would not violate his freedom. I would not tempt him out of his dignity. Behind my burning eyes, my locked lips, my breath stilled like an ocean in which the tide suddenly ceases to operate, I joined him in his silence. I joined him. "Talk to him," she said. I went to my room and got into bed. I was six years old, and I would never see my grandfather again. For five days, I kept mute, like Pa—we protested together—and no entreaty on my parents' part was strong enough to sunder that connection, no wooing or threat capable of interrupting that long, long conversation.

THE COSTA BRAVA, 1959

WARD JUST

Ward Just is the author of six novels and two collections of short stories. He lives in Andover, Massachusetts.

Ted had been terribly sick in Saulieu, a combination of too much wine and a poisonous fish soup, and no one to blame but himself. He had chosen the night in Saulieu to be difficult about money, explaining to Bettina that a room and dinner for two plus wine at the glorious Côte d'Or was an extravagance they could not afford. It was only their third day in France, and he was not yet comfortable in francs. Gasoline was expensive, and it was necessary to keep a reserve for contingencies. The travel agent had said that Spain would be cheap, but she had also said that it would be warm in Europe; and when they had landed at Orly it was cold, 40 degrees, and raining. And the room at the Continental had been very expensive, though he had wisely prepaid in Chicago.

They had driven hesitantly into the parking lot at the Côte d'Or, their little rented Renault conspicuous between two black Citröen sedans. The Côte d'Or had the appearance of an elegant country house. A bushy cat lay dozing on the doormat, and the trees in the courtyard were changing in a blaze of red and gold. Bettina read the specialties from the Michelin guide: *terrine royal, timbale de quenelles de brochet eminance, poularde de Bresse belle-aurore.* Two stars, 23 rooms. She rolled down the window and smiled slowly, arching her eyebrows. They could smell the kitchen.

He asked if she minded, and she said she didn't.

It's so damned expensive, he said.

She said, "I'm so tired."

Ted said, "We'll take a nap before dinner."

They booked into the shabby hotel down the street, and Ted took a stroll around town while she slept. In the Basilique St.-Andoche he sat a moment in meditation, and then in prayer—her good health, his good health, their future together. Then he lit a taper and stood watching it burn; the air was chilly and damp inside the church. Later, they had an aperitif in a cafe and returned to the hotel to dine at a table by the front window. From the window they could see the Côte d'Or through the trees, a little privet hedge in front and a rosy glow within. It had begun to rain, and the hotel dining room was drafty and cold. Ted ordered the fish soup and roast chicken and knew right away that he had made a terrible mistake. Bettina ordered a plain omelet, and they ate in silence, looking out the window through the rain at the alluring Côte d'Or. He knew he had been very stupid; it was one of the best restaurants in France. To kill the taste of the soup, he drank two bottles of wine. Bettina, exhausted, went to bed immediately after dinner. Ted walked across the street alone to have a cognac at the tiny bar off the dining room of the Côte d'Or. There were two large parties still at table, and much laughter; they were talking back and forth. Ted's French was not good enough to eavesdrop seriously, but they seemed to be talking about American politics, John F. Kennedy, and the primary campaign, still months away. He heard, "Weees-consin" and "Wes Virginia" and then a blast of laughter. He wondered who they were, to have such detailed knowledge of American elections. The room was very warm. Ted picked up a copy of *Le Monde,* but the text was impossible to read. Inside, however, was a piece on the Kennedy *stratégie.* It depressed him, not speaking French or reading it. It would be better in Spain, where he knew the language and admired the culture. His stomach was already sour, and he had three cognacs before returning to the hotel to be sick.

The weather improved as they drove south. They had a cheerful, lovely drive on secondary roads to Perpignan. They lunched on bread and cheese, choosing pretty places off the road to eat. And Bettina's strength returned. Her color improved, and she lost the preoccupied look she had had for three weeks, ever since the miscarriage. Five months pregnant, and it had seemed to Ted that she could get no larger. When she began to cramp early one evening, neither of them knew what it was, or what it meant; she was alarmed, but passed it off as an upset stomach. At midnight he had rushed her to the hospital, and in two hours knew that she had lost the babies, a boy and a girl. She had been pregnant with twins, and that was such a surprise because there were no twins on either side of the family. Of course there was no chance of saving either one, they were so tiny and undeveloped. The doctor said that Bettina was perfectly healthy, it was just something that had happened; she would have other children. Ted listened to all this in a stunned state. He did not know the mechanics of it, and when the doctor explained, he listened carefully but did not know the right questions to ask; there were certain obvious questions, but he did not want to seem a fool. Bettina had been wonderfully brave that evening, and later in the car rushing to the hospital, displaying a dignity and serenity that he had not known she possessed. It was the first crisis for either of them, and she had been great. To Ted, the doctor said that the twins were a shock to her system. She was a perfectly normal, healthy girl but this was her first pregnancy and twins after all, what a surprise; it was simply too much. All this in the corridor outside Bettina's room, the two of them whispering together as if it were a conspiracy. The doctor had taken him out of earshot, but the door was open and Ted could see Bettina in her bed, and he knew she was watching them even though she was supposed to be asleep. Dr. McNab put his hand on Ted's shoulder and spoke confidentially, man-to-man. Ted gathered that this was information best kept to himself, the "shock to her system." He was flattered that the doctor would confide in him; the night before, the nurses had been brusque. He had sat in the waiting room for two hours with no word from anyone, and no idea what was happening except that it was precarious. The truth was, he had not had time to become accustomed to the idea of being a father; and now he wouldn't be one, at least not this year. But he accepted without question the doctor's explanation (such as it was) and cheerful prognosis. Of course they would have other children.

Bettina was not communicative, lying in her bed, the stack of books unread, staring out the window or at the ceiling. She cried only once, the next morning, when he arrived in her room with a dozen roses. No, she said, there was no pain; there had been, the night before. Now she was—uncomfortable. She wondered if, really, she were not the slightest bit relieved. She looked at him and frowned. Wrong word. Not *relieved*, exactly. But they had been married only a year and hardly knew each other, and children were a responsibility. Wasn't that what her mischievous friend Evie had said? Didn't everyone say that children would change their life together, and not absolutely for the better: diapers, three A.M. feedings, colic, tantrums, unreliable baby sitters. She had quoted an Englishman to him: *The pram in the hallway is the enemy of art.* Ted was not amused. So she had reassured him, of course, that was no argument for not having children, children were adorable and everyone wanted a family; but still. As the doctor said, they were both young. And they were happy on the practical surface of things, their house, their friends, Ted's job. And Ted was preoccupied, too; as it happened, he was working with the senior partner on his first big case. The senior partner was a legend on La Salle Street, and he seemed to look on Ted as a protégé. Ted described the case in detail to her as she lay in the narrow hospital bed; and as if to confirm his estimate of his excellent prospects with Estabrook, Mozart they were interrupted by the nurse bearing an aspidistra with a get-well card signed by the man himself in his muscular scrawl, E. L. Mozart.

Bettina was home in four days. She went immediately to her desk in the bedroom, to look at the poem she had been writing. She had been very excited about it, but now the poem seemed—frivolous. About one inch deep, she said to Ted that night at dinner. And derivative, and the odd part was that it was derivative of a poet she did not admire: e. e. cummings, with his erratic syntax and masculine sensibility. She had not seen that when she was working on the poem, nor had it seemed to her one inch deep. As she spoke, she knew that her life was changed in some unfathomable way. It was not simply the miscarriage, it was something more; the miscarriage had released hidden emotions. How strange a word it was, "miscarriage," as in miscarriage of justice. And the form that Ted had been given to sign did not use the word at all; the word on the form was "abortion."

That night he got the idea of a vacation.

Europe, he blurted. It was entirely spur-of-the-moment, and she doubted it would ever happen. What about Mozart and the big case? The trip would have to wait until the case was settled—as, miraculously, it was, the following week, a fine out-of-court settlement for the client. This was an omen, and Ted was elated. He had never been to Europe or even out of America. Bettina had been two years before, the summer of her senior year in college. Ted was courting her then and wrote her every day from Chicago, where he was in his final year at law school. She had given him an itinerary, carefully typed by her father's secretary. Ted had sent her three or four long letters to every city on the itinerary, places he knew only from an atlas, London, Amsterdam, Paris, Lausanne, Venice, Florence, Rome. The letters were his way of holding her. Ted was terrified that she would meet someone sexy in Europe and would have a love affair that would change her forever. And then she would be lost to him. Later, he learned that the letters were the cause of much hilarity, some of it forced. Bettina was traveling with her roommates, the three of them determined to have an adventure before settling down and marrying someone. The letters were somehow inhibiting, and irritating in their wordy insistence and blunt postmark, *CHICAGO.*

All those damned letters, Evie St. John said later. *God,* Ted. It was like being followed by your family, *watched.* Just once we wanted to arrive at the hotel and find nothing at the desk. It was as if you were on the trip with us, and it was supposed to be girls-only. Or maybe Peggy and I were jealous. The only letters we got were from our mothers, asking us about the weather and reminding us to wash our underwear. But *really,* it was a bit much, don't you think? Bettina couldn't get away from you, even when we found those boys in Florence, *especially* when we found those boys in Florence. The cutest one was after Bettina. But there were four letters of yours at the hotel in Florence and it just made her sick with—it wasn't guilt.

What was it? he had asked.

I don't know, Evie replied. Disloyalty, perhaps.

Well, he said. What happened in Florence?

Laughing: I'll never tell.

They arrived at last on the Costa Brava. Spain was everything he imagined. They chose a pretty whitewashed town with a small bullring, a lovely 14th-century church, and two plain hotels. The hotel they chose was near the church, perched on a cliff overlooking the sea. The room was primitive, but they would use it only for sleeping. It was late afternoon, and they changed immediately and went to the beach. Bettina smiled happily; it was a great relief being out of the car.

The path to the beach wound through a stand of sweet-smelling pines. They spread their towels on the rough sand, side-by-side. Bettina was carrying a thick poetry miscellany. She murmured, "Isn't this nice," and at once lay down and went to sleep. She didn't say another word. Her forehead was beaded with sweat. She was lying on her side, her thighs up against her stomach, her cheek dead against her small fists. Her brown hair fell lifeless and tangled in a fan over her forearm. She looked defenseless, fast alseep. Ted looked down at her, his shadow falling across her stomach. He thought she needed a new bathing suit, something Bardot might favor, black or red, snug against the skin. The one she had on was heavy and loose, made in America. In her Lake Forest bathing suit she looked complacent and matronly, though she was obviously worn out from the drive, all day long in their small car on narrow roads, dodging diesel trucks and ox carts and every 50 kilometers a three-man patrol, the *Guardia Civil,* Franco's men, sinister in their black tricorns and green capes and carbines, though they looked scarcely older than boys, nodding impassively when Bettina waved. She thought they looked more droll than sinister; as Americans, she and

Ted had nothing to fear from the *Guardia Civil.* He stepped back and looked at Bettina again. From her rolled-up position on the towel, she might have been at home in bed on the North Shore instead of on a sunny Mediterranean beach. Her skin was very white in the fading sun.

Ted turned and walked to the water's edge. There were no waves. The water seemed to slide up the sand, pause, and die. He looked left and right. The beach was wide, crescent-shaped and cozy. There were two other couples nearby, middle-aged people reading under beach umbrellas. Down the beach a girl stood staring out to sea. Presently a man joined her and they stood together. They were very tan, and Ted was conscious of his own white skin and frayed madras trunks. The girl wore a white bikini, and the man had a black towel around his waist. The girl stood with her legs apart, her arm around the man's dark shoulders; they were both wearing sunglasses. Ted looked back at Bettina. She was faced in his direction, but she had not moved. He turned back to the water, thinking how different it was from the shore at Lake Michigan—the fragrance of the beach, pine mixed with sea and sand, and the swollen bulk of two great rocks a hundred feet offshore. This coast was complicated and diverse, a place to begin or continue a love affair *sin vergüenza.* It was nothing at all like mediocre Lake Michigan; it was as different from Lake Michigan as he was from his American self. He walked into the water, chilly around his ankles. The woman in the bikini and the man in the towel were walking up the beach in the direction of the hotel, holding hands.

Ted began to swim in a slow crawl, feeling the water under his fingernails. He wished Bettina were with him at his side. The water slid around his thighs, slippery, a sexual sensation. He imagined them swimming together nude, unfettered in the Mediterranean. He swam steadily, kicking slowly, hot and knotted inside, his throat dusty and the sun warm on his back. Bettina would never swim nude but now and again he could coax her out of her bra and she would swim around and around in circles; this was always late at night in the deserted pool of the country club, after a party, illicit summer adventures before they were married. He slowed a little, lost in the sentimental memory of them together. The sensation mounted, a thick giddiness, incomplete. Ahead were the great rocks rising from the water ten feet apart. From his perspective they looked like skyscrapers, and beyond them nothing but the serene blue-gray Mediterranean and the milky sky overhead. He wanted to climb the nearest rock to the summit and sit in the last of the afternoon sun. But above the waterline the rock was smooth, no hand holds anywhere. The stone was warm to his touch and smooth as skin. When he tried to climb, his hands kept slipping, and at last he gave up and floated, the curve of the brown rocks always on the edges of his vision. Then on impulse he took a deep breath and dove, kicking and corkscrewing through the murky water. He could not see the bottom. Almost immediately the water chilled, offering resistance. He did not fight it, saving strength and breath. He struggled deeper, hanging in the heavy water, darkness all around him, the bottom out of sight. Something nudged his arm, and he felt a moment of panic. Lost, he had the sensation of rising in an elevator. The elevator was crowded with old men, their faces grim. Mozart was in front of him, lecturing in his flat prairie accent. There was a ringing in his ears, and he tried to push forward to get out through the heavy doors, away from the old men. He was dazzled by a profusion of winking red lights, a multitude of floors, all forbidden. Mozart would not yield, and the elevator came slowly to a halt, the atmosphere morbid and unspeakably oppressive. He recognized the faces of those around him, friends, colleagues, clients. Then his hand struck stone and the hallucination vanished. He had arched his back like a high-diver in mid-air, hanging upside down, watching afternoon light play on the flat surface of the water. Losing breath, he thought of the girl in the white bikini, so trim and self-possessed, and provocative as she stared out to sea. He wondered if she had had many lovers. Certainly a few, more than he had had; and more than Bettina, though they would all be about the same age. It was hard to know exactly how old she was, she could be 18 or 25; but a hard-muscled and knowing 18 or 25, having grown up in Europe. If the three of them met, what would they have to say to each other? He could describe for her the ins and outs of an Illinois Land Trust and the genius of E. L. Mozart. Bettina could talk to her about pregnancy or e. e. cummings. Well, there would be no common experience. And Bettina was so shy and he so green. She looked like a girl who would know her own mind, where she had been and where she was going. The cavalier with her looked like he knew his own mind, too. She moved beautifully, like a dancer or athlete. He thought of embracing her in the darkness and silence of the deep water.

When he broke the surface, gasping, he heard his name and turned to see Bettina on the beach, calling. The people under the umbrellas had put their books down and were rising, curious. Bettina saw him and dropped her hands, in an abrupt gesture of irritation and relief. She stood quietly a moment, shaking her head, then walked slowly back to the towel. The bells of the church began to toll, the dull sounds reaching him clearly across the water. He smiled, never having heard church bells on a beach. He shook his head to clear his ears of water. The bells stopped, and there was no echo; the girl and her escort had disappeared down the beach. Ted remained a moment, treading water, looking closely at the rocks and knowing there was a way up somehow. There was always a way up. Perhaps on the far side, he could look on it as the north face of the Eiger, an incentive for tomorrow's swim. He pushed off and began a slow crawl back to the shore, where Bettina was already gathering their things.

They went directly to their room and made love, quickly and wordlessly; a model of efficiency, she thought but did not say. Ted had been ardent and a little rough, and now they lay together in the semidarkness, smoking and listening to two workmen gossip outside their window. Ted lay staring at the ceiling, blowing smoke rings. She was looking into an oval mirror atop their dresser beyond the foot of the bed. She was nearsighted and could not see her features clearly, but she knew how drained she looked, her sallow complexion, dead eyes, and oily hair, the pits. She hadn't washed her hair in a week, since they left Chicago. She touched it with her fingertips, then worked it into a single braid and brought it over her shoulder and smelled it—sweat, fish, and seaweed, ugh. It had to be washed, but she had no energy for that or for anything; no energy, or taste for food, drink, or sex. She had loved listening to the bells, though. The truth was, she looked the way she felt. Her looks were a mirror of her state of mind as surely as the mirror on her dresser reflected her looks, and there was no disguise she could wear. What should she do, put on a party hat? Pop a Miltown? No chance of that; she distrusted tranquilizers and had not filled the prescription the doctor gave her. She disliked suburban life as it was—how much more would she dislike it tranquilized? She felt as if half of her was empty. She was a fraction, half empty. She thought that something had been stolen from her, some valuable part of herself, and it was more than a fetus; but she did not know what it was or who had taken it. She felt so alone. She inhabited a country of which she was the only citizen; one citizen, speaking to herself in a personal tongue. Sometimes in her poetry she could hear a multitude of voices, a vivifying rialto in the dead suburban city. On the beach she had felt abandoned; and when she looked across the water and did not see him, she didn't know what to do; he had been there a moment before, looking at that girl. So she had gone to the water's edge and called, in a jokey way; then she was filled with a sudden dread and called again, yelled really, just as he broke the surface, spraying water every which way, his arm straight up—and looked at her so shamefacedly, as if he had been caught red-handed. Then the bells began to toll and she listened, startled at first; they were so mournful and exact, church bells from the middle ages, tolling an unrecognizable dirge. The church would have been built around the time of the beginning of the Inquisition, and she imagined the altar and the simulacrum behind it, an emaciated, bloody, mortified Christ, wearing a crown of thorns sharp and deadly as razor blades, the thorns resembling birds' talons. And for a long moment, within hearing of the bells, everything stopped, a kind of ecstatic suspension of all sound and motion. She turned away, fighting a desire to cry; she wanted tears, evidence of life.

She felt a movement next to her, Ted extinguishing his cigarette, sighing, and closing his eyes. Smoke from the Spanish tobacco hung in layers in the air, its odor pungent and unfamiliar. She stubbed out her own Chesterfield. He murmured, "Forty winks before dinner, Bee." She absently put her hand on his chest, his skin slick with sweat though the room was no longer warm—watching herself do this in the mirror, her hand rising slowly from her stomach, making its arc, and then falling, and he covering her hand with his own. He had nice hands, dry and light, uncalloused. She felt his heart flutter, and the tension still inside him; she wondered if he could feel her tension as she felt his. Probably not, she was so emotionally dense sometimes, and he was not that kind of man.

It was almost dark now. The workmen had gone and she could hear gentler voices, hotel guests moving along the path to the terrace.

She said, "Teddy?"

He made a sound and squeezed her hand.

"Nothing," she said.

He said, "No, what?" in a muddy voice.

She said, "Go back to sleep, Teddy." He stirred and did not reply. It was quiet outside. She said quietly, "It's silly." She looked at the ceiling, there was a ghost of a shadow from the light outside. "Are you still sexy?"

He laughed softly. "A little."

She said, "Me, too."

He rolled over on his side, facing her.

She smiled at him, wrinkling her nose in a way that he liked; this was a sign of absolution. "Did you know that?"

He grunted ambiguously and kissed her stomach. Then he reached over her shoulder and took one of the Chesterfields from the pack on the bedside table, lit it, and offered it to her. She shook her head, watching all this dimly in the mirror; she had to crane her neck to see over him when he reached for the cigarette. Then the flare of the match in the glass.

She turned to look at him squarely. "I'll bet you didn't."

He said, "Did too."

She shook her head. "Huh uh."

"I know all about you, Bettina."

Dense, she thought; an underbrush. Her poetry was dense, too, but she liked it that way.

He began to make jokes about the various ways he knew all about her, "Bettina through the ages." He always knew what she was thinking, as she was an open book; she wore her heart on her sleeve, more or less. Then he began to talk about himself, his disappointment with his white skin and college-boy bathing suit, as obvious as a fingerprint or a sore thumb. He said he wanted to lose his nationality, and she should lose hers, too. They would become inconspicuous in Europe, part of the continent's mass. Perhaps he would become an international lawyer with offices in Lisbon and Madrid, master of half a dozen languages, a cosmopolitan. They would have a little villa on the Costa Brava within sight of the sea, a weekend place. He knew they would love the Costa Brava. He described swimming alone to the rocks, thinking of her, then diving, the water cold and heavy below the surface, and the hallucination that had transported him to La Salle Street, an elevator crowded with old men, red lights everywhere and no exit, a morbid oppression. The stone was slippery and warm to the touch, unfamiliar, the rocks sheer as Alps, no inhibitions on the Costa Brava—though what that had to do with it, with *her,* he couldn't say. At any event, he didn't.

She said, "Thinking about me? And then a real hallucination?"

He said, "Yes."

She said, "Nuts. You were watching that *femme fatale* in the bikini. The one with the flat stomach."

"No," he said. "It was you. You're my favorite."

She lay quietly, holding her breath; she had a moment of déjà vu, come and gone in an instant. She tried to recapture it, but the memory feathered away. Distracted, she said, "I'll never have a flat stomach, ever again." She prodded her soft belly. It was as if there was an empty place in her stomach, an empty room, a VACANCY. There was no spring or bounce to her, her muscles were loose. Almost a month, and she had not returned to normal; depressed, always tired, petulant, negative, frequently near tears. But what was normal? She was an anomaly. She had a young mother's flabby body, but she was not a young mother. "And I need a new bathing suit." She looked at the coral-colored Jantzen lying crumpled in the corner; ardent Teddy, he couldn't wait. He couldn't get it off fast enough. What a surprising boy he was in Europe, so curious about things, a young *husband.* At home he was reserved, wanting so to fit in. They both looked at the bathing suit. There were bones in the bra and she didn't need bones. She didn't need bones any more than the *femme fatale* did, except now she might, now that she looked like a young mother. Was her body changed forever? She looked at him in the darkness and then turned away, blinking back tears. She wanted him to touch her and say that he loved her body, would love it always, that it was a beautiful young body even in the coral-colored Jantzen, Marshall Field chic. His cigarette flared and he blew a smoke ring. She sighed; there would be no tears after all. And he would not tell her that she had a beautiful young body, even if he believed it. Tomorrow she would buy a new bathing suit, a bathing suit à la mode. No bikinis, though. Bikinis were unforgiving. She said, "He was much too old for her."

"Who was?" Teddy rose and stepped to the window, peeking out through the blind.

"That man she was with. That señorito in the black towel."

"So," he said. "You were watching him."

"Why not?" she said. "Jesus, he was a handsome man."

She took her time bathing and dressing, selecting a white skirt and a blue silk shirt and the pearls Teddy had given her at their wedding. She washed her hair, and took care making up her eyes. It was nine before they presented themselves on the terrace. Lanterns here and there threw a soft light. Each table had a single candle and a tiny vase of flowers and a jar of wine. The tables were set for two or four; they were round tables with heavy ladderback chairs. One of the waiters looked up, smiling, and indicated they could sit anywhere. It was an informal seating. The terrace was not crowded, and conversation was subdued in the balmy night. The handsome señorito and his girl were at a table on the edge of the terrace, overlooking the sea. They were holding hands and talking earnestly. Bettina led the way to an empty table nearby, also on the edge.

The moon was full and brilliant. The sea spread out before them, steely in the moonlight, seeming to go on forever. The drop to the sea was sheer, and although it was a hundred feet or more Ted felt he could lean over the iron railing and touch the water. The rocks were off to their left, dark masses in the water. From the terrace the rocks did not look as large as skyscrapers. A way out to sea there was a single light, a freighter bound for Barcelona. Ted looked at Bettina, but she was lost in some private thought, absently twisting her pearls around her index finger, her eyes in shadows. She did it whenever she was nervous or distracted, and he wondered what she was thinking about now, so withdrawn; probably the handsome couple at the table nearby. She had seated herself so that she could look at them, and perhaps guess their provenance. She loved inventing exotic histories for strangers.

The waiter arrived and took their order. Conversation on the terrace rose and fell in a low murmur. There was laughter and a patter of French behind him. Bettina looked up, raising her chin to look over his shoulder, her fingers working at the pearls. Ted sat uncomfortably a moment, then poured wine into both their glasses. Bettina touched hers with her fingernails, *click,* and smiled thanks. She was still looking past him, concentrating as if committing something to memory.

"Isn't it pretty?"

She said, "Another world."

"Did you imagine it like this? I didn't."

She said, "I didn't know what to expect."

He said, "You're twisting your pearls."

"You gave them to me." She took a sip of wine. "I have a right to twist them, if I want to." She said after a moment, "I wish I had brought my poem with me, the one I was working on. It was the one that began as one thing and then when I got out of the hospital it was another thing, the one I told you about after, that night. There's one part of it that I can't remember. Isn't it a riot? I wrote it and now I can't remember it."

"Begin another," Ted said. "That's the great thing about writing poetry, all you need is a pencil and a piece of paper." And a memory, he thought but did not say.

"No, there's this one part. I have to know what it is because I want to revise it. I want to revise it here. It means a lot to me, and I know I'll remember if I try."

"Is it the beginning or the end?"

"The middle," she said.

"Good," he said and laughed.

She looked at him, confused.

"I figured the poem was about me. Or us. Us together."

"No," she said. "It wasn't."

"What was it about, Bee?"

She looked away, across the water, her chin in her hands. The breeze, freshening, moved her hair, and she tilted her chin and shook her head lightly, evidently enjoying the sensation. "Me, the baby, that's what the poem was about." She smiled without irony or guile. "What happens when things are pregnant." She took a sip of wine, holding the glass by its stem in front of her eyes. She said, "I'll never be able to think of them separately, as distinct and different personalities, a brother and a sister. It'll always be just, 'the baby.' "

"You were extremely brave," he said.

She gestured impatiently. "No," she said. "That isn't it."

"Still," he began, then didn't finish the sentence. Why was she so reluctant to take the credit that was hers? If you couldn't take the credit you deserved, you couldn't take the blame either and you ended up with nothing, always in debt to someone else. But he did not want to argue, so he said, "I didn't know what was going on."

"Like the other night in Saulieu."

"What night was that? You mean, when I got so sick?"

"Teddy," she said. "Sometimes, you know, you could just *ask.*"

"All right then," he said. "I'm asking."

She looked at him innocently, the beginnings of a smile. "I thought a lawyer never asked a question without knowing the answer to it." When he reacted, she said, "Please, don't be angry. This is so pretty, and I'm happy to be here. I feel like a human being for the first time in ages, and I feel that it's *possible,* right here. This country is so old, and it's gone through so much." She glanced over his shoulder and smiled; he heard a flurry of laughter. "You know, we're not so dumb. We don't know everything. Probably we don't know as much as those two, but we can learn. I feel." She leaned toward him across the table, sliding her hand forward like a gambler wagering a stack of chips. "I feel we don't try for the best there is. We're surrounded by nonentities, like you in your elevator, all those organization men. What did you call it? You called it morbid, that atmosphere."

He nodded, touched by her sincerity. But what they didn't know would fill an encyclopedia. And he didn't like her reference to organization men, and he didn't know what she meant about the night in Saulieu; then he got it. "It was just a restaurant, Bee. I didn't have the money straight and didn't know how expensive things were. And how lousy that hotel would be. I thought it was important to keep a reserve for emergencies."

She nodded, Sure.

"See?"

She looked at him across the table, wondering if she could make clear what it was that she felt. She wanted him to listen—and here, this terrace, this table, the Mediterranean, this was the place. She had been stupid to mention Saulieu, off the subject. She took another sip of wine. "But there are times when you shouldn't leave me. The night in Saulieu was one of the times, and the night in the hospital another. You and McNab in the corridor, talking about *me.* You wouldn't look at me while you were talking to him, and I didn't know what it was that was so secret. If it was secret, it couldn't be anything good, isn't that right? So I thought something was being kept from me, and I felt excluded, you two men in the corridor and me in bed."

He said, "I didn't know. I thought you were asleep. It's what McNab wanted. I didn't know what he was talking about, and I was too dumb to ask the right questions." He looked around him, embarrassed; their voices were sharp in the subdued ambiance of the terrace.

"It's that you have to stand up for what's yours, Teddy." She filled his wineglass and her own. She looked at both glasses, full, and smiled. She watched him closely, wondering if he had really listened, and if he understood. Probably he had, he looked bothered. In the candlelight she thought him good-looking, a good-looking American; he only needed a few years. The Costa Brava became him. And her, too. Spain gave her courage. She gave a bright laugh. "I was brave, was I?"

"Yes."

"Tell me how brave?"

He said, "Brave as can be." Her eyes were sparkling, brilliant in the soft light.

"Oh," she said suddenly, lowering her voice. "Oh, Teddy. Turn around."

He did as she directed. The handsome señorito and the girl were embracing. She had her bare arms around his neck. Her head was thrown back as she leaned into him, on tiptoe. Against the light and motion of the moon and the sea, it was an exalted moment. Bettina whispered, "I know who they are." She commenced a dreamy narrative, a vivid sketch of him, a romantic poet and playwright like Garcia Lorca, close to the Spanish people. There was definitely something literary and slightly dangerous about him. As for her, she was a political, a young Pasionaria, a woman of character and resolve. They had been in love for ages, exiled together, now returned to Catalonia incognito . . . .

Bettina took his hand and held it. She described the poem she had been working on, reciting a few of the lines, the ones she could remember. She was going to write another poem, and McNab would be a character in it. She was going to write it tomorrow on the beach, while he climbed to the summit of the largest rock. What better place to write? The Costa Brava was a tonic. In time she would be as healthy and resolute as the girl in the bikini, and he would be as lean and dangerous as the man in the towel.

Ted opened his mouth to make a comment, then thought better of it. He looked out to sea and it occurred to him suddenly that they were sitting literally on the edge of Europe, the precipice at their feet a boundary as clear and present as the Urals or the Atlantic. He had never considered the Mediterranean a European sea, and Spain herself was always on the margins of modern history. A puff of wind caused the candles to flicker and dance. Ted imagined the air originating in north Africa, bringing the scent and languor of the Sahara or the Casbah. There were two lights now on the horizon. What a distance it was, from their stronghold in the heart of America to the rim of Europe! Was it true that everything was possible in Europe? Ted thought of the Spanish war and the 20 years of peace, the *veinte anos de paz,* that had followed. Franco's hard-faced *paz.* He had read all the books but could not imagine what it had been like in Catalonia. He had thought he knew but now, actually in the country, face to face with the people and the terrain, he had no idea at all.

UNCLE GEORGE AND UNCLE STEFAN

PETER MEINKE

Peter Meinke is a poet and short story writer whose latest book is *Trying to Surprise God* (Pitt Poetry Series). This is his second story chosen for the O. Henry collections. He is director of the Writing Workshop at Eckerd College in St. Petersburg, Florida.

It has always seemed strange to me that our houses outlive us. When a house has really been lived in it should be retired, like a star's locker; or dismantled and discarded like yesterday's theatre set: the play's over, make way for the new.

We had such good times in our house! Especially when Uncle George and Uncle Stefan were together: they would drive us kids crazy with laughter.

"Tamara!" Uncle Stefan would frown at me across the dinner table. "Eat every carrot and pea on your plate!"

"Yes sir," I would say, while the others whooped and hollered. I was a slow learner, and my older sister Elizabeth would shake her head in disgust at my gullibility.

Neither Uncle Stefan nor Uncle George was a mean man: their eyes bulged with high spirits. They loved us kids (more than our parents did, we thought), they loved to show off, and they loved to drink. At some point during most parties, Uncle George would stick toothpicks into his mouth in a way that made his jaw jut out like an ape's and would lurch after us, his knuckles dragging across the floor; until Uncle Stefan, using the fireplace poker as a rifle, would leap in front of the roaring creature and shoot him through the heart. George would collapse in a moaning heap, whereupon we children would leap on him like gnats on a bull: Uncle George was *big.* One time, in an excess of fearsome invention, he jumped on our wooden cocktail table, which exploded into splinters so quickly that there was a minute of confusion while everyone tried to figure out what happened. The first sound was my mother's wail—"Oooo Noooo"—which became our house motto:

"Oooo Noooo!" we'd cry whenever Uncle George or Uncle Stefan would arrive. "Oooo Yeeesss!" they would answer in their lovely deep voices.

Those were happy times, and there were many of them, but today I am remembering what Stefan said to me in 1947 when the war was over and George was living with us and I had just turned fifteen. God help me, fifteen is a tough age: I wouldn't be fifteen again for all the coke in China. At that time we had no shower and no lock on our bathroom door, and whenever I'd take a bath my younger brother would "accidentally" barge in on me. And if I stayed in over five minutes everyone would begin talking, congregating in the dark hallway under Grandfather's ancient German cuckoo clock, like some demented town meeting.

"What's Tammy *doing* in there?"

"Must be boring"—my father's voice—"there are only so many things you can play with."

"I have to go tinkle."

"Jesus, Billy, don't say *tinkle!* You're twelve years old!"

We lived in a tall skinny three-story house on Fairland Avenue: Grandpa, Mother, Father, Uncle George, and the four kids. The children were symmetrically arranged: Elizabeth (blond hair, blue eyes), me (brown hair, brown eyes), Stephen (blond hair, blue eyes), and Billy (brown hair, brown eyes). It was as if the Polish-German genes of our parents had been politely taking turns. Uncle Stefan said, "Half you kids look like gypsies and half like Nazis. I don't know which is worse."

Grandpa actually *was* a Nazi. At least, when the war broke out in 1939, before he came to live with us, he was squarely pro-German—as were many in our neighborhood, full of German delicatessens, bakeries, and the Lutheran Church. He wanted us to go in on Hitler's side and bomb the hell out of Britain. He hated the English, among many other large groups: Grandpa was a cornucopia of prejudices, though he would occasionally waffle them in consideration of our guests. In his old age, in the fifties, he became repetitive as a parrot, and when we'd ask him how things were going he would shake his head and mutter, "Aah, the Jews and the Ginnies is ruining the world." I warned my college roommate, Carmen Esposito, about this when she came home with me for a visit in 1951; she said not to worry, she was a tough gal from Newark. So when we all sat down in the living room and asked Grandpa how things were going, he looked at Carmen—swarthy and black-haired—paused, and said, "Aah, the Jews is ruining the world." Carmen and I winked at each other.

We drank in prejudice with our mother's milk—it seemed to be part of the Christian experience: Jews, Blacks, Italians specifically, because they were encroaching on our neighborhood; but in a general way, almost anyone not related to the family: Russians, Austrians, Chinese, dwarfs. World War II was therefore a great puzzle, as we tried to sort out the complicated relationships.

Our mother had come to America in 1910 from Danzig, now the beautiful and disturbed Polish city of Gdansk, but then under German control. She and her twin brother, Stefan, were brought here by their mother to stay with relatives when their father died in a boating accident. Mother and Uncle Stefan retained a fierce Polish patriotism that went far past anything they could possibly remember: it was in their bones. Between the wars they went back to visit their house, after Danzig became a "free city"—*Freie Stadt Danzig*—in 1920. This was a powerful experience for them, although they have not gone back since, partly because Mother married Father in 1929, and partly because their house did not survive the second war. And of course, they're in their seventies now, playing chess in a condominium.

Both my grandfathers were fishermen, which may explain my aversion to fish. Wilhelm Schmidt (Grandpa) came over from Schweinfurt in the 1890s and lived as a fisherman on Sheepshead Bay, before they knocked down all those wonderful shacks on stilts to fill in the bay for that idiotic golf course. Somebody made a lot of money on that boondoggle, and to my mind Brooklyn has never recovered from the loss. Some of my earliest memories are of lying on my stomach at the end of Grandpa's ramshackle dock, loving the smell of mud flats and salt air, catching blue claw crabs by lowering a piece of bacon on a string and slowlyslowlyslowly bringing it up again till the crab could be netted. Grandpa was wonderful then, before he noticed I was only a girl, taking me out in his boat while he fished for weakfish, porgies, fluke, and the occasional eel that would terrify me by banging around the rowboat long after it was caught. When we got back, his two sons—William (my father) and Uncle George—would be broiling fish for the grown-ups and hamburgers for the grandchildren on the outdoor grill. It breaks my heart to remember it. There is nothing there now but deserted landfill: even the fiddler crabs have gone.

Uncle Stefan would be there, with his wife, Nina. Their arrival was always greeted by loud cheering, because Stefan would bring the liquor, a habit that lasted well past Prohibition. Stefan was an accountant and made good money, even during the Depression. He would come with bottles, jars, and cans, and something for the children, too: licorice sticks for the girls, war cards with bubblegum for the boys. Nina was one of those gay and amusing women who remain gay but become less amusing as they grow older. She was indefatigably girlish and Stefan and we kids soon tired of her and wished her dead. At least that's what he yelled at her one night, and we (behind the door, listening wide-eyed to the grown-ups misbehaving) were on his side.

Uncle Stefan often misbehaved, so the children naturally loved him. Small, dark, dapper, with a pencil-thin moustache and a quick tongue, he was the center of our parties. He liked to embarrass the girls.

"Elizabeth, what are ant holes for?" he'd ask.

"What?" she'd say suspiciously. Elizabeth was born suspicious.

"Uncles, of course!" he'd cry, while my mother giggled and Aunt Nina arched her artificial eyebrows and said, *"Really,* Stefan."

"Tamara, how do you make holy water?"

I always tried to answer his questions. "Let me think," I'd say. Priestly rites, laboratory bottles sprang to my mind.

"You boil the hell out of it!"

It's a great gift, to remember jokes; no one else in our family ever could. It was typical for one of us to say, "Charlie Morrison told a terrific joke at school today"; and then sit in stunned silence as the joke evaporated before our disbelieving eyes. But Uncle Stefan could tell short ones, long ones, jokes with accents, musical jokes. He had a fine baritone voice, and could sing anything from raunchy beer hall ballads to sentimental songs in Polish and German that brought tears to Grandpa's eyes.

Perhaps his biggest fan was Uncle George. In 1947, when I was fifteen, George was paralyzed and in a wheelchair, but ten years earlier he and Uncle Stefan were inseparable. They were both masculine men, cigar-smoking drinkers, but George was much larger: perhaps a shade over six feet, he had a stocky peasant build that went straight down from his shoulders to his thick ankles, and no visible neck. If Uncle George weren't with us when Stefan arrived, Stefan would hunch his head into his shoulders and lurch around the room, swinging his arms and crying, "Vere ees Quassimodo? Vere ees Quassimodo?" with the children shrieking and sweeping behind him like so many quail in a covey.

Because Stefan was argumentative, and not a good drinker, Uncle George was often required to save him at the local taverns. They would come home, noisy and disheveled, with Stefan bragging how George had picked up "that bum Rafferty and threw him over the bar." He would describe George as the instigator, "this fearful brute," but that was just his ritual humor: we could all picture Uncle George sitting there, smiling at his friend's needling chatter, and then stepping in to rescue him when he went too far. Aunt Nina, of course, disapproved of such behavior in general and of their friendship in particular—she felt they led each other astray—so it was a great relief to everybody when she stopped coming to the house. There was much whispering on her absence at family get-togethers, not for children's ears: we know now that Nina was suing Uncle Stefan for divorce on grounds of adultery. She was a tough and practical lady behind those painted eyebrows, and not only got the house and the car, but silverware and furniture that came over from Poland when Stefan and our mother were children. Stefan didn't care; he was in love.

The third party in the divorce was Jessie Patterson, a schoolteacher who lived in the neighborhood. She taught music at P.S. 223, where we would have gone if we lived one block over: after we met her, we all wished we did. She had red hair, a pale ethereal face, and a substantial fanny, which on her at least was a nice combination. At first it was difficult for us to tell whom she was with, Uncle George or Uncle Stefan: they made a threesome. George, who never married, was shy around women, but Jessie had the knack of opening him up. He would talk to her about his job at the Brooklyn Navy Yard, the excitement of building the big ships, the noise and the difficulties.

"These aren't boats like you see around here, Jessie," he said. "Not like Grandpa's fishing boats or those sight-seeing barges along the pier. These are floating cities, you need a map to get around 'em. Tammy could go in there"—he'd put his big hand over my head like he was testing a melon—"and disappear for a year."

"Hooray," said Elizabeth.

Jessie was separated from a husband who wouldn't give her a divorce. She was what we called a lapsed Catholic: it sounded exciting and I resolved to be a lapsed Lutheran when I grew up. Her husband lived in Detroit and Uncle Stefan was all for going there and breaking his legs.

"He'll give you a divorce after I talk to him, you can bet on that."

"No, it would just make him more stubborn; besides, he's a crazy maniac and is liable to shoot you or something."

"Then George can come with me. Bullets bounce off George. George takes crazy maniacs and bites holes in their necks, don't you, George?" At that, Stevie and Billy began chasing Elizabeth and me, trying to bite holes in our necks.

Uncle Stefan stood up at Christmas dinner in 1938 and said, holding up his glass, "I propose a toast to Jessie Louise Patterson, the light of my life, the most beautiful woman in Brooklyn, New York, which has the most beautiful women in the world"—here he pointed his glass at Mother—"and who, in an act of enormous and foolhardy courage, has consented to marry me at the earliest possible moment." There was much applause, and Uncle George leaped up with tears in his eyes to lead a chorus of "For They Are Jolly Good Fellows." It's clear to me now that Uncle George was in love with Jessie, but he never seemed to question the idea that she and Uncle Stefan belonged together.

We always had big family dinners at holidays. My mother's mother died before I was born, and Grandpa's wife died when I was just a baby, so mainly I remember my mother, slim and intense like her twin, Uncle Stefan, working on the huge turkey in the kitchen, with first Nina, then Jessie, and finally Elizabeth and me to help her: men were not allowed in the kitchen. There were Polish side orders of bigos, barszcz, pierogis, ciastka; the house was thick for weeks with delicious smells. Father, who was a quiet solid man along the lines of his brother George, though thinner, would mix the manhattans, always serving Grandpa first. Grandpa was the patriarch, and accepted our deference aristocratically, without noticing it. On such occasions, we children—Billy and I small and dark, Elizabeth and Stevie tall and fair—would hang around the two uncles like diminutive clones, waiting to get the whiskey-soaked cherries from their cocktails. These were the good times, and we were a happy family, with no problems that we didn't think we could handle: America the melting pot, the Land of Opportunity. World War II changed all that.

When Germany invaded Poland in 1939 our family was split down the middle. We had grown up singing German songs for Grandpa, eating Polish food that Mother loved to prepare, hearing about Danzig from Uncle Stefan and about Munich from Uncle George. They would kid each other good-naturedly.

"You shrimpy Polack, when're you going to grow up?"

"Listen to Heinie Keplotz! He's speaking English, almost."

But after 1939 this kind of ribbing became dangerous and filled with tension. Stefan, particularly, had all he could do to hold in anti-German diatribes. "The swine," he would mutter, and walk out of the room, as the Nazis marched across Europe. To his chagrin, he was turned down for military service: something wrong with his feet, one eye that was uncorrectable. To make it worse for him, Uncle George enlisted in the Navy, and got to stay almost at his same job in the Navy Yard. In 1942 Father was drafted and went off with the Army to the South Pacific.

We survived as a family for some time by more or less pretending that the war was solely against the Japanese.

1943 was a bad year. The war dragged on in a bloody and discouraging manner, we saw less of Grandpa and Uncle Stefan than usual, Jessie was still not divorced (though now living with Stefan), Mother took a part-time job to aid in the war effort, and in October our father was wounded at Guadalcanal. So Christmas was a glum affair. Jessie and Mother tried to be cheerful for our sake, but the men were edgy, and drank without the usual banter.

"I heard from William this week," Mother said. "He says he's fine, and may get sent home soon."

"That would be a blessing," said Jessie.

"Daddy got shot in the stomach," I said, avoiding Elizabeth's eyes. Elizabeth was almost fourteen and found everything I said painful.

Grandpa said, "Tammy, sing 'Stille Nacht' for me." For years at Christmas we had sung 'Stille Nacht' for Grandpa, and then he would give us each a quarter.

"No," I said.

There was a silence so sudden and complete that I nearly fell over from fright.

Grandpa said, "What do you mean, no?"

"I'll sing it in English," I said.

"Listen, Tammy," said Uncle George, "what is this nonsense? Sing it for your Grandpa. We're still the same people we always were."

"That's right," said Uncle Stefan. "Nazis!"

Uncle Stefan was almost out of his mind with frustration on all fronts. He got up a little unsteadily and began goose-stepping around the room, singing.

> *"Und der Fuhrer says*
> *Ve are der Master Race*
> *So ve Heil* (spit) *Heil* (spit)
> *Right in der Fuhrer's face!"*

Grandpa turned white and speechless. Mother said later she thought he was having a heart attack. As Stefan swung around and began again, Uncle George jumped up and pushed him down into one of the big overstuffed chairs. Stefan bounced out of it as if it were a trampoline and stood clenching his fists.

"That's right," he said again. "Nazis! Thieves and bullies with the brains of pigs!"

"Stop that," said Uncle George, moving toward him.

"Come on! You're a Nazi pig and a coward," yelled Uncle Stefan, and spit on the carpet as Uncle George came at him. He hit George several times sharply in the face, bringing blood to his eyes and mouth, but it was a short fight. George was so much stronger and heavier he just bulled through the smaller man's punches, fell on top of him, and banged his head on the bare floor by the fireplace until Uncle Stefan stopped moving.

"You've killed him!" shrieked Mother, and indeed her brother lay as if dead.

"Good," said George, and made as if to kick Stefan as my mother shrieked again.

Ten minutes later Uncle George was staring out the window, holding a cold washcloth to his mouth, when Uncle Stefan got up and, swinging with all his wiry strength, hit him on the back of his neck with the iron poker from the fireplace. Uncle George went down without a sound; in fact, he never spoke again.

Four years after that, when the war was over, and I was fifteen, one of my jobs was pushing Uncle George in a wheelchair around the park near our house. He had got so heavy so fast that only Uncle Stefan could move him for any length of time. George had been in the Navy hospital for a year, with the best treatment, but the vertebrae were crushed and there was nothing they could do. He not only could not walk or talk, but his mouth was frozen in a permanent scowl that frightened little Billy. He could write with difficulty, but seemed to have no trouble understanding: he enjoyed watching TV and listening to people talk.

Uncle Stefan would have liked to have been arrested, but no one would testify against him, so he had to punish himself, which he did by becoming a drunk and chasing Jessie Patterson away. This was hard to do. As if to torture Stefan more, Jessie's crazy maniac husband was killed on V-E Day, a war hero. Jessie went up to Detroit to settle the estate, and sent a telegram, through Mother, that Stefan should join her there; they could get married and start all over. On the train, Uncle Stefan got so drunk that he wound up in Minneapolis with another woman. He eventually made it back to Detroit, but what he and Jessie said to each other no one knows but themselves. He came back to Brooklyn, alone, to help take care of Uncle George.

It was a good thing, too, at least for Mother. Grandpa moved in with us permanently after Uncle George was hurt, and Father came home from the war in 1945. As Uncle George got fatter, my father got thinner, and Grandpa got older. Mother had her hands full, and needed all the help she could get, even though we kids pretty much took care of ourselves.

On that day when I was fifteen I came out of the bath and saw Uncle Stefan kneeling beside George's wheelchair. George was nodding, and making feeble motions with his hands. Stefan saw me and came over. The odor of manhattans washed over us as he hugged me to him: I was his favorite because I could sing.

"There's no end to it," he said. "I want you to remember that for when you get older." His voice was breaking. "There's no forgiveness."

"We can forget it, can't we?" I said.

"No forgetting, no forgiveness," he said. "You're a bright girl, Tamara, you've read Shakespeare."

"A little."

"Remember King Lear," he said. In my room I had a large Polish poster, *Krol Lear* in stark blacks and reds, that he had given me. "The answer to your question, whether you like it or not, whether it's . . . fair . . . or not, is: *'Never, never, never, never, never.'* "

I didn't believe that, and still don't, at least about the forgiveness part. But he couldn't forgive himself; even I could see that.

Well, that was a while ago. Most of the grown-ups are dead now, except for the twins, Mother and Uncle Stefan. George got up to about 300 pounds before his heart attack in 1950. My father never really recovered his health, and died in the early sixties, followed within the month by Grandpa, as if the old man were embarrassed at outliving both of his sons.

The grandchildren scattered to their various destinies. I have continued the family tradition by having twins; Elizabeth, more practical, has them one at a time. Stevie, a fine athlete, was killed in an automobile accident right after he graduated from high school. After his death, Mother sold the house and moved in with Uncle Stefan, and we were on our own. When Stefan retired, on a good pension, he and Mother moved down to Florida. I try to see them once a year, but there is no talk of reviving the old holiday get-togethers. None of us ever saw Jessie again.

I'm the only one still within striking distance of the neighborhood, and I am often drawn to drive slowly by the old house, despite the tears that almost floated it away—O childhood harbor, even you were unsafe! I suppose I'm happy to see it cared for and lived in again; and particularly at holiday time, my mind's eye flies through the lighted window, and there is Uncle George peering around the corner with a smile, while Uncle Stefan leaps up and down shouting, "Vere ees Quassimodo? Vere ees Quassimodo?" Myself, I'm still a slow learner, but I'm studying, and I'm learning.

BIG BERTHA STORIES

BOBBIE ANN MASON

Bobbie Ann Mason is the author of *In Country*, a novel published by Harper & Row, 1985, and *Shiloh and Other Stories*, Harper & Row, 1982, for which she won the Ernest Hemingway Foundation Award for best first fiction. She has received a number of other awards and grants, including a Guggenheim Fellowship. Her stories have been published in *The New Yorker, The Atlantic, Redbook*, and other magazines. A native of Mayfield, Kentucky, Bobbie Ann Mason lives in Pennsylvania.

Donald is home again, laughing and singing. He comes home from Central City, Kentucky, near the strip mines, only when he feels like it, like an absentee landlord checking on his property. He is always in such a good humor when he returns that Jeannette forgives him. She cooks for him—ugly, pasty things she gets with food stamps. Sometimes he brings steaks and ice cream, occasionally money. Rodney, their child, hides in the closet when he arrives, and Donald goes around the house talking loudly about the little boy named Rodney who used to live there—the one who fell into a septic tank, or the one stolen by Gypsies. The stories change. Rodney usually stays in the closet until he has to pee, and then he hugs his father's knees, forgiving him, just as Jeannette does. The way Donald saunters through the door, swinging a six-pack of beer, with a big grin on his face, takes her breath away. He leans against the door facing, looking sexy in his baseball cap and his shaggy red beard and his sunglasses. He wears sunglasses to be like the Blues Brothers, but he in no way resembles either of the Blues Brothers. I should have my head examined, Jeannette thinks.

The last time Donald was home, they went to the shopping center to buy Rodney some shoes advertised on sale. They stayed at the shopping center half the afternoon, just looking around. Donald and Rodney played video games. Jeannette felt they were a normal family. Then, in the parking lot, they stopped to watch a man on a platform demonstrating snakes. Children were petting a 12-foot python coiled around the man's shoulders. Jeannette felt faint.

"Snakes won't hurt you unless you hurt them," said Donald as Rodney stroked the snake.

"It feels like chocolate," he said.

The snake man took a tarantula from a plastic box and held it lovingly in his palm. He said, "If you drop a tarantula, it will shatter like a Christmas ornament."

"I hate this," said Jeannette.

"Let's get out of here," said Donald.

Jeannette felt her family disintegrating like a spider shattering as Donald hurried them away from the shopping center. Rodney squalled and Donald dragged him along. Jeannette wanted to stop for ice cream. She wanted them all to sit quietly together in a booth, but Donald rushed them to the car, and he drove them home in silence, his face growing grim.

"Did you have bad dreams about the snakes?" Jeannette asked Rodney the next morning at breakfast. They were eating pancakes made with generic pancake mix. Rodney slapped his fork in the pond of syrup on his pancakes. "The black racer is the farmer's friend," he said soberly, repeating a fact learned from the snake man.

"Big Bertha kept black racers," said Donald. "She trained them for the 500." Donald doesn't tell Rodney ordinary children's stories. He tells him a series of strange stories he makes up about Big Bertha. Big Bertha is what he calls the huge strip-mining machine in Muhlenberg County, but he has Rodney believing that Big Bertha is a female version of Paul Bunyan.

"Snakes don't run in the 500," said Rodney.

"This wasn't the Indy 500, or the Daytona 500, none of your well-known 500s," said Donald. "This was the Possum Trot 500, and it was a long time ago. Big Bertha started the original 500, with snakes. Black racers and blue racers mainly. Also some red-and-white striped racers, but those are rare."

"We always ran for the hoe if we saw a black racer," Jeannette said, remembering her childhood in the country.

In a way, Donald's absences are a fine arrangement, even considerate. He is sparing them his darkest moods, when he can't cope with his memories of Vietnam. Vietnam had never seemed such a meaningful fact until a couple of years ago, when he grew depressed and moody, and then he started going away to Central City. He frightened Jeannette, and she always said the wrong thing in her efforts to soothe him. If the welfare people find out he is spending occasional weekends at home, and even bringing some money, they will cut off her assistance. She applied for welfare because she can't depend on him to send money, but she knows he blames her for losing faith in him. He isn't really working regularly at the strip mines. He is mostly just hanging around there, watching the land being scraped away, trees coming down, bushes flung in the air. Sometimes he operates a steam shovel, and when he comes home his clothes are filled with the clay and it is caked on his shoes. The clay is the color of butterscotch pudding.

At first, he tried to explain to Jeannette. He said, "If we could have had tanks over there as big as Big Bertha, we wouldn't have lost the war. Strip mining is just like what we were doing over there. We were stripping off the top. The topsoil is like the culture and the people, the best part of the land and the country. America was just stripping off the top, the best. We ruined it. Here, at least the coal companies have to plant vetch and loblolly pines and all kinds of trees and bushes. If we'd done that in Vietnam, maybe we'd have left that country in better shape."

"Wasn't Vietnam a long time ago?" Jeannette asked.

She didn't want to hear about Vietnam. She thought it was unhealthy to dwell on it so much. He should live in the present. Her mother is afraid Donald will do something violent, because she once read in the newspaper that a veteran in Louisville held his little girl hostage in their apartment until he had a shootout with the police and was killed. But Jeannette can't imagine Donald doing anything so extreme. When she first met him, several years ago, at her parents' pit-barbecue luncheonette, where she was working then, he had a good job at a lumberyard and he dressed nicely. He took her out to eat at a fancy restaurant. They got plastered and ended up in a motel in Tupelo, Mississippi, on Elvis Presley Boulevard. Back then, he talked nostalgically about his year in Vietnam, about how beautiful it was, how different the people were. He could never seem to explain what he meant. "They're just different," he said.

They went riding around in a yellow 1957 Chevy convertible. He drives too fast now, but he didn't then, maybe because he was so protective of the car. It was a classic. He sold it three years ago and made a good profit. About the time he sold the Chevy, his moods began changing, his even-tempered nature shifting, like driving on a smooth interstate and then switching to a secondary road. He had headaches and bad dreams. But his nightmares seemed trivial. He dreamed of riding a train through the Rocky Mountains, of hijacking a plane to Cuba, of stringing up barbed wire around the house. He dreamed he lost a doll. He got drunk and rammed the car, the Chevy's successor, into a Civil War statue in front of the courthouse. When he got depressed over the meaninglessness of his job, Jeannette felt guilty about spending money on something nice for the house, and she tried to make him feel his job had meaning by reminding him that, after all, they had a child to think of. "I don't like his name," Donald said once. "What a stupid name. Rodney. I never did like it."

Rodney has dreams about Big Bertha, echoes of his father's nightmare, like TV cartoon versions of Donald's memories of the war. But Rodney loves the stories, even though they are confusing, with lots of loose ends. The latest in the Big Bertha series is "Big Bertha and the Neutron Bomb." Last week it was "Big Bertha and the MX Missile." In the new story, Big Bertha takes a trip to California to go surfing with Big Mo, her male counterpart. On the beach, corn dogs and snow cones are free and the surfboards turn into dolphins. Everyone is having fun until the neutron bomb comes. Rodney loves the part where everyone keels over dead. Donald acts it out, collapsing on the rug. All the dolphins and the surfers keel over, everyone except Big Bertha. Big Bertha is so big she is immune to the neutron bomb.

"Those stories aren't true," Jeannette tells Rodney.

Rodney staggers and falls down on the rug, his arms and legs akimbo. He gets the giggles and can't stop. When his spasms finally subside, he says, "I told Scottie Bidwell about Big Bertha and he didn't believe me."

Donald picks Rodney up under the armpits and sets him upright. "You tell Scottie Bidwell if he saw Big Bertha he would pee in his pants on the spot, he would be so impressed."

"Are you scared of Big Bertha?"

"No, I'm not. Big Bertha is just like a wonderful woman, a big fat woman who can sing the blues. Have you ever heard Big Mama Thornton?"

"No."

"Well, Big Bertha's like her, only she's the size of a tall building. She's slow as a turtle and when she crosses the road, they have to reroute traffic. She's big enough to straddle a four-lane highway. She's so tall she can see all the way to Tennessee, and when she belches, there's a tornado. She's really something. She can even fly."

"She's too big to fly," Rodney says doubtfully. He makes a face like a wadded-up washrag and Donald wrestles him to the floor again.

Donald has been drinking all evening, but he isn't drunk. The ice cubes melt and he pours the drink out and refills it. He keeps on talking. Jeannette cannot remember him talking so much about the war. He is telling her about an ammunitions dump. Jeannette had the vague idea that an ammo dump is a mound of shotgun shells, heaps of cartridge casings and bomb shells, or whatever is left over, a vast waste pile from the war, but Donald says that is wrong. He has spent an hour describing it in detail, so that she will understand.

He refills the glass with ice, some 7-Up, and a shot of Jim Beam. He slams doors and drawers, looking for a compass. Jeannette can't keep track of the conversation. It doesn't matter that her hair is uncombed and her lipstick eaten away. He isn't seeing her.

"I want to draw the compound for you," he says, sitting down at the table with a sheet of Rodney's tablet paper.

Donald draws the map in red-and-blue ballpoint, with asterisks and technical labels that mean nothing to her. He draws some circles with the compass and measures some angles. He makes a red dot on an oblique line, a path that leads to the ammo dump.

"That's where I was. Right there," he says. "There was a water buffalo that tripped a land mine and its horn just flew off and stuck in the wall of the barracks like a machete thrown backhanded." He puts a dot where the land mine was, and he doodles awhile with the red ballpoint pen, scribbling something on the edge of the map that looks like feathers. "The dump was here and I was there and over there was where we piled the sandbags. And here were the tanks." He draws tanks, a row of squares with handles—guns sticking out.

"Why are you going to so much trouble to tell me about a buffalo horn that got stuck in a wall?" she wants to know.

But Donald just looks at her as though she has asked something obvious.

"Maybe I *could* understand if you'd let me," she says cautiously.

"You could never understand." He draws another tank.

In bed, it is the same as it has been since he started going away to Central City—the way he claims his side of the bed, turning away from her. Tonight, she reaches for him and he lets her be close to him. She cries for a while and he lies there, waiting for her to finish, as though she were merely putting on make-up.

"Do you want me to tell you a Big Bertha story?" he asks playfully.

"You act like you're in love with Big Bertha."

He laughs, breathing on her. But he won't come closer.

"You don't care what I look like anymore," she says. "What am I supposed to think?"

"There's nobody else. There's not anybody but you."

Loving a giant machine is incomprehensible to Jeannette. There must be another woman, someone that large in his mind. Jeannette has seen the strip-mining machine. The top of the crane is visible beyond a rise along the Western Kentucky Parkway. The strip mining is kept just out of sight of travelers because it would give them a poor image of Kentucky.

For three weeks, Jeannette has been seeing a psychologist at the free mental health clinic. He's a small man from out of state. His name is Dr. Robinson, but she calls him The Rapist, because the word *therapist* can be divided into two words, *the rapist.* He doesn't think her joke is clever, and he acts as though he has heard it a thousand times before. He has a habit of saying, "Go with that feeling," the same way Bob Newhart did on his old TV show. It's probably the first lesson in the textbook, Jeannette thinks.

She told him about Donald's last days on his job at the lumberyard—how he let the stack of lumber fall deliberately and didn't know why, and about how he went away soon after that, and how the Big Bertha stories started. Dr. Robinson seems to be waiting for her to make something out of it all, but it's maddening that he won't tell her what to do. After three visits, Jeannette has grown angry with him, and now she's holding back things. She won't tell him whether Donald slept with her or not when he came home last. Let him guess, she thinks.

"Talk about yourself," he says.

"What about me?"

"You speak so vaguely about Donald that I get the feeling that you see him as somebody larger than life. I can't quite picture him. That makes me wonder what that says about you." He touches the end of his tie to his nose and sniffs it.

When Jeannette suggests that she bring Donald in, the therapist looks bored and says nothing.

"He had another nightmare when he was home last," Jeannette says. "He dreamed he was crawling through tall grass and people were after him."

"How do *you* feel about that?" The Rapist asks eagerly.

"I didn't have the nightmare," she says coldly. "Donald did. I came to you to get advice about Donald, and you're acting like I'm the one who's crazy. I'm not crazy. But I'm lonely."

Jeannette's mother, behind the counter of the luncheonette, looks lovingly at Rodney pushing buttons on the jukebox in the corner. "It's a shame about that youngun," she says tearfully. "That boy needs a daddy."

"What are you trying to tell me? That I should file for divorce and get Rodney a new daddy?"

Her mother looks hurt. "No, honey," she says. "You need to get Donald to seek the Lord. And you need to pray more. You haven't been going to church lately."

"Have some barbecue," Jeannette's father booms, as he comes in from the back kitchen. "And I want you to take a pound home with you. You've got a growing boy to feed."

"I want to take Rodney to church," Mama says. "I want to show him off, and it might do some good."

"People will think he's an orphan," Dad says.

"I don't care," Mama says. "I just love him to pieces and I want to take him to church. Do you care if I take him to church, Jeannette?"

"No. I don't care if you take him to church." She takes the pound of barbecue from her father. Grease splotches the brown wrapping paper. Dad has given them so much barbecue that Rodney is burned out on it and won't eat it anymore.

Jeannette wonders if she would file for divorce if she could get a job. It is a thought—for the child's sake, she thinks. But there aren't many jobs around. With the cost of a babysitter, it doesn't pay her to work. When Donald first went away, her mother kept Rodney and she had a good job, waitressing at a steak house, but the steak house burned down one night—a grease fire in the kitchen. After that, she couldn't find a steady job, and she was reluctant to ask her mother to keep Rodney again because of her bad hip. At the steak house, men gave her tips and left their telephone numbers on the bill when they paid. They tucked dollar bills and notes in the pockets of her apron. One note said, "I want to hold your muffins." They were real-estate developers and businessmen on important missions for the Tennessee Valley Authority. They were boisterous and they drank too much. They said they'd take her for a cruise on the Delta Queen, but she didn't believe them. She knew how expensive that was. They talked about their speedboats and invited her for rides on Lake Barkley, or for spins in their private planes. They always used the word *spin.* The idea made her dizzy. Once, Jeannette let an electronics salesman take her for a ride in his Cadillac, and they breezed down The Trace, the wilderness road that winds down the Land Between the Lakes. His car had automatic windows and a stereo system and lighted computer-screen numbers on the dash that told him how many miles to the gallon he was getting and other statistics. He said the numbers distracted him and he had almost had several wrecks. At the restaurant, he had been flamboyant, admired by his companions. Alone with Jeannette in the Cadillac, on The Trace, he was shy and awkward, and really not very interesting. The most interesting thing about him, Jeannette thought, was all the lighted numbers on his dashboard. The Cadillac had everything but video games. But she'd rather be riding around with Donald, no matter where they ended up.

While the social worker is there, filling out her report, Jeannette listens for Donald's car. When the social worker drove up, the flutter and wheeze of her car sounded like Donald's old Chevy, and for a moment Jeannette's mind elapsed back in time. Now she listens, hoping he won't drive up. The social worker is younger than Jeannette and has been to college. Her name is Miss Bailey, and she's excessively cheerful, as though in her line of work she has seen hardships that make Jeannette's troubles seem like a trip to Hawaii.

"Is your little boy still having those bad dreams?" Miss Bailey asks, looking up from her clipboard.

Jeannette nods and looks at Rodney, who has his finger in his mouth and won't speak.

"Has the cat got your tongue?" Miss Bailey asks.

"Show her your pictures, Rodney." Jeannette explains, "He won't talk about the dreams, but he draws pictures of them."

Rodney brings his tablet of pictures and flips through them silently. Miss Bailey says, "Hmm." They are stark line drawings, remarkably steady lines for his age. "What is this one?" she asks. "Let me guess. Two scoops of ice cream?"

The picture is two huge circles, filling the page, with three tiny stick people in the corner.

"These are Big Bertha's titties," says Rodney.

Miss Bailey chuckles and winks at Jeannette. "What do you like to read, hon?" she asks Rodney.

"Nothing."

"He can read," says Jeannette. "He's smart."

"Do you like to read?" Miss Bailey asks Jeannette. She glances at the pile of paperbacks on the coffee table. She is probably going to ask where Jeannette got the money for them.

"I don't read," says Jeannette. "If I read, I just go crazy."

When she told The Rapist she couldn't concentrate on anything serious, he said she read romance novels in order to escape from reality. "Reality, hell!" she had said. "Reality's my whole problem."

"It's too bad Rodney's not here," Donald is saying. Rodney is in the closet again. "Santa Claus has to take back all these toys. Rodney would love this bicycle! And this Pac-Man game. Santa has to take back so many things he'll have to have a pickup truck!"

"You didn't bring him anything. You never bring him anything," says Jeannette.

He has brought doughnuts and dirty laundry. The clothes he is wearing are caked with clay. His beard is lighter from working out in the sun, and he looks his usual joyful self, the way he always is before his moods take over, like migraine headaches, which some people describe as storms.

Donald coaxes Rodney out of the closet with the doughnuts.

"Were you a good boy this week?"

"I don't know."

"I hear you went to the shopping center and showed out." It is not true that Rodney made a big scene. Jeannette has already explained that Rodney was upset because she wouldn't buy him an Atari. But she didn't blame him for crying. She was tired of being unable to buy him anything.

Rodney eats two doughnuts and Donald tells him a long, confusing story about Big Bertha and a rock-and-roll band. Rodney interrupts him with dozens of questions. In the story, the rock-and-roll band gives a concert in a place that turns out to be a toxic-waste dump and the contamination is spread all over the country. Big Bertha's solution to this problem is not at all clear. Jeannette stays in the kitchen, trying to think of something original to do with instant potatoes and leftover barbecue.

"We can't go on like this," she says that evening in bed. "We're just hurting each other. Something has to change."

He grins like a kid. "Coming home from Muhlenberg County is like R and R—rest and recreation. I explain that in case you think R and R means rock-and-roll. Or maybe rumps and rears. Or rust and rot." He laughs and draws a circle in the air with his cigarette.

"I'm not that dumb."

"When I leave, I go back to the mines." He sighs, as though the mines were some eternal burden.

Her mind skips ahead to the future: Donald locked away somewhere, coloring in a coloring book and making clay pots, her and Rodney in some other town, with another man—someone dull and not at all sexy. Summoning up her courage, she says, "I haven't been through what you've been through and maybe I don't have a right to say this, but sometimes I think you act superior because you went to Vietnam, like nobody can ever know what you know. Well, maybe not. But you've still got your legs, even if you don't know what to do with what's between them anymore." Bursting into tears of apology, she can't help adding, "You can't go on telling Rodney those awful stories. He has nightmares when you're gone."

Donald rises from bed and grabs Rodney's picture from the dresser, holding it as he might have held a hand grenade. "Kids betray you," he says, turning the picture in his hand.

"If you cared about him, you'd stay here." As he sets the picture down, she asks, "What can I do? How can I understand what's going on in your mind? Why do you go there? Strip mining's bad for the ecology and you don't have any business strip mining."

"My job is serious, Jeannette. I run that steam shovel and put the topsoil back on. I'm reclaiming the land." He keeps talking, in a gentler voice, about strip mining, the same old things she has heard before, comparing Big Bertha to a supertank. If only they had had Big Bertha in Vietnam. He says, "When they strip off the top, I keep looking for those tunnels where the Viet Cong hid. They had so many tunnels it was unbelievable. Imagine Mammoth Cave going all the way across Kentucky."

"Mammoth Cave's one of the natural wonders of the world," says Jeannette brightly. She is saying the wrong thing again.

At the kitchen table at 2 a.m., he's telling about C-5A's. A C-5A is so big it can carry troops and tanks and helicopters, but it's not big enough to hold Big Bertha. Nothing could hold Big Bertha. He rambles on, and when Jeannette shows him Rodney's drawing of the circles, Donald smiles. Dreamily, he begins talking about women's breasts and thighs—the large, round thighs and big round breasts of American women, contrasted with the frail, delicate beauty of the Orientals. It is like comparing oven broilers and banties, he says. Jeannette relaxes. A confession about another lover from long ago is not so hard to take. He seems stuck on the breasts and thighs of American women—insisting that she understand how small and delicate the Orientals are, but then he abruptly returns to tanks and helicopters.

"A Bell Huey Cobra—my God, what a beautiful machine. So efficient!" Donald takes the food processor blade from the drawer where Jeannette keeps it. He says, "A rotor blade from a chopper could just slice anything to bits."

"Don't do that," Jeannette says.

He is trying to spin the blade on the counter, like a top. "Here's what would happen when a chopper blade hits a power line—not many of those over there!—or a tree. Not many trees, either, come to think of it, after all the Agent Orange." He drops the blade and it glances off the open drawer and falls to the floor, spiking the vinyl.

At first, Jeannette thinks the screams are hers, but they are his. She watches him cry. She has never seen anyone cry so hard, like an intense summer thundershower. All she knows to do is shove Kleenex at him. Finally, he is able to say, "You thought I was going to hurt you. That's why I'm crying."

"Go ahead and cry," Jeannette says, holding him close.

"Don't go away."

"I'm right here. I'm not going anywhere."

In the night, she still listens, knowing his monologue is being burned like a tattoo into her brain. She will never forget it. His voice grows soft and he plays with a ballpoint pen, jabbing holes in a paper towel. Bullet holes, she thinks. His beard is like a bird's nest, woven with dark corn silks.

"This is just a story," he says. "Don't mean nothing. Just relax." She is sitting on the hard edge of the kitchen chair, her toes cold on the floor, waiting. His tears have dried up and left a slight catch in his voice.

"We were in a big camp near a village. It was pretty routine and kind of soft there for a while. Now and then we'd go into Da Nang and whoop it up. We had been in the jungle for several months, so the two months at this village was a sort of rest—an R and R almost. Don't shiver. This is just a little story. Don't mean nothing! This is nothing, compared to what I could tell you. Just listen. We lost our fear. At night there would be some incoming and we'd see these tracers in the sky, like shooting stars up close, but it was all pretty minor and we didn't take it seriously, after what we'd been through. In the village I knew this Vietnamese family—a woman and her two daughters. They sold Cokes and beer to GIs. The oldest daughter was named Phan. She could speak a little English. She was really smart. I used to go see them in their hooch in the afternoons—in the siesta time of day. It was so hot there. Phan was beautiful, like the country. The village was ratty, but the country was pretty. And she was beautiful, just like she had grown up out of the jungle, like one of those flowers that bloomed high up in the trees and freaked us out sometimes, thinking it was a sniper. She was so gentle, with these eyes shaped like peach pits, and she was no bigger than a child of maybe 13 or 14. I felt funny about her size at first, but later it didn't matter. It was just some wonderful feature about her, like a woman's hair, or her breasts."

He stops and listens, the way they used to listen for crying sounds when Rodney was a baby. He says, "She'd take those big banana leaves and fan me while I lay there in the heat."

"I didn't know they had bananas over there."

"There's a lot you don't know! Listen! Phan was 23, and her brothers were off fighting. I never even asked which side they were fighting on." He laughs. "She got a kick out of the word *fan.* I told her that *fan* was the same word as her name. She thought I meant her name was banana. In Vietnamese the same word can have a dozen different meanings, depending on your tone of voice. I bet you didn't know that, did you?"

"No. What happened to her?"

"I don't know."

"Is that the end of the story?"

"I don't know." Donald pauses, then goes on talking about the village, the girl, the banana leaves, talking in a monotone that is making Jeannette's flesh crawl. He could be the news radio from the next room.

"You must have really liked that place. Do you wish you could go back there to find out what happened to her?"

"It's not there anymore," he says. "It blew up."

Donald abruptly goes to the bathroom. She hears the water running, the pipes in the basement shaking.

"It was so pretty," he says when he returns. He rubs his elbow absentmindedly. "That jungle was the most beautiful place in the world. You'd have thought you were in paradise. But we blew it sky-high."

In her arms, he is shaking, like the pipes in the basement, which are still vibrating. Then the pipes let go, after a long shudder, but he continues to tremble.

They are driving to the Veterans Hospital. It was Donald's idea. She didn't have to persuade him. When she made up the bed that morning —with a finality that shocked her, as though she knew they wouldn't be in it again together—he told her it would be like R and R. Rest was what he needed. Neither of them had slept at all during the night. Jeannette felt she had to stay awake, to listen for more.

"Talk about strip mining," she says now. "That's what they'll do to your head. They'll dig out all those ugly memories, I hope. We don't need them around here." She pats his knee.

It is a cloudless day, not the setting for this sober journey. She drives and Donald goes along obediently, with the resignation of an old man being taken to a rest home. They are driving through southern Illinois, known as Little Egypt, for some obscure reason Jeannette has never understood. Donald still talks, but very quietly, without urgency. When he points out the scenery, Jeannette thinks of the early days of their marriage, when they would take a drive like this and laugh hysterically. Now Jeannette points out funny things they see. The Little Egypt Hot Dog World, Pharaoh Cleaners, Pyramid Body Shop. She is scarcely aware that she is driving, and when she sees a sign, Little Egypt Starlite Club, she is confused for a moment, wondering where she has been transported.

As they part, he asks, "What will you tell Rodney if I don't come back? What if they keep me here indefinitely?"

"You're coming back. I'm telling him you're coming back soon."

"Tell him I went off with Big Bertha. Tell him she's taking me on a sea cruise, to the South Seas."

"No. You can tell him that yourself."

He starts singing a jumpy tune, "Won't you let me take you on a sea cruise?" He grins at her and pokes her in the ribs.

"You're coming back," she says.

Donald writes from the VA Hospital, saying that he is making progress. They are running tests, and he meets in a therapy group in which all the veterans trade memories. Jeannette is no longer on welfare because she now has a job waitressing at Fred's Family Restaurant. She waits on families, waits for Donald to come home so they can come here and eat together like a family. The fathers look at her with downcast eyes, and the children throw food. While Donald is gone, she rearranges the furniture. She reads some books from the library. She does a lot of thinking. It occurs to her that even though she loved him, she has thought of Donald primarily as a husband, a provider, someone whose name she shared, the father of her child, someone like the fathers who come to the Wednesday night all-you-can-eat fish fry. She hasn't thought of him as himself. She wasn't brought up that way, to examine someone's soul. When it comes to something deep inside, nobody will take it out and examine it, the way they will look at clothing in a store for flaws in the manufacturing. She tries to explain all this to The Rapist, and he says she's looking better, got sparkle in her eyes. "Big deal," says Jeannette. "Is that all you can say?"

She takes Rodney to the shopping center, their favorite thing to do together, even though Rodney always begs to buy something. They go to Penney's perfume counter. There, she usually hits a sample bottle of cologne—Chantilly or Charlie or something strong. Today she hits two or three and comes out of Penney's smelling like a flower garden.

"You stink!" Rodney cries, wrinkling his nose like a rabbit.

"Big Bertha smells like this, only a thousand times worse, she's so big," says Jeannette impulsively. "Didn't Daddy tell you that?"

"Daddy's a messenger from the devil."

This is an idea he must have gotten from church. Her parents have been taking him every Sunday. When Jeannette tries to reassure him about his father, Rodney is skeptical. "He gets that funny look on his face like he can see through me," the child says.

"Something's missing," Jeannette says, with a rush of optimism, a feeling of recognition. "Something happened to him once and took out the part that shows how much he cares about us."

"The way we had the cat fixed?"

"I guess. Something like that." The appropriateness of his remark stuns her, as though, in a way, her child has understood Donald all along. Rodney's pictures have been more peaceful lately, pictures of skinny trees and airplanes flying low. This morning he drew pictures of tall grass, with creatures hiding in it. The grass is tilted at an angle, as though a light breeze is blowing through it.

With her paycheck, Jeannette buys Rodney a present, a miniature trampoline they had seen advertised on television. It is called Mr. Bouncer. Rodney is thrilled about the trampoline, and he jumps on it until his face is red. Jeannette discovers that she enjoys it, too. She puts it out on the grass, and they take turns jumping. She has an image of herself on the trampoline, her sailor collar flapping at the moment when Donald returns and sees her flying. One day a neighbor driving by slows down and calls out to Jeannette as she is bouncing on the trampoline, "You'll tear your insides loose!" Jeannette starts thinking about that, and the idea is so horrifying she stops jumping so much. That night, she has a nightmare about the trampoline. In her dream, she is jumping on soft moss, and then it turns into a springy pile of dead bodies.

"I DON'T BELIEVE THIS"

MERRILL JOAN GERBER

Merrill Joan Gerber has published two collections of short stories, *Stop Here, My Friend* and *Honeymoon,* and three novels. Her stories have appeared in *The New Yorker, The Atlantic, Redbook, The Sewanee Review, The Virginia Quarterly Review,* and elsewhere. She was born in Brooklyn, New York, and now teaches fiction writing at Pasadena City College.

After it was all over, a final detail emerged, one so bizarre that my sister laughed crazily, holding both hands over her ears as she read the long article in the newspaper. I had brought it across the street to show to her; now that she was my neighbor, I came to see her and the boys several times a day. The article said that the crematorium to which her husband's body had been entrusted for cremation had been burning six bodies at a time and dumping most of the bone and ash into plastic garbage bags, which went directly into their dumpsters. A disgruntled employee had tattled.

"Can you imagine?" Carol said, laughing. "Even that! Oh, his poor mother! His poor *father!*" She began to cry. "I don't believe this," she said. That was what she had said on the day of the cremation, when she had sat in my back yard in a beach chair at the far end of the garden, holding on to a washcloth. I think she was prepared to cry so hard that an ordinary handkerchief would never have done. But she remained dry-eyed. When I came outside after a while, she said, "I think of his beautiful face burning, of his eyes burning." She looked up at the blank blue sky and said, "I just don't believe this. I try to think of what he was feeling when he gulped in that stinking exhaust. What could he have been thinking? I know he was blaming me."

She rattled the newspaper. "A dumpster! Oh, Bard would have loved that. Even at the end he couldn't get it right. Nothing ever went right for him, did it? And all along I've been thinking that I won't ever be able to go in the ocean again, because his ashes are floating in it! Can you believe it? How that woman at the mortuary promised they would play Pachelbel's Canon on the little boat, how the remains would be scattered with 'dignity and taste'? His mother even came all the way down with that jar of his father's ashes that she had saved for thirty years, so father and son could be mixed together for all eternity. Plastic garbage baggies! You know," she said, looking at me, "life is just a joke, a bad joke, isn't it?"

Bard had not believed me when I'd told him that my sister was in a shelter for battered women. Afraid of *him?* Running away from *him?* The world was full of dangers from which only *he* could protect her! He had accused me of hiding her in my house. "Would I be so foolish?" I had said. "She knows it's the first place you'd look."

"You better put me in touch with her," he had said, menacingly. "You both know I can't handle this for long."

It had gone on for weeks. On the last day, he called me three times, demanding to be put in touch with her. "Do you understand me?" he shouted. "If she doesn't call here in ten minutes, I'm checking out. Do you believe me?"

"I believe you," I said. "But you know she can't call you. She can't be reached in the shelter. They don't want the women there to be manipulated by their men. They want them to have space and time to think."

"Manipulated?" He was incredulous. "I'm checking *out,* this is *IT.* Good-bye forever!"

He hung up. It wasn't true that Carol couldn't be reached. I had the number. Not only had I been calling her but I had also been playing tapes for her of his conversations over the phone during the past weeks. This one I hadn't taped. The tape recorder was in a different room.

"Should I call her and tell her?" I asked my husband.

"Why bother?" he said. He and the children were eating dinner; he was becoming annoyed by this continual disruption of our lives. "He calls every day and says he's killing himself and he never does. Why should this call be any different?"

Then the phone rang. It was my sister. She had a fever and bronchitis. I could barely recognize her voice.

"Could you bring me some cough syrup with codeine tomorrow?" she asked.

"Is your cough very bad?"

"No, it's not too bad, but maybe the codeine will help me get to sleep. I can't sleep here at all. I just can't sleep."

"He just called."

"Really," she said. "What a surprise!" But the sarcasm didn't hide her fear. "What this time?"

"He's going to kill himself in ten minutes unless you call him."

"So what else is new?" She made a funny sound. I was frightened of her these days. I couldn't read her thoughts. I didn't know if the sound was a cough or a sob.

"Do you want to call him?" I suggested. I was afraid to be responsible. "I know you're not supposed to."

"I don't know," she said. "I'm breaking all the rules anyway."

The rules were very strict. No contact with the batterer, no news of him, no worrying about him. Forget him. Only female relatives could call, and they were not to relay any news of him—not how sorry he was, not how desperate he was, not how he had promised to reform and never do it again, not how he was going to kill himself if she didn't come home. Once, I had called the shelter for advice, saying that I thought he was serious this time, that he was going to do it. The counselor there—a deep-voiced woman named Katherine—had said to me, very calmly, "It might just be the best thing; it might be a blessing in disguise."

My sister blew her nose. "I'll call him," she said. "I'll tell him I'm sick and to leave you alone and to leave me alone."

I hung up and sat down to try to eat my dinner. My children's faces were full of fear. I could not possibly reassure them about any of this. Then the phone rang again. It was my sister.

"Oh, God," she said. "I called him. I told him to stop bothering you, and he said, *I have to ask you one thing, just one thing. I have to know this. Do you love me?*" My sister gasped for breath. "I shouted *No*—what else could I say? That's how I *felt.* I'm so sick, this is such a nightmare; and then he just hung up. A minute later I tried to call him back to tell him that I didn't mean it, that I did love him, that I *do,* but he was gone." She began to cry. "He was gone."

"There's nothing you can do," I said. My teeth were chattering as I spoke. "He's done this before. He'll call me tomorrow morning, full of remorse for worrying you."

"I can hardly breathe," she said. "I have a high fever and the boys are going mad cooped up here." She paused to blow her nose. "I don't believe any of this. I really don't."

Afterward she moved right across the street from me. At first she rented the little house, but then it was put up for sale, and my mother and aunt found enough money to make a down payment so that she could be near me and I could take care of her till she got her strength back. I could see her bedroom window from my bedroom window—we were that close. I often thought of her trying to sleep in that house, alone there with her sons and the new, big watchdog. She told me that the dog barked at every tiny sound and frightened her when there was nothing to be frightened of. She was sorry she had got him. I could hear his barking from my house, at strange hours, often in the middle of the night.

I remembered when she and I had shared a bedroom as children. We giggled every night in our beds and made our father furious. He would come in and threaten to smack us. How could he sleep, how could he go to work in the morning, if we were going to giggle all night? That made us laugh even harder. Each time he went back to his room, we would throw the quilts over our heads and laugh till we nearly suffocated. One night our father came to quiet us four times. I remember the angry hunch of his back as he walked, barefoot, back to his bedroom. When he returned for the last time, stomping like a giant, he smacked us, each once, very hard, on our upper thighs. That made us quiet. We were stunned. When he was gone, Carol turned on the light and pulled down her pajama bottoms to show me the marks of his violence. I showed her mine. Each of us had our father's handprint, five red fingers, on the white skin of her thigh. She crept into my bed, where we clung to each other till the burning, stinging shock subsided and we could sleep.

Carol's sons, living on our quiet, adult street, complained to her that they missed the shelter. They rarely asked about their father and only occasionally said that they wished they could see their old friends and their old school. For a few weeks they had gone to a school near the shelter; all the children had had to go to school. But one day Bard had called me and told me he was trying to find the children. He said he wanted to take them out to lunch. He knew they had to be at some school. He was going to go to every school in the district and look in every classroom, ask everyone he saw if any of the children there looked like his children. He would find them. "You can't keep them from me," he said, his voice breaking. "They belong to me. They love me."

Carol had taken them out of school at once. An art therapist at the shelter held a workshop with the children every day. He was a gentle, soft-spoken man named Ned, who had the children draw domestic scenes and was never once surprised at the knives, bloody wounds, or broken windows that they drew. He gave each of them a special present, a necklace with a silver running-shoe charm, which only children at the shelter were entitled to wear. It made them special, he said. It made them part of a club to which no one else could belong.

While the children played with crayons, their mothers were indoctrinated by women who had survived, who taught the arts of survival. The essential rule was *Forget him, he's on his own, the only person you have to worry about is yourself.* A woman who was in the shelter at the same time Carol was had had her throat slashed. Her husband had cut her vocal cords. She could speak only in a grating whisper. Her husband had done it in the bathroom, with her son watching. Yet each night she sneaked out and called her husband from a nearby shopping center. She was discovered and disciplined by the administration; they threatened to put her out of the shelter if she called him again. Each woman was allowed space at the shelter for a month, while she got legal help and made new living arrangements. Hard cases were allowed to stay a little longer. She said that she was sorry, but that he was the sweetest man, and when he loved her up, it was the only time she knew heaven.

Carol felt humiliated. Once each week the women lined up and were given their food: three very small whole frozen chickens, a package of pork hot dogs, some plain-wrapped cans of baked beans, eggs, milk, margarine, white bread. The children were happy with the food. Carol's sons played in the courtyard with the other children. Carol had difficulty relating to the other mothers. One had ten children. Two had black eyes. Several were pregnant. She began to have doubts that what Bard had done had been violent enough to cause her to run away. Did mental violence or violence done to furniture really count as battering? She wondered if she had been too hard on her husband. She wondered if she had been wrong to come here. All he had done—he said so himself, in the taped conversations, dozens of times—was to break a lousy hundred-dollar table. He had broken it before, he had fixed it before. Why was this time different from any of the others? She had pushed all his buttons, that's all, and he had gotten mad, and he had pulled the table away from the wall and smashed off its legs and thrown the whole thing out into the yard. Then he had put his head through the wall, using the top of his head as a battering ram. He had knocked open a hole to the other side. Then he had bitten his youngest son on the scalp. What was so terrible about that? It was just a momentary thing. He didn't mean anything by it. When his son had begun to cry in fear and pain, hadn't he picked the child up and told him it was nothing? If she would just come home, he would never get angry again. They'd have their sweet life. They'd go to a picnic, a movie, the beach. They'd have it better than ever before. He had just started going to a new church that was helping him to become a kinder and more sensitive man. He was a better person than he had ever been; he now knew the true meaning of love. Wouldn't she come back?

One day Bard called me and said, "Hey, the cops are here. You didn't send them, did you?"

"Me?" I said. I turned on the tape recorder. "What did you do?"

"Nothing. I busted up some public property. Can you come down and bail me out?"

"How can I?" I said. "My children . . ."

"How can you *not?*"

I hung up and called Carol at the shelter. I said, "I think he's being arrested."

"Pick me up," she said, "and take me to the house. I have to get some things. I'm sure they'll let me out of the shelter if they know he's in jail. I'll check to make sure he's really there. I have to get us some clean clothes, and some toys for the boys. I want to get my picture albums. He threatened to burn them."

"You want to go to the house?"

"Why not? At least we know he's not going to be there. At least we know we won't find him hanging from a beam in the living room."

We stopped at a drugstore a few blocks away and called the house. No one was there. We called the jail. They said their records showed that he had been booked, but they didn't know for sure whether he'd been bailed out. "Is there any way he can bail out this fast?" Carol asked.

"Only if he uses his own credit card," the man answered.

"I *have* his credit card," Carol said to me, after she had hung up. "We're so much in debt that I had to take it away from him. Let's just hurry. I hate this! I hate sneaking into my own house this way."

I drove to the house and we held hands going up the walk. "I feel his presence here, that he's right here seeing me do this," she said, in the dusty, eerie silence of the living room. "Why do I give him so much power? It's as if he knows whatever I'm thinking, whatever I'm doing. When he was trying to find the children, I thought that he had eyes like God, that he would go directly to the school where they were and kidnap them. I had to warn them, 'If you see your father anywhere, run and hide. Don't let him get near you!' Can you imagine telling your children that about their father? Oh, God, let's hurry."

She ran from room to room, pulling open drawers, stuffing clothes in paper bags. I stood in the doorway of their bedroom, my heart pounding as I looked at their bed with its tossed covers, at the phone he used to call me. Books were everywhere on the bed—books about how to love better, how to live better; books on the occult, on meditation; books on self-hypnosis for peace of mind. Carol picked up an open book and looked at some words underlined in red. "*You can always create your own experience of life in a beautiful and enjoyable way if you keep your love turned on within you—regardless of what other people say or do,*" she read aloud. She tossed it down in disgust. "He's paying good money for these," she said. She kept blowing her nose.

"Are you crying?"

"No!" she said. "I'm allergic to all this dust."

I walked to the front door, checked the street for his car, and went into the kitchen.

"Look at this," I called to her. On the counter was a row of packages, gift-wrapped. A card was slipped under one of them. Carol opened it and read it aloud: "I have been a brute and I don't deserve you. But I can't live without you and the boys. Don't take that away from me. Try to forgive me." She picked up one of the boxes and then set it down. "I don't believe this," she said. "God, where are the children's picture albums! I can't *find* them." She went running down the hall.

In the bathroom I saw the fishbowl, with the boys' two goldfish swimming in it. The water was clear. Beside it was a piece of notebook paper. Written on it in his hand were the words *Don't give up, hang on, you have the spirit within you to prevail.*

Two days later he came to my house, bailed out of jail with money his mother had wired. He banged on my front door. He had discovered that Carol had been to the house. "Did *you* take her there?" he demanded. "*You* wouldn't do that to me, would you?" He stood on the doorstep, gaunt, hands shaking.

"Was she at the house?" I asked. "I haven't been in touch with her lately."

"Please," he said, his words slurred, his hands out for help. "Look at this." He showed me his arms; the veins in his forearms were black and blue. "When I saw that Carol had been home, I took the money my mother sent me for food and bought three packets of heroin. I wanted to OD. But it was lousy stuff; it didn't kill me. It's not so easy to die, even if you want to. I'm a tough bird. But please, can't you treat me like regular old me? Can't you ask me to come in and have dinner with you? I'm not a monster. Can't anyone, *anyone,* be nice to me?"

My children were hiding at the far end of the hall, listening. "Wait here," I said. I went and got him a whole ham I had. I handed it to him where he stood on the doorstep and stepped back with distaste. Ask him in? Let my children see *this?* Who knew what a crazy man would do? He must have suspected that I knew Carol's whereabouts. Whenever I went to visit her at the shelter, I took a circuitous route, always watching in my rearview mirror for his blue car. Now I had my tear gas in my pocket; I carried it with me all the time, kept it beside my bed when I slept. I thought of the things in my kitchen: knives, electric cords, mixers, graters, elements that could become white-hot and sear off a person's flesh.

He stood there like a supplicant, palms up, eyebrows raised in hope, waiting for a sign of humanity from me. I gave him what I could—a ham, and a weak, pathetic little smile. I said, dishonestly, "Go home. Maybe I can reach her today; maybe she will call you once you get home." He ran to his car, jumped in it, sped off. I thought, coldly, *Good, I'm rid of him. For now we're safe.* I locked the door with three locks.

Later Carol found among his many notes to her one that said, "At least your sister smiled at me, the only human thing that happened in this terrible time. I always knew she loved me and was my friend."

He became more persistent. He staked out my house, not believing I wasn't hiding her. "How could I possibly hide her?" I said to him on the phone. "You know I wouldn't lie to you."

"I know you wouldn't," he said. "I trust you." But on certain days I saw his blue car parked behind a hedge a block away, saw him hunched down like a private eye, watching my front door. One day my husband drove away with my daughter beside him, and an instant later the blue car tore by. I got a look at him then, curved over the wheel, a madman, everything at stake, nothing to lose, and I felt he would kill, kidnap, hold my husband and child as hostages till he got my sister back. I cried out. As long as he lived he would search for her, and if she hid, he would plague me. He had once said to her (she told me this), "You love your family? You want them alive? Then you'd better do as I say."

On the day he broke the table, after his son's face crumpled in terror, Carol told him to leave. He ran from the house. Ten minutes later he called her and said, in the voice of a wild creature, "I'm watching some men building a house, Carol. I'm never going to build a house for you now. Do you know that?" He was panting like an animal. "And I'm coming back for you. You're going to be with me one way or the other. You know I can't go on without you."

She hung up and called me. "I think he's coming back to hurt us."

"Then get out of there," I cried, miles away and helpless. "Run!"

By the time she called me again, I had the number of the shelter for her. She was at a gas station with her children. Outside the station were two phone booths. She hid her children in one; she called the shelter from the other. I called the boys in their booth and I read to them from a book called *Silly Riddles* while she made arrangements to be taken in. She talked for almost an hour to a counselor at the shelter. All the time I was sweating and reading riddles. When it was settled, she came into her children's phone booth and we made a date to meet in forty-five minutes at Sears, so that she could buy herself some underwear and her children some blue jeans. They were still in their pajamas.

Under the bright fluorescent lights in the department store we looked at price tags, considered quality and style, while her teeth chattered. Our eyes met over the racks, and she asked me, "What do you think he's planning now?"

My husband got a restraining order to keep him from our doorstep, to keep him from dialing our number. Yet he dialed it, and I answered the phone, almost passionately, each time I heard it ringing, having run to the room where I had the tape recorder hooked up. "Why is she so afraid of me? Let her come to see me without bodyguards! What can happen? The worst I could do is kill her, and how bad could that be, compared with what we're going through now?"

I played her that tape. "You must never go back," I said. She agreed; she had to. I took clean nightgowns to her at the shelter; I took her fresh vegetables, and bread that had substance.

Bard had hired a psychic that last week, and had gone to Las Vegas to confer with him, taking along a $500 money order. When Bard got home, he sent a parcel to Las Vegas containing clothing of Carol's and a small gold ring that she often wore. A circular that Carol found later under the bed promised immediate results: *Gold has the strongest psychic power—you can work a love spell by burning a red candle and reciting "In this ring I place my spell of love to make you return to me." This will also prevent your loved one from being unfaithful.*

Carol moved in across the street from my house just before Halloween. We devised a signal so that she could call me for help if some maniac cut her phone lines. She would use the antique gas alarm our father had given to me. It was a loud wooden clacker that had been used in the war. She would open her window and spin it. I could hear it easily. I promised her that I would look out my window often and watch for suspicious shadows near the bushes under her windows. Somehow neither of us believed he was really gone. Even though she had picked up his wallet at the morgue, the wallet he'd had with him while he breathed his car's exhaust through a vacuum-cleaner hose and thought his thoughts, told himself she didn't love him and so he had to do this and do it now; even though his ashes were in the dumpster; we felt that he was still out there, still looking for her.

Her sons built a six-foot-high spider web out of heavy white yarn for a decoration and nailed it to the tree in her front yard. They built a graveyard around the tree, with wooden crosses. At their front door they rigged a noose and hung a dummy from it. The dummy, in their father's old blue sweat shirt with a hood, swung from the rope. It was still there long after Halloween, swaying in the wind.

Carol said to me, "I don't like it, but I don't want to say anything to them. I don't think they're thinking about him. I think they just made it for Halloween, and they still like to look at it."

RESURRECTION

GORDON LISH

Gordon Lish is the author of the novel *Dear Mr. Capote.* He has published three anthologies of short fiction: *New Sounds in American Fiction, The Secret Life of Our Time,* and *All Our Secrets Are the Same.* For some years he was fiction editor of *Esquire;* since that time he has been an editor at Knopf. Awarded a Guggenheim fellowship in 1984, he teaches regularly at both Columbia and New York University. His latest novel is *Peru,* published by Dutton in January.

The big thing about this is deciding what it's all about. I mean, by way of theme, what, what? Sure, it gives you the event that got me sworn off whiskey forever. But does that make it a tale of how a certain person got himself a good scare, put aside drunkenness, took up sobriety in high hopes of a permanent shift? I don't think so. Me, I keep feeling it's going to be more about Jews and Christians than about this thing of matching another man glass for glass. But I could be wrong in both connections. Maybe what this story is really getting at is something I'd be afraid to know it is.

Either way or whatever, it happened last Easter, which doesn't mean a thing to me because of me being Jewish. To my wife it's something, though, and I am more or less willing to play along—providing things don't get dangerously out of hand. Egg hunts for the kids, this is okay, and maybe a chocolate bunny wrapped in colored tinfoil. But I draw the line when it comes to a whole done-up basket. I don't see why that's called for, strands of candy-store grass getting stuck between floorboards and you can't get the stuff up even with the vacuum.

As for the Easter that I am talking about, not much of all of that was ever at issue. This was because we got invited out to somebody's place. I think the question just got answered this way—whatever they do, that'll be it, that'll be Easter—no reason for us to have to make any decisions. Which was a relief, of course—the whys and wherefores of which I am sure you do not need me to explicate for you. But my wife and I, we found something else to get into a fuss about, anyway. And that's the best I can do—say "something else." Because I don't remember what. Not that it was anything trifling. I'm certain it must have been something pretty substantial. I mean, aside from the whole routine thing of Easter.

But our boy got us reasonably jolly just in time for our arrival. What happened was, you just caught it from him, his thrill at getting into the country thing. You see, I think he really suffers in the city—I think my wife and I agree on this—not that you could ever actually get a confession of his agony out of him. He's all stoic, this kid of ours—God knows from what sources. Twelve years old and tough as a stump, though to my mind that is still nowhere near as tough as what I think you have to be. At any rate, he was out and gone as soon as we pulled up into the driveway. Trees, I guess. That boy, in him we're looking at a mighty passion to get up high on anything, his mother and his dad always hollering, "Come down from there! You're giving us heart trouble!"

The host and hostess, they were swell people. No need to say more. Nice folks. I was going to say "for Christians," but it is never necessary to actually say it, is it? As for the house-guest thing, we can skip right from Friday when we got there to Saturday before supper, them having over a few neighbors to meet us, three couples, more Christians. There was this one fellow among them, he seemed to take me for a person of special interest. We got to talking with what was surely more gusto than the rest. I don't know what about so much as I know it had to do with a lot of different municipal things—the houses around there, the gardening, getting the old estates up to snuff with fabulous renovations. There were these trays of Rob Roys going from hand to hand, and dishes of tiny asparagus spears and something lemony in a small porcelain bowl, kids underfoot, and the light in there was that country light, this burnished thing the April light can sometimes get to be at maybe five o'clock when you are indoors in a low-slung, high-gloss, many-windowed room. Well, I might as well tell you now, the fellow had a little girl there, maybe half the age of our boy. Harelipped—that was the thing—a girl with a bad face to go through life with, and I think I got drunk enough to say to the man, "Aw, God—aw, shit."

That's it. The story stops short right then and there where I am. Because the next thing I know, it's morning and I am waking up in one of the upstairs beds. But I cannot tell you how I got there. I cannot even tell you what was what between when I was having those Rob

Roys and just standing there and when I was lying down and pulling away the comforter from my head.

There was a carillon across the street. Or across the town. Who knows? It was playing hymns. Or what I think are hymns. As for me, I felt entirely terrific—feeling nothing, not even a tremor, of what you would expect in the way of after-shocks. I mean, I had gotten so bad off that I had actually lost time, lost hours of real life. But there I was, waking up and never sprightlier, never more refurbished in spirit and fiber. Restored, I tell you—I could have said to you, "Look at me, for Christ's sake, look at me—I am in the pink!" Except for this thing of a whole night having vanished on me—that was something I wasn't going to think about yet—or didn't really actually even believe yet—whereas I kept trying to figure out how a thing like this sort of worked, one minute you're on your feet blazing away with a great new friend, the next minute you've skipped over no knowing what, and how did you get to here and to this from that and whatever that was?

Thing was, I knew I couldn't ask my wife. Christ, are you kidding? But I could smell the bacon down there, and went down, thinking that if I don't get a certain kind of a look, then that will mean I must have behaved passably enough, even if I was actually out like a light behind my eyes. And that's how the whole thing down there turned out, all of them downstairs—host, hostess, wife, our boys—and nobody—wife least of all—seeming to regard me as other than an immoderately late-riser and late-comer to the table.

Coffee is poured, conversation reinstalled.

But here is where the story stops short again. Because—just by way of making an effort to add myself to the civilities—I said, "Wretchedest luck, that guy, and such a handsome woman, his espoused, the two of them such a damnably attractive couple, and that little girl with the, you know, the thing, the lip." I mean, I did a speech as an offering, as a show of my harmless presence, the hearty closing up of the morning circle, the one that's formed to ward off night spells.

Not stops short enough, though. Because somebody was taking me up on it, converting ceremony to sermon. My wife, of course—her, of course—with that carillon going wild behind her. I tell you, whoever it was, and whatever he was playing, the man was good on the thing, the man was getting something colossal from those community bells.

But back to my wife, please—for she nips off a bit of toast and says, "You call that bad luck? Knowing what you know, how could you call that such a piece of bad luck, just a harelip?"

Ah, but this is madness, this is treachery—saying anything about a thing like this when I know it is a thing that ought to be left unsaid. Besides, we had no business being where we were. Even if it had meant keeping to the city and to squabbling over everything in sight, here is where we belong, where we should have stayed, where all the trees worth climbing are in a park. Those were rich people. My drink, when I was drinking, it had never been anything too mixed.

I mean, what the hell was she getting at, just a harelip?

I didn't give her the satisfaction. I didn't ask. What I did was go to work on it with my own good sense—trying harder to remember, or to make things up—the result being that on the way home, I came up with a thing that goes roughly like this—the fellow with the little girl sort of producing himself from out of the midst of the rest, me not tracking his features any too clearly, my vision already diminished by at least half.

"Ah, yes," he says, and with his glass he gives my glass a click. He says, "Great to meet the neighbors, don't you say?" He says, "See the fucking neighbors?" He says, "Here's to fucking us."

And me, what did I do? Say l'chaim? Click his glass back?

"Oh, sure, sure," I hear him say. "Sure, sure—right, right."

I know. We drank.

Did I ever say, "Surgery can handle that"? Is that what I said? Or "It's nothing—a good man can fix that right up"?

I mean, what had I said to him to get him to say to me, "Had a little chap of his measure once," and lift his Rob Roy in salute to my boy? Except that I am just guessing that he was doing that—because by then it was too hard for me to see if the man was really pointing anybody out. "Bloody garage door took his fucking head off, don't you see? No, really, old chap. Brand new automatic sort of thing. Automated, I mean."

We were coming up on a toll-booth, my wife and I. In real life, that is. But I don't have to tell you that I wasn't there with all my wits. "Take this!" my wife was saying, and I took a hand off the wheel to take the coins from her hand, meanwhile still making up sentences to keep filling in the blanks.

"Nothing against the old homestead, though—no fucking hard feelings."

That's what I think the man said next. Or something like, "The fucker drops like a shot the day they finish the wiring up."

I don't think I ever got his name, the man who came for cocktails when the neighbors came over and who then left so that the hostess could finally sit us down to something—my wife says cold lamb. She also says she was standing right there and heard every single word, him saying how they'd lost a son but that God had made it up to them with the girl. My wife says the man said to me, "I'd spotted you, you know," and that I said, "For what?" and that the man said, "For a Jew."

But maybe my wife was making that up, just the way I am making this up, especially the part about me hearing him say, "Happy fucking Easter," and me seeing myself get a hand up out of my pocket to hold his chin in place so that I could aim for right on his lips when that was where I kissed him.

For what it's worth, that's the whole story, and notice who just told it cold-sober.

EXCERPTS FROM SWAN LAKE

PETER CAMERON

Peter Cameron grew up in Pompton Plains, New Jersey. He works for the Trust for Public Land in New York City. *One Way or Another,* a collection of stories, will be published by Harper & Row in May.

"What is that called again?" my grandmother asks, nodding at my lover's wok.

"A wok," I say.

"A wok," my grandmother repeats. The word sounds strange coming out of her mouth. I can't remember ever hearing her say a foreign word. She is sitting at the kitchen table smoking a Players cigarette. She saw an ad for them in *Time* magazine and wanted to try them, so after work I drove her down to the 7-Eleven and she bought a pack. She also bought a Hostess cherry pie. That was for me.

Keith, my lover, is stir-frying mushrooms in the wok. My grandmother thinks he is my friend. I am slicing tomatoes and apples. We are staying at my grandmother's house while my parents go on a cruise around the world. It is a romance cruise, stopping at the "love capitals" of the world. My mother won it. Keith and I are making mushroom curry. Keith isn't wearing a shirt, and his chest is sweating. He always sweats when he cooks. He cooks with a passion.

"I wish I could help," my grandmother says. "Let me know if I can."

"We will," says Keith.

"I don't think I've ever seen a wok before," my grandmother says.

"Everyone has them now," says Keith. "They're great."

The doorbell rings, the front door opens, and someone shouts, "Yoohoo!"

"Who's that?" I say.

"Who's what?" my grandmother says. She's a little deaf.

I walk into the living room to investigate. A woman in a jogging suit is standing in the front hall. "Who are you?" she says.

"Paul," I say.

"Where's Mrs. Andrews?" she asks.

"In the kitchen," I say. "I'm her grandson."

"Oh," she says. "I thought you were some kind of maniac. What with that knife and all." She nods at my hand. I am still holding the knife.

"Who are you?" I ask.

"Who's there?" my grandmother shouts from the kitchen.

The woman shouts her name to my grandmother. It sounds like Gloria Marsupial. Then she whispers to me, "I'm from Meals on Wheels. I bring Mrs. Andrews dinner on Tuesday nights. Your mother bowls on Tuesdays."

"Oh," I say.

Mrs. Marsupial walks past me into the kitchen. I follow her. "There you are," she says to my grandmother. "I thought he had killed you."

"Nonsense," my grandmother says. "What are you doing here? You come on Tuesdays."

"It *is* Tuesday," says Mrs. Marsupial. She opens the oven. "We've got to warm this up," she says.

"I don't need it tonight," my grandmother says. "They're making me dinner."

Mrs. Marsupial eyes the wok, the mushrooms, and Keith disdainfully.

"What do you have?" Keith asks.

Mrs. Marsupial takes a tinfoil tray out of the paper bag she is holding. It has a cardboard cover on it. "Meat loaf," she says. "And green beans. And a nice pudding."

"What kind of pudding?" my grandmother asks.

"Rice pudding," says Mrs. Marsupial.

"No thanks," says my grandmother.

"What are you making?" Mrs. Marsupial asks Keith.

"Mushroom curry," says Keith. "We're lacto-vegetarians."

"I'm sure you are," Mrs. Marsupial replies. She turns to my grandmother. "Well, do you want this or not?"

"I could have it tomorrow night," my grandmother says. "If I remember."

"Then I'll stick it in the fridge." Mrs. Marsupial opens the refrigerator and frowns at the beer Keith and I have installed. She moves a six-pack of Dos Equis aside to make room for the container. "I'll put it right here," she says into the refrigerator, "and tomorrow night you just pop it into the oven at about 300 and warm it up, and it will be as good as new." She closes the refrigerator and looks at my grandmother. "Are you sure you're all right, now?" she says.

"What kind of bush is that out there?" my grandmother asks. She points out the window.

"That's not a bush, dear," Mrs. Marsupial says. "That's the clothesline."

"I know that's the clothesline," my grandmother says. "I mean behind it. With the white flowers."

"It's a lilac bush," I say.

"A lilac? Are you sure?"

"It's a lilac," confirms Keith. "You can smell it when you hang out the wash." He opens the window and sticks his head out. "You can smell it from here," he says. "It's beautiful."

"Do you want me to take your blood pressure?" Mrs. Marsupial asks my grandmother. "I left the sphygmomanometer in the van."

"No," my grandmother says. "My blood pressure is fine. It's my memory that's no good."

I dump the sliced tomatoes and apples into the wok and lower the domelike cover. Then I stick my head out the window beside Keith's. It's getting dark out. The lilac bush, the clothesline, the collapsing grape arbor are all disappearing.

"I don't want to be late for my next drop-off," Mrs. Marsupial says. "I guess I'll be running along."

No one says anything. Keith has taken my hand; we are holding hands outside the kitchen window where my grandmother and Mrs. Marsupial can't see us. The smell of curry mixes with the scent of lilacs and intoxicates me. I feel as if I'm leaning on the balcony of a Mediterranean villa, not the window of my grandmother's house in Cheshire, Connecticut, five feet above the dripping spigot.

After dinner my grandmother tells Keith and me stories about "growing up on the farm." She didn't really grow up on a farm—she just visited a friend's farm one summer—but these memories are particularly vivid and make for good telling. I have heard them many times, but Keith hasn't. He is lying on the floor at my feet, exhausted from cooking. My grandmother is sitting on the love seat and I am sitting across from her on the couch, stroking Keith's bare back with my bare foot, a gesture that is hidden by the coffee table. At least I think it is.

"There was an outhouse with a long bench and three holes—a little one, a medium one, and a big one."

"Like the three bears," says Keith. His eyes are closed.

"Like who?" says my grandmother. She doesn't like being interrupted.

"The three bears," repeats Keith. "Cinderella and the three bears."

"Goldilocks," I correct.

"Little Red Riding Hood," murmurs Keith.

"You've lost me," my grandmother says. "Anyway, we used to eat outside, on a big plank table under a big tree. Was it an oak tree? No, it was a mulberry tree. I remember because mulberries would fall off it if the wind blew. You'd be eating mashed potatoes and suddenly there would be a mulberry in them. They looked like black raspberries. In between courses we would run down to the barn and back—run down the hill to the barn, touch it, and run back up the hill. You'd always be hungry again when you got back up." She pauses. "We should turn on some light," she says. "We shouldn't sit in the dark."

No one says anything. No one turns on a light, because light damages the way that words travel. Suddenly my grandmother says, "How many times was I married?"

"Once," I say. "Just once."

"Are you sure just once?"

"As far as I know," I say.

"Maybe you had affairs," suggests Keith.

"Oh, I'm sure I had affairs," says my grandmother. "Although I couldn't tell you with whom. I can't remember the faces at all. It all gets fuzzy. Sometimes I'm not even sure who you are."

"I'm Paul," I say. "Your beloved grandson."

"I'm Keith," says Keith. "Paul's friend."

"I know," my grandmother says. "I know now. But I'll wake up tonight and I'll have no idea. I won't even know where I am. Or what year it is."

"But none of that matters," I say.

"What?" my grandmother asks.

"Who cares what year it is?" I say. I rest both my feet lightly on Keith's back. It moves as though he is sleeping. I think about explaining how none of that matters: names or ages or whereabouts. But before I can explain this to my grandmother, or attempt to, a new thought occurs to me: someday, I'll forget Keith, just like my grandmother has forgotten the great love of her life. And then I think: is Keith the great love of my life? Or is that one still coming, to be forgotten too?

After my grandmother goes to bed at nine o'clock, Keith and I redo the dishes. She likes to wash them if we make the dinner, but she doesn't do such a hot job anymore. There are always little pieces of muck stuck to her pink glass plates. Keith washes and I dry. I am using a dish towel from the 1964 World's Fair. On it, a geisha girl embraces an eskimo, who in turn embraces an Indian squaw embracing a man in a kilt. My grandmother took my sister and me to the World's Fair, but I don't remember her buying this dish towel.

"I think I'm going to move back into the apartment," Keith says.

"Why?" I ask.

"I feel funny here. I don't feel comfortable."

"But I thought you wanted to get out of the city in the summer."

"I did. I do. But this isn't working out." Keith motions with his wet, sudsy hand, indicating my grandmother's kitchen: the African violets on the windowsill, the humming refrigerator, the cookie jars filled with Social Teas. I insert the plate I am drying into the slotted dish rack. It seems to stand on its own accord, gleaming.

"Are you mad?" asks Keith.

"I don't know," I say. "Sad. But not mad."

"There is another thing, too," Keith says. He chases the suds down the drain with the sprayer thing.

"What?"

"I feel like when we're sleeping together she might come in. I don't feel right about it."

"She sleeps all night," I say. "She thinks you sleep on the porch. Plus she's senile."

"I know," says Keith, "but I still don't feel right about it. I just can't relax."

I sit down at the kitchen table and light one of my grandmother's Players cigarettes. Keith washes his hands, dries them, and carefully folds the World's Fair dish towel. He comes over and curls his fingers around my throat, lightly, affectionately throttling me. Keith's clean hands smell like the English Lavender soap my grandmother keeps in a pump dispenser by the sink. Keith's hands smell like my grandmother's hands.

I exhale and look at our reflection in the window. I only smoke about one cigarette a month, and every time I do I experience a wonderful dizzy feeling that quickly gives way to nausea.

"It's no big deal," says Keith. "It's just not cool here."

I think about answering, but I can't. I close my eyes and feel myself floating. The occasional cigarette is a wonderful thing.

My mother sends me a postcard from Piraeus. This is what it says:

> Dear Paul,
> Piraeus is a lovely city considering I had never even heard of it. I'm not sure why it's a Love Capital except the movie "Never on Sunday" was filmed here. Have you seen it? Hope you're okay. Are you taking good care of Grandma?
>
> Love, Mom

About a week after Keith moves out, the ballet comes to town, and my grandmother asks to see it. There are commercials for it on TV, showing an excerpt from "Swan Lake," while across the bottom of the screen a phone number for charging tickets appears and reappears. The dancers' feet blur into the flashing numbers.

My grandmother claims she has never been to the ballet. I don't know if I should believe her or not. Whenever the commercial comes on, she turns it up loud and calls for me to come watch. I do not understand her sudden zeal for the ballet. She gave up on movies long ago, because they were "just nonsense." Besides, she falls asleep at 9:00, no matter where she is.

Nevertheless, I buy three tickets to "Swan Lake" for my grandmother's 88th birthday. Keith comes to her special birthday dinner, bringing a Carvel ice cream cake with him. At my grandmother's request, we are eating tomatoes stuffed with tuna salad. She must have seen an ad for it somewhere. I tried to scallop the edges of the tomatoes as she described, but I failed: they look hacked-up, like something that would be served in a punk restaurant. But they taste okay.

"It's just like old times, having Keith here," my grandmother says.

"I've only been gone a week," Keith says.

"It seems like longer," my grandmother says. "It seems like ages. We were lonely without you. Weren't we, Paul?"

I don't answer. I never admit to being lonely.

After dinner Keith and I do the dishes because my grandmother is the birthday girl and not allowed to help. Keith is telling her the story of "Swan Lake." "The chief swan turns into a girl and falls in love with the prince, but then she gets turned back into a swan."

"Why?" my grandmother asks.

"I don't know," Keith says. "It's morning or something. They have to part. But the prince goes back to the lake the next night and finds her, and because they truly love one another, she changes back into a girl. I think that's it. Basically."

"It sounds ridiculous," says my grandmother.

"I thought you especially wanted to see 'Swan Lake,' " I say.

"I do," my grandmother says. "It just sounds silly." She looks out the window. "What kind of bush is that out there?" She points at the lilac bush.

"A lilac," I say.

"That's a lilac?" she says. "I thought lilacs had tiny purple flowers."

"They do," I say. "But that's a white lilac. The flowers grow in bunches."

"That's not a lilac," my grandmother says. "I remember lilacs."

"It is a lilac," confirms Keith. "Maybe you're thinking of wisteria. Or dogwood."

"I can't see it from here," my grandmother says. "I'm going to go out and look at it." She gets up and walks down the hall. The back door opens and then slams shut.

"If she asks me that one more time," I say, "I think I'll go crazy."

"I think it's sweet," Keith says. "I think your grandmother's great."

"I know," I say. "She is."

Keith puts the remaining, melting, Carvel cake back into the freezer, and then stands there, with the freezer door open, pinching the lavender roses with his fingers. "I wish your grandmother knew we were lovers," he says.

I laugh. "I don't think she'd want to know that," I say. I sit down at the kitchen table.

"Why do you say that?" Keith says. "I think you should tell her. I wouldn't be surprised if she hadn't figured it out."

"What do you mean?" I say.

"What do you mean, what do I mean?" Keith says.

"She doesn't know," I say. "No one knows."

"I know no one knows." Keith closes the freezer and sits down next to me. "That's the problem."

I don't see the problem. I look out the window. My grandmother is walking slowly down the backyard. She is an old lady, and I love her, and I love Keith too, but I don't see the problem in all this. "I don't see the problem in all this," I say.

"You don't?" Keith says. "Really, you don't?"

I shake my head no. Keith shrugs and gets up. He opens the refrigerator and stands silhouetted in the glow from the open door. He is looking for nothing in particular. Outside, my grandmother reaches up and pulls a lilac blossom towards her face, because she has forgotten what they are.

Keith is disgusted with me, and leaves the ballet at intermission. My grandmother falls asleep as Prince Siegfried is reunited with Odile. Her hands are crossed in her lap. She is wearing a pair of white, mismatched gloves—one has tiny pearls sewn on the back of the hand and the other doesn't.

I watch the dancing, unamused. The ballet is such a lie. No one—not my grandmother, not Keith, not I—no one in real life ever moves that beautifully.

MOLLY'S DOG

ALICE ADAMS

Alice Adams grew up in Chapel Hill, North Carolina, and graduated from Radcliffe; since then she has lived mostly in San Francisco. Her most recent novel, *Superior Women,* was published by Knopf in 1984, and a collection of short stories, *Return Trips,* appeared in 1985.

Accustomed to extremes of mood, which she experienced less as 'swings' than as plunges, or more rarely as soarings, Molly Harper, a newly retired screenwriter, was nevertheless quite overwhelmed by the blackness—the horror, really, with which, one dark pre-dawn hour, she viewed a minor trip, a jaunt from San Francisco to Carmel, to which she had very much looked forward. It was to be a weekend, simply, at an inn where in fact she had often stayed before, with various lovers (Molly's emotional past had been strenuous). This time she was to travel with Sandy Norris, an old non-lover friend, who owned a bookstore. (Sandy usually had at least a part-time lover of his own, one in a series of nice young men.)

Before her film job, and her move to Los Angeles, Molly had been a poet, a good one—even, one year, a Yale Younger Poet. But she was living, then, from hand to mouth, from one idiot job to another. (Sandy was a friend from that era; they began as neighbors in a shabby North Beach apartment building, long since demolished.) As she had approached middle-age, though, being broke all the time seemed undignified, if not downright scary. It wore her down, and she grabbed at the film work and moved down to L.A. Some years of that life were wearing in another way, she found, and she moved from Malibu back up to San Francisco, with a little saved money, and her three beautiful, cross old cats. And hopes for a new and calmer life. She meant to start seriously writing again.

In her pre-trip waking nightmare, though, which was convincing in the way that such an hour's imaginings always are (one sees the truth, and sees that any sunnier ideas are chimerical, delusions) at three, or four a.m., Molly pictured the two of them, as they would be in tawdry, ridiculous Carmel: herself, a scrawny sun-dried older woman, and Sandy, her wheezing, chain-smoking fat queer friend. There would be some silly awkwardness about sleeping arrangements, and instead of making love they would drink too much.

And, fatally, she thought of another weekend, in that same inn, years back: she remembered entering one of the cabins with a lover, and as soon as he, the lover, had closed the door they had turned to each other and kissed, had laughed and hurried off to bed. Contrast enough to make her nearly weep—and she knew, too, at four in the morning, that her cherished view of a meadow, and the river, the sea, would now be blocked by condominiums, or something.

This trip, she realized too late, at dawn, was to represent a serious error in judgment, one more in a lifetime of dark mistakes. It would weigh down and quite possibly sink her friendship with Sandy, and she put a high value on friendship. Their one previous lapse, hers and Sandy's, which occurred when she stopped smoking and he did not (according to Sandy she had been most unpleasant about it, and perhaps she had been) had made Molly extremely unhappy.

But, good friends as she and Sandy were, why on earth a weekend together? The very frivolousness with which this plan had been hit upon seemed ominous; simply, Sandy had said that funnily enough he had never been to Carmel, and Molly had said that she knew a nifty place to stay. And so, why not? they said. A long time ago, when they both were poor, either of them would have given anything for such a weekend (though not with each other) and perhaps that was how things should be, Molly judged, at almost five. And she thought of all the poor lovers, who could never go anywhere at all, who quarrel from sheer claustrophobia.

Not surprisingly, the next morning Molly felt considerably better, although imperfectly rested. But with almost her accustomed daytime energy she set about getting ready for the trip, doing several things simultaneously, as was her tendency: packing clothes and breakfast food (the cabins were equipped with little kitchens, she remembered), straightening up her flat and arranging the cats' quarters on her porch.

By two in the afternoon, the hour established for their departure, Molly was ready to go, if a little sleepy; fatigue had begun to cut into her energy. Well, she was not twenty any more, or thirty or forty, even, she told herself, tolerantly.

Sandy telephoned at two-fifteen. In his raspy voice he apologized; his assistant had been late getting in, he still had a couple of things to do. He would pick her up at three, three-thirty at the latest.

Irritating: Molly had sometimes thought that Sandy's habitual lateness was his way of establishing control; at other times she thought that he was simply tardy, as she herself was punctual (but why?). However, wanting a good start to their weekend, she told him that was really okay; it did not matter what time they got to Carmel, did it?

She had begun a rereading of *Howards End,* which she planned to take along, and now she found that the book was even better than she remembered it as being, from the wonderful assurance of the first sentence, "We may as well begin with Helen's letter to her sister—" Sitting in her sunny window, with her sleeping cats, Molly managed to be wholly absorbed in her reading—not in waiting for Sandy, nor in thinking, especially, of Carmel.

Just past four he arrived at her door: Sandy, in his pressed blue blazer, thin hair combed flat, his reddish face bright. Letting him in, brushing cheeks in the kiss of friends, Molly thought how nice he looked, after all: his kind blue eyes, sad witty mouth.

He apologized for lateness. "I absolutely had to take a shower," he said, with his just-crooked smile.

"Well, it's really all right. I'd begun *Howards End* again. I'd forgotten how wonderful it is."

"Oh well. *Forster.*"

Thus began one of the rambling conversations, more bookish gossip than 'literary,' which formed, perhaps, the core of their friendship, its reliable staple. In a scattered way they ran about, conversationally, among favorite old novels, discussing characters not quite as intimates but certainly as contemporaries, as alive. *Was* Margaret Schlegel somewhat prudish? Sandy felt that she was; Molly took a more sympathetic view of her shyness. Such talk, highly pleasurable and reassuring to them both, carried Molly and Sandy, in his small green car, past the dull first half of their trip: down the Bayshore Highway, past San Jose and Gilroy, and took them to where (Molly well remembered) it all became beautiful. Broad stretches of bright green early summer fields; distant hills, grayish blue; and then islands of sweeping dark liveoaks.

At the outskirts of Carmel itself a little of her pre-dawn apprehension came back to Molly, as they drove past those imitation Cotswold cottages, fake-Spanish haciendas, or bright little gingerbread houses. And the main drag, Ocean Avenue, with its shops, shops—all that tweed and pewter, 'imported' jams and tea. More tourists than ever before, of course, in their bright synthetic tourist clothes, their bulging shopping bags—Japanese, French, German, English tourists, taking home their awful wares.

"You turn left next, on Dolores," Molly instructed, and then heard herself begin nervously to babble. "Of course if the place has really been wrecked we don't have to stay for two nights, do we. We could go on down to Big Sur, or just go home, for heaven's sake."

"In any case, sweetie, if they've wrecked it, it won't be your fault." Sandy laughed, and wheezed, and coughed. He had been smoking all the way down, which Molly had succeeded in not mentioning.

Before them, then, was their destination: the Inn, with its clump of white cottages. And the meadow. So far, nothing that Molly could see had changed. No condominiums. Everything as remembered.

They were given the cabin farthest from the central office, the one nearest the meadow, and the river and the sea. A small bedroom, smaller kitchen, and in the living room a studio couch. Big windows, and that view.

"Obviously, the bedroom is yours," Sandy magnanimously declared, plunking down his bag on the studio couch.

"*Well,*" was all for the moment that Molly could say, as she put her small bag down in the bedroom, and went into the kitchen with the sack of breakfast things. From the little window she looked out to the meadow, saw that it was pink now with wildflowers, in the early June dusk. Three large brown cows were grazing out there, near where the river must be. Farther out she could see the wide, gray-white strip of beach, and the dark blue, turbulent sea. On the other side of the meadow were soft green hills, on which—yes, one might have known—new houses had arisen. But somehow inoffensively; they blended. And beyond the beach was the sharp, rocky silhouette of Point Lobos, crashing waves, leaping foam. All blindingly undiminished: a miraculous gift.

Sandy came into the kitchen, bearing bottles. Beaming Sandy, saying, "Mol, this is the most divine place. We must celebrate your choice. Immediately."

They settled in the living room with their drinks, with that view before them; the almost imperceptibly graying sky, the meadow, band of sand, the sea.

And, as she found that she often did, with Sandy, Molly began to say what had just come into her mind. "You wouldn't believe how stupid I was, as a very young woman," she prefaced, laughing a little. "Once I came down here with a lawyer, from San Francisco, terribly rich. Quite famous, actually." (The same man with whom she had so quickly rushed off to bed, on their arrival—as she did not tell Sandy.) "Married, of course. The first part of my foolishness. And I was really broke at the time—*broke,* I was poor as hell, being a typist to support my poetry habit. You remember. But I absolutely insisted on bringing all the food for that stolen, illicit weekend, can you imagine? What on earth was I trying to prove? Casseroles of crabmeat, endive for salads. Honestly, how crazy I was!"

Sandy laughed agreeably, and remarked a little plaintively that for him she had only brought breakfast food. But he was not especially interested in that old, nutty view of her, Molly saw—and resolved that that would be her last 'past' story. Customarily they did not discuss their love affairs.

She asked, "Shall we walk out on the beach tomorrow?"

"But of course."

Later they drove to a good French restaurant, where they drank a little too much wine, but they did not get drunk. And their two reflections, seen in a big mirror across the tiny room, looked perfectly all right: Molly, gray-haired, dark-eyed and thin, in her nice flowered silk dress; and Sandy, tidy and alert, a small plump man, in a neat navy blazer.

After dinner they drove along the beach, the cold white sand ghostly in the moonlight. Past enormous millionaire houses, and blackened wind-bent cypresses. Past the broad sloping river beach, and then back to their cabin, with its huge view of stars.

In her narrow bed, in the very small but private bedroom, Molly thought again, for a little while, of that very silly early self of hers: how eagerly self-defeating she had been—how foolish, in love. But she felt a certain tolerance now for that young person, herself, and she even smiled as she thought of all that intensity, that driven waste of emotion. In many ways middle age is preferable, she thought.

In the morning, they met the dog.

After breakfast they had decided to walk on the river beach, partly since Molly remembered that beach as being far less populated than the main beach was. Local families brought their children there. Or their dogs, or both.

Despite its visibility from their cabin, the river beach was actually a fair distance off, and so instead of walking there they drove, for maybe three or four miles. They parked and got out, and were pleased to see that no one else was there. Just a couple of dogs, who seemed not to be there together: a plumy, oversized friendly Irish setter, who ran right over to Molly and Sandy; and a smaller, long-legged, thin-tailed dark gray dog, with very tall ears—a shy young dog, who kept her distance, running a wide circle around them, after the setter had ambled off somewhere else. As they neared the water, the gray dog sidled over to sniff at them, her ears flattened, seeming to indicate a lowering of suspicion. She allowed herself to be patted, briefly; she seemed to smile.

Molly and Sandy walked near the edge of the water; the dog ran ahead of them.

The day was glorious, windy, bright blue, and perfectly clear; they could see the small pines and cypresses that struggled to grow from the steep sharp rocks of Point Lobos, could see fishing boats far out on the deep azure ocean. From time to time the dog would run back in their direction, and then she would rush toward a receding wave, chasing it backwards in a seeming happy frenzy. Assuming her (then) to live nearby, Molly almost enviously wondered at her sheer delight in what must be familiar. The dog barked at each wave, and ran after every one as though it were something new and marvelous.

Sandy picked up a stick and threw it forward. The dog ran after the stick, picked it up and shook it several times, and then, in a tentative way, she carried it back toward Sandy and Molly—not dropping it, though. Sandy had to take it from her mouth. He threw it again, and the dog ran off in that direction.

The wind from the sea was strong, and fairly chilling. Molly wished she had a warmer sweater, and she chided herself: she could have remembered that Carmel was cold, along with her less practical memories. She noted that Sandy's ears were red, and saw him rub his hands together. But she thought, I hope he won't want to leave soon, it's so beautiful. And such a nice dog. (Just that, at that moment: a very nice dog.)

The dog, seeming for the moment to have abandoned the stick game, rushed at a just-alighted flock of seagulls, who then rose from the wet waves'-edge sand with what must have been (to a dog) a most gratifying flapping of wings, with cluckings of alarm.

Molly and Sandy were now close to the mouth of the river, the gorge cut into the beach, as water emptied into the sea. Impossible to cross—although Molly could remember when one could, when she and whatever companion had jumped easily over some water, and had then walked much farther down the beach. Now she and Sandy simply stopped there, and regarded the newish houses that were built up on the nearby hills. And they said to each other:

"What a view those people must have!"

"Actually the houses aren't too bad."

"There must be some sort of design control."

"I'm sure."

"Shall we buy a couple? A few million should take care of it."

"Oh sure, let's."

They laughed.

They turned around to find the dog waiting for them, in a dog's classic pose of readiness: her forelegs outstretched in the sand, rump and tail up in the air. Her eyes brown and intelligent, appraising, perhaps affectionate.

"Sandy, throw her another stick."

"You do it this time."

"Well, I don't throw awfully well."

"Honestly, Mol, she won't mind."

Molly poked through a brown tangle of seaweed and small broken sticks, somewhat back from the waves. The only stick that would do was too long, but she picked it up and threw it anyway. It was true that she did not throw very well, and the wind made a poor throw worse: the stick landed only a few feet away. But the dog ran after it, and then she ran about with the stick in her mouth, shaking it, holding it high up as she ran, like a trophy.

Sandy and Molly walked more slowly now, against the wind. To their right was the meadow, across which they could just make out the cottages where they were staying. Ahead was a cluster of large, many-windowed ocean-front houses—in one of which, presumably, their dog lived.

Once their walk was over, they had planned to go into Carmel and buy some wine and picnic things, and to drive out into the valley for lunch. They began to talk about this now, and then Sandy said that first he would like to go by the Mission. "I've never seen it," he explained.

"Oh well, sure."

From time to time on that return walk one or the other of them would pick up a stick and throw it for the dog, who sometimes lost a stick and then looked back to them for another. Who stayed fairly near them but maintained, still, a certain shy independence.

She was wearing a collar (Molly and Sandy were later to reassure each other as to this) but at that time, on the beach, neither of them saw any reason to examine it. Besides, the dog never came quite that close. It would have somehow seemed presumptuous to grab her and read her collar's inscription.

In a grateful way Molly was thinking, again, how reliable the beauty of that place had turned out to be: their meadow view, and now the river beach.

They neared the parking lot, and Sandy's small green car.

An older woman, heavy and rather bent, was just coming into the lot, walking her toy poodle, on a leash. *Their* dog ran over for a restrained sniff, and then ambled back to where Molly and Sandy were getting into the car.

"Pretty dog!" the woman called out to them. "I never saw one with such long ears!"

"Yes—she's not ours."

"She isn't lost, is she?"

"Oh no, she has a collar."

Sandy started up the car; he backed up and out of the parking lot, slowly. Glancing back, Molly saw that the dog seemed to be leaving too, heading home, probably.

But a few blocks later—by then Sandy was driving somewhat faster—for some reason Molly looked back again, and there was the dog. Still. Racing. Following them.

She looked over to Sandy and saw that he too had seen the dog, in the rear-view mirror.

Feeling her glance, apparently, he frowned. "She'll go on home in a minute," he said.

Molly closed her eyes, aware of violent feelings within herself, somewhere: anguish? dread? She could no more name them than she could locate the emotion.

She looked back again, and there was the dog, although she was now much farther—hopelessly far behind them. A small gray dot. Racing. Still.

Sandy turned right in the direction of the Mission, as they had planned. They drove past placid houses with their beds of too-bright, unnatural flowers, too yellow or too pink. Clean glass windows, neat shingles. Trim lawns. Many houses, all much alike, and roads, and turns in roads.

As they reached the Mission, its parking area was crowded with tour busses, campers, vans and ordinary cars.

There was no dog behind them.

"You go on in," Molly said. "I've seen it pretty often. I'll wait out here in the sun."

She seated herself on a stone bench near the edge of the parking area —in the sun, beside a bright clump of bougainvillea, and she told herself that by now surely the dog had turned around and gone on home, or back to the beach. And that even if she and Sandy had turned and gone back to her, or stopped and waited for her, eventually they would have had to leave her, somewhere.

Sandy came out, unenthusiastic about the church, and they drove into town to buy sandwiches and wine.

In the grocery store, where everything took a very long time, it occurred to Molly that probably they should have checked back along the river beach road, just to make sure that the dog was no longer there. But by then it was too late.

They drove out into the valley; they found a nice sunny place for a picnic, next to the river, the river that ran on to their beach, and the sea. After a glass of wine Molly was able to ask, "You don't really think she was lost, do you?"

But why would Sandy know, any more than she herself did? At that moment Molly hated her habit of dependence on men for knowledge —any knowledge, any man. But at least, for the moment, he was kind. "Oh, I really don't think so," he said. "She's probably home by now." And he mentioned the collar.

Late that afternoon, in the deepening, cooling June dusk, the river beach was diminishingly visible from their cabin, where Molly and Sandy sat with their pre-dinner drinks. At first, from time to time, it was possible to see people walking out there: small stick figures, against a mild pink sunset sky. Once, Molly was sure that one of the walkers had a dog along. But it was impossible, at that distance, and in the receding light, to identify an animal's markings, or the shape of its ears.

They had dinner in the inn's long dining room, from which it was by then too dark to see the beach. They drank too much, and they had a silly outworn argument about Sandy's smoking, during which he accused her of being bossy; she said that he was inconsiderate.

Waking at some time in the night, from a shallow, winy sleep, Molly thought of the dog out there on the beach, how cold it must be, by now —the hard chilled sand and stinging waves. From her bed she could hear the sea's relentless crash.

The pain that she experienced then was as familiar as it was acute.

They had said that they would leave fairly early on Sunday morning and go home by way of Santa Cruz: a look at the town, maybe lunch, and a brief tour of the university there. And so, after breakfast, Molly and Sandy began to pull their belongings together.

Tentatively (but was there a shade of mischief, of teasing in his voice? could he sense what she was feeling?) Sandy asked, "I guess we won't go by the river beach?"

"No."

They drove out from the inn, up and onto the highway; they left Carmel. But as soon as they were passing Monterey, Pacific Grove, it began to seem intolerable to Molly that they had not gone back to the beach. Although she realized that either seeing or *not* seeing the dog would have been terrible.

If she now demanded that Sandy turn around and go back, would he do it? Probably not, she concluded; his face had a set, stubborn look. But Molly wondered about that, off and on, all the way to Santa Cruz.

For lunch they had sandwiches in a rather scruffy, open-air place; they drove up to and in and around the handsome, almost deserted university; and then, anxious not to return to the freeway, they took off on a road whose sign listed, among other destinations, San Francisco.

Wild Country: thickly wooded, steeply mountainous. Occasionally through an opening in the trees they could glimpse some sheer cliff, gray sharp rocks; once a distant small green secret meadow. A proper habitat for mountain lions, Molly thought, or deer, at least, and huge black birds. "It reminds me of something," she told Sandy, disconsolately. "Maybe even someplace I've only read about."

"Or a movie," he agreed. "God knows it's melodramatic."

Then Molly remembered: it was indeed a movie that this savage scenery made her think of, and a movie that she herself had done the screenplay for. About a quarrelling alcoholic couple, Americans, who were lost in wild Mexican mountains. As she had originally written it, they remained lost, presumably to die there. Only, the producer saw fit to change all that, and he had them romantically rescued by some good-natured Mexican bandits.

They had reached a crossroads, where there were no signs at all. The narrow, white roads all led off into the woods. To Molly, the one on the right looked most logical, as a choice, and she said so, but Sandy took the middle one. "You really like to be in charge, don't you," he rather unpleasantly remarked, lighting a cigarette.

There had been a lot of news in the local papers about a murderer who attacked and then horribly killed hikers and campers, in those very

Santa Cruz mountains, Molly suddenly thought. She rolled up her window and locked the door, and she thought again of the ending of her movie. She tended to believe that one's fate, or doom, had a certain logic to it; even, that it was probably written out somewhere, even if by one's self. Most lives, including their endings, made a certain sort of sense, she thought.

The gray dog then came back powerfully, vividly to her mind: the small heart pounding in that thin, narrow rib cage, as she ran, ran after their car. Unbearable: Molly's own heart hurt, as she closed her eyes and tightened her hands into fists.

"Well, Christ," exploded Sandy, at that moment. "We've come to a dead end. Look!"

They had; the road ended abruptly, it simply stopped, in a heavy grove of cypresses and redwoods. There was barely space to turn around.

Not saying, Why didn't you take the other road, Molly instead cried out, uncontrollably, "But why didn't we go back for the dog?"

"Jesus, Molly." Red-faced with the effort he was making, Sandy glared. "That's what we most need right now. Some stray bitch in the car with us."

"What do you mean, stray bitch? She chose us—she wanted to come with us."

"How stupid you are! I had no idea."

"You're so selfish!" she shouted.

Totally silent, then, in the finally righted but possibly still lost car, they stared at each other: a moment of pure dislike.

And then, "Three mangy cats, and now you want a dog," Sandy muttered. He started off, too fast, in the direction of the crossroads. At which they made another turn.

Silently they travelled through more woods, past more steep gorges and ravines, on the road that Molly had thought they should have taken in the first place.

She had been right; they soon came to a group of signs which said that they were heading toward Saratoga. They were neither to die in the woods nor to be rescued by bandits. Nor murdered. And, some miles past Saratoga, Molly apologized. "Actually I have a sort of headache," she lied.

"I'm sorry, too, Mol. And you know I like your cats." Which was quite possibly also a lie.

They got home safely, of course.

But somehow, after that trip, their friendship, Molly and Sandy's, either 'lapsed' again, or perhaps it was permanently diminished; Molly was not sure. One or the other of them would forget to call, until days or weeks had gone by, and then their conversation would be guilty, apologetic.

And at first, back in town, despite the familiar and comforting presences of her cats, Molly continued to think with a painful obsessiveness of that beach dog, especially in early hours of sleeplessness. She imagined going back to Carmel alone to look for her; of advertising in the Carmel paper, describing a young female with gray markings. Tall ears.

However she did none of those things. She simply went on with her calm new life, as before, with her cats. She wrote some poems.

But, although she had ceased to be plagued by her vision of the dog (running, endlessly running, growing smaller in the distance) she did not forget her.

And she thought of Carmel, now, in a vaguely painful way, as a place where she had lost, or left something of infinite value. A place to which she would not go back.

TRANSACTIONS IN A FOREIGN CURRENCY

DEBORAH EISENBERG

Deborah Eisenberg was born in Winnetka, Illinois, and has lived for many years in New York City. Her first collection of stories, *Transactions in a Foreign Currency,* is being published in the spring of 1986 by Alfred A. Knopf, Inc. Her play *Pastorale* was performed at The Second Stage in Manhattan in 1982.

I had lit a fire in my fireplace, and I'd poured out two coffees and two brandies, and I was settling down on the sofa next to a man who had taken me out to dinner when Ivan called after more than six months. I turned with the receiver to the wall as I absorbed the fact of Ivan's voice, and when I glanced back at the man on my sofa, he seemed like a scrap of paper, or the handle from a broken cup, or a single rubber band—a thing that has become dislodged from its rightful place and intrudes on one's consciousness two or three or many times before one understands that it is just a thing best thrown away.

"Still in Montreal?" I said into the phone.

"Yeah," Ivan said. "I'm going to stay for a while."

"What's it like?" I said.

"Cold," he said.

"It's cold in New York, too," I was able to answer.

"Well, when can you get here?" he said. "We'll warm each other up."

I'd begun to think that this time there would be no end to the waiting, but here he was, here was Ivan, dropping down into my life again and severing the fine threads I'd spun out toward the rest of the world.

"I can't just leave," I said. "I have a job, you know."

"They'll give you a few weeks, won't they?" he said. "Over Christmas?"

"A few weeks?" I said, but when he was silent I was sorry I'd said it.

"We'll talk it all over when you get up here," he said finally. "I know it's hard. It's hard for me, too."

I turned slightly, to face the window. The little plant that sat on the sill was almost leafless, I noticed, and paint was peeling slightly from the ceiling above it. How had I made myself believe this apartment was my home? This apartment was nothing.

"O.K.," I said. "I'll come."

I replaced the receiver, but the man on the sofa just sat and moved his spoon back and forth in his cup of coffee with a little chiming sound.

"An old friend," I said.

"So I assumed," he said.

"Well," I said, but then I couldn't even remember why that man was there. "I think I'd better say good night."

The man stood. "Going on a trip?"

"Soon," I said.

"Well, give me a call when you get back," he said. "If you want to."

"I'm not sure that I'll be coming back," I said.

"Uh-huh, uh-huh," he said, nodding as if I were telling him a long story. "Well, then, good luck."

I flew up early one morning, leaving my apartment while it was still dark outside. I had packed, and flooded my plant with water in a hypocritical gesture that would delay, but not prevent, its death, and then I'd sat waiting for the clock face to arrive at the configuration that meant it was time I could reasonably go.

The airport was shaded and still in the pause before dawn, and the scattering of people there seemed to have lived for days in flight's distended light or dark; for them, this stop was no more situated in space than a dream is.

How many planes and buses and trains I had taken, over the years, to see Ivan! And how inevitable it always felt, as if I were being conveyed to him by some law of the universe made physical. We'd met when I was nineteen, in Atlanta, where I was working for a photographic agency. He lived with his wife, Linda, who had grown up there, and their one-year-old, Gary. But he travelled frequently, and when he would call and ask me to go with him or meet him for a weekend somewhere—well, Ivan was one of those men, and just standing next to him I felt as if I were standing in the sun, and it never occurred to me to hesitate or to ask any questions.

And Ivan warmed with me. After their early marriage, Linda had grown increasingly fearful and demanding, he told me, and years of trying to work things out with her had imposed on him the cautious reserve of an unwilling guardian. It was a habit he seemed eager to discard.

After a time, there was a divorce, and Ivan moved about from place to place, visiting and taking photographs, and I got a job in New York. But he would call, and I would lock the door of whatever apartment I was living in and go to him in strange cities, leaving each before I could break through the transparent covering behind which it lay, mysterious and inert. And I always felt the same when I saw Ivan—like an animal raised in captivity that, after years of caged, puzzled solitude, is instantly recalled by the touch of a similar creature to the natural blazing consciousness of its species.

The last time we were together, though, we had lain on a slope overlooking a sunny lake, and a stem trembled in my hand while I explained, slowly and quietly, that it would not do any longer. I was twenty-eight now, I said, and he would have to make some sort of decision about me.

"Are you talking about a decision that can be made honestly?" He held my chin up and looked into my eyes.

"That is what a decision is," I said. "If the next step is self-evident, we don't call it a decision."

"I don't want to be unfair," he said, finally. And I came to assume, because I hadn't heard from him since, that the decision had been made.

Soft winter light was rolling up onto the earth as the plane landed, and the long corridors of the airport reflected a mild, dark glow.

An official opened my suitcase and turned over a stack of my underpants. "SOMETHING TO DECLARE," "NOTHING TO DECLARE," I saw on signs overhead, and strange words below each message. Oh, yes—part of this city was English-speaking, part French-speaking. A sorry-looking Christmas wreath hung over the lobby, and I thought of something Ivan had said after one of his frequent trips to see Gary and Linda in Atlanta: "I can't really have much sympathy for her. When she senses I'm not as worried about her as she'd like me to be, she takes a slight, semi-accidental overdose of something or gets herself into a little car crash."

"She loves you that much?" I asked.

"It isn't love," he said. "For all her dependence, she doesn't love me."

"But," I said, "is that what she thinks? Does she think she loves you that much?"

He stood up and stretched, and for a moment I thought that he hadn't registered my question. "Yeah," he said. "That's what she thinks."

Near the airport exit, there was a currency-exchange bureau, and I understood that I would need new money. The man behind the cage counted out the variegated, colorful Canadian bills in front of me. "Ah," he said, noticing my expression—he spoke with a faint but unfamiliar accent—"an unaccustomed medium of exchange, yes?"

I was directed by strangers to a little bus that took me across a plain to the city, a stony outcropping perched at the cold top of the world. There were solitary houses, heavy in the shallow film of light, and rows of low buildings, and many churches. I found a taxi and circumvented the question of language by handing the driver a piece of paper with Ivan's address on it, and I was brought in silence to a dark, muscular Victorian house that loomed from a brick street in a close row with others of its kind.

Ivan came downstairs bringing the morning gold with him and let me in. His skin and hair were wheat and honey colors, and he smelled as if he had been sleeping in a sunny field. "Ivan," I said, taking pleasure in speaking his name. As he held me, I felt ebbing from me a terrible pain that I had been unaware of until that moment. "I'm so tired."

"Want to wake up, or want to go to sleep?" he said.

"Sleep," I said, but for whole minutes I couldn't bring myself to move.

Upstairs, the morning light, gathering strength, made the melting frost on the bedroom window glow. I slept as if I hadn't slept for a week, and then awoke, groping hurriedly through my life to place myself. Understanding, I looked out the window through the city night shine of frost: I was in Montreal with Ivan, and I had missed the day.

I stood in the doorway of the living room for a moment, looking. Ivan was there, sharing a bottle of wine with two women. One of them was striking and willowy, with a spill of light curls, and the other was small and dark and fragile-looking. When had Ivan become so much older?

The small woman was studying a photograph, and her shiny hair fell across her pretty little pointy face. "No, it is wonderful, Ivan," she was saying. She spoke precisely, as if picking her way through the words, with the same accent I had heard at the airport. "It is a portrait of an entire class. A class that votes against its own interests. It is . . . a *photograph* of false consciousness."

"Well, it's a damn good print, anyway," the other woman said. "Lovely work, Ivan."

"We're playing Thematic Apperception Test," Ivan said, and the dark girl blushed and primly lowered her eyes. "We've had responses from Quebec and England. Let's hear from our U.S. representative." He handed me the photograph. "What do you see?"

Two women who, to judge from this view, were middle-aged, overweight, and poor stood gazing into a shopwindow at a display of tawdry lingerie. High up in the window was a reflection of mounded clouds, and trees in full leaf. I did not feel like discussing the picture.

"Hello," the small girl said, intercepting my gaze as I looked up. "I am Micheline, and this is my friend Fiona."

Fiona reached lazily over to shake hands. "Hello," I said, allowing our attention to flow away from the photograph. "Do you live here, Fiona, or in England?"

"Oh, let's see," she said. "Where do I live? Well, it's been quite some time since I've even seen England. I've been in Montreal for a while, and before that I was in L.A."

"Really," I said. "What were you doing there?"

"What one does," she said. "I was working in film."

"The industry!" Micheline said. A hectic flush beat momentarily under her white skin, as if she'd been startled by her own exclamation. "There is much money to be made there, but at what personal expense!"

"Fiona has a gallery here," Ivan said.

"No money, no personal expense." Fiona smiled.

"It is excellent," Micheline said. "Fiona exhibits the most important new photographs in Canada. Soon she will have a show of Ivan's work."

"Wonderful," I said, but none of the others added anything. "We're rather on display here, Ivan," I said. "Are you planning to do something about curtains?"

Ivan smiled. "No." Ivan's rare smile always stopped me cold, and I smiled back as we looked at each other.

"It is not important," Micheline said, reclaiming the conversation. "The whole world is a window."

"That's ridiculous," Fiona said good-naturedly, and yawned.

"Yes, but that is true, Fiona," Micheline said. "Privacy is a—what is that?—*debased* form of dignity. It is dignity's . . . atrophied corpse."

"How good your English has become," Fiona said, smiling, but Ivan had nodded approvingly.

"The rigorous Northern temperament," Fiona said to me. "Sometimes I long for just a weekend in Los Angeles again."

"Not me!" Micheline said. She kicked her feet impatiently.

"Have you lived there as well?" I asked.

"No," she said. "But I am sure. Beaches, hotels, drinks with little hats—"

"That's Hawaii, I think," I said.

"Perhaps," Micheline said, looking sideways at me out of her doll's face.

"So what about it?" Ivan said. "Have you two decided to stay for dinner?"

"No," Micheline said, jumping to her feet. "Come, Fiona. We must go." She held out her hand to Fiona, blushing deeply. "We must go."

"All right." Fiona yawned and stood. "But let's have a rain check, Ivan. Micheline raves about your cooking. Maybe we'll come back over the weekend for Micheline's things. Sorry to have left them so long. We've been a while sorting things out."

"No problem," Ivan said. "Plenty of closet space."

At the door, Micheline was piling on layers and layers of clothing and stamping like a little pony in anticipation of the snow.

"Tell me about them," I said to Ivan after dinner, as we lay on the sofa, our feet touching. "Who are they?"

"What do you mean, 'who'?" he said. "You met them."

"Come on, Ivan," I said. "All I meant was that I'd like to know more about your friends. How did you meet them? That sort of thing."

"Actually," he said, "I hardly know Fiona. Micheline just brought her over once before."

"Micheline's so extreme," I said, smiling.

"She's very young," Ivan said.

"I used to be young," I said. "But I was never that extreme, was I?"

"She's a purist," Ivan said. "She's a very serious person."

"She seemed a bit of a silly person to me," I said. "Have she and Fiona been together long?"

"Just a month or so," he said.

"Micheline doesn't seem as if she's really used to being with another woman, somehow," I said. Ivan glanced at a page of newspaper lying on the floor below him. Some headline had caught his eye, apparently.

"She was sort of defiant," I said. "Or nervous. As if she were making a statement about being gay."

"On the contrary," Ivan said. "She considers that to be an absolutely fraudulent opposition of categories—gay, straight. Utterly fraudulent."

"Do you?" I said.

"What is this?" Ivan said. "Are you preparing your case against me? Yes, 'The People of the United States of America versus Ivan Augustine Olmstead.' I know."

"How long did she live here?" I said.

"Three months," he said, and then neither of us said anything or moved for about fifteen minutes.

"Ivan," I said. "I didn't call you. You wanted me to come up here."

He looked at me. "I'm sorry," he said. "But we're both very tense."

"Of course I'm tense," I said. "I don't hear from you for six months, then out of the blue you summon me for some kind of audience, and I don't know what you're going to say. I don't know whether you want some kind of future with me, or whether we're having our last encounter, or what."

"Look," he said. He sat upright on the sofa. "I don't know how to say this to you. Because, for some reason, it seems very foreign to you, to your way of thinking. But it's not out of the blue for me at all, you see. Because you're always with me. But you seem to want to feel rejected."

"I don't want to feel rejected," I said. "But if I've been rejected I'd just as soon know it."

"You haven't been rejected," he said. "You can't be rejected. You're a part of me. But instead of enjoying what happens between us, you always worry about what *has* happened between us, or what *will* happen between us."

"Yes," I said. "Because there is no such thing as an independent present. How can I not worry each time I see you that it will be the last?"

"You act as if I had all the power between us," he said. "You have just as much power as I do. But I can't give it to you. You have to claim it."

"If that were true," I said, "we'd be living together at least half the time."

"And if we were living together," he said, "would you feel that you had to go to work with me or stay with me in the darkroom to see whether my feelings about you changed minute by minute? It's not the quantity of time we spend together that makes us more close or less close. People are to each other what they are."

"But that can change," I said. "People's interests are at odds sometimes."

"Not really," he said. "Not fundamentally. And you would understand that if you weren't so interested in defending your isolating, competitive view of things."

"What on earth are you talking about, Ivan? Are you really saying that there's no conflict between people?"

"What I'm saying is that it's absurd for people to be obsessed with their own little roles. People's situations are just a fraction of their existence—the difference between those situations is superficial, it's arbitrary. In actuality, we're all part of one giant human organism, and one part can't survive at the expense of another part. Would you take off your sock and put it on your hand because you were cold? Look—does the universe care whether it's you or Louis Pasteur that's Louis Pasteur? No. From that point of view, we're all the same."

"Well, Ivan," I said, "if we're all the same, why drag me up here? Why not just keep Micheline around? Or call in a neighbor?"

He looked at me, and he sighed. "Maybe you're right," he said. "Maybe I just don't care about you in the way that you need. I just don't know. I don't want to falsify my feelings."

But when I saw how exhausted he looked, and miserable, loneliness froze my anger, and I was ashamed that I'd allowed myself to become childish. "Never mind," I said. I wished that he would touch me. "Never mind. We'll figure it out."

It was not until the second week that I regained my balance and Ivan let down his guard, and we were able to talk without hidden purposes and we remembered how it felt to be happy together. Still, it seemed to me as if I were remembering every moment of happiness even as it occurred, and, remembering, mourning its death.

One day, Ivan was already dressed and sitting in the kitchen by the time I woke up. "Linda called this morning," he said. "She let the phone ring about a hundred times before I got it. I'm amazed you slept through it."

I poured myself a cup of coffee and sat down.

"I wonder why people do that," he said. "It's annoying, and it's pointless."

"It wasn't pointless in this case," I said. "You woke up."

"Want some toast?" Ivan asked. "Eggs?"

"No, thanks," I said. I hardly ever ate breakfast. "So, is she all right?"

"Fine," he said. "I guess."

"Well, that's good," I said.

"Remember that apartment I had in Washington?" he said. "I loved that place. It was the only place I ever lived where I could get the paper delivered."

"How's Gary?" I said.

"Well, I don't know," Ivan said. "According to Linda, he's got some kind of flu or something. She's gotten it into her head that it's psychosomatic, because this is the first time since he was born that I haven't come home for Christmas."

"Home," I said.

"Well," Ivan said. "Gary's home."

"Maybe you should go," I said.

"He'll have to adjust sometime," Ivan said. "This is just Linda's way of manipulating the situation."

I shrugged. "It's up to you." I wondered, really for the first time, what Ivan's son looked like. "Do you have a picture of Gary?"

"Somewhere, I think," Ivan said.

"I'd like to see one," I said.

"Sure," he said. "You mean now?"

"Well, I'd like to," I said.

Steam rose from my coffee and faded into the bright room. Outside the window, light snow began to fall. In a few minutes Ivan came back with a wallet-sized snapshot.

"How did you get into this picture?" I said.

He took it from me and peered at it. "Oh. Some friends of Linda's were over that day. They took it."

"So that's Linda," I said. For nine years I'd been imagining the wrong woman—someone tired and aggrieved—but the woman in the photograph was finely chiselled, like Ivan. Even in her jeans, she appeared aristocratic, and her expression was somewhat set, as if she had just disposed of some slight inconvenience. She and Ivan could have been brother and sister. The little boy between them, however, looked clumsy and bereft. His head was large and round and wobbly-looking, and the camera had caught him turning, his mouth open in alarm, as if he had fallen through space into the photograph. A current of fury flowed through me, leaving me as depleted as the child in the picture looked. "What if he *is* sick?" I said.

"Kids get sick all the time," Ivan said.

"You could fly down Christmas Eve and come back the twenty-sixth or twenty-seventh."

"Flying on Christmas Eve's impossible anyhow," he said.

"Well, you could go down tomorrow."

"What about you?" he said.

"What about me?" I said.

"If I can even still get reservations," he said.

"Call and see," I said. "I'll call." Linda had probably never, in awe of Ivan's honey-colored elegance that was so like her own, hesitated to touch him as I sometimes did. As I did right now.

The next day, Ivan bought some toys, much more cheerful and robust than the child they were for, and then I watched him pack. And then we went out to the airport together.

I took the little airport bus back alone, and I felt I had been equipped by a mysterious agency: I knew without asking how to transport myself into a foreign city, my pockets were filled with its money, and in my hand I had a set of keys to an apartment there. The snow still fell lightly, detaching itself piece by piece from the white sky, absorbing all the sound. And the figures past which we rode looked almost immobile in their heavy clothing, and not quite formed, as if they were bodies waiting to be inhabited by displaced souls. In the dark quiet of the bus, I let myself drift. Cities, the cities where I visited Ivan, were repositories of these bodies waiting to be animated, I thought sleepily, but how did a soul manage to incarnate itself in one?

All night long I slept easily, borne away on the movements of my new unfettered life, but I awoke to a jarring silence. Ivan had taken the clock.

I looked around. It was probably quite late. The sun was already high, and the frost patterns, which seemed always on the verge of meaning, were being sucked back to the edges of the window as I stared. In the kitchen I sat and watched the light pooling in rich winter tints across the linoleum, and eventually the pink-and-pewter evening came, and frost patterns encroached on the windows again. How quickly the day had disappeared. The day had sat at the kitchen window, but the earth had simply rolled away from under it.

It was light again when I woke. I thought suddenly of the little plant on my windowsill in New York. It would be dead by now. I felt nauseated, but then I remembered I hadn't eaten the day before.

There was nothing in the refrigerator, but in the freezer compartment I found a roll of chocolate-chip-cookie dough. How unlike Ivan to have such a thing—what circumstances had prompted him to buy it? Ah—I saw Micheline and Ivan with a shopping cart, laughing: the purists' night off.

I searched through the pots and pans—what a lot of clatter—but there was a cookie sheet. Good. I turned on the oven and sawed through the frozen dough. Soon the kitchen was filling with warmth. But an assaultive odor underlay it, and when I opened the oven door, I found the remains of a leg of lamb from earlier in the week that we'd forgotten to put away. The bone stood out, almost translucent, and the porous sheared face of meat was still red in the center. "Get rid of all this old stuff," I heard myself say out loud in a strange, cheerful voice, and I jabbed a large fork into it. But I had to sit for several minutes breathing deeply with my head lowered before I managed to dump the lamb into the garbage can along with the tray of dough bits and get myself back into bed, where I stayed for the rest of the day.

The next afternoon, it seemed to me that I was ready to go out of the apartment. I took a hot bath, cleansing myself carefully. Then I looked through my clothing, taking it out and putting it away, piece by piece. None of the things I'd brought with me seemed right. Steam poured from the radiators, but the veil of warmth hardly softened the little pointed particles of cold in the room.

The hall closet was full of women's clothes, and there I found everything I needed. I supposed it all belonged to Micheline, but everything felt roomy enough, even though she looked so small. I selected a voluminous skirt, a turtleneck jersey, and a long, heavy sweater. There was a pair of boots as well—beautiful boots, fine-grained and sleek. If they belonged to Micheline, they must have been a gift. Surely she never would have chosen them for herself.

The woman who stood in the mirror was well assembled, but the face, above the heavy dark clothing, was indistinct in the brilliant sunlight. I made up my eyes heavily, and then my mouth with a red lipstick that was sitting on Ivan's bureau, and checked back with the mirror. Much better. Then I found a jacket that probably belonged to Ivan, and a large shawl, which I arranged around my head and shoulders.

Outside, everything was outlined in a fluid brilliance, and underfoot the snow emitted an occasional dry shriek. The air was as thin as if it might break, fracturing the landscape along which I walked: broad, flat-roofed buildings with blind windows, low upon the endless sky. There were other figures against the landscape, all bundled up like myself against the cold, and although the city was still unfathomable, I could recall no other place, and the rudiments of a past seemed to be hidden here for me somewhere, beyond my memory.

I entered a door and was plunged into noise and activity. I was in a supermarket arranged like a hallucination, with aisles shooting out in unexpected directions, and familiar and unfamiliar items perched side by side. If only I had made a list! I held my cart tightly, trusting the bright packages to draw me along correctly and guide me in my selections.

The checkout girl rang up my purchases: eggs (oh, I'd forgotten butter; well, no matter, the eggs could always be boiled, or used in something); a replacement roll of frozen cookie dough; a box of spaghetti; a jar of pickled okra from Texas; a package of mint tea; foil; soap powder; cleanser; violet toilet paper (an item I'd never seen before); and a bottle of aspirin. The girl took my money, glancing at me.

Several doors along, I stopped at a little shop filled with pastries. There were trays of jam tarts and buns, and plates piled up with little chocolate diamond shapes, and pyramids of caramelized spheres, and shelves of croissants and tortes and cookies, and the most wonderful aroma surged around me. "Madame?" said a woman in white behind the counter.

I looked up at her, over a shelf of frosted cakes that held messages coded into French. On one of them a tiny bride and groom were borne down upon by shining sugar swans, and my heart fluttered high up against my chest like a routed moth. I spoke, though, resolutely in English: "Everything looks so good." Surely that was an appropriate thing to say—surely people said that. "Wait." I pointed at a tray of evergreen-shaped cookies covered with green sugar crystals. Tiny bright candies had been placed on them at intervals to simulate ornaments. "There."

"Very good," the woman said. "The children like these very much."

"Good," I said. What had she meant? "I'll take a dozen."

"Did you have a pleasant Christmas?" she asked me, nestling my cookies into a box.

"Yes," I said, perhaps too loudly, but she didn't seem to notice the fire that roared over me. "And you?"

"Very good," she said. "I was with my sister. All the children were home. But now today it feels so quiet." She smiled, and I understood that her communication had been completed, and we both inclined our heads slightly as I left.

"Hello," I said uncertainly to the butcher in the meat market next door. It had occurred to me that I ought to stop and get something nourishing.

"What can I do for you?" the butcher asked in easy English.

"Actually," I said, dodging a swift memory of the leg of lamb in Ivan's garbage can, "I'd like something for supper." Ah! I had to smile—what the woman in the bakery had been telling me was how it felt to be a person when one's sister and some children were around.

"Something in particular?" the butcher asked. "If I'm not being too nosy?"

"Please," I said across a wall of nausea. "Sausages." That had been good thinking—at least they would be in casings.

"Sausages," he said. "How many sausages?"

"Not so many," I said, trying not to think too concretely about the iridescent hunks of meat all around me.

"Let's see," he said. "Should we say . . . for two?"

"Good," I said. Fortunately there was a chair to wait in. "Did you have a pleasant Christmas?" I asked.

"Excellent," the butcher said. "Goose. And yours?"

"Oh, excellent," I said. I supposed from his silence that that had been insufficient, so I continued. "It feels so quiet today, though. All the children have gone back."

"Oh, I know that quiet," the butcher said. "When they go."

"They're not exactly my children, of course," I said. "They're my sister's. Stepsister's, I mean. My sister would be too young a person to have children old enough to go back anywhere. You know," I said, "I have a friend who believes that in a sense it doesn't matter whether I'm a person with a stepsister who has children or whether someone else is."

The butcher looked at me. "Interesting point," he said. "That's five seventy-eight with tax."

"I know it sounds peculiar," I said, counting out the price. "But this friend really believes that, assuming there's a person with a stepsister, it just doesn't ultimately matter—to the universe, for instance—whether that person happens to be me or whether that person happens to be someone else. And I was thinking—does it actually matter to you whether that person is me or that person is someone else?"

"To me . . . does it matter to me . . ." The butcher handed me my package. "Well, to me, sweetheart, you *are* someone else."

"Well." I laughed uneasily. "No. But do you mean—wait—I'm not sure I understand. That is, did you mean that I might as well be the person with the stepsister? That it's an error to identify oneself as the occupant of a specific situation?" The butcher looked at me again. "I mean, how would you describe the difference between the place you occupy in the world and the place I occupy?"

"Well"—his eyes narrowed thoughtfully—"I'm standing over here, I see you standing over there, like that."

"Oh—" I said.

"So," he said. "Got everything? Know where you are?"

"Thanks," I said. "Yes."

"You're all set, then," he said. "Enjoy the sausages."

Back at the apartment, I unpacked my purchases and put them away. Strange, that I missed Ivan so much more when we were together than when we were apart.

I was dozing when I heard noises in the kitchen. I went to investigate, and found a man with black hair and pale, pale skin standing near the table and holding the bakery box to his ear as if it were a seashell.

"Sorry," he said, putting it down. "The door was open. Where's Ivan?"

"Gone," I said.

"Oh," he said. "Be back soon?"

"No," I said. Well, I was up. I put on the kettle.

"Sit down," he said. "Relax. I don't bite." He laughed—the sound of breaking dishes. "Name's Eugene." He held out a hand to me. "Mind if I sit for a minute, too? Foot's killing me."

He pulled up a chair across from me and sat, his long-lashed eyes cast down.

"What's the matter with your foot?" I said after a while.

"Well, I'm not exactly sure. Doctor told me it was a calcium spur. Doesn't bother me much, except just occasionally." He fell silent for a minute. "Maybe I should see the guy again, though. Sometimes things . . . become *exacerbated,* I guess is how you'd put it. Turn into other things, almost."

I nodded, willing him toward the door. I wanted to sleep. I wanted to have a meal.

"I was walking around, though," he said, "and I thought I'd drop in to see Ivan."

"I'm going to have a cup of tea," I said. "Do you want one?"

"He doesn't have any herb tea, does he?" Eugene said. "It's good for the nerves. Soothing." He was wearing heavy motorcycle boots, I saw, that were soaking wet. No wonder his feet hurt. "Yeah, Ivan owes me some money," he said. "Thought I'd drop by and see if he had it on him by some chance."

I put the teapot and cups on the table. I wondered how soon I could get Eugene to go.

"Where're you from?" Eugene said. "You're not from here, are you?"

"New York," I said. I also wanted to get out of these clothes. They were becoming terribly uncomfortable.

"Yeah, that's what I thought. I thought so." He laughed miserably again. "Good old rotten apple."

"Don't like it much, huh?" I said.

"Oh, I like it all right," Eugene said. "I love it. I was born and raised there. Whole family's there. Yeah, I miss it a lot. From time to time." He sipped delicately at his tea, still looking down. Then he tossed his thick black hair from his face, as if he were aware of my stare.

"Aren't you cold?" I asked suddenly. "Walking around like that?" I reached over to his leather jacket.

"Oh, I'm fine, thank you, dear," he said. "I enjoy this. Of course I've got a scarf on, too. Neck's a very sensitive part of the body. Courting disaster to expose the neck to the elements. But this is my kind of weather. I'd live outside if I could." He lifted his eyes to me. They were pale and shallow, and they caught the light strangely, like pieces of bottle glass under water. "Candy?" he said, taking a little vial from his pocket and shaking some of its powdery contents out onto the table.

"No, thanks," I said.

"Mind if I do?" He drew a wad of currency from another pocket and peeled off a large bill.

"That's pretty," I said, watching him roll it into a tight brown tube stippled with green and red. "I've never seen that one before."

"Pretty," he said. "You bet it's pretty. It's a cento. Still play money to me, though. A lot better than that stingy little monochrome crap back home, huh?"

Eugene tipped some more from the vial onto the table.

"So why don't you go back?" I said. "If you like it so much."

"Go back." He sniffed loudly, eyes closed. "You know, I don't feel this stuff the way a woman does. They say it's a woman's drug. I don't get that feeling at the back of my head, like you can." His light eyes rested on my face. "Well, I can't go back. Not unless they extradite me."

"For what?" Maybe I could just ask Eugene to go. Or maybe I could grab his teacup and smash it on the floor.

"Shot a guy," he said.

"Yes?" I tucked my feet under me. This annoying skirt! I hated the feeling of wool next to my skin.

"Now, don't get all nervous," Eugene said. "It was completely justified. Guy tried to hurt me. I'd do it again, too. Fact, I said so to the judge. My lawyer kept telling me, 'Shut up, maniac, shut up.' And he told the judge, 'Your Honor, you can see yourself my client's as crazy as a lab rat.' How do you like that? So I said, 'Listen, Judge. What would you do if some slimebag pulled a knife on you? I may be crazy, but I'm no fool.' " Eugene leaned back and put his hands against his eyes.

I poured myself some more tea. It felt thick going down. I hadn't even had water, I remembered, for some time. "Would you like another cup?" I asked.

"Yeah," Eugene said. "Thanks."

"You know Ivan a long time?" he asked.

"Nine years," I said.

"Nine years. A lot of bonds can be forged in nine years. So how come I never met you? Ivan and I hang out."

"Oh, God, I don't know," I said. "It's an on-and-off type of thing. We're thrashing it out together now."

"You're thrashing it out together," he said. "You're thrashing it out together, but I only see one of you."

"Right," I said. "So how did you get to Canada, anyhow?"

"Oh. They put me in the hospital," he said. "But I've got friends. Here," he said. "Look." He emptied a pocket onto the table. There was a key chain, and an earring, and something that I presumed was a switchblade, and a bundle of papers—business cards and phone numbers and all sorts of miscellany—that he started to read out to me. "Jesus," he said, noticing me inspecting his knife. "You'll take your whole arm off that way. Do it like this." He demonstrated, flashing the blade out, then he folded it up and put it back in his pocket. "Here—look at this one." He handed me a card covered with a meaningless mass of dots. "Now hold it up to the light." He grabbed it back and placed it over a lamp near me. The dots became a couple engaged in fellatio. "Isn't that something?"

"Yes," I said. "I think you should go now, though. I have to do some things." His face was changing and changing in front of me. He receded, rippling.

"Wait—" he said. "You don't look good. Have you been eating right?"

"I'm all right," I said. "I don't care. Please leave."

"You're in bad shape, lady," he said. "You're not well. Sure you don't want any of this?" He offered me the vial. "Pick you right up. Then we'll fix you some more tea or something. Get some vitamins into you."

"No, no. It's just these clothes," I said, plucking at them. "I've got to get out of these clothes." He was beautiful, I saw. He was beautiful. He sparkled with beauty; it streamed from him in glistening sheets, as if he were emerging from a lake of it. I kicked at Micheline's boots, but Eugene was already kneeling, and he drew them off, and the thick stockings, too, and my legs appeared, very long, almost shining in the growing dark, from beneath them.

"Got 'em," he said, standing.

"Yes," I said, holding my arms up. "Now get this one," and he pulled the sweater over my head.

"Sh-h-h," he said, folding the sweater neatly. "It's O.K." But I was rattling inside my body like a Halloween skeleton as he carried me to Ivan's bed and wrapped a blanket around me.

"Look how white," I said. "Look how white your skin is."

"When I was in the jungle it was like leather," he said. "Year and a half, shoe leather. Sh-h-h," he said again, as I flinched at a noise. "It's just this." And I understood that it was just his knife, inside his pocket, that had made the noise when he'd dropped his clothes to the floor. "You like that, huh?" he said holding the knife out for me.

Again and again and again I made the blade flash out, severing air from air, while Eugene waited. "That's enough now," he said. "First things first. You can play with that later."

When we finished making love, the moon was a perfect circle high in the black window. "How about that?" Eugene said. "Nature." We leaned against each other and looked at it. "You got any food here, by the way?" he asked. "I'm famished."

By the time I'd located a robe—a warm, stripy thing in Ivan's closet—Eugene was rummaging through the icebox. "You got special plans for this?" he said, holding up the violet toilet paper that apparently I'd refrigerated.

"Let's see . . ." I said. "There're some sausages."

"Sausages," he said. "Suckers are delicious, but they'll kill you. Preservatives, unsaturated fats. Loaded with PCBs, too."

"Really?" I said.

"Don't you know that?" he said. "What are you smiling about? You think I'm kidding? Listen, Americans eat too much animal protein anyhow. Fibre's where it's at." He nodded at me, his eyebrows raised. "What else you got?"

"There's some pickled okra," I said.

"Ivan's into some heavy stuff here, huh?" he said.

"Well . . ." It was true that I hadn't shopped very efficiently. "Oh, there are these." I undid the bakery box.

"Holy Christ," Eugene said. "How do you like that—little Christmas trees. Isn't that something!" He arranged them into a forest on the table and walked his fingers among them. "Here we come awassailing among the leaves so green," he sang, and it sounded like something he didn't often do.

> Here we come awandering
>   so fair to be seen.
> Love and joy come to you,
>   and to you your wassail too,
> And God bless you and send you
>   a happy New Year,
> And God send you a happy New Year.

"What's the matter?" he said. "You don't like Christmas carols?" So I did harmony as he sang another verse:

> We are not daily beggars
>   that beg from door to door,
> But we are neighbors' children
>   whom you have seen before.
> Love and joy come to you,
>   and to you your wassail too,
> And God bless you and send you
>   a happy New Year,
> And God send you a happy New Year.

Eugene clapped. Then he made an obscene face and stuck a cookie into his mouth. "Oh, lady," he said, holding the cookie out for me to finish. "These are abso-*lute*ly scrumptious."

That was true. They were awfully good, and we munched on them quietly in the moonlit kitchen.

"So what about you and Ivan?" Eugene asked.

"I don't know," I said. "I'm starving with Ivan, but my life away from him—my own life—I've just let it dry up. Turn into old bits and pieces."

"Well, honey," Eugene said, "that's not right. It's your life."

"But nothing changes or develops," I said. "Ivan just can't seem to decide what he wants."

"No?" Eugene looked away tactfully, and I laughed out loud in surprise.

"That's true," I said. "I guess he decided a long time ago." I stared down at the table, into our diminished cookie forest, and I felt Eugene staring at me. "Well, I didn't want to be the one to end it, you know?" I said. "But time does change things even if you can't see it happen, and eventually someone has to be the one to say 'Well, now things are different.' Anyhow, it's not his fault. He's given me what he could."

Eugene nodded. "Ivan's a solitary kind of guy. I respect him."

"Yes," I said. "But I wish things were different."

"I understand, dear." Eugene patted my hand. "I hear you."

"What about you?" I said. "Do you have a girlfriend?"

"Who, me?" he said. "No, I'm just an old whore. I've got a wife down in the States. Couldn't live with her anymore, though." He sighed and looked around. "Sixteen years. So what else you got to eat here? I'm still hungry."

"Well," I said. "There's a roll of cookie dough in the freezer, but it's Ivan's, really."

"We should eat it, then." Eugene laughed. "Serve the arrogant bastard right." I looked at him. "Don't mind me, honey," he said. "You know I'm crazy."

I woke up once in the night, with Eugene snoring loudly next to me, and when I butted my head gently into his shoulder to quiet him down he wrapped his marvellous white arms around me. "Thought I forgot about you, huh?" he said distinctly, and started to snore again.

Sunlight forced my eyes open hours later. "Jesus," said a voice near me. "What time is it?" The sun had bleached out Eugene's luminous beauty. With his pallor and coarse black hair, he looked like a phantom that one registers peripherally on the streets. "I've got a business appointment at noon," he said, pulling on his jeans. "Think it's noon?"

"I don't know," I said. It felt pleasantly early. "No clock."

"I better hit the road," he said. "Christ."

"Here," I said, holding out his knife.

"Yeah, thanks." He pocketed it and looked at me. "You be O.K. now, lady? Going to take care of yourself for a change?"

"Yes," I said. "By the way, how much does Ivan owe you?"

"Huh?" he said. "Hey, there's my jacket. Right on the floor. Very nice."

"Because he mentioned it before he left," I said.

"Yeah?" Eugene said. "Well, it doesn't matter. I'll come back for it, like—when? When's that sucker going to get back?"

"No," I said. There was really no point in waiting for Ivan. I wanted to conclude this business myself right now. "He forgot to tell me how much it was, but he left me plenty to cover."

Eugene looked down at his boots. "Two bills."

I put on the robe and counted out two hundred dollars from my purse. It was almost all I had left of the lively cash. "And he said thanks," I said.

I stood at the open door until Eugene went through it. "Yeah, well," he said. "Thanks yourself."

At the landing he turned back to me. "Have a good one," he called up.

I went back inside and put some eggs on to boil. Then I twirled slowly, making the stripes on the robe flare.

How on earth had I forgotten butter? The eggs were good, though. I enjoyed them.

After breakfast I rooted around and found a pail and sponges. It made me sad that Ivan had let the apartment get so filthy. He used to enjoy taking care of things. Then I sat down with a mystery I found on a shelf, and by the time Ivan walked in, late in the afternoon, I'd almost finished it.

"Looks great in here," he said after he kissed me.

"I did some cleaning," I said.

"That's great," he said. I thought of my own apartment. There would be a lot to do when I got home. "Jesus. Am I exhausted! That was some trip."

"How's Gary?" I said.

"Well, he was running a little fever when I got there, but he's fine now," Ivan said.

"Good," I said. "Did he like his presents?"

"Uh-huh." Ivan smiled. "Particularly that game that the marble rolls around in. He and I both got pretty good at it after the first few hundred hours."

"I liked that one, too," I said.

"He's a good kid," Ivan said. "He really is. I just hope Linda doesn't make him into some kind of nervous wreck."

"How's she doing?" I asked.

"Well, she's all right, I think. She's trying to get a life together for herself at least. She's getting a degree in dance therapy."

"That's good," I said.

"She'll be O.K. if she can just get over her dependency," he said. "I'll be interested to see how she does with this new thing."

He would be monitoring her closely, I knew. What a tight family they had established, Ivan and Linda—not much room for anyone else. Of course, Gary and I had our own small parts in it. I'd probably been quite important in fencing out, oh, Micheline, for instance, just as Gary had been indispensable in fencing me out.

"Hey," Ivan said. "Who's been sitting in my chair?" He bent down and picked up a scarf.

"Someone named Eugene stopped by," I said. "He said you owed him money."

"Jesus. That's right," Ivan said. "Well, I'll get around to it in the next day or so."

"I took care of it myself," I said.

"Really? Well, thanks. That's great. I'll reimburse you. Sorry you had to deal with him, though."

"I liked him," I said.

"You did?" Ivan said.

"You like him enough to do business with him," I said.

"Yeah, I know I should be more compassionate," Ivan said. "It's just that he's so hard to take."

"Is any of that stuff true that he says?" I asked. "That he shot some guy? That he lived in the jungle?"

"Shot some guy? I don't know. He has a pretty extensive fantasy life. But he fought in the war, yeah."

"Oh," I said. "I see. Jungle—Vietnam."

"I keep forgetting," Ivan said. "You're really just a baby."

"That must have been awful," I said.

"Well, he could have gotten out of it if he didn't want to do it," Ivan said.

"He probably thought it was a good thing to do," I said. "Besides, people can't arrange their lives exactly the way they'd like to."

"I disagree," Ivan said. "People only like to think they can't."

"You know," I said, trying to recall the events of the day before, "I was having some sort of conversation with a butcher about that yesterday."

"A butcher?" Ivan said.

"Yes," I said. "And, as I remember, he was saying something to the effect that people are only free to the extent that they recognize the boundaries of their lives."

"Sounds pretty grim," Ivan said. "And pretty futile."

"Not exactly futile," I said. "At least, I think his point was that if I know that over here is where I'm standing, well, that's what gives rise to the consciousness that over there is where you're standing, and automatically I get a map, a compass. So my situation—no matter how bad it is—is my source of power."

"Well," Ivan said. "That's a very dangerous way of thinking, because it's just that point of view that can be used to rationalize a lot of selfishness and oppression and greed. I'll bet you were talking to that thief over by St. Lawrence who weighs his thumb, right?"

"Well, maybe I'm misrepresenting him," I said. "He was pretty enigmatic."

Ivan looked at me and smiled, but I could hardly bear the sweetness of it, so I turned away from him and went to the window.

How handsome he was! How I wished I could contain the golden, wounding hope of him. But it had begun to diverge from me—oh, who knew how long before—and I could feel myself already re-forming: empty, light.

"So how are you?" Ivan said, joining me at the window.

"All right," I said. "It's good not to be waiting for you."

"I'm sorry I missed Christmas here," he said. "Montreal's a nice place for Christmas. Next year, what do you say we try to do it right?"

He put his arm around me, and I leaned against his shoulder while we looked out at the place where I'd been walking the day before. The evening had arrived at the moment when everything is all the same soft color of a shadow, and the city seemed to be floating close, very close, outside the window. How familiar it was, as if I'd entered and explored it over years. Well, it had been a short time, really, but it would certainly be part of me, this city, long after I'd forgotten the names of the streets and the colors of the light, long after I'd forgotten the feel of Ivan's shirt against my cheek, and the darkening sight separated from me now by a sheet of glass I could almost reach out to shatter.

THE GARDEN OF REDEMPTION

ANTHONY DIFRANCO

Anthony DiFranco was born and grew up in New York City, and now lives in Fort Salonga, Long Island. A Fordham University graduate, he teaches English at Suffolk County Community College, and is coeditor of *Long Pond Review.* His first novel, *The Streets of Paradise,* was published in 1984. He has twice won a Catholic Press Association award for fiction, and is nearing completion of a second novel, inspired by "The Garden of Redemption."

The villa stands on the mountainside overlooking the town of Vaiano, about twelve miles north of Florence. Even today the townspeople refer to its walled garden by the old name of Golgotha, though its famous statue of the praying Jesus was destroyed by the Nazis nearly two generations ago. Other atrocities too took place in that garden during the period of the occupation and the Resistance, when the Allied advance up the boot was stalled at the Arno and the Nazis had turned the villa into their local headquarters of reprisal. Just how many partisans were tortured and murdered there will never be known, for the villagers have never disturbed the graves except to plant rose and hawthorn bushes over them; taciturn by nature, they avoid the subject of the war in general. To a visitor who is trusted, though, an old person, over a glass of wine, will occasionally tell a story of that time in words whose plainness and stark brutality mark them as the truth.

The young Nazi commandant seemed surprised to see the priest being ushered into his office. He put down the tin of rations he'd been eating at his desk, waiting in silence until the escorting soldier withdrew and shut the door. "So you've come, have you?" he remarked in careful but correct Italian.

The priest nodded. Though the heat of the day was yet to come, his face was streaked with sweat from the uphill climb. He was a short, heavily built man of about forty, with spectacles, swarthy skin, large features. Far from handsome, he looked physically powerful, though there was an obvious gentleness about him, and even a daintiness in the way he carried his black bag.

"You didn't have to come, you know," the commandant said, not standing up. His uniform was unbuttoned, his undershirt frayed and sweat-stained. "The corporal made that clear when he arrived to fetch you, didn't he?"

"Yes," the priest said quietly, "I understood that I wasn't obliged to come."

"And yet here you are." There was a note of wonder in the Nazi's voice, yet he didn't smile or strike any of those cruelly elegant poses practiced by his comrades in the town. Only one eyebrow went up for a moment as he observed the priest. He had the look of a direct man, not a sadist but a brute who did his killing without playing at it. "You should have stayed away, you know. You should have begged off." He shrugged. "But now it's too late."

The priest, his lips compressed and his face pale, nodded. "Let's get it over with, then. I've come prepared to hear this woman's confession. Will you take me to her?"

The Nazi stood up and came around the desk. Compact, brusque in movement, he gave the impression of careless and lethal force. He snatched the bag from the priest's hand, opened it, looked inside, returned it. "Schmidt!" he barked toward the closed door. The coarse tone of voice, the sloppiness of the uniform, the faint stable smell in the room, all worked to convince the priest that he was among thugs, not officers, not civilized men. He didn't need this lesson. He'd seen enough in the garden on his way in.

The room was on the second floor. There were many doors on the corridor, all padlocked. From behind one came the sound of breathing, from another, someone stirring. There were no voices.

Once the priest had entered the small, dim room, the door was quickly locked behind him. His flesh went cold at that. The room appeared empty and unused and he supposed that, if there truly was a woman in need of him, she would be brought to him. He crossed to the window, and was relieved to see that the garden and its horrors did not extend around to this side of the house. Instead the hillside sloped away steeply from the foundation, leaving the upstairs windows some twenty feet above the ground. The casement itself was made of metal and secured by an old-fashioned hasp which evidently required a key. Through the panes he could see Vaiano down in the valley, its roofs glowing in the midmorning sun. The church was easily distinguishable, and so was the pitched red roof of the rectory. Both seemed hopelessly far away.

A creaking noise from behind him made him whirl around. The woman was already in the room. She was sitting on the bed in the alcove behind the door, her back against the wall, her legs drawn up as if she were cold. Her gaze was on him, uncertain. He drew near her, eyeing her intently in the poor light. "It is I, Don Paolo," he said reassuringly. "Are you the one who asked for me?"

"Yes, Don Paolo, I'm the one." Her voice was weak and hoarse. "It was wrong of me to put you in danger . . . and yet I didn't think you would truly come. You must forgive me . . ."

He waved away those words, humiliating to him. "But who are you? What have they done to you?" In spite of the bruises on her face, he could see that she was quite young—twenty-five, perhaps; no, more like twenty. Her hair, where it wasn't matted with blood, was soft and fine, and her clothing was of good quality.

"Don't you know me, Don Paolo?" she said. "Look, look! It is I, Adriana Lastra."

"Adriana!" His breath came out sharply, and suddenly he was terrified, more so than he had been even passing through that desecrated garden with its corpses and open graves; this was to be much harder than he'd dared to think. "Adriana, dear child," he whispered. "Then it's true, what I heard. The boy, the sacristan's helper, told me . . ."

"Yes, what the boy said is true. I'm with the partisans, and the boy is with us too. But me, I've been caught. Last night on the road to Mercatale, they caught me with letters and money inside my coat." She shook her head, and for a moment her eyes grew sad. "I tried to get away. Perhaps if I hadn't run, if I'd tried to talk my way out of it . . ."

"But why you?" the priest demanded. "Why were you involved in such a dangerous thing?"

"Why not?" she answered quickly. "I have no sweetheart to tell me I must stay out of harm's way. The boy I loved was killed two years ago, even before these swine took over." She turned her keen, dark eyes on the priest, and the beauty of her young face momentarily emerged—the delicate brow and high, proud cheekbones, the straight nose and finely cut jaw. "I know, you're fooled by my looks, just as I've fooled these Nazis for so long. Do you think I'm soft inside, as I seem to be on the outside?"

He didn't think she was soft either inside or out. Beautiful, yes, and her bare legs on the bed, shapely and white, had the smooth strength of stone; but soft—that would never be the word for her.

"What do you suppose they got out of me for all their trouble?" she declared, motioning with her head toward the corridor. "Nothing! Look at what the brutes have done to me!" In an instant she had pulled open her blouse.

Don Paolo looked away, his eyes filled with tears. He was afraid; since the knock on the rectory door that morning, and all the way up the treacherous trail to the villa, he'd been afraid, and now on top of it all he was afraid of her.

"Don't be embarrassed, Don Paolo," she said, covering herself. "It's no sin to look at a corpse. In a little while, perhaps less than an hour, I'll be dead." Her own manner was as free from embarrassment as it was from fright. "All morning they've been shooting people out in the garden—haven't you heard them from the town?"

"Yes, I heard the shooting," he said. His hands trembling, he opened his bag and groped for the stole. "Come, Adriana. It was to hear your confession that you summoned me, was it not? I fear they'll not allow us much time together."

"Yes, when I asked for you I thought I wanted to confess. I have things on my conscience, Don Paolo, awful things. Do you remember how, when I was a little girl, I always made sure to get you in the confessional, and not Don Sebastiano? That's because you were so kind, I thought I could tell you anything."

"Don Sebastiano was a good man, a far braver man than I. He died a martyr, that poor old man, at the hands of these savages." This too touched Don Paolo in the wound of his cowardice—even the memory of Adriana as a child hurt him, that fatherless waif with the white face and bold eyes and dark frame of hair, and he a young priest, naïvely hopeful, at peace with his vocation . . . "But come, let us begin," he persisted, putting the stole around his neck. He was determined to get this thing done with before fear got the better of him.

"No, no, I've changed my mind," the girl said. "I was afraid before, but now I'm not. And the things I've done, I'm not really ashamed of them either, even the worst of them. Besides, Don Paolo, why should I drag you down along with me? Whatever secrets I utter, they'll torture you to get out of you. No, don't shake your head; your priestly vows count for nothing among these barbarians." She shifted on the bed and, in obvious pain, brought her feet to the floor. "I regret now that I asked for you. I was half out of my senses, and just speaking a wish aloud. I was terribly frightened, you see—but I suppose you can't imagine what it is to be so afraid."

Don Paolo looked at her in amazement. "Is that what you think, Adriana? If only you knew what a pitiful coward I really am!"

She shook her head. "If you were a coward, you would never have come here."

The priest ground his teeth. "Dear God, it's my cowardice that brought me here! I only came because my shame had finally grown more unbearable than my fear—if not I'd be hiding in the rectory yet!"

He turned away from her and paced the floor to the window and back, running his hands through his coarse gray hair. Stopping at the bedside, he gazed down at the girl whose punished beauty brought a quivering to his insides, a queer mixture of despair and some other violent feeling. "Can you imagine how I've tormented myself this past year and a half? One after another, good men have spoken out or taken their stand against this evil, and one by one they've died. Even Don Sebastiano had the courage to speak the truth from the pulpit, and I watched them come and take that poor white-haired man away. And what have I done in all this time? Nothing. Nothing." He shook his head. "I'm ashamed of myself just for being alive, for keeping still and avoiding trouble and eating my supper in my room and saying Mass for the old women who come to church. I'm ashamed for thinking that this would all soon be over, and that I must just keep out of the way a little longer, and then things would be the way they were before, and I could go back to playing soccer in the alley with the schoolboys."

He sat down on the bed beside her, surprised at his outburst and painfully aware of his clumsy build and the dull planes of his face; yet he couldn't stop himself. "I'm a useless man who even misunderstood the priesthood, thinking it was for peaceful souls who wanted nothing out of the world except what no one else had use for. Yes, don't look at me so, Adriana, for just the sight of you fills me with shame for the littleness of my wants." He glanced bitterly at the welts and burns on her slender arms. "It is I who should have been tortured here, not you. Did you know that the partisans had sought my help—and I turned them down? Yes, it would have been far safer for me to carry messages than for you, but I was frightened, thinking of what happened to the two priests at Pratolino when they were caught. And so I refused, and left the danger to mere children. There—now it is I who have made my confession! How can you ever forgive me for such cowardice, Adriana, me a man you used to look up to?"

"You've nothing to be ashamed of, Don Paolo," she replied, gazing at him with pity in her eyes, and with something more, a redeeming wisdom as if she had witnessed such outpourings before from men who felt the nearness of death. "Deep down, none of us is any braver than the next." She got to her feet and walked slowly, stiffly to the window. The daylight filtered through her hair as if she were wearing a veil of gauze. "In spite of what you say, you had the courage to stay where you were and do your job. You're the last priest in Vaiano, or Sesto—or Pratolino, for that matter; do you realize that? And when you were told that a woman was about to die and wanted to confess her sins, you came. That's all there is to say."

He stood and followed her to the window. "As God is my witness, I came suspecting that there was no woman, and that if there was, the Nazis had simply turned her to account to lure me to my death. Perhaps I was a fool for fancying that my faith and my vocation were being put to the test at last—but I saw my chance and I took it. You must not blame yourself for what happens to me, for even now I'm relieved to have entered this trap while there is still a shred of value to my dying. Yes, I mean that—look at this face, so ugly and useless that only a mother could love it! What loss will it be to anyone when I'm gone?"

The girl turned to look into his eyes. "Is that what you think, Don Paolo? And don't you know how many people have loved you? I'm one of them, and I'm not ashamed to say it." She put her small, white hand on the windowsill to steady herself. A blush spread upward from her throat. "It was no accident that my mind turned to you, and not to one of those young men hiding in the mountains, when I knew I was to die. Yes, it was your face I longed to see. Don't you think that the memory of you playing with the children or leading the procession on St. Pascal's day is carried in the hearts of many of us as we do what we must? Where would we find the courage to do such unspeakable things if it weren't for thoughts of you and your goodness?"

She raised a hand and stroked his cheek, leaving a trail of warmth on his coarse skin. "You must never make fun of this face of yours, for to me it has always been the image of what is kind and manly. I've seen how love spreads out from you and touches those around you. If this were a dream world and not real, I would want such love and no other for myself."

The priest flushed, and that quivering feeling began in his insides, squirming and distending and grappling with the incumbent weight of fear; he ached as if something deep in his physical bulk were straining to pull free. "You're only trying to comfort me, child," he whispered sadly, "when it is I who should be comforting you." It was more than the incredible beauty of the girl that tormented him—it was the thought of her destruction, of the awful waste of her life, her love, the children she might bring forth, the goodness that could be brought to the world through her.

So distracted and unhappy was he that at first he scarcely noticed the distant thunder which broke fitfully along the mountain range to the south. But the girl's eyes instantly widened, and she turned to peer through the window. "Listen," she breathed. "Do you hear?" The rumbling had spread slowly across the spine of the range from west to east. "It's happening . . . they've kept their word, the English and Americans."

She was right—it was not thunder but artillery fire that had erupted, a massive barrage along the entire front below the river. Don Paolo stared at her in wonder for a moment before turning to the window. "It's true!" he exclaimed with a surge of hope. "By the sound of it, it must be a full-scale assault—the Americans are coming at last!"

She nodded. "We in the mountains knew it was to be today. Perhaps the Nazis knew it too—but it'll do them no good. By tonight they'll be on the run north to their new 'Gothic' line."

The somber note of vindication in her voice quickly turned the priest's excitement to bitterness. Could she face her death so stoically even now, knowing that rescue was so close at hand? He studied those dark eyes, eyes filled with childlike faithfulness and resolve. How innocent was the glow in them, how ready for life and yet unafraid to throw life away. He groaned; that taut, tormented thing inside him stretched to its limit and parted at last.

Suddenly he was on his knees rummaging through his bag, his mind and hands groping for any instrument of escape. *She must live,* that was all he knew! A half-plan, formulated earlier and rejected, dangled before him, and when his fingers closed around the big bronze crucifix with its tapered base, a reckless hope rose up in his heart. "Stand away from the window!" he commanded, and in another instant he had applied the tool to the hasp of the casement.

"But what are you doing?" the girl protested. "Stop it!—You've still a chance to leave here alive! Stop it, I say!"

His only thought was that the girl had to be freed at any cost, that she must remain in the world of the living. "Hush—do you want them to hear? There! It's done!" The old lock yielded with a snap, and the window, heavy but well-balanced, swung outward on its hinges.

"Now you've done it!" the girl reproached him. "What are you thinking? Don't you see how far down the ground is from here?"

His eyes darted around the room. It had been stripped of all but the bed and its flimsy mattress. Outside, the barrage seemed to draw nearer and more furious as the breeze swung the window further ajar. Surely within minutes the nervous jailers would be flinging open the door. His hands went to the stole around his neck, tore it off. "Use this!" he hissed. "Here—quick!" He draped the long silk garment over the windowsill. "You go first—once you're clear, I'll fasten the cloth somehow and drop down after you. Come, don't argue with me! It's too late to turn back now!"

She did argue, but he put his hands on her and lifted her forcibly to the sill. She was a long-legged girl, strong, but weakened by her ordeal. The pumps fell off her feet as she struggled, one dropping to the ground below.

Winding the end of the stole around his wrist, he braced himself and succeeded in forcing her through the window. It took all his strength to hold her once she'd put her weight on the garment. She'd gone only halfway down when it began to rip. As it parted, he staggered back, recovered himself, and thrust his head out the window.

The girl was getting to her feet, shaken but evidently able to walk. She motioned anxiously for him to follow her. He shook his head, showing her the tattered remnant of the stole.

"Don Paolo!" she whispered, her eyes pleading.

He shook his head again. To try dropping from the window, he knew, would mean broken bones for a man of his bulk, and the end of her chance for escape, as she would feel compelled to stay with him. He was not afraid now for himself, but only desperate that she should get away.

"Don Paolo!" she entreated again. There were tears in her eyes. Didn't she know how gladly his heart was racing right now, how happy he was to give his life for hers? He motioned toward the south, where her freedom lay through woods and brush.

Still the girl waited for him, crouched, stubborn. He dropped her other shoe to her and pulled the window shut. For a long while he stood out of sight beside the window jamb, his eyes on that soft huddle of roofs in the distance. Only when he saw her stealing at last down the slope toward the forest did he turn away.

He sank down on the bed with his back to the wall. There was no sound from outside except for the rumble of the barrage. Perhaps the coming assault had already driven the Nazi pickets out of the woods on the hillside. Good. Let them all come back to the villa, let them come through that door right now. He could face them now without being afraid, without saying or doing anything shameful. He'd been given this last chance, and he wouldn't spoil it. If only they would come now.

The minutes passed. He pulled his legs up onto the bed and wrapped his arms around them against the chill. A smile formed on his face.

They took him outside to the garden and stood him against a bullet-chewed section of the wall. The air had grown warmer, and the bright sun made a pocket of heat against the stucco. The sky was splendid.

For a minute or two the artillery barrage ceased, and there was talk of bringing him back inside to the "interrogation" room. But then the shells began to come down again, nearer—it meant that the Allies had broken through and had raised their fire ahead of the assault. A funnel of black smoke rose up from the direction of the town.

Papers were being burned on the veranda, soldiers busily cramming equipment into rucksacks. The young commandant, calm, efficient, oversaw all with an occasional terse command. He stayed a comfortable distance to the rear of the firing squad, avoiding the priest's eye.

From inside the villa, shots rang out—a few poor patriots were being murdered in their cells. Even then Don Paolo's courage didn't fail. He stood facing the men who would kill him, ignoring the repeated orders to turn toward the wall. His hands remained unbound, and the blood-stained wooden chair into which earlier victims had been roped lay toppled on its side.

His senses were very keen. He could smell blackthorn and oak in the fire the soldiers had made. His gaze took in everything—the mutilated statuary of the garden, the vista of gray-green slopes and peaks through the open gate, the fresh pit beside him which, an hour earlier, had seemed like a red wound in the earth.

He was not afraid or even unhappy. He felt magnificently strong; in a single morning his whole life had been reinvented, the Don Paolo of the past obliterated. The soldiers with their guns and their doglike commands seemed small and powerless—he pitied them their ugliness. Perhaps they would never feel his exhilaration at this moment, the fearlessness he enjoyed in the certainty that his death was right and useful. It didn't matter that no one would know what had become of him; he understood now the reckless sacrifices of the partisans, their lives thrown like stones beneath the treads of the Nazi bloodlust—not futile, no, but all part of a big, fundamental struggle . . .

There was an interruption, then, as two soldiers came shouting through the gate, dragging between them a half-naked human being. Their captive, languid and broken as a doe, was a woman. Oh, they were thorough, these Nazis—persistent and grudging as hounds! It was Adriana they had brought back.

For a moment Don Paolo was afraid now that he would lose it all and sink down, down. But then she saw him, and their eyes met and held. He barely heard the instructions growled by the commandant, and never saw the man's face to know whether there was irony or expedience in it; his eyes were on the girl as she was dragged to his side. Through the tatters of her skirt, he could see the fresh blood streaked down her legs. Her shoes were gone. "Adriana!" he whispered.

Leaning on his arm, she straightened herself with effort beside him, her eyes too proud for comforting. "It's a splendid morning, Don Paolo," was all she would say. "A fine day to die."

Yes. Yes. The sunlight making creases of shadow in the distant ravines, the rising yellow blossoms of smoke and the rumble of justice coming up, up the range, so close that the shell bursts cracked like flints on the hard flanks of the hills. The perfect square of the garden, the cold throat of the pit waiting for its meal, the crooked little line of soldiers, poor, motley, contemptible boys—it was all so intensely lovely.

As the commands were given he edged in front of her, his arms half raised, and she, bless her, standing tall as she could, not trembling, allowed him.

When he heard the explosion, he thought for a moment that a shell had fallen directly in the garden, and that it was not finished yet . . . but he was falling backward then, and that stark little row of boys was still standing, and he knew. She kept her grip on his arm as they fell, and though he couldn't see her, he could feel the touch of her, warm.

His lips quivered and a final prayer formed on them—"Receive, O Lord . . . among those . . . whom Thou hast redeemed . . ."—though the sound of it never reached the air.

DIRT ANGEL

JEANNE WILMOT

Jeanne Wilmot lives in New York City and is completing a collection of short fiction entitled *Said's*. She grew up in Kansas City.

It is the time of year the gypsies come out of hibernation. The ochre-faced children make an altar of plastic roses when they see me heading down Broadway straight to Said's. I recognize the little ones who are new to the marketplace even though the willful charcoal eyes and the con are familiar. They learn to spit at grace young here. Immediately after returning from the hospital I changed out of the summer seersucker I wear under my white resident's coat by day, into a red two-piece halter and shawl that match the first spring air. When I enter the club, Page is holding court from his usual corner, speaking in chants that are in keeping with the cadence of his gang days, stabbing down into the air with his fingers, floating high on The Hawk with the dust of an angel. I haven't been to Said's for a while. Haven't seen Page for longer. Tonight I needed to be back home. I like my life now all right, but this place, Page and the people here manage to sustain something close to the sense of silent *commotion* I associate with home—there is no routine, crisis is our energy and the silence is just the waiting for something to happen.

Page glances at me quick as I rock into the center of the club, swivel-headed and a little coked up. A beautiful sandy-haired woman-child straddling a stool at the bar fixes on my small breasts. She looks as white as I look black, and for all her sexual smugness, I can smell the captive in her. Tall ferns and palms sway to a breeze propelled by a wind machine that rocks the third-sex lovers lined up against the street windows. Instead of looking out onto the fantastical tropics of Macao, they see a homeland of yellow cabs and midwestern boys with swollen hormonal breasts. I rhyme with the chants until the music starts playing and Page strolls over to kiss my ear, aiming intuitively through burnt red eyes. In '59 we'd been kids together on John R and Brush in

Detroit, playing bobo bedetton dotton games with sticks, balls and jump ropes. Half the snowfiends in the club are from blocks like mine; and although some might say I fucked destiny standing up, I could still catch the disease. The sandy-haired girl with the translucent skin was probably destined for the Henderson, North Carolina Junior League and she's caught it. Page calls her Pandy.

I look more closely at this girl Pandy. She wants me to watch her, and for a moment it's as if I'm in the presence of royalty, the red and blue lights of Said's reaching through her rich blonde curls and across the tiny features placed perfectly upon Pandy's anglo-saxon face. However, there is a trapped expression in her eyes as they embrace mine. She stands up and immediately I see that she is pregnant. Probably close to seven months. She is surrounded by the sycophants and true admirers of her court. The French silk and sequin shirt she wears covers her filled belly. She gracefully strides over to the dance floor. Her transition from empress to royal mother is effortless. It could humble the barren. She has engaged me without having to say a word. Page says she always wears sequins. That she is referred to as The Sequin.

My eyes follow The Sequin's stride to the middle of the neon room where she automatically demands center spot. Her competition plays fierce and violent around her for a few minutes until it is absorbed into her dance. Joyfully the other dancers join the girl, not puzzled in the slightest by her grace and agility. She has two partners, likewise her partners, seven in all trading off girl for boy, boy for girl—little ambidextrous babies riding high on the mania of pills and madness. They dance fast. Jerky to the beat, step to step on sparkling shoes with stilt-heels, dervish turns Latin style, calling out high-pitched expletives meant to dot the same place in each skull. I watch the naked backs of the dancing boys, their greased spines like healthy roots, with my eyes clinging tenuously to their ancient strength. Go down, go down on your boy, hump him from the back, hump him in the front—girl to girl, belly to belly, boy to boy up to down—fast now not Latin erotic-smooth, fast bumping here and there, fast computer motions clicking on the upstroke, a slighter downbeat, bent knees, flamboyant male arms, rigid but cool female arms.

Pandy's earthbound body compels her partners to remain rooted. The floor chants, *she's so cool, she's ice-box cool.* Little thirteen-year-old girls undulate involuntarily on the sidelines, their firm little bodies seasonably in need of the bizarre, calling back *I'm so cool, I'm ice-box cool,* while their boys move next to them—each forsaking the other with the fantasy of making it with this sequined mothergirl and her androgynous entourage. I smirk at her glitter but its blood-color takes me captive. I fight her glory, yet her urgency wins. It might be the coke, or it might be that we each know about stepping out of one world into others, being watched as travelers always in-between, claiming a love or a hate for some recent home whose legacy we daily tangle into more lie than truth, or it might be that our lives intersect at a place beyond the gypsies, who, afoot for the spring thaw, remind us both that rebirth applies to all things. Whatever it is, she's taken my night from me, and maybe more.

A little girl painted head to toe in white paint over her dark skin, wearing a black hood over her hair, pasties over her breasts and a g-string-like facade over her tiny cunt, grabs my hand suddenly and pulls me out to the dance floor. She doesn't belong here. Someone must have brought her as a mascot, a cruel joke. She belongs downtown. Page grins as she high-steps smoothly around me, softly leading me into a sensual counterpoint to the erratic moves of the dancers around us. We dance a slow hypnotic grind at first, half-time to the chant. Only our knees move, deliberately and in unison. The Sequin struts out and stands opposite us. Her stomach is thrust forward and proud. The seven-headed Dancing Machine stops to watch their girl come on cold. She is the star here. The Sequin turns her misshapen body to me, grasps me around the waist, and pulls me against her groin. I initiate a gesture of contempt; but knowing he has to get Pandy away from me fast, Page slithers up laughing. He grabs Pandy around her waist and flips her toward him, twirling her the way a father would his child, gleefully offering a moment's different reality in the sweeping motion of a top, then releases her on the sideline before returning to me. Page's attention has short-circuited the tension and The Sequin becomes no more than one of the sweet dancing girls I grew up with. The touch of a man has lessened the weight of her child so that she laughs as if through liquid. I continue to dance, waiting patiently while Page slides down off his sloppy high. He holds me close as the song comes to its end.

Page had been my first and I float along with that memory. He was tall and light-skinned. Almost pretty. Considered one of the lucky ones in those days. But he didn't deal in lucky. He had a brutal and facile mind. He chose me. I had style, no great beauty, but could go toe to toe with him on any scheme. None of us thought he'd ever get hooked. We dance until his eyes return to the bright they used to be after he'd beat me at stick ball, and at the very moment this nostalgic mist could have turned into regret and accusation, Pandy touches me on the shoulder. Dugie takes you up and dugie takes you down, so part of the glitter of a sequin is the artificiality of its evanescence. I choose to sleep the tragedy of what has made me one thing and Page a junkie, and decide instead to caress those blazing eyes that seem to leap from the dark rims set into Pandy's face. Drug solitude is common here, so I let her hold me from behind and dance with us.

I smell the rot of Pandy's imminent death. Someone else might miss the agony of her exile and sensationalize the choices she must have made, but I imagine that within Pandy's doom there is something pure and hyperbolic. There are separate, individual pains that are more vile in their means to exile than exile itself. It is an organic condition, not metaphor, and I want to flee from it. I want to walk right out of Said's and out of New York, out of the universe for that matter.

But instead, I take Pandy home with me that night, passing through streets littered with pigeon bone and bottle caps. My place is between Ninth and Tenth Avenues in the fifties. She uses my egg poacher as a cooker and shoots up at the kitchen table while we talk about setting the styles with rags, bandanas and second-hand acetate Gucci's later sells to the weary rich. As Pandy speaks, she plucks the air with her long fingers, drawing bows and barrettes and ankle bracelets on the air. I soon tire of her meanderings.

"Why are you having this baby? You're doing everything you possibly can to maim it."

She looks straight at me, not at all surprised by my brash change of subject.

"I'm not really a junkie. I just like to get high sometimes."

"All the time looks like to me."

"No, that's not really true. I go a day or two without nothin."

"Why do you say *nothin?* Was that the way you were taught to talk?"

"Don't be so hard on me. I'd like to be your friend."

"Sorry, I don't make friends easily. And they never make me."

I turn on her. She can't hold her head up any longer. She nods onto the table so I carry her to the chair and try to make her as comfortable as possible, surrounding her with old clothes I shape into pillows. I put an extra blanket my mother had left in the project when she died over Pandy's birdlike ankles and legs—they could have been my mother's. She half-dozes as I rinse out the dishes in the sink and prepare for bed. I'm angry with myself for finding Pandy so compelling.

She startles me when she speaks out.

"Why did you cover my legs with the blanket and tuck me into a bed you made if you hate me?"

"I don't hate you, I just don't know what you want from me, and I know it's something."

The twilight color of pre-dawn lights up one square foot on the rug in my first floor room. Pandy leaves the nest I made her, twists her hair up into a little knot on top of her head and angles around the room. I light a joint and sit on the edge of my bed, following her transit around the room. She watches me a minute. I don't say anything. Finally she does.

"You know, I used to be a cheerleader."

"So did I."

I can visualize Pandy's light hair in a flip and her lithe body wrapped in a red uniform as a highlight to the Henderson, North Carolina School Yearbook.

I am hooked by her vulnerability and decay in the same way I was by my mother's in the days before her death. But their decay is also my anger and defense. My mother's swollen alcoholic belly pressing against an organ that eventually turned her yellow and filled her tissues with the excrement of a body gone mad was my ticket out.

I decide to get ready for bed. I go first into the little room that holds the toilet, strip and grab a towel from the closet, then out to the screened-in area around the sink and bathtub. I stay behind the matchstick curtains for an unusually long time. Still, Pandy is not asleep when I pull the blanket back on my bed.

"I'll take you home with me tomorrow night."

Her unpredictability is as engaging as her vulnerability. Again, reminscent. I would pay a lot of money if this were not the case. If I could resist.

In the morning I leave for rounds at my usual time, tired but this isn't the first time. I trust Pandy to be there with nothing missing when I return in the evening. Our intimacy is automatic and for me, uncomfortable. That night when I come home, she is dressed up in a plaid pleated skirt designed in such a way that she barely looks pregnant. She is a very small woman anyway. Her baby looks like it might be as well. She has cleaned my apartment, probably shot up for the day, been to her own place and gone shopping.

"You're coming over for dinner."

I'm not wild about the idea but decide to go anyway. We take the IRT express up to "125th" and then walk crosstown. I don't know East

Harlem all that well and the further east we go, the more uneasy I become. We don't talk much. We zigzag uptown, turn off the avenue and onto a rural mud street, heading toward the East River. We could be anywhere. Empty lots filled with city weeds and brick dust shroud the uneven boundaries of the street. I notice the wild dogs snarling in harmony with each other when we pass them in the brush.

We leave the path, abandoned totally now by the city's compass of light. Pandy strikes a match and pokes her foot into the familiar earth as we continue to walk. Eventually we hit metal. I assume it is the old tracks from trains that used to carry the rich out of the city. Along the tracks a cement slab interrupted by periodic holes covered with gratings gives Pandy the direction she needs. The only peculiarity that makes these openings different from sewer covers is the large padlocks evidently holding sections of the gratings together. Pandy takes out a cylindrical key and opens one of these locks. She does it with a brief finesse that claims it as her home.

Pandy lifts the city grate up and drops it against the cement, then unlocks another padlock and shoves something heavy and metal inward. A gaslight globe lights our way down a flight of cement steps which opens onto a cave charmed only slightly by the touch of humanity. I notice the lamp immediately. The floor is packed mud, the walls cinder block, and in the center a small generator Pandy has switched on offers a glitter to the room. There is no bathroom. The generator seems also to hype up an hydraulic pump that brings water to a tiny sink Pandy uses to both wash her hands and to pee in. The lamp possesses one corner, a bentwood rocker belonging in a young married's apartment another, a pile of neatly folded clothing the third, and finally, standing on an orange crate, a bowl filled with goldfish floating on top of scummy water. The bed is swung up against the wall exposing bits and pieces draped onto the wire tapestry at odd intervals. Between the aquarium and the clothes, a metal door covered with posters of dark, dead jazz musicians stands ajar.

"Come and see the neighborhood."

"Is this where you live all the time?"

"It's my home, if that's what you mean."

The doorway leads out to the old subway tracks unused by the city since the 'twenties. The backs of an entire community of these part-mud part-cement huts, all with doorways leading out to the tracks, line the ledge that eventually falls off into the pit of dead rails. From the stench it is obvious that this area is used for all forms of refuse, consumed daily by the rats that now slink around our legs.

I know rats. I move cautiously, remembering their feel on my face babied with milk, back in Detroit. Here the constant motion their squat bodies create imprisons me. In fact, the tracks themselves are fur-lined with the backs of these Norwegian city squirrels used to eating babies' faces and the mothers' arms that hold them. The hebephrenic calm of shock allows me a moment to adjust; yet even as I stand paralyzed, I can see that the rats are like pets in this neighborhood. Doglike in their sensibility, the rats know if they don't graze on the flesh of their strange life-fellows, they will be fed a daily menu of garbage and human feces. Whirring armies of flying beetles the size of small mice stop just short of attacking my head. I sense in their kingdom the same peculiar fear and curiosity the families of a small village might experience when confronted by a stranger. Although the insects don't bite, Pandy runs into her home and brings out a foul-smelling root that she smears over my head and hair. With the odor signaling my rite-of-passage into their ranks, they move away to sit happily on the backs of the rats dozing on the forgotten tracks. In this symbiotic hell of the cryptozoa, the bugs live off the maggots that spontaneously appear in the garbage the rats leave behind; and although my fascination impoverishes my fear, there exists a dread far beneath the surface that has to do with Pandy and her comfort at my being here with her.

Halfway down the tracks I can see a bonfire being fed rags by a man with thick dreadlocks. Pandy tentatively explains that the groups of people I now begin to see around other bonfires strung along the edge of the pit as it curves to the left, would be outlawed up on the streets. The people in the nicer homes living within the cinder and mud igloos provide these people with food and necessities, even though the longer the outlaws remain, the less they desire anything but their own sludge-fires, their own conversation and a meal every so often.

For several moments there is silence between Pandy and me. Pandy moves from foot to foot restlessly. It is a graceful gesture. Her limbs sway to a silent chorus. Then:

"You shocked by where I live?"

"Is that what you want me to be? Is that why you live here?"

Her glow fades as I continue.

"Look, I know you don't have to live like this—that dress you wore last night cost more than a year's rent on my apartment. You have antiques in your mud hut. What kind of joke are you playing on yourself and the people who *have* to live here?"

Pandy spreads her hands out in all directions.

"Why shouldn't I live like this if they do?"

I am not amused by martyrs—their innocence a luxury I could never afford.

"Come on, we're going to have a talk. All you are is a mixed up kid."

But she stands her ground, narcotized though she is.

"But why? Why shouldn't I live like they do?"

She won't budge. I lose patience and shout.

"What about that baby in your belly?"

I grab her by the hand, expecting resistance, and find that she has gone limp. Her acquiescence to me seems total so I lead her back to her hut. The usual distance and tension the drugs maintain are gone, and within seconds it is as if she is dissembling from a drug reaction. It doesn't make sense. She enters a kind of reticent confusion, not wanting to submit or admit to anything, but allowing me to move her about.

She cries uncontrollably as I pack a few things and lock the door to her hut. I can't understand the words she is trying to form. Her lack of control is all so sudden. We take a subway back to my house and I hold her in the back of one of the cars. When I finally get to my apartment I stick her in the bathtub and her full stomach looks hard and mottled, as if her own flesh is all that can protect the jewel lying hidden inside. I consider shooting her up with an I.V. of valium and demerol, but the bath seems to be calming her down. She calls to me that she has to return to get her lamp, she never travels without it; and then she dopes herself. Finally I get her into my bed to rest.

She must have left after I went to buy food at the Ninth Avenue markets. When I come back and can't find her, I call Page. If I have to return to her hut, I don't want to go alone. I tell him to meet me at 125th and First, we can walk from there.

Page is drugged to a fine tuning and in complete control.

I don't have a landmark or a key so when I find the gratings, I start knocking. The silence beyond each padlock does not unnerve me. I walk five blocks and, like a machine programmed for solution, I keep knocking and screaming Pandy's name. Page follows me. We cross a patch that looks familiar. There is a stark sapling standing cold, new, out-of-place and memorable for its solitude—and the bricks some caretaker has built around it—in the middle of the path. I wait. I think I hear the tinny sound of a transistor radio.

Page sucks the wind through his teeth as I holler, the matches burning in my fist illuminating the ground around us and one of the padlocked grates. All at once the noise stops and the grate is thrown open so suddenly that the only thing I glimpse is a dark head as it descends some steps into a pit below. Words pierce the darkness.

"All right. All right. My baby is me."

I follow the screams down the steps, turning around three times to beckon Page to follow. He stands riveted to the clammy slab of cement, as if he is a watchdog bred in the bushes with the other wild dogs. He tells me to wait for him, but instead I continue into the deep black room at the bottom of the steps. I light another match and glance quickly around to get my bearings. The room is empty except for a sink like the one at Pandy's and a cot shoved up against the wall. The person who opened the door squats in the middle of the floor, cuddling what I presume to be an infant and screeching a lullaby in that high-pitched voice I mistook for a small radio.

The blanket swaddling the infant looks familiar. It takes a few minutes for my eyes to adjust to the lack of light, but gradually I can discern color and detail. An orange glow shines under the bottom and through the sides of the backdoor, stippling the mud floor around the woman. Pandy's neighbor holds a light brown child mottled from new birth. I feel very afraid. The neighbor is an old black-skinned woman with a goiter that hangs down to her breast where she is trying to suckle the child. The taunting shriek announces her insanity less vividly than the look in her eyes: "It's my baby see, it's my baby, please, you can't have my baby, my baby is me."

The old woman repeats the singsong over and over again. She pulls at the extra skin hanging from beneath her chin as the rhyme becomes a hymnal refrain. I step back and glance up to see if Page is still at the top of the stairs, but he has already slowly begun his descent. Obviously the sounds from below have both alerted and disoriented him. Like a night animal, once his eyes can make use of the available light, he adjusts to the situation. He sees my fear. In a guttural voice pitched against the noise of the old woman, he speaks to me.

"Get the fuck outta here. I'll stop her. Get the fuck outta here!"

"Ask her about Pandy, please ask her."

Just as I speak I am whiplashed; it is as if the "God of Time" has decided to make me understand endlessness. For a person as godless as myself, and so dependent upon the finite, this particular sensation aggravates my worst fear. I hear Page from the twilight.

"If you don't get outta here, I'll walk right out and leave you *and* Pandy."

Page stalks the distance between this creature and myself with an exorbitant hatred toward me for getting him into the mess. Out of habit, he begins rolling up his sleeves. When he is certain that the poor woman is reasonably harmless, although unpredictable, he very calmly addresses himself to her.

"Por favor, dónde está su amiga Pandy?"

I hadn't heard the latin accent in her song. Page stares kindly and repeats his sentence. I try to focus.

"Por favor, dónde está su amiga Pandy?"

Without missing a beat or altering her expression, the old woman drops the baby and jumps back, hissing the words of the hymn in Spanish. I run to the baby and discover it is very recently stillborn. The goiter flaps as the old woman takes off around the room. When she races to her sink in the corner, sticking first one leg and then the other into the bowl, I run out the backdoor which leads to the tracks. Page follows. Without thinking, I run deep into the city behind the huts and stop when I feel safe. Page grabs me. My fever makes me a dangerous friend. It matches the heat of the sludge-fires warming the dread-locked men.

"Cut it out. What's happening to you? We're on a mission. Don't go *saditty* on me now."

Page has reached far back into our parents' past. I stare at him. In the glow of a hundred different bonfires I fight the demon that is trying to terrorize me. Page doesn't respond to my stillness. He is watching something over my shoulder. I twist around so fast I am thrown off balance and fall. The palms of my hands touch a thin layer of mud before sinking with the weight of my body into the hideous rat food. The immediate impact of the odor makes me cry out, just as a voice above me begins to speak. Squatting there, arms thrown back for support, vulnerable to the dungeon and its recent tradition, I begin to weep.

The voice offers me a rag. I feel a need to be proper.

"Oh, thank you."

I stand up and peer into the face of a man who could have been the shadow with the thick dreadlocks I saw yesterday down near the main bonfire. He nods to me and watches peacefully as I primly clean off my hands. He repeats the words he has spoken before, and this time I hear what he means.

"She left you a note."

"What do you mean—left?"

"She's dead. Do you want me to take you to her?"

"How do you know who I am?"

"She said you would be coming. She expected you."

"What about the old woman? She's got Pandy's baby."

"We'll take care of that here."

We follow the man through the tunnel, past clots of people, their yellow fire lighting our way and the activity of the nether world, past the old woman's screams, down to Pandy's house which I can now see is in a cul-de-sac where the direction of the old train track takes a sharp turn to the right. All of the houses on the same line with Pandy's have colorful flower pots filled with plastic flowers outside their doors. Page follows the rats with his eyes. He never stops and never asks a question. The bugs are clustered in halos over Page's head and my own. Page does not try to brush them away. He keeps his fists clenched and his arms free to swing. Pandy's backdoor is open. Inside, the single murphy bed is suspended halfway to the floor, swinging gently to the rock of the subway rumble. The springs and the legs are eaten away by rats. Earlier in the day Pandy told me that wherever she goes to stay she carries with her the bronze lamp given her by her grandmother. Here the piece is more a touch of art in a room made barren by deliberate poverty. The base is broad—and carved out in bronze, against the light shining through a red tiffany glass, is a small lady carrying a parasol as she descends a flight of steps into a Japanese garden. It is the little red light that now illuminates Pandy hanging in the center of the room. A gnarl of veins bulge through her needle-pocked skin like a blue worm reappearing in the nape of her neck, in her arms and in her legs. Even the femoral artery in her groin is swollen.

Page's nose begins to run as we three stand. Pandy's *commotion* is mostly over. The roar of a subway crossing town to head up to the Bronx echoes in another part of the catacombs. The immediate stillness is interrupted each time Page sniffs. I shake a little, never taking my eyes from Pandy and the homely afterbirth which hangs from her.

The man is the first to speak, and he speaks to Page.

"If you want to leave, I'll watch over your friend."

"No, there's no more either of us can do, I think we should both leave."

I have many things to do yet. "You leave. I have things to do here. Don't worry. I'm not frightened."

"I can't just leave you."

"Please. I'd rather. And besides," I gesture to our guide, "he'll make sure nothing happens."

Page nods to the man, walks up the cement steps with the keys to the padlocks the man has handed him, unclasps the lock to the metal door, then the one for the grating covering the door and throws the keys back down to me at the bottom of the steps and climbs out, leaving the door open, but closing the top grate. The man walks out the backdoor and stations himself next to it.

I close the door and look again at Pandy. I stand on the orange crate that has held the dead goldfish and lift Pandy out of her noose. I pull the bed down and lay her on it. Her pink sheets are covered with little rosebuds. Then, finally, I look at the note underneath the lamp. She bequeathed me her grandmother's lamp. She had believed we had a preordained connection so strong that the force of her death would make itself known to me through a means beyond logic and information. What kind of ritual execution had been in her mind I can only crudely imagine; however, she probably had made peace in her final bargain: if the baby survived, it was meant to and she had protected and nurtured it as far as she could; if the baby died, then it was meant to because her poison had already begun to enter it. Understanding this primitive gesture binds me to Pandy in a way she would have wanted. Yet seeing that she could go no further into motherhood than expectancy does not surprise me. The Dancing Machine could come to life for a night in the afterglow of medicine, but it could not share a life with her. She wouldn't have wanted it to become her language. She was alone. And she had chosen it that way.

Touched briefly by clarity earlier today, she had seemed to understand what her choices meant. While Pandy was taking her bath in my apartment, after she calmed down a bit, she began talking about things she had read back in the days when she kept books. I tried to encourage her to confide in me but before I could stop her she shot up right in the bathtub and what might have become an explanation turned into babble. Instead of speech she spoke in tongues made feathery by the legs of spiders she claimed to feel spilling and prancing through her veins. It was this frustration that precipitated my leaving for the market. Yet now as I stand next to her nearly alive body, I remember from the rubble of her monologue that there was an intaglio engraved upon her life; and that it is in a similar design to mine.

I ask the subway man to take me down to the old woman's home. He explains to her for me that she will have to give the baby back. That we have come for the baby. A group of people gather outside her door merely to overhear our conversation. They lean in to each other for comfort in the way old ladies might hold hands on the street. The woman hides in a corner and begins to sing the hymn again as she performs the ritual of wrapping the dead infant in the blanket, rolling the baby this way and that, murmuring her refrain until all of the blanket is tucked and folded around the infant. It is a boy. His little body stiffened into permanent innocence. I take him down to his mother's bed and fit him neatly inside the curve of her elbow.

I nod to the subway man and close the door to the rats, put the groceries Pandy bought earlier over my arm, pick up the lamp and climb the stairs. There is a picture of Stevie Wonder I hadn't noticed before, on the wall leading to the street. The photo is a familiar one—from the days when Yolanda beaded and wove his hair. Page is waiting near the little sapling down the mud from me. I slam the street door onto the darkness inside. We walk home. On Broadway a little gypsy girl comes up to us and offers Page a plastic rose. I cook dinner with Pandy's groceries and Page stays with me until I tell him to go. I put the lamp in the closet where my mother's blanket had been, and that is the end of it.

Page is in the hospital today. Watershedding. He decided two days ago. Last night I brought him here. He hadn't shot up for 36 hours and the pain was ripping his gut to hell. I went with him to the hospital and I'll see him again tomorrow after work. He'll be in a cell, screaming maybe, or perhaps silent. Then he'll get out. He's my homeboy.

THE COUSINS

ELIZABETH SPENCER

Elizabeth Spencer was born and raised in Carrollton, Mississippi, and educated in Jackson and Nashville, where she attended Vanderbilt University. She lived for a number of years in Italy, and now lives in Montreal, Quebec. She is the author of eight novels, including *The Light in the Piazza, The Voice at the Back Door, The Snare,* and, most recently, *The Salt Line.* A collection of her short fiction, *The Stories of Elizabeth Spencer,* was published by Doubleday in 1981. In 1983, she was awarded the Award of Merit Medal of the American Academy of Arts and Letters, for the Short Story, and has recently been elected to membership in the American Academy/Institute's Department of Literature. "The Cousins" was written during a sojourn in Italy at Bellagio as a guest of the Rockefeller Foundation.

I could say that on the train from Milan to Florence, I recalled the events of thirty summers ago and the curious affair of my cousin Eric. But it wouldn't be true. I had Eric somewhere in my mind all the time, a constant. But he was never quite definable, and like a puzzle no one could ever solve, he bothered me. More recently, I had felt a restlessness I kept trying without success to lose, and I had begun to see Eric as its source.

The incident that had triggered my journey to find him had occurred while lunching with my cousin Ben in New York, his saying: "I always thought in some way I can't pin down—it was your fault we lost Eric." Surprising myself, I had felt stricken at the remark as though the point of a cold dagger had reached a vital spot. There was a story my cousins used to tell, out in the swing, under the shade trees, about a man found dead with no clues but a bloody shirt and a small pool of water on the floor beside him. Insoluble mystery. Answer: He was stabbed with a Dagger of Ice! I looked up from eating bay scallops. "*My* fault! Why?"

Ben gave some vague response, something about Eric's need for staying indifferent, no matter what. "But he could do that in spite of me," I protested. "Couldn't he?"

"Oh, forget it." He filled my glass. "I sometimes speculate out loud, Ella Mason."

Just before that he had remarked how good I was looking—good for a widow just turned fifty, I think he meant. But once he got my restlessness so stirred up, I couldn't lose it. I wanted calming, absolving. I wanted freeing and only Eric—since it was he I was in some way to blame for, or he to blame for me—could do that. So I came alone to Italy, where I had not been for thirty years.

For a while in Milan, spending a day or so to get over jet lag, I wondered if the country existed any more in the way I remembered it. Maybe, even back then, I had invented the feelings I had, the magic I had wanted to see. But on the train to Florence, riding through the June morning, I saw a little town from the window, in the bright, slightly hazy distance. I don't know what town it was. It seemed built all of a whitish stone, with a church, part of a wall cupping round one side and a piazza with a few people moving across it. With that sight and its stillness in the distance and its sudden vanishing as the train whisked past, I caught my breath and knew it had all been real. So it still was, and would remain. I hadn't invented anything.

From the point of that glimpsed white village, spreading outward through my memory, all its veins and arteries, the whole summer woke up again, like a person coming out of a trance.

Sealed, fleet, the train was rocking on. I closed my eyes with the image of the village, lying fresh and gentle against my mind's eye. I didn't have to try, to know that everything from then would start living now.

Once at the hotel and unpacked, with my dim lamp and clean bathroom and view of a garden—Eric had reserved all this for me: we had written and talked—I placed my telephone call. "Pronto," said the strange voice. "Signor Mason," I said. "Ella Mason, is that you?" So there was his own Alabama voice, not a bit changed. "It's me," I said, "tired from the train." "Take a nap. I'll call for you at seven."

Whatever southerners are, there are ways they don't change, the same manners to count on, the same tone of voice, never lost. Eric was older than I by about five years. I remember he taught me to play tennis, not so much how to play because we all knew that, as what not to do. Tennis manners. I had wanted to keep running after balls for him when they rolled outside the court, but he stopped me from doing that. He would take them up himself, and stroke them underhand to his opponent across the net. "Once in a while's all right," he said. "Just go sit down, Ella Mason." It was his way of saying there was always a right way to do things. I was only about ten. The next year it was something else I was doing wrong, I guess, because I always had a lot to learn. My cousins had this constant fondness about them. They didn't mind telling what they knew.

Waking in Florence in the late afternoon, wondering where I was, then catching on. The air was still and warm. It had the slight haziness in the brightness that I had seen from the train, and which I had lost in the bother of the station, the hastening of the taxi through the annoyance of crowds and narrow streets, across the Arno. The little hotel, a pensione, really, was out near the Pitti Palace.

Even out so short a distance from the center, Florence could seem the town of thirty years ago, or even the way it must have been in the Brownings' time, narrow streets and the light that way and the same flowers and gravel walks in the gardens. Not that much changes if you build with stone. Not until I saw the stooped grey man hastening through the pensione door did I get slapped by change, in the face. How could Eric look like that? Not that I hadn't had photographs, letters. He at once circled me, embracing, my head right against him, sight of him temporarily lost in that. As was his of me, I realized, thinking of all those lines I must have added, along with twenty extra pounds and a high count of grey among the reddish-brown hair. So we both got bruised by the sight of each other, and hung together, to blot each other out and soothe the hurt.

The shock was only momentary. We were too glad to see each other. We went some streets away, parked his car, and climbed about six flights of stone stairs. His place had a view over the river, first a great luxurious room opening past the entrance, then a terrace beyond. There were paintings, dark furniture, divans and chairs covered with good, rich fabric. A blonde woman's picture in a silver frame—poised, lovely. Through an alcove, the glimpse of an impressive desk, spread with papers, a telephone. You'd be forced to say he'd done well.

"It's cooler outside on the terrace," Eric said, coming in with drinks. "You'll like it over the river." So we went out there and talked. I was getting used to him now. His profile hadn't changed. It was firm, regular, Cousin Lucy Skinner's all over. That was his mother. We were just third cousins. Kissing kin. I sat answering questions. How long would it take, I wondered, to get around to the heart of things? To whatever had carried him away, and what had brought me here?

We'd been brought up together back in Martinsville, Alabama, not far from Birmingham. There was our connection and not much else in that little town of seven thousand and something. Or so we thought. And so we would have everybody else think. We did, though, despite a certain snobbishness—or maybe because of it—have a lot of fun. There were three leading families, in some way "connected." Eric and I had had the same great-grandfather. His mother's side were distant cousins, too. Families who had gone on living around there, through the centuries. Many were the stories and wide ranged the knowledge, though it was mainly of local interest. As a way of living, I always told myself, it might have gone on for us, too, right through the present and into an endless future, except for that trip we took that summer.

It started with ringing phones.

Eric calling one spring morning to say, "You know, the idea Jamie had last night down at Ben's about going to Europe? Well, why don't we do it?"

"This summer's impossible," I said, "I'm supposed to help Papa in the law office."

"He can get Sister to help him—" That was Eric's sister Chessie, one way of making sure she didn't decide to go with us. "You all will have to pay her a little, but she wants a job. Think it over, Ella Mason, but not for very long. Mayfred wants to, and Ben sounds serious, and there's Jamie and you makes five. Ben knows a travel agent in Birmingham. He thinks we might even get reduced rates, but we have to hurry. We should have thought this up sooner."

His light voice went racing on. He read a lot. I didn't even have to ask him where we'd go. He and Ben would plan it, both young men who had studied things, knew things, read, talked, quoted. We'd go where they wanted to go, love what they planned, admire them. Jamie was younger, my uncle Gale's son, but he was forming that year—he was becoming grown-up. Would he be like them? There was nothing else to be but like them, if at all possible. No one in his right mind would question that.

Ringing phones. . . . "Oh, I'm thrilled to death! What did your folks say? It's not all that expensive what with the exchange, not as much as staying here and going somewhere like the Smokies. You can pay for the trip over with what you'd save."

We meant to go by ship. Mayfred who read up on the latest things, wanted to fly, but nobody would hear to it. The boat was what people talked about when they mentioned their trip. It was a phrase: "On the boat going over. . . . On the boat coming back. . . ." The train was what we'd take to New York, or maybe we could fly. Mayfred, once redirected, began to plan everybody's clothes. She knew what things were drip-dry and crush-proof. On and on she forged through slick-paged magazines.

"It'll take the first two years of law practice to pay for it, but it might be worth it," said Eric. "J'ai très hâte d'y aller," said Ben. The little French he knew was a lot more than ours.

Eric was about twenty-five that summer, just finishing law school, having been delayed a year or so by his army service. I wasn't but nineteen. The real reason I had hesitated about going was a boy from Tuscaloosa I'd been dating up at the university last fall, but things were running down with him, even though I didn't want to admit it. I didn't love him so much as I wanted him to love me, and that's no good, as Eric himself told me. Ben was riding high, having gotten part of his thesis accepted for publication in the *Sewanee Review.* He had written on "The Lost Ladies of Edgar Allan Poe" and this piece was the chapter on "Ulalume." I pointed out they weren't so much lost as dead, or sealed up half-dead in tombs, but Ben didn't see the humor in that.

The syringa were blooming that year, and the spirea and bridal wreath. The flags had come and gone but not the wisteria, prettier than anybody could remember. All our mothers doted on their yards, while not a one of us ever raised so much as a petunia. No need to. We called each other from bower to bower. Our cars kept floating us through soft spring twilights. Travel folders were everywhere and Ben had scratched up enough French grammars to go around so we could practice some phrases. He thought we ought at least to know how to order in a restaurant and ask for stationery and soap in a hotel. Or buy stamps and find the bathroom. He was on to what to say to cab drivers when somebody mentioned that we were spending all this time on French without knowing a word of Italian. What did *they* say for Hello, or How much does it cost? or Which way to the post office? Ben said we didn't have time for Italian. He thought the people you had to measure up to were the French. What Italians thought of you didn't matter all that much. We were generally over at Eric's house because his mother was away visiting his married sister Edith and the grandchildren, and Eric's father couldn't have cared less if we had drinks of real whiskey in the evening. In fact, he was often out playing poker and doing the same thing himself.

The Masons had a grand house. (Mason was Mama's maiden name and so my middle one.) I loved the house especially when nobody was in it but all of us. It was white, two-story with big high-ceilinged rooms. The tree branches laced across it by moonlight, so that you could only see patches of it. Mama was always saying they ought to thin things out, take out half the shrubs and at least three trees (she would even say which trees), but Cousin Fred, Eric's father, liked all that shaggy growth. Once inside, the house took you over—it liked us all—and we were often back in the big kitchen after supper fixing drinks or sitting out on the side porch making jokes and talking about Europe. One evening it would be peculiar things about the English, and the next, French food, how much we meant to spend on it, and so on. We had a long argument about Mont St. Michel, which Ben had read about in a book by Henry Adams, but everybody else, though coaxed into reading at least part of the book, thought it was too far up there and we'd better stick around Paris. We hoped Ben would forget it: he was bossy when he got his head set. We wanted just to see Ver-sigh and Fontaine-blow.

"We could stop off in the southern part of France on our way to Italy," was Eric's idea. "It's where all the painting comes from."

"I'd rather see the paintings," said Mayfred. "They're mostly in Paris, aren't they?"

"That's not the point," said Ben.

Jamie was holding out for one night in Monte Carlo.

Jamie had shot up like a weed a few years back and had just never filled out. He used to regard us all as slightly opposed to him, as though none of us could possibly want to do what he most liked. He made, at times, common cause with Mayfred, who was kin to us only by a thread, so complicated I wouldn't dream of untangling it.

Mayfred was a grand-looking girl. Ben said it once: "She's got class." He said that when we were first debating whether to ask her along or not (if not her, then my roommate from Texas would be invited), and had decided that we had to ask Mayfred or smother her because we couldn't have stopped talking about our plans if our lives depended on it and she was always around. The afternoon Ben made that remark about her, we were just the three of us—Ben, Eric, and me—out to help Mama about the annual lining of the tennis court, and had stopped to sit on a bench, being sweaty and needing some shade to catch our breath in. So he said that in his meditative way, hitting the edge of a tennis racket on the ground between his feet and occasionally sighting down it to see if it had warped during a winter in the press. And Eric, after a silence in which he looked off to one side until you thought he hadn't heard (this being his way), said: "You'd think the rest of us had no class at all." "Of course we have, we just never mention it," said Ben. So we'd clicked again. I always loved that to happen.

Mayfred had a boyfriend named Donald Bailey, who came over from Georgia and took her out every Saturday night. He was fairly nice-looking was about all we knew, and Eric thought he was dumb.

"I wonder how Mayfred is going to get along without Donald," Ben said.

"I can't tell if she really likes him or not," I said. "She never talks about him."

"She just likes to have somebody," Ben said tersely, a thread of disapproval in his voice, the way he could do.

Papa was crazy about Mayfred. "You can't tell what she thinks about anything and she never misses a trick," he said. His unspoken thought was that I was always misjudging things. "Don't you *see*, Ella Mason," he would say. But are things all that easy to see?

"Do you remember," I said to Eric on the terrace, this long after, "much about Papa?"

"What about him?"

"He wanted me to be different, some way."

"Different how?"

"More like Mayfred," I said, and laughed, making it clear that I was deliberately shooting past the mark, because really I didn't know where it was.

"Well," said Eric, looking past me out to where the lights were brightening along the Arno, the towers standing out clearly in the dusky air, "I liked you the way you were."

It was good, hearing him say that. The understanding that I wanted might not come. But I had a chance, I thought, and groped for what to say, when Eric rose to suggest dinner, a really good restaurant he knew, not far away; we could even walk.

". . . Have you been to the Piazza? No, of course, you haven't had time. Well, don't go. It's covered with tourists and pigeon shit; they've moved all the real statues inside except the Cellini. Go look at that and leave quick. . . ."

"You must remember Jamie, though, how he put his head in his hands our first day in Italy and cried, 'I was just being nice to him and he took all the money!' Poor Jamie, I think something else was wrong with him, not just a couple of thousand lire."

"You think so, but what?"

"Well, Mayfred had made it plain that Donald was her choice of a man, though not present. And of course there was Ben. . . ." My voice stopped just before I stepped on a crack in the sidewalk.

". . . Ben had just got into Yale that spring before we left. He was hitching to a *fu*ture, man!" It was just as well Eric said it.

"So that left poor Jamie out of everything, didn't it? He was young, another year in college to go, and nothing really outstanding about him, so he thought, and nobody he could pair with."

"There were you and me."

"You and me," I repeated. It would take a book to describe how I said that. Half-question, half-echo, a total wondering what to say next. How, after all, did *he* mean it? It wasn't like me to say nothing. "He might just have wondered what *we* had?"

"He might have," said Eric. In the corner of the white-plastered restaurant, where he was known and welcomed, he was enjoying grilled chicken and artichokes. But suddenly he put down his fork, a pause like a solstice. He looked past my shoulder: Eric's way.

"Ben said it was my fault we 'lost' you. That's how he put it. He told me that in New York, the last time I saw him, six weeks ago. He wouldn't explain. Do you understand what he meant?"

" 'Lost,' am I? It's news to me."

"Well, you know, not at home. Not even in the States. Is that to do with me?"

"We'll go back and talk." He pointed to my plate. "Eat your supper, Ella Mason," he said.

My mind began wandering pleasantly. I fell to remembering the surprise Mayfred had handed us all when we got to New York. We had come up on the train, having gone up to Chattanooga to catch the Southern. Three days in New York and we would board the Queen Mary for Southampton. "Too romantic for anything," Mama had warbled on the phone. ("Elsa Stephens says, 'Too romantic for anything,' " she said at the table. "No, Mama, you said that, I heard you." "Well, I don't care who said it, it's true.") On the second afternoon in New York, Mayfred vanished with something vague she had to do. "Well, you know she's always tracking down dresses," Jamie told me. "I think she wants her hair restyled somewhere," I said. But not till we were having drinks in the hotel bar before dinner did Mayfred show up with Donald Bailey! She had, in addition to Donald, a new dress and a new hairstyle, and the three things looked to me about of equal value, I was thinking, when she suddenly announced with an earsplitting smile: "We're married!" There was a total silence, broken at last by Donald, who said with a shuffling around of feet and gestures: "It's just so I could come along with y'all, if y'all don't mind." "Well," said Ben, at long last, "I guess you both better sit down." Another silence followed, broken by Eric, who said he guessed it was one excuse for having champagne.

Mayfred and Donald had actually gotten married across the state line in Georgia two weeks before. Mayfred didn't want to discuss it because, she said, everybody was so taken up with talking about Europe, she wouldn't have been able to get a word in edgewise. "You better go straight and call yo' Mama," said Ben. "Either you do, or I will."

Mayfred's smile fell to ashes and she sloshed out champagne. "She can't do a thing about it till we get back home! She'll want me to explain everything. Don't y'all make me . . . please!"

I noticed that so far Mayfred never made common cause with any one of us, but always spoke to the group: Y'all. It also occurred to me both then and now that that was what had actually saved her. If one of us had gotten involved in pleading for her with Ben, he would have overruled us. But Mayfred, a lesser cousin, was keeping a distance. She could have said—and I thought she was on the verge of it—that she'd gone to a lot of trouble to satisfy us; she might have just brought him along without benefit of ceremony.

So we added Donald Bailey. Unbeknownst to us, reservations had been found for him and though he had to share a four-berth, tourist-class cabin with three strange men, after a day out certain swaps were effected, and he wound up in second class with Mayfred. Eric overheard a conversation between Jamie and Donald which he passed on to me. Jamie: Don't you really think this is a funny way to spend a honeymoon? Donald: It just was the best I could do.

He was a polite squarish sort of boy with heavy, dark lashes. He and Mayfred used to stroll off together regularly after the noon meal on board. It was a serene crossing, for the weather cleared two days out of New York and we could spend a lot of time on deck playing shuffleboard and betting on races with wooden horses run by the purser. (I forgot to say everybody in our family but Ben's branch were inveterate gamblers and had played poker in the club car all the way up to New York on the train.) After lunch every day Mayfred got seasick and Donald in true husbandly fashion would take her to whichever side the wind was not blowing against and let her throw up neatly over the rail, like a cat. Then she'd be all right. Later, when you'd see them together they were always talking and laughing. But with us she was quiet and trim, with her fashion-blank look, and he was just quiet. He all but said "Ma'am" and "Sir." As a result of Mayfred's marriage, I was thrown a lot with Eric, Ben, and Jamie. "I think one of you ought to get married," I told them. "Just temporarily, so I wouldn't feel like the only girl." Ben promised to take a look around and Eric seemed not to have heard. It was Jamie who couldn't joke about it. He had set himself to make a pair, in some sort of way, with Mayfred, I felt. I don't know how seriously he took her. Things run deep in our family—that's what you have to know. Eric said out of the blue, "I'm wondering when they had time to see each other; Mayfred spent all her time with us." (We were prowling through the Tate Gallery.) "Those Saturday night dates," I said, studying Turner. At times she would show up with us, without Donald, not saying much, attentive and smooth, making company. Ben told her she looked Parisian.

Eric and Ben were both well into manhood that year, and were so future conscious they seemed to be talking about it even when they weren't saying anything. Ben had decided on literature, had finished a master's at Sewanee and was going on to Yale, while Eric had just stood law school exams at Emory. He was in some considerable debate about whether he shouldn't go into literary studies, too, for unlike Ben, whose interest was scholarly, he wanted to be a writer, and he had some elaborate theory that actually studying literature reduced the possibility of your being able to write it. Ben saw his point and though he did not entirely agree, felt that law might just be the right choice—it put you in touch with how things actually worked. "Depending, of course, on whether you tend to fiction or poetry. It would be more important in regard to fiction because the facts matter so much more." So they trod along ahead of us—through London sights, their heels coming down in tandem. They might have been two dons in an Oxford street, debating something. Next to come were Jamie and me, and behind, at times, Donald and Mayfred.

I was so fond of Jamie those days. I felt for him in a family way, almost motherly. When he said he wanted a night in Monte Carlo, I sided with him, just as I had about going at least once to the picture show in London. Why shouldn't he have his way? Jamie said one museum a day was enough. I felt the same. He was all different directions with himself: too tall, too thin, big feet, small head. Once I caught his hand: "Don't worry," I said, "everything good will happen to you." The way I remember it, we looked back just then, and there came Mayfred, alone. She caught up with us. We were standing on a street corner near Hyde Park and, for a change, it was sunny. "Donald's gone home," she said, cheerfully. "He said tell you all goodbye."

We hadn't seen her all day. We were due to leave for France the next morning. She told us, for one thing, that Donald had persistent headaches and thought he ought to see about it. He seemed, as far as we could tell, to have limitless supplies of money, and had once taken us all for dinner at the Savoy, where only Mayfred could move into all that glitter with an air of belonging to it. He didn't like to bring up his illness and trouble us, Mayfred explained. "Maybe it was too much honeymoon for him," Eric speculated to me in private. I had to say I didn't know. I did know that Jamie had come out like the English sun —unexpected, but marvelously bright.

I held out for Jamie and Monte Carlo. He wasn't an intellectual like Ben and Eric. He would listen while they finished up a bottle of wine and then would start looking around the restaurant. "That lady didn't have anything but snails and bread," he would say, or, of a couple leaving, "He didn't even know that girl when they came in." He was just being a small town boy. But with Mayfred he must have been different, she laughed so much. "What do they talk about?" Ben asked me, perplexed. "Ask them," I advised. "You think they'd tell me?" "I doubt it," I said. "They wouldn't know what to say," I added, "they would just tell you the last things they said." "You mean like, Why do they call it the Seine if they don't seine for fish in it? Real funny."

Jamie got worried about Mayfred in Paris because the son of the hotel owner, a young Frenchman so charming he looked like somebody had made him up whole cloth, wanted to take her out. She finally consented with some trepidation on our part, especially from Ben, who in this case posed as her uncle, with strict orders from her father. The Frenchman, named Paul something, was not disturbed in the least: Ben fit right in with his ideas of how things ought to be. So Mayfred went out with him, looking, except for her sunny hair, more French than the natives—we all had to admit being proud of her. I also had invitations, but none so elegant. "What happened?" we all asked, the next day. "Nothing," she insisted. "We just went to this little nightclub place near some school . . . begins with an 'S.' " "The Sorbonne," said Ben, whose bemusement, at that moment, peaked. "Then what?" Eric asked. "Well, nothing. You just eat something, then talk and have some wine and get up and dance. They dance different. Like this." She locked her hands together in air. "He thought he couldn't talk good enough for me in English, but it was OK." Paul sent her some marrons glacés which she opened on the train south, and Jamie munched one with happy jaws. Paul had not suited him. It was soon after that, he and Mayfred began their pairing off. In Jamie's mind we were moving on to Monte Carlo, and had been ever since London. The first thing he did was find out how to get to the Casino.

He got dressed for dinner better than he had since the Savoy. Mayfred seemed to know a lot about the gambling places, but her attitude was different from his. Jamie was bird-dogging toward the moment; she was just curious. "I've got to trail along," Eric said after dinner, "just to see the show." "Not only that," said Ben, "we might have to stop him in case he gets too carried away. We might have to bail him out." When we three, following up the rear (this was Jamie's night), entered the discreetly glittering rotunda, stepped on thick carpets beneath the giant, multiprismed chandeliers, heard the low chant of the croupier, the click of roulette, the rustle of money at the bank, and saw the bright rhythmic movements of dealers and wheels and stacks of chips, it was still Jamie's face that was the sight worth watching. All was mirrored there. Straight from the bank, he visited card tables and wheels, played the blind dealing-machine—chemin-de-fer—and finally turned, a small sum to the good, to his real goal: roulette. Eric had by then lost a hundred francs or so, but I had about made up for it, and Ben wouldn't play at all. "It's my Presbyterian side," he told us. His mother had been one of those. "It's known as 'riotous living,' " he added.

It wasn't riotous at first, but it was before we left, because Jamie, once he advanced on the roulette, with Mayfred beside him—she was wearing some sort of gold blouse with long peasant sleeves and a low-cut neck she had picked up cheap in a shop that afternoon, and was not speaking to him but instead, with a gesture so European you'd think she'd been born there, slipping her arm through his just at the wrist and leaning her head back a little—was giving off the glow of somebody so magically aided by a presence every inch his own that he could not and would not lose. Jamie, in fact, looked suddenly aristocratic, overbred, like a Russian greyhound or a Rumanian prince. Both Eric and I suspended our own operations to watch. The little ball went clicking around as the wheel spun. Black. Red. And red. Back to black. All wins. People stopped to look on. Two losses, then the wins again, continuing. Mayfred had a look of curious bliss around her mouth—she looked like a cat in process of a good purr. The take mounted.

Ben called Eric and me aside. "It's going on all night," he said. We all sat down at the little gold and white marble bar and ordered Perriers.

"Well," said Eric, "what did he start with?"

"Couldn't have been much," said Ben, "if I didn't miss anything. He didn't change more than a couple of hundred at the desk."

"That sounds like a lot to me," said Eric.

"I mean," said Ben, "it won't ruin him to lose it all."

"You got us into this," said Eric to me.

"Oh, gosh, I know it. But look. He's having the time of his life."

Everybody in the room had stopped to watch Jamie's luck. Some people were laughing. He had a way of stopping everybody and saying: "What's *that* mean?" as if only English could or ought to be spoken in the entire world. Some man near us said, "Le cavalier de l'Okla-hum," and another answered, "Du Texas, plutôt." Then he took three more in a row and they were silent.

It was Mayfred who made him stop. It seemed like she had an adding machine in her head. All of a sudden she told him something, whispered in his ear. When he shook his head, she caught his hand. When he pulled away, she grabbed his arm. When he lifted his arm, she came up with it, right off the floor. For a minute I thought they were both going to fall over into the roulette wheel.

"You got to stop, Jamie!" Mayfred said in the loudest Alabama voice I guess they'd ever be liable to hear that side of the ocean. It was curdling, like cheering for 'Bama against Ole Miss in the Sugar Bowl. "I don't have to stop!" he yelled right back. "If you don't stop," Mayfred shouted, "I'll never speak to you again, Jamie Marshall, as long as I live!"

The croupier looked helpless, and everybody in the room was turning away like they didn't see us, while through a thin door at the end of the room, a man in black tie was approaching who could only be called the "management." Ben was already pulling Jamie toward the bank. "Cash it in now, we'll go along to another one . . . maybe tomorrow we can. . . ." It was like pulling a stubborn calf across the lot, but he finally made it with some help from Mayfred, who stood over Jamie while he counted everything to the last sou. She made us all take a taxi back to the hotel because she said it was common knowledge when you won a lot they sent somebody out to rob you, first thing. Next day she couldn't rest till she got Jamie to change the francs into travelers' checks, U.S. He had won well over two thousand dollars, all told.

The next thing, as they saw it, was to keep Jamie out of the Casino. Ben haggled a long time over lunch, and Eric, who was good at scheming, figured out a way to get up to a village in the hills where there was a Matisse chapel he couldn't live longer without seeing. And Mayfred took to handholding and even gave Jamie on the sly (I caught her at it) a little nibbling kiss or two. What did they care? I wondered. I thought he should get to go back and lose it all.

It was up in the mountain village that afternoon that I blundered in where I'd rather not have gone. I had come out of the chapel where Ben and Eric were deep in discussion of whether Matisse could ever place in the front rank of French art, and had climbed part of the slope nearby where a narrow stair ran up to a small square with a dry stone fountain. Beyond that, in the French manner, was a small café with a striped awning and a few tables. From somewhere I heard Jamie's voice, saying, "I know, but what'd you do it for?" "Well, what does anybody do anything for? I wanted to." "But what would you want to *for,* Mayfred?" "Same reason you'd want to, sometime." "I wouldn't want to except to be with you." "Well, I'm right here, aren't I? You got your wish." "What I wish is you hadn't done it." It was bound to be marrying Donald that he meant. He had a frown that would come at times between his light eyebrows. I came to associate it with Mayfred. How she was running him. When they stepped around the corner of the path, holding hands (immediately dropped), I saw that frown. Did I have to dislike Mayfred, the way she was acting? The funny thing was, I didn't even know.

We lingered around the village and ate there and the bus was late, so we never made it back to the casinos. By then all Jamie seemed to like was being with Mayfred, and the frown disappeared.

Walking back to the apartment, passing darkened doorways, picking up pieces of Eric's past like fragments in the street.

". . . And then you did or didn't marry her, and she died and left you the legacy. . . ."

"Oh, we did get married, all right, the anticlimax of a number of years. I wish you could have known her. The marriage was civil. She was afraid the family would cause a row if she wanted to leave me anything. That was when she knew she hadn't long to live. Not that it was any great fortune. She had some property out near Pasquallo, a little town near here. I sold it. I had to fight them in court for a while, but it did eventually clear up."

"You've worked, too, for this other family . . . ?"

"The Rinaldi. You must have got all this from Ben, though maybe I wrote you, too. They were friends of hers. It's all connections here, like anywhere else. Right now they're all at the sea below Genoa. I'd be there too, but I'd some business in town, and you were coming. It's the export side I've helped them with. I do know English, and a little law, in spite of all."

"So it's a regular Italian life," I mused, climbing stairs, entering his salotto where I saw again the woman's picture in a silver frame. Was that her, the one who had died? "Was she blonde?" I asked, moving as curiously through his life as a child through a new room.

"Giana, you mean? No, part Sardinian, dark as they come. Oh, you mean her. No, that's Lisa, one of the Rinaldi, Paolo's sister . . . that's him up there."

I saw then, over a bookshelf, a man's enlarged photo: tweed jacket, pipe, all in the English style.

"So what else, Ella Mason?" His voice was amused at me.

"She's pretty," I said.

"Very pretty," he agreed.

We drifted out to the terrace once more.

It is time I talked about Ben and Eric, about how it was with me and with them and with the three of us.

When I look back on pictures of myself in those days, I see a girl in shorts, weighing a few pounds more than she thought she should, low-set, with a womanly cast to her body, chopped-off reddish hair, and a wide, freckled, almost boyish grin, happy to be posing between two tall boys, who happened to be her cousins, smiling their white tentative smiles. Ben and Eric. They were smart. They were fun. They did everything right. And most of all, they admitted me. I was the audience they needed.

I had to run to keep up. I read Poe because of Ben's thesis; and Wallace Stevens because Eric liked his poetry. I even, finding him referred to at times, tried to read Plato. (Ben studied Greek.) But what I did was not of much interest to them. Still, they wanted me around. Sometimes Ben made a point of "conversing" with me—what courses, what books, etc.—but he made me feel like a high school student. Eric, seldom bothering with me, was more on my level when he did. To one another, they talked at a gallop. Literature turned them on, their ideas flowed, ran back and forth like a current. I loved hearing them.

I think of little things they did. Such as Ben coming back from Sewanee with a small Roman statue, copy of something Greek—Apollo, I think—just a fragment, a head, turned aside, shoulders and a part of a back. His professor had given it to him as a special mark of favor. He set it on his favorite pigeon-hole desk, to stay there, it would seem, for always, to be seen always by the rest of us—by me.

Such as Eric ordering his "secondhand but good condition" set of Henry James's novels with prefaces, saying, "I know this is corny but it's what I wanted," making space in his Mama's old upright secretary with glass-front bookshelves above, and my feeling that they'd always be there. I strummed my fingers across the spines lettered in gold. Some day I would draw down one or another to read them. No hurry.

Such as the three of us packing Mama's picnic basket (it seems my folks were the ones with the practical things—tennis court, croquet set: though Jamie's set up a badminton court at one time, it didn't take) to take to a place called Beulah Woods for a spring day in the sun near a creek where water ran clear over white limestone then plunged off into a swimming hole. Ben sat on a bedspread reading Ransom's poetry aloud and we gossiped about the latest town scandal, involving a druggist, a real estate deal where some property went cheap to him, though it seemed now that his wife had been part of the bargain, being lent out on a regular basis to the man who sold him the property. The druggist was a newcomer. A man we all knew in town had been after the property and was now threatening to sue. "Do you think it was written in the deed, so many nights a week she goes off to work the property out," Ben speculated. "Do you think they calculated the interest?" It wasn't the first time our talk had run toward sexual things; in a small town, secrets didn't often get kept for long.

More than once I'd dreamed that someday Ben or Eric would ask me somewhere alone. A few years before the picnic, romping through our big old rambling house at twilight with Jamie, who loved playing hide-and-seek, I had run into the guest room where Ben was standing in the half-dark by the bed. He was looking at something he'd found there in the twilight, some book or ornament, and I mistook him for Jamie and threw my arms around him crying, "Caught you!" We fell over the bed together and rolled for a moment before I knew then it was Ben, but knew I'd wanted it to be; or didn't I really know all along it was Ben, but pretended I didn't? Without a doubt when his weight came down over me, I knew I wanted it to be there. I felt his body, for a moment so entirely present, draw back and up. Then he stood, turning away, leaving. "You better grow up," was what I think he said. Lingering feelings made me want to seek him out the next day or so. Sulky, I wanted to say, "I *am* growing up." But another time he said, "We're cousins, you know."

Eric for a while dated a girl from one of the next towns. She used to ask him over to parties and they would drive to Birmingham sometimes, but he never had her over to Martinsville. Ben, that summer we went to Europe, let it be known he was writing and getting letters from a girl at Sewanee. She was a pianist named Sylvia. "You want to hear music played softly in the 'drawing room,' " I clowned at him. " 'Just a song at twilight.' " "Now, Ella Mason, you behave," he said.

I had boys to take me places. I could flirt and I got a rush at dances and I could go off the next to the highest diving board and was good in doubles. Once I went on strike from Ben and Eric for over a week. I was going with that boy from Tuscaloosa and I had begun to think he was the right one and get ideas. Why fool around with my cousins? But I missed them. I went around one afternoon. They were talking out on the porch. The record player was going inside, something of Berlioz that Ben was onto. They waited till it finished before they'd speak to me. Then Eric, smiling from the depths of a chair, said, "Hey, Ella Mason"; and Ben, getting up to unlatch the screen, said, "Ella Mason, where on earth have you been?" I'd have to think they were glad.

Ben was dark. He had straight, dark brown hair, dry-looking in the sun, growing thick at the brow, but flat at night when he put a damp comb through it, and darker. It fit close to his head like a monk's hood. He wore large glasses with lucite rims. Eric had sandy hair, softly appealing and always mussed. He didn't bother much with his looks. In the day they scuffed around in open-throated shirts and loafers, crinkled seersucker pants, or shorts; tennis shoes when they played were always dirty white. At night, when they cleaned up, it was still casual but fresh laundered. But when they dressed, in shirts and ties with an inch of white cuff laid crisp against their brown hands: they were splendid!

"Ella Mason," Eric said, "if that boy doesn't like you, he's not worth worrying about." He had put his arm around me coming out of the picture show. I ought to drop it, a tired romance, but couldn't quite. Not till that moment. Then I did.

"Those boys," said Mr. Felix Gresham from across the street. "Getting time they started earning something 'stead of all time settin' around." He used to come over and tell Mama everything he thought, though no kin to anybody. "I reckon there's time enough for that," Mama said. "Now going off to France," said Mr. Gresham, as though that spoke for itself. "Not just France," Mama said, "England, too, and Italy." "Ain't nothing in France," said Mr. Gresham. "I don't know if there is or not," said Mama, "I never have been." She meant that to hush him up, but the truth is, Mr. Gresham might have been to France in World War I. I never thought to ask. Now he's dead.

Eric and Ben. I guess I was in love with both of them. Wouldn't it be nice, I used to think, if one were my brother and the other my brother's best friend, and then I could just quietly and without so much as thinking about it find myself marrying the friend (now which would I choose for which?) and so we could go on forever? At other times, frustrated, I suppose, by their never changing toward me, I would plan on doing something spectacular, finding a Yankee, for instance, so impressive and brilliant and established in some important career, that they'd have to listen to him, learn what he was doing and what he thought and what he knew, while I sat silent and poised throughout the conversation, the cat that ate the cream, though of course too polite to show satisfaction. Fantasies, one by one, would sing to me for a little while.

At Christmas vacation before our summer abroad, just before Ben got accepted to Yale and just while Eric was getting bored with law school, there was a quarrel. I didn't know the details, but they went back to school with things still unsettled among us. I got friendly with Jamie then, more than before. He was down at Tuscaloosa, like me. It's when I got to know Mayfred better, on weekends at home. Why bother with Eric and Ben? It had been a poor season. One letter came from Ben and I answered it, saying that I had come to like Jamie and Mayfred so much; their parents were always giving parties and we were having a grand time. In answer I got a long, serious letter about time passing and what it did, how we must remember that what we had was always going to be a part of ourselves. That he thought of jonquils coming up now and how they always looked like jonquils, just absent for a time, and how the roots stayed the same. He was looking forward, he said, to spring and coming home.

Just for fun I sat down and wrote him a love letter. I said he was a fool and a dunce and didn't he know while he was writing out all these ideas that I was a live young woman and only a second cousin and that through the years while he was talking about Yeats, Proust, and Edgar Allan Poe that I was longing to have my arms around him the way they were when we fell over in the bed that twilight romping with Jamie and why in the ever-loving world couldn't he see me as I was, a live girl, instead of a cousin-spinster, listening to him and Eric make brilliant conversation? Was he trying to turn me into an old maid? Wasn't he supposed, at least, to be intelligent? So why couldn't he see what I was really like? But I didn't mail it. I didn't because, for one thing, I doubted that I meant it. Suppose, by a miracle, Ben said, "You're right, every word." What about Eric? I started dating somebody new at school. I tore the letter up.

Eric called soon after. He just thought it would do him good to say hello. Studying for long hours wasn't his favorite sport. He'd heard from Ben, the hard feelings were over, he was ready for spring holidays already. I said, "I hope to be in town, but I'm really not sure." A week later I forgot a date with the boy I thought I liked. The earlier one showed up again. Hadn't I liked him, after all? How to be sure? I bought a new straw hat, white-and-navy for Easter, with a ribbon down the back, and came home.

Just before Easter, Jamie's parents gave a party for us all. There had been a cold snap and we were all inside, with purplish-red punch, and a buffet laid out. Jamie's folks had this relatively new house, with new carpets and furnishings and the family dismay ran to what a big mortgage they were carrying and how it would never be paid out. Meantime his mother (no kin) looked completely unworried as she arranged tables that seemed to have been copied from magazines. I came alone, having had to help Papa with some typing, and so saw Ben and Eric for the first time, though we'd talked on the phone.

Eric looked older, a little worn. I saw something drawn in the way he laughed, a sort of restraint about him. He was standing aside and looking at a point where no one and nothing were. But he came to when I spoke and gave that laugh and then a hug. Ben was busy "conversing" with a couple in town who had somebody at Sewanee, too. He smoked a pipe now, I noticed, smelly when we hugged. He had soon come to join Eric and me, and it was at that moment, the three of us standing together for the first time since Christmas, and change having been mentioned at least once by way of Ben's letter, that I knew some tension was mounting, bringing obscure moments with it. We turned to one another but did not speak readily about anything. I had thought I was the only one, sensitive to something imagined—having "vapors," as somebody called it—but I could tell we were all at a loss for some reason none of us knew. Because if Ben and Eric knew, articulate as they were, they would have said so. In the silence so suddenly fallen, something was ticking.

Maybe, I thought, they just don't like Martinsville anymore. They always said that parties were dull and squirmed out of them when they could. I lay awake thinking, They'll move on soon; I won't see them again.

It was the next morning Eric called and we all grasped for Europe like the drowning, clinging to what we could.

After Monte Carlo, we left France by train and came down to Florence. The streets were narrow there and we joked about going single file like Indians. "What I need is moccasins," said Jamie, who was always blundering over the uneven paving stones. At the Uffizi, the second day, Eric, in a trance before Botticelli, fell silent. Could we ever get him to speak again? Hardly a word. Five in number, we leaned over the balustrades along the Arno, all silent then from the weariness of sightseeing, and the heat; and there I heard it once more, the ticking of something hidden among us. Was it to deny it we decided to take the photograph? We had taken a lot, but this one, I think, was special. I have it still. It was in the Piazza Signoria.

"Which monument?" we kept asking. Ben wanted Donatello's lion, and Eric the steps of the Old Palace, Jamie wanted Cosimo I on his horse. I wanted the Perseus of Cellini, and Mayfred the Rape of the Sabines. So Ben made straws out of toothpicks and we drew and Mayfred won. We got lined up and Ben framed us. Then we had to find somebody, a slim Italian boy as it turned out, to snap us for a few hundred lire. It seemed we were proving something serious and good, and smiled with our straight family smiles, Jamie with his arm around Mayfred, and she with her smart new straw sun hat held to the back of her head, and me between Ben and Eric, arms entwined. A photo outlasts everybody, and this one with the frantic scene behind us, the moving torso of the warrior holding high the prey while we smiled our ordinary smiles—it was a period, the end of a phase.

Not that the photograph itself caused the end of anything. Donald Bailey caused it. He telephoned the pensione that night from Atlanta to say he was in the hospital, gravely ill, something they might have to operate for any day, some sort of brain tumor was what they were afraid of. Mayfred said she'd come.

We all got stunned. Ben and Eric and I straggled off together while she and Jamie went to the upstairs sitting room and sat in the corner. "Honest to God," said Eric, "I just didn't know Donald Bailey had a brain." "He had headaches," said Ben. "Oh, I knew he had a head," said Eric, "we could see that."

By night it was settled. Mayfred would fly back from Rome. Once again she got us to promise secrecy—how she did that I don't know, the youngest one and yet not even Ben could prevail on her one way or the other. By now she had spent most of her money. Donald, we knew, was rich; he came of a rich family and had, furthermore, money of his own. So if she wanted to fly back from Rome, the ticket, already purchased, would be waiting for her. Mayfred got to be privileged, in my opinion, because none of us knew her family too well. Her father was a blood cousin but not too highly regarded—he was thought to be a rather silly man who "traveled" and dealt with "all sorts of people"—and her mother was from "off," a Georgia girl, fluttery. If it had been my folks and if I had started all this wild marrying and flying off, Ben would have been on the phone to Martinsville by sundown.

One thing in the Mayfred departure that went without question: Jamie would go to Rome to see her off. We couldn't have sealed him in or held him with ropes. He had got on to something new in Italy, or so I felt, because where before then had we seen in gallery after gallery, strong men, young and old, with enraptured eyes, enthralled before a woman's painted image, wanting nothing? What he had gotten was an idea of devotion. It fit him. It suited. He would do anything for Mayfred and want nothing. If she had got pregnant and told him she was a virgin, he would have sworn to it before the Inquisition. It could positively alarm you for him to see him satisfied with the feelings he had found. Long after I went to bed, he was at the door or in the corridor with Mayfred, discussing baggage and calling a hotel in Rome to get a reservation for when he saw her off.

Mayfred had bought a lot of things. She had an eye for what she could wear with what, and she would pick up pieces of this and that for putting costumes and accessories together. She had to get some extra luggage and it was Jamie, of course, who promised to see it sent safely to her, through a shipping company in Rome. His two thousand dollars was coming in handy, was all I could think.

Hot, I couldn't sleep, so I went out in the sitting room to find a magazine. Ben was up. The three men usually took a large room together, taking turns for the extra cot. Ever since we got the news, Ben had had what Eric called his "family mood." Now he called me over. "I can't let those kids go down there alone," he said. "They seem like children to me—and Jamie . . . about all he can say is Grazie and Quanto." "Then let's all go," I said, "I've given up sleeping for tonight anyway." "Eric's hooked on Florence," said Ben. "Can't you tell? He counts the cypresses on every knoll. He can spot a Della Robbia a block off. If I make him leave three days early, he'll never forgive me. Besides, our reservations in that hotel can't be changed. We called for Jamie and they're full; he's staying third-class somewhere till we all come. I don't mind doing that. Then we'll all meet up just the way we planned, have our week in Rome, and go catch the boat from Naples." "I think they could make it on their own," I said, "it's just that you'd worry every minute." He grinned; "our father for the duration," was what Eric called him. "I know I'm that way," he said.

Another thing was that Ben had been getting little caches of letters at various points along our trek from his girl friend Sylvia, the one he'd been dating up at Sewanee. She was getting a job in New York that fall which would be convenient to Yale. She wrote a spidery hand on thick rippled stationery, cream colored, and had promised in her last dispatch, received in Paris, to write to Rome. Ben could have had an itch for that. But mainly he was that way, careful and concerned. He had in mind what we all felt, that just as absolutely anything could be done by Mayfred, so could absolutely anything happen to her. He also knew what we all knew, that if the Colosseum started falling on her, Jamie would leap bodily under the rocks.

At two A.M. it was too much for me to think about. I went to bed and was so exhausted, I didn't even hear Mayfred leave.

I woke up about ten with a low tapping on my door. It was Eric. "Is this the sleep of the just?" he asked me, as I opened the door. The air in the corridor was fresh: it must have rained in the night. No one was about. All the guests, I supposed, were well out into the day's routine, seeing what next tour was on the list. On a trip you were always planning something. Ben planned for us. He kept a little notebook.

Standing in my doorway alone with Eric, in a loose robe with a cool morning breeze and my hair not even combed, I suddenly laughed. Eric laughed, too. "I'm glad they're gone," he said, and looked past my shoulder.

I dressed and went out with him for some breakfast, cappucino and croissants at a café in the Signoria. We didn't talk much. It was terrible, in the sense of the Mason Skinner Marshall and Phillips sense of family, even to think you were glad they were gone, let alone say it. I took Eric's silence as one of his ironies, what he was best at. He would say, for instance, if you were discussing somebody's problem that wouldn't ever have any solution, "It's time somebody died." There wasn't much to say after that. Another time, when his daddy got into a rage with a next-door neighbor over their property line, Eric said, "You'd better marry her." Once he put things in an extreme light, nobody could talk about them anymore. Saying "I'm glad they're gone," was like that.

But it was a break. I thought of the way I'd been seeing them. How Jamie's becoming had been impressing me, every day more. How

Mayfred was a kind of spirit, grown bigger than life. How Ben's dominance now seemed not worrisome, but princely, his heritage. We were into a Renaissance of ourselves, I wanted to say, but was afraid they wouldn't see it the way I did. Only Eric had eluded me. What was he becoming? For once he didn't have to discuss Poe's idea of women, or the southern code of honor, or Henry James's views of France and England.

As for me, I was, at least, sure that my style had changed. I had bought my little linen blouses and loose skirts, my sandals and braided silver bracelets. "That's great on you!" Mayfred had cried. "Now try this one!" On the streets, Italians passed me too close not to be noticed; they murmured musically in my ear, saying I didn't know just what; waiters leaned on my shoulder to describe dishes of the day.

Eric and I wandered across the river, following narrow streets lined with great stone palaces, seeing them open into small piazzas whose names were not well known. We had lunch in a friendly place with a curtain of thin twisted metal sticks in the open door, an amber-colored dog lying on the marble floor near the serving table. We ordered favorite things without looking at the menu. We drank white wine. "This is fun," I suddenly said. He turned to me. Out of his private distance, he seemed to be looking down at me. "I think so, too."

He suddenly switched on to me, like somebody searching and finding with the lens of a camera. He began to ask me things. What did you think of that, Ella Mason? What about this, Ella Mason? Ella Mason, did you think Ben was right when he said . . . ? I could hardly swing on to what was being asked of me, thick and fast. But he seemed to like my answers, actually to listen. Not that all those years I'd been dumb as a stone. I had prattled quite a lot. It's just that they never treated me one to one, the way Eric was doing now. We talked for nearly an hour, then, with no one left in the restaurant but us, stopped as suddenly as we'd started. Eric said, "That's a pretty dress."

The sun was strong outside. The dog was asleep near the door. Even the one remaining waiter was drowsing on his feet. It was the shutting-up time for everything and we went out into streets blanked out with metal shutters. We hugged the shady side and went single file back to home base, as we'd come to call it, wherever we stayed.

A Vespa snarled by and I stepped into a cool courtyard to avoid it. I found myself in a large yawning mouth, mysterious as a cave, shadowy, with the trickling sound of a fountain and the glimmer in the depths of water running through ferns and moss. Along the interior of the street wall, fragments of ancient sculpture, found, I guess, when they'd built the palazzo, had been set into the masonry. One was a horse, neck and shoulder, another an arm holding a shield, and a third at about my height the profile of a woman, a nymph or some such. Eric stopped to look at each, for as Ben had said, Eric loved everything there, and then he said, "Come here, Ella Mason." I stood where he wanted, by the little sculptured relief, and he took my face and turned it to look at it closer, then with a strong hand (I remembered tennis), he pressed my face against the stone face and held it for a moment. The stone bit into my flesh and that was the first time that Eric, bending deliberately to do so, kissed me on the mouth. He had held one side of me against the wall, so that I couldn't raise my arm to him, and the other arm was pinned down by his elbow, the hand that pressed my face into the stone was that one, so that I couldn't move closer to him, as I wanted to do, and when he dropped away suddenly, turned on his heel and walked rapidly away, I could only hasten to follow, my voice gone, my pulses all throbbing together. I remember my anger, the old dreams about him and Ben stirred to life again, thinking, *If he thinks he can just walk away,* and knowing with anger, too, *It's got to be now,* as if in the walled land of kinship, thicker in our illustrious connection than any fortress in Europe, a door had creaked open at last. Eric, Eric, Eric. I'm always seeing your retreating heels, how they looked angry; but why? It was worth coming for, after thirty years, to ask that. . .

"That day you kissed me in the street, the first time," I asked him. Night on the terrace; a bottle of chianti between our chairs. "You walked away. Were you angry? Your heels looked angry. I can see them still."

"The trip in the first place," he said, "it had to do with you partly. Maybe you didn't understand that. We were outward bound, leaving you, a sister in a sense. We'd talked about it."

"I adored you so," I said. "I think I was less than a sister, more like a dog."

"For a little while you weren't either one." He found my hand in the dark. "It was a wonderful little while."

Memories: Eric in the empty corridor of the pensione. How Italy folds up and goes to sleep from two to four. His not looking back for me, going straight to his door. The door closing, but no key turning and me turning the door handle and stepping in. And he at the window already with his back to me and how he heard the sliding latch on the door—I slid it with my hands behind me—heard it click shut, and turned. His face and mine, what we knew. Betraying Ben.

: Walking by the Arno, watching a white and green scull stroking by into the twilight, the rower a boy or girl in white and green, growing dimmer to the rhythm of the long oars, vanishing into arrow shape, then pencil thickness, then movement without substance, on. . .

: A trek the next afternoon through twisted streets to a famous chapel. Sitting quiet in a cloister, drinking in the symmetry, the silence. Holding hands. "D for Donatello," said Eric. "D for Della Robbia," I said. "M for Michelangelo," he continued. "M for Medici." "L for Leonardo." "I can't think of an L," I gave up. "Lumbago. There's an old master." "Worse than Jamie." We were always going home again.

: Running into the manager of the pensione one morning in the corridor. He'd solemnly bowed to us and kissed my hand. "Bella ragazza," he remarked. "The way life ought to be," said Eric. I thought we might be free forever, but from what?

At the train station waiting the departure we were supposed to take for Rome, "Why do we have to go?" I pleaded. "Why can't we just stay here?"

"Use your common sense, Ella Mason."

"I don't have any."

He squeezed my shoulder. "We'll get by all right," he said. "That is, if you don't let on."

I promised not to. Rather languidly I watched the landscape slide past as we glided south. I would obey Eric, I thought, for always. "Once I wrote a love letter to you," I said. "I wrote it at night by candlelight at home one summer. I tore it up."

"You told me that," he recalled, "but you said you couldn't remember if it was to me or Ben."

"I just remembered," I said. "It was you. . . ."

"Why did we ever leave?" I asked Eric, in the dead of the night, a blackness now. "Why did we ever decide we had to go to Rome?"

"I didn't think of it as even a choice," he said. "But at that point, how could I know what was there, ahead?"

We got off the train feeling small—at least, I did. Ben was standing there, looking around him, tall, searching for us, then seeing. But no Jamie. Something to ask. I wondered if he'd gone back with Mayfred. "No, he's running around Rome." The big smooth station, echoing, open to the warm day. "Hundreds of churches," Ben went on. "Millions. He's checking them off." He helped us in a taxi with the skill of somebody who'd lived in Rome for ten years, and gave the address. "He's got to do something now that Mayfred's gone. It's getting like something he might take seriously, is all. Finding out what Catholics believe. He's either losing all his money, or falling in love, or getting religion."

"He didn't lose any money," said Eric. "He made some."

"Well, it's the same thing," said Ben, always right and not wanting to argue with us. He seemed a lot older than the two of us, at least to me. Ben was tall.

We had mail in Rome; Ben brought it to the table that night. I read Mama's aloud to them: "When I think of you children over there, I count you all like my own chickens out in the yard, thinking I've got to go out in the dark and make sure the gate's locked because not a one ought to get out of there. To me, you're all my own, and thinking of chickens is my way of saying prayers for you to be safe at home again."

"You'd think we were off in a war," said Eric.

"It's a bold metaphor," said Ben, pouring wine for us, "but that never stopped Cousin Charlotte."

I wanted to giggle at Mama, as I usually did, but instead my eyes filled with tears, surprising me, and a minute more and I would have dared to snap at Ben. But Eric, who had got some mail, too, abruptly got up and left the table. I almost ran after him, but intent on what I'd promised about not letting on to Ben, I stayed and finished dinner. He had been pale, white. Ben thought he might be sick. He didn't return. We didn't know.

Jamie and Ben finally went to bed. "He'll come back when he wants to," said Ben.

I waited till their door had closed, and then, possessed, I crept out to the front desk. "Signor Mason," I said, "the one with the capelli leggero—" My Italian came from the dictionary straight to the listener. I found out later I had said that Eric's hair didn't weigh much. Still, they understood. He had taken a room, someone who spoke English explained. He wanted to be alone. I said he might be sick, and I guess they could read my face because I was guided by a porter in a blue working jacket and cloth shoes, into a labyrinth. Italian buildings, I knew by now, are constructed like dreams. There are passages departing from central hallways, stairs that twist back upon themselves, dark silent doors. My guide stopped before one. "Ecco," he said and left. I knocked softly, and the door eventually cracked open. "Oh, it's you." "Eric. Are you all right? I didn't know. . . ."

He opened the door a little wider. "Ella Mason—" he began. Maybe he was sick. I caught his arm. The whole intensity of my young life in that moment shook free of everything but Eric. It was as though I'd traveled miles to find him. I came inside and we kissed and then I was sitting apart from him on the edge of the bed and he in a chair, and a letter, official looking, the top of the envelope torn open in a ragged line, lay on a high black-marble-topped table with bowed legs, between us. He said to read it and I did, and put it back where I found it.

It said that Eric had failed his law exams. That in view of the family connection with the university (his father had gone there and some cousin was head of the board of trustees), a special meeting had been held to grant his repeating the term's work so as to graduate in the fall, but the evidences of his negligence were too numerous and the vote had gone against it. I remember saying something like, "Anybody can fail exams—" as I knew people who had, but knew also that those people weren't "us," not one of our class or connection, not kin to the brilliant Ben, nor nephew of a governor, nor descended from a great Civil War general.

"All year long," he said, "I've been acting like a fool, as if I expected to get by. This last semester especially. It all seemed too easy. It is easy. It's easy and boring. I was fencing blindfold with somebody so far beneath me it wasn't worth the trouble to look at him. The only way to keep the interest up was to see how close I could come without damage. Well, I ran right into it, head on. God, does it serve me right. I'd read books Ben was reading, follow his interests, instead of boning over law. But I wanted the degree. Hot damn, I wanted it!"

"Another school," I said. "You can transfer credits and start over."

"This won't go away."

"Everybody loves you," I faltered, adding, "Especially me."

He almost laughed, at my youngness, I guess, but then said, "Ella Mason," as gently as feathers falling, and came to hold me a while, but not like before, the way we'd been. We sat down on the bed and then fell back on it and I could hear his heart's steady thumping under his shirt. But it wasn't the beat of a lover's heart just then; it was more like the echo of a distant bell or the near march of a clock; and I fell to looking over his shoulder.

It was a curious room, one I guess they wouldn't have rented to anybody if Rome hadn't been, as they told us, so full. The shutters were closed on something that suggested more of a courtyard than the outside as no streak or glimmer of light came through, and the bed was huge, with a great dark tall rectangle of a headboard and a footboard only slightly lower. There were brass sconces set ornamentally around the moldings, looking down, cupids and fawns and smiling goat faces, with bulbs concealed in them, though the only light came from the one dim lamp on the bedside table. There were heavy, dark engravings of

Rome—by Piranesi or somebody like that—the avenues, the monuments, the river. And one panel of small pictures in a series showed some familiar scenes in Florence.

My thoughts, unable to reach Eric's, kept wandering off tourist-fashion among the myth faces peeking from the sconces, laughing down, among the walks of Rome—the arched bridge over the Tiber where life-sized angels stood poised; the rise of the Palatine, mysterious among trees; the horseman on the Campidoglio, his hand outstretched; and Florence, beckoning still. I couldn't keep my mind at any one set with all such around me, and Eric, besides, had gone back to the table and was writing a letter on hotel stationery. When my caught breath turned to a little cry, he looked up and said, "It's my problem, Ella Mason. Just let me handle it." He came to stand by me, and pressed my head against him, then lifted my face by the chin. "Don't go talking about it. Promise." I promised.

I wandered back through the labyrinth, thinking I'd be lost in there forever like a Poe lady. Damn Ben, I thought, he's too above it all for anybody to fall in love or fail an examination. I'm better off lost, at this rate. So thinking, I turned a corner and stepped out into the hotel lobby.

It was Jamie's and Ben's assumption that Eric had picked up some girl and gone home with her. I never told them better. Let them think that.

"Your Mama wrote you a letter about some chickens once, how she counted children like counting chickens," Eric said, thirty years later. "Do you remember that?"

We fell to remembering Mama. "There's nobody like her," I said. "She has long talks with Daddy. They started a year or so after he died. I wish I could talk to him."

"What would you say?"

"I'd ask him to look up Howard. See'f he's doing all right."

"Your husband?" Eric wasn't that sure of the name.

I guess joking about your husband's death isn't quite the thing. I met Howard on a trip to Texas after we got home from abroad. I was visiting my roommate. Whatever else Eric did for me, our time together had made me ready for more. I pined for him alone, but what I looked was ripe and ready for practically anybody. So Howard said. He was a widower with a Texas-size fortune. When he said I looked like a good breeder, I didn't even get mad. That's how he knew I'd do. Still, it took a while. I kept wanting Eric, wanting my old dream: my brilliant cousins, princely, cavalier.

Howard and I had two sons, in their twenties now. Howard got killed in a jeep accident out on his cattle ranch. Don't think I didn't get married again, to a wild California boy ten years younger. It lasted six months exactly.

"What about that other one?" Eric asked me. "Number two."

I had gotten the divorce papers the same day they called to say Howard's tombstone had arrived. "Well, you know, Eric, I always was a little bit crazy."

"You thought he was cute."

"I guess so."

"You and I," said Eric, smooth as silk into the deep silent darkness that now was ours—even the towers seemed to have folded up and gone home—"we never worked it out, did we?"

"I never knew if you really wanted to. I did, God knows. I wouldn't marry Howard for over a year because of you."

"I stayed undecided about everything. One thing that's not is a marrying frame of mind."

"Then you left for Europe."

"I felt I'd missed the boat for everywhere else. War service, then that law school thing. It was too late for me. And nothing was of interest. I could move but not with much conviction. I felt for you—maybe more than you know—but you were moving on already. You know, Ella Mason, you never are still."

"But you could have told me that!"

"I think I did, one way or another. You sat still and fidgeted." He laughed.

It's true that energy is my middle name.

The lights along the river were dim and so little was moving past by now they seemed fixed and distant, stars from some long dead galaxy maybe. I think I slept. Then I heard Eric.

"I think back so often to the five of us—you and Ben, Jamie and Mayfred and me. There was something I could never get out of mind. You remember when we were planning everything about Europe Europe Europe, before we left, and you'd all come over to my house and we'd sit out on the side porch, listening to Ben mainly but with Jamie asking some questions, like, 'Do they have bathtubs like us?' Remember that? You would snuggle down in one of those canvas chairs like a sling, and Ben was in the big armchair—Daddy's—and Jamie sort of sprawled around on the couch among the travel folders, when we heard the front gate scrape on the sidewalk and heard the way it would clatter when it closed. A warm night and the streetlight filtering in patterns through the trees and shrubs and a smell of honeysuckle from where it was all baled up on the yard fence, and a cape jessamine outside, I remember that, too—white flowers in among the leaves. And steps on the walk. They stopped, then they walked again, and Ben got up (I should have) and unlatched the screen. If you didn't latch the screen it wouldn't shut. Mayfred came in. Jamie said, 'Why'd you stop on the walk, Mayfred?' She said, 'There was this toadfrog. I almost stepped on him.' Then she was among us, walking in, one of us. I was sitting back in the corner, watching, and I felt, If I live to be a thousand, I'll never feel more love than I do this minute. Love of these, my blood, and this place, here. I could close my eyes for years and hear the gate scrape, the steps pause, the door latch and unlatch, hear her say, 'There was this toadfrog. . . .' I would want literally to embrace that one minute, hold it forever."

"But you're not there," I said, into the dark: "You're here. Where we were. You chose it."

"There's no denying that," was all he answered.

We had sailed from Naples, a sad day under mist, with Vesuvius hardly visible and damp clinging to everything—the end of summer. We couldn't even make out the outlines of the ship, an Italian-line monster from those days, called the *Independence.* It towered white over us and we tunneled in. The crossing was rainy and drab. Crossed emotions played around amongst us, while Ben, noble and aware, tried to be our mast. He read aloud to us, discussed, joked, tried to get our attention.

Jamie wanted to argue about Catholicism. It didn't suit Ben for him to drift that way. Ben was headed toward Anglican belief: that's what his Sylvia was, not to mention T. S. Eliot. But Jamie had met an American Jesuit from Indiana in Rome and chummed around with him; they'd even gone to the beach. "You're wrong about that," I heard him tell Ben. "I'm going to prove it by Father Rogers when we get home."

I worried about Eric; I longed for Eric; I strolled the decks and stood by Eric at the rail. He looked with grey eyes out at the grey sea. He said: "You know, Ella Mason, I don't give a damn if Jamie joins the Catholic Church or not." "Me either," I agreed. We kissed in the dark beneath the lifeboats, and made love once in the cabin while Ben and Jamie were at the movies, but in a furtive way, as if the grown people were at church. Ben read aloud to us from a book on Hadrian's Villa where we'd all been. There was a half-day of sun.

I went to the pool to swim, and up came Jamie, out of the water. He was skinny, string beans and spaghetti. "Ella Mason," he said, in his dark croak of a voice, "I'll never be the same again." I was tired of all of them, even Jamie. "Then gain some weight," I snapped, and went pretty off the diving board.

Ben knew about the law school thing. The first day out, coming from the writing lounge, I saw Eric and Ben standing together in a corner of an enclosed deck. Ben had a letter in his hand, and just from one glance I recognized the stationery of the hotel where we'd stayed in Rome and knew it was the letter Eric had been writing. I heard Ben: "You say it's not important, but I know it is—I knew that last Christmas." And Eric, "Think what you like, it's not to me." And Ben, "What you feel about it, that's not what matters. There's a right way of looking at it. Only to make you see it." And Eric, "You'd better give up; you never will."

What kept me in my tracks was something multiple, yet single, the way a number can contain powers and elements that have gone into its making, and can be unfolded, opened up, nearly forever. Ambition and why some had it, success and failure and what the difference was, and why you had to notice it at all. These matters, back and forth across the net, were what was going on.

What had stopped me in the first place, though, and chilled me, was that they sounded angry. I knew they had quarreled last Christmas; was this why? It must have been. Ben's anger was attack and Eric's self-defense, defiance. Hadn't they always been like brothers? Yes, and they were standing so, intent, a little apart, in hot debate, like two officers locked in different plans of attack at dawn, stubbornly held to the point of fury. Ben's position, based on rightness, classical and firm. Enforced by what he was. And Eric's wrong, except in and for himself, for holding on to himself. How to defend that? He couldn't, but he did. And equally. They were just looking up and seeing me, and nervous at my intrusion I stepped across the high shipboard sill to the deck, missed clearing it and fell sprawling. "Oh, Ella Mason!" they cried at once and picked me up, the way they always had.

One more thing I remember from that ship. It was Ben, finding me one night after dinner alone in the lounge. Everyone was below: we were docking in the morning. He sat down and lighted his pipe. "It's all passed so fast, don't you think?" he said. There was such a jumble in my mind still, I didn't answer. All I could hear was Eric saying, after we'd made love: "It's got to stop now; I've got to find some shape to things. There was promise, promises. You've got to see we're saying they're worthless, that nothing matters." What did matter to me, except Eric? "I wish I'd never come," I burst out at Ben, childish, hurting him, I guess. How much did Ben know? He never said. He came close and put his arm around me. "You're the sister I never had," he said. "I hope you change your mind about it." I said I was sorry and snuffled a while, into his shoulder. When I looked up, I saw his love. So maybe he did know, and forgave us. He kissed my forehead.

At the New York pier, who should show up but Mayfred.

She was crisp in black and white, her long blonde hair wind-shaken, her laughter a wholesome joy. "Y'all look just terrible," she told us with a friendly giggle, and as usual made us straighten up, tuck our tummies in and look like quality. Jamie forgot religion, and Eric quit worrying over a missing bag, and Ben said, "Well, look who's here!" "How's Donald?" I asked her. I figured he was either all right or dead. The first was true. They didn't have to do a brain tumor operation; all he'd had was a pinched nerve at the base of his cortex. "What's a cortex?" Jamie asked. "It sounds too personal to inquire," said Eric, and right then they brought him his bag.

On the train home, Mayfred rode backwards in our large drawing room compartment (courtesy of Donald Bailey) and the landscape, getting more southern every minute, went rocketing past. "You can't guess how I spent my time when Donald was in the hospital. Nothing to do but sit."

"Working crossword puzzles," said Jamie.

"Crocheting," said Eric, provoking a laugh.

"Reading *Vogue,*" said Ben.

"All wrong! I read Edgar Allan Poe! What's more, I memorized that poem! That one Ben wrote on. You know? That 'Ulalume'!"

Everybody laughed but Ben, and Mayfred was laughing, too, her grand girlish sputters, innocent as sun and water, her beautiful large white teeth, even as a cover girl's. Ben, courteously at the end of the sofa, smiled faintly. It was best not to believe this was true.

" 'The skies they were ashen and sober;
    The leaves they were crisped and sere—
    The leaves they were withering and were:
It was the night in the lonesome October
    Of my most immemorial year. . . .' "

"By God, she's done it," said Ben.

At that point Jamie and I began to laugh, and Eric, who had at first looked quizzical, started laughing, too. Ben said, "Oh, cut it out, Mayfred," but she said, "No, sir, I'm not! I *did* all that. I know *every* word! Just wait, I'll show you." She went right on, full speed, to the "ghoul-haunted woodland of Weir."

Back as straight as a ramrod, Ben left the compartment. Mayfred stopped. An hour later, when he came back, she started again. But it wasn't till she got to Psyche "uplifting her finger" (Mayfred lifted hers) saying, "Ah, fly!—let us fly!—for we must," and all that about the "tremulous light, the crystalline light," etc., that Ben gave up and joined in the general merriment. She actually did know it, every word. He followed along open-mouthed through "Astarte" and "Sybillic," and murmured, "Oh, my God" when she got to

> " 'Ulalume—Ulalume—
> 'Tis the vault of thy lost Ulalume!' "

because she let go in a wail like a hound's bugle and the conductor, who was passing, looked in to see if we were all right.

We rolled into Chattanooga in the best of humor and filed off the train into the waiting arms of my parents, Eric's parents, and selected members from Ben's and Jamie's families. There was nobody from Mayfred's, but they'd sent word. They all kept checking us over, as though we might need washing, or might have gotten scarred some way. "Just promise me one thing!" Mama kept saying, just about to cry. "Don't y'all ever go away again, you hear? Not all of you! Just promise you won't do it! Promise me right now!"

I guess we must have promised, the way she was begging us to.

Ben married his Sylvia, with her pedigree and family estate in Connecticut. He's a big professor, lecturing in literature, up East. Jamie married a Catholic girl from West Virginia. He works in her father's firm and has sired a happy lot of kids. Mayfred went to New York after she left Donald and works for a big fashion house. She's been in and out of marriages, from time to time.

And Eric and I are sitting holding hands on a terrace in far off Italy. Midnight struck long ago, and we know it. We are sitting there, talking, in the pitch black dark.

THE YEAR OF THE HOT JOCK

IRVIN FAUST

Irvin Faust is the author of six novels, and two short story collections. He has a master's and doctorate degree from Columbia Teachers College. This is his second appearance in the O. Henry collections. He was born in Brooklyn, New York. "Hot Jock" is the title story of his latest book.

Had a great day. Four-bagger at Aqueduct. Tenth time in my career. Almost nailed two more. Lost one on photo, lost one on bob of the nose. They say you can't win them all. Who are they? I say why not? On way home bought Ramona fur wrap, Olga bracelet, Lorenzo Walkman . . .

Inform them as watch me kick in fourth winner have to ride Stir Krazy Hialeah. In Bougainvillea, Jan. 30. Ramona responds with her mourning face, kids understand 100%. Learn a lot from kids. But what can she say after fur wrap? Not much.

Catch 8 A.M. La Guardia. Have to rescue Jeff Kahn Hialeah. Tough but fair trainer who got a bad trip from Ben Gotch last time out. Jock can lose for Jeff, but must lose good. Can always win bad, but better lose good.

Eastern pilot comes through with real nice trip. Relax with *Racing Form,* beats mysteries, plus learn something. Know it all, but always learning. An extra. Full of extras. Over Delaware notice blonde next seat peeking over. Not unusual. Over Virginia give her a break. Pardon me, you into horses? Oh yes, she's into horses. Loves the gorgeous creatures. Gorgeous but dumb as shit; don't tell her that. Agree, some lovely animals. Likes words like lovely from a man. Sensitive. Terrific parlay, strength and sensitive. She just knows has seen me somewhere, maybe Gulfstream, Calder, Belmont. Well, guess you have, happen to be Pablo Dega. Have to slip that in fast, they can't tell us apart—Hernandez, Cordero, Santiago, Dega. Rings a great bell, she saw me win Woodward Belmont, beautiful race. Can't argue, I stole it.

When she gets up to go to john see she goes easy five-nine and velvety all over. Not young, but fine condition. When returns tell her contact me Fontainebleau if care for a box for Bougainvillea, very decent race. Expect to do rather well. Modest. Goes with sensitive. Gives me soft, velvet look, just might take you up on that. Forget it, she's hooked.

Jeff meets plane, very jumpy, hustles me out to track. Stir Krazy still a nut job, been that way since he hit the ground, but can run like Slew on uppers when in the mood. That's his problem, mood. Take him for a ride and croon Spanish lullaby and he gentles right down. Remember that from two years ago Turf Paradise. Another extra. Inform Jeff his horse will be fine, he sighs, calms right down. Have to play trainers like horses.

Check into Fontainebleau. They go into their act. Yes, Mr. Dega, of course not, Mr. Dega, anything else, Mr. Dega? All bullshit, but love it. Earned every bob of the head, every open door, paid some heavy dues. No brothers, uncles in the business like Jeff. Thirteen years ago. Thirteen. Just another dark monkey-on-a-stick. Toss a whip, hit ten of us. Hole up on a straw mattress in grooms' quarters. Live on white bread and OJ. Whothehell is this kid Dega? Eighty million in purses later, Jock of the Year, a Wood, a Woodward, a Travers, a Preakness, ho hum, maybe they know who is Dega, yes?

Hit the big round bed for two hours. Action, rest, action, rest, law of nature. Phone. Bounce up, walk slow, one guess. Helena Stadler, velvet blonde from plane. Accept your generous offer. Smile at phone, my pleasure, *hasta la vista.* Little Spanish, not too much. Call Jeff. Set her up in owner's box, he's fishing for tuna off Lauderdale. Jeff: Pablo, please don't screw around till after the race. Relax, Mr. Kahn, I know my priorities. Can hear his sigh, he loves those words.

Call down to room service. Order filet mignon, baked potato, the works. Tip kid ten, autograph menu for him. Eat very careful, very slow. Then very careful, very slow, walk to john, flip up whole goddam thing. Ah, still got it. Sensational will power. You got that, you got it all. Providing God bless you with hands of steel, a brain, fantastic ability. Thank you, God. Gargle Listerine.

Call Miami Motors, order Mercedes. Tip kid fifty. Drive slow and easy through city to track. Cuba all the way. Ten years ago. Green kid on the move. Win the Flamingo, meet Ramona. Sixteen years old and don't know a horse from a chicken. But busting out all over. And backside never stops flicking at me. And same size. Five and change. Don't realize can handle tall stuff till I win Preakness three years later.

Don't count. Did her number on me. But give her this: Ramona very religious. Oh yes. Gives me many glimpses heaven, but won't open gates till she gets me in church . . .

Hialeah not what it used to be, what is? But still lakes and thick grass and sensational birds. They don't know racing, but great for tourists. Walk into jocks' quarters, hand out friendly hellos. They interrupt their ping pong and poker, mumble hello, track me around the room the way I used to watch Hartack and Baeza. Love it.

Walk out to Mr. Gracklin's box. Owner Stir Krazy, poor bastard. Poor rich bastard. Delighted I'm here. Me too, Mr. Gracklin. Mean it. He likes Spanish jocks. Well, he likes winners.

Next day Jan. 30. Come into feature after riding fourth, sixth race. Win fourth from here to West Palm, nice price. Finish third in sixth on nag who chucks it final 16th. Off at 2–1 and crowd blames me, but Jeff don't. Knows this horse hates to win, professional runner-up. But hope springs eternal, especially when the trainer got Dega.

Check certain box. Yes, she's there. In large floppy hat, with guy: chestnut tan, wearing cabana shirt. Back to priorities.

Bougainvillea goes nine and half furlongs. Mile and then some. Krazy got sire to go distance, but mother a nut. Up to Dega, wipe her out of his head. Jeff talks, I listen. Always follow orders 100%. Not my fault if orders are rotten. He tells me take Krazy back and keep him sane. Move off final turn. These orders very okay.

Do just that. Hold him easy but firm. He behaves, knows he can trust me. Come off turn, show him the whip, only show. The saved-up power switches on. He fires whooooosh. I hand-ride him in by length and a half. Have worked harder in sweat box. Good ones alway make it look easy. Flip my stick to grinning groom, hop down, pose in winner's circle with Jeff, Mr. Gracklin. As I turn toward jocks' room he slips me a crisp grand.

Change, take my sweet time. Walk out to Mercedes. Note on wiper with Helena Stadler's number. Take some more time, then call. Drive slow, careful, wind up party in Boca. Sweet little condo, part of her divorce deal. She introduces me all around, they eat me up. Few won bundle on me. Circulate. Polite. When asked for tip, say Pleasant Colony sure thing to win Derby. Always big hit, plus message: Don't pump Dega.

Crowd thins out around 3:30. At 4:20 just me and the tanned guy from box left. He's watching TV as Helena and prime guest go upstairs. She informs me her first time with a jock, but says believes in variety of experience. Can't argue with that. She likes to play horsey.

Nothing very new there. Up and out at 6:37. Quiet, tan guy shakes my hand, wishes me luck. Not a bad guy but leads a strange life. Watching TV as I walk out to catch 8 A.M. back to NY. After action, sleep. All the way.

Ramona has to greet me with problems. Don't even ask did I come out of race sound? Always check the horse, why not a top jock? Okay, now what? Lorenzo and Olga. Fresh mouths, get off their case. Just log three thousand miles, ride my ass off, make two grand plus, and this my reward. Tell her, politely, kids are her department. Informs me, not so politely, they're 50% mine. Bite my tongue; Panama woman never give me that routine. Ramona's family skipped out of Cuba one length ahead of Castro. She didn't have a pot to sit on till she nailed King Pablo. Now she gives me long division. Thank you, Fidel.

Lecture kids in English. Strictly English. Tell them I do it all for them, expect loyalty in return. If mother sometimes don't make sense, nobody is perfect. Ground them both two weeks. Tears could fill up Atlantic Ocean. Make it one week.

Steaming so hard, go out next day and ride three winners Aqueduct. In rain, cold, mud. Work through five pairs of goggles in sixth. Feel human again. On way home, order moped for Lorenzo, 8-inch color TV for Olga.

Now my agent. Hy Platkin. Complains I don't consult enough on big races. Just a phone call, catching a plane, seeya. Whole world complains and all I do is make them money. But explain, politely, Jeff Kahn in tough spot and I always bail out old friends. Anyhow, won and we both make out okay. Hy not the hustler he once was, but he spotted Dega, so he don't have to be. Earned him 200 big ones last year. But Pablo Dega is a U.S. Marine—always faithful. Remind him. Hy relaxes, lights up. How about I go back down to Florida Feb. 13 for Donn Handicap Gulfstream? Can get me on that nice 3-year-old colt, Wineglo. He's a good one, Hy. You telling me? And Lester Pawkins wants you, Paul. Lovely old man. Spotted me Government Riding School Panama. Liked my hands, head, way I sat a horse. My style. Even then, the Dega style. Brought me to Florida, rest is history.

I'm a Marine elephant, always faithful and never forget. You got it, Hy. Tell Mr. Pawkins Pablo Dega ride for him on the moon. Hy pats my face, father never did that once, walks off to do some relaxed hustling.

Ride splendid into February Big A. Shooting for eleven million this year, off to big start. Freeze nuts off, so what? Maybe the hot shot bug boys learn a lesson when they see Dega pound through snow, rain, mud, come back for more. Maybe they learn; don't bet your eating money.

Day before Donn Handicap call school, tell them, politely, Lorenzo has virus, take him with me to airport. Begs me go to Florida, never saw me ride there. True. Doing nothing important in school. Wellll. Write a composition, My Father and Me and a Horse. Done.

We fly first class, behave myself entire trip. Got my kid with me. Land and call Ramona first thing. Screams so loud, phone jumps. Are you *crazy?* Beautiful trip. *Crazy.* Thought I'd take him off your hands few days; should learn the business. Screaming louder now, people looking: he's going to college, he don't need your business. Stay calm, not easy: I didn't go to college and I can buy one or two, don't worry, I called his school. She hangs up. Can you make them happy?

Rent new Imperial at airport and drive to Gulfstream. Love me in Gulfstream. Introduce big-eyed Lorenzo all around and ask assistant trainer Karl Witkin keep an eye on kid, show him a thing or two while I take care of business. Sure, Pablo. They take off around backstretch, kid seventh heaven. Get this at Harvard?

Mr. Pawkins getting on and takes my arm as we walk down shed row, talk about old, happy days. Had a Derby winner hundred years ago; Pablo, one more classic winner and I die happy.

Maybe it's Wineglo. Maybe. Long, long way to paydirt. But Mr. Pawkins a pro. He discovered me. Look his baby over. Smallish colt. Chestnut. Pretty blaze. *Very* well formed, tight, front legs out of same hole. Mr. P. says he runs with his head down, like he's looking for uncashed tickets. Love that. Give me those low runners, they mean business. Can't stand a high head, run like trotters. Abnormal. Decent but not great sire and dam. He's a maybe, nice maybe, but maybe. Get acquainted. Say this, a real gentleman. Could mean something. Or nothing. Will meet some older horses in Donn. Learn something. Maybe. Trainer Tim Seelen. Gives me polite hello. Wanted someone like Fell or even Shoe. But Mr. Pawkins one owner who says this, not that, you do this. So from Tim polite hello.

Pick up Lorenzo, still sky-high, drive to hotel Hallendale, check in, make him take hot bath calm down, feed him first class. Never make it as jock, too many vitamins, maybe a trainer. Or first dark president NY Racing Assoc. Tuck him in, click TV. Be back soon, sonny, have to talk strategy with Mr. Pawkins and Tim. Eyes tiny slits as I tiptoe out.

Saddle up, point Imperial at Bal Harbor. Twenty minutes later relaxing 110th Street, thirty-fifth-floor condo overlooking smooth, calm ocean. With Ginny Gottlieb. Who listens to all my sadness and does nothing but nod her head and keep quiet. Whips up neat, nutritious salad. Then takes care of *me.*

Get back to hotel 3 A.M. Lorenzo in dreamland with late late show. Turn it down but not off, likes a voice in his room. Catch five hours real sleep. If felt better, I'd see a doctor.

Next day just ride feature. Set kid up with Mr. Pawkins. Instant hit. His grandchildren spoiled rotten. Check in and change. Silks orange and black, colors Princeton College. Left after two years to enter real world, but still loyal. Respect that, common bond. And college didn't hurt him. Report to Tim in paddock. He talks fast but good. Wants a wire job. Nod. Have very respectful nod. Paddock judge gives us Riders up! Best two words English language. Step out to post parade, back to gate.

Give Tim his wire job, win by a neck. Hold him on rail entire trip. Rail golden. Like inside my head. Tim can't play with that. Only Dega can.

Lorenzo jumping out of pants next to me winner's circle, along with Mr. P. and Tim. Very good thing kid see his father a hero. Make sure never be a faggot. My case, had uncles who stepped in. Had to. My old man hardly ever home. Worked all the time. Shoe factory Balboa. When he got home, never talked. Not a bad man, just tired. And no hero. Didn't even argue when Mr. Pawkins wanted me to go to States. Should have. Then give in. Silence. Now they own the canal.

Ginny waves to me from her box. Back in hotel, bouquet of flowers. Someone giving *me* something. Two-day vacation. Catch plane back to NY. Beautiful sleep. Get home and Lorenzo can't stop talking. Olga can't stop crying. Why does he go and I stay? That's the way it is. But *why?* Kids born that word in their mouth. From Romana finally get something. Closed gates.

Terrific week. Typical. Fifteen winners 6 days. Buy Ramona Zuni necklace for 3 thou. Loves that Indian stuff, makes her feel like a princess. Loosens her up for her prince. Pablo, the Prince of Great Neck. Peace.

Hy gets me on Sugar Blue for Barbara Fritchie Bowie last week February. Grade III Stake but worth a hundred bigs. Sugar supposed to be best filly since Risk. But just like Ramona, blows hot and cold. Run out of your picture one race, act like having her period the next. Trainer Abe Pilky. Talks with marbles in mouth, but I understand him.

Thinks change of jocks could help. Might have a point. Red-haired stewardess checks me out, but don't blink; too short. Some trip, take off, fire, land, wham.

Out at track meet Abe and darling Sugar. One look, all I need. Hates people. You can change jocks, can't change their heads. Don't tell Abe. He jabbers, I nod. Adds up to, don't let her loaf; if have to, kick the shit out of her. Sugar looks at me, I look at her. Sure.

Dwells at gate. Studying the crowd. Finally consents to run. Work her like crazy, finally in gear after first half. Switch hit her entire final eighth, get her up to 3rd. Far as she'll go, that's it. Miracle get show money. Crowd gets on jock, what else is new? Abe disappointed, but says maybe we get em next time. Next time he tries Migliore or Cordero. Good luck baby.

Fly away home. Ramona extremely considerate. Likes it when I lose now and then. Long as I'm in the money. Cooks up tremendous Cuban dinner, paella, beans, the works. Tell her she knows I can't eat fat. Answers can't kill you once in a while. It can, but don't want jeers or tears. Shovel it in. Don't even flip. Sweat box, here I come. What I do for peace. Pope Pablo . . .

Mar. 6 and we drive to Keystone in my green Mercedes, green for all my lettuce, me and Hy. Hit seventy on Jersey Turnpike, could hit a hundred. Easy. If not Paul the Great might settle for Richard Petty, racing is racing, except on four wheels it's snow white. Maybe buy way in when retire, $ make me Pale the Great . . .

At Keystone win 50 thou Cotillion on big ugly filly, Outamyway, so easy almost boring except a win and nice $ always interesting. Tap her just once, wave stick like it's sugar cane. She fires like a moon shot, bye bye baby.

On way back stop off Atlantic City, blow fifteen hundred, easy come, so on, so forth. But find a cushion. Connect with waitress who has so much might be illegal. Goes six-one easy, amaze her with speed and power in compact package, by time I leave has dropped "cute" routine which I hate, so pretty fair night after all. Hymie drives us home while I curl up in back and sleep like brand new foal . . .

Pick up Big A where I left off, but hit a snag, or envy, or both. Set down Mar. 10 for tough but 100% honest ride against new bug boy, everybody's darling. Never protect me like that when I come up, now they stand on head to protect every new hot shot, even Spanish, *especially* Spanish. Dear Public, no prejudice here.

Sit around for entire week, nothing to do except work some horses, listen to Ramona and kids on phone. Plus stuff face and go nuts. Get so crazy absolutely necessary get some relief. Not what you think, I *do* have other outlets. Drive into Manhattan, 114th Street, Third Avenue, residence of best and oldest friend in U.S.A. Rafael Laguna. Who came to states together with yrs truly way back when, is true blue while I am likewise ditto. Rafael the greatest shortstop in Panama, hell, all Central America, even at five-three, another Freddie Patek, better glove. Reached top minors, up to Oneonta, that's it. Couldn't hit change-up, fastball. Not even satin glove carry that, or great arm. One summer, whoosh, down and so long *béisbol*, you no so good to him. But Happiness Inc. Blows all his money on horses, never complains, always smiling, ballplayer's beerbelly. Maybe knows something I don't know . . . ?

Sit in his flaking, secondhand kitchen while his latest woman who could use the sweat box sits inside and jumps when he says jump. Breaks out some real beer, the light stuff makes him sick. I relax first time all week, Rafael never even asks for a tip, that's friendship baby. Ramona can't stand him, real plus for Rafael. She says he got eyes for her. Have told her a hundred times she's nuts, watches too much "General Hospital" where everybody screwing everybody. She tells me she knows men's eyes. Tell her that's all she better know or she's a dead Cuban, but she's dreaming. Dreams okay long as she don't wake up and perform. Anyway Rafael likes them fat and sloppy and accommodating. Ramona just make one out of three: fat. Beautiful evening, beer and old times. Can't sit still in Great Neck, loose as a goose el Barrio. Figure that out, I write a book . . .

Get home very late, tell her had to work out Jack La Lanne's. Pablo Dega got more stories than loser at track. But idea always makes sense. Like this one. Next day hit sweat box for three hours, hit it every day left in suspension. Cut down to 113, not great but ride better at 113 than Joe Blow at 90. First day back got head of steam like horse coming into Derby. Win four, in money five, give you a piece of something every race if you play jocks. Hot jocks. Hot *jock.* Crowd even applauds on fourth winner, 12–1 shot. Don't mean a thing, crowd applaud Hitler he kicks in 12–1 shot.

Pablo the Great is back, life is life again. Trainers get on line. Hymie's phone rings more than Olga's. Consults me, he better. Pick and choose, get some nice horses, make them nicer. Some nice races, especially one. Dominion Day, Woodbine, north of the border, 75 thou, Mar. 20. Connections get screwed up, so fly Toronto same morning, check in with Rip Kelly who almost has heart attack thinking I won't show. Buy him drink at airport, another on the way, talk low and calm and tell him all about his horse: gelding, Bay Rummy, old friend, rode him Laurel as a four-year-old, Rip leans back, sighs. Sits up, says he's six now, then was then, now is now. Does he still run like he's chasing his *cojones?* Sits back, I know his horse . . .

Race goes distance of ground, mile and an eighth. Take firm hold, he's strong as Tarzan, shoulders ache like bad tooth, but strategy works. Two apprentices kill each other off while we lay fifth, off final turn old pro goes wide, circles field, we win by one. Rip says I'm the best, I say one of the best, he says the best. Don't argue.

Before dinner call Ramona, tell her catch me 11 o'clock news, answers sure and lets kids stay up. So amazed go out and buy her Zuni bracelet. Then celebrate with Shana O'Toole, hostess in hotel restaurant, we go back five Dominion Days, terrific hostess.

Fly home 6 A.M. Presents for everybody.

I'm a bitch April. Recapture $ lead Aqueduct, number 3 in wins. Redhot bug boy number 1, they ride every race, weight allowance, so why not? However, develop certain problem, although real nice one: Which of two Derby horses gets Dega? Offered Wineglo by Mr. Pawkins and Scoliosis, California horse. Loyal Mr. P., but his little nag loves germs and accidents, catches this, steps on that. If superstitious (I'm not), say evil eye got him. Out on coast, Scoliosis going great this year, big, healthy, solid, excellent paper, daddy won Arlington Classic, mama daughter Preakness winner. Trainer Arnold Lewisohn, smart man, likes strong jock on strong horse, guess who? Tell Hy. Rocks on eight-hundred-dollar Tony Lama boots, okay boss, damn right okay. Call down to Mr. Pawkins, break tough news, takes it like real thoroughbred, good luck Pablo. Almost change mind, don't, once I move, I move. Tell Ramona it's California. Sigh. After ninth race Aqueduct call Brenda Burlington, English actress hooked on horses and dark, strong jocks. Jock. California, here he comes.

April 10. Santa Anita Derby mile and an eighth. Scoliosis rank in paddock. Determined show NY star who's boss. Hates gate, almost kicks it to Catalina, hands almost raw meat by time we break. Get off dead last, bust behind to crank him up, finally fires and we close to 2nd. Winner Fat Bat, another Derby hopeful. His jock Cal Jones, King of the Koast. Swivels head at wire, informs me this ain't your turf, *señor.* Give me another 16th, even with this bad actor and I show him whose turf it is. Don't say a word. Crowd takes care of that. *Two* words: you bum.

We got trouble, Arnold and me. Scoliosis starts limping on way back to barn. Big healthy brute looks at me like I did it. Arnold not so happy either, avoids my eyes, tells press we'll know story tomorrow. Reporters look at me: Thanks a lot, New York. Smile, look back, drop dead.

Change, meet Brenda Burlington our private spot, drive out Holmby Hills her BMW. Still not talking, losing hurts, losing on favorite kills me, my horse comes up lame, kills me dead. Brenda real track fan, understands. Lot like Ginny, only bigger. Says very quiet, you gave him a great trip, big bum lucky to get place money. By time we reach her house, almost smiling, checking out Technicolor profile.

Small party that night, intimate, exclusive, suntans, penny loafers, dresses down to the south pole. Producers, few directors, some movie stars who'd love to be in real life, never make it. Loosen up on coke, sound like horses blowing out, only blow in. One of them in a custom shirt and new nose challenges me to hand wrestle. Pin pathetic bastard five seconds, toss him in pool. Loves it, toss him in six times. Smash hit, they all love it. Line up, toss them all in, keep on tossing, can't get enough, me, me, me. Pissing in their custom jeans, still me, me, happy to oblige, work off loss and limpy Scoliosis, one terrific bitch. Toss for two hours till Brenda blows cop's whistle, yells CUT. Beg, plead, Brenda one tough limey, cut and out, the man is tired, he ran a big race today. Shake my hand, file out, wet but happy, two girls slip me phone numbers, I play dumb, Brenda watching, one jealous star, don't screw with her man.

Alone beside pool, like to tell me something. In that Brit voice, soft, cool, opposite Ramona, tells me only man she knows a bitch without coke or ludes. Inform her losing does that, she says fine, take out frustration on Great Britain, we have no business in Malvinas anyway. Don't give a shit about Malvinas, don't say so, she can have them, but take care of frustration, God Save the Queen, wind up in pool, playing sea horsey. Win that one.

Next morning send her to studio happy, borrow third or fourth car, report to track. Should have known, Scoliosis bowed tendon, most likely out of Derby. Give him best dirty look, walk away, call Hy, tell him. He has great news, Wineglo training splendid, entered Bluegrass Keeneland, prepping for Derby. All I need. Big, tough nag breaks down, tender lambchop breezes, call Brenda, California there he goes.

Catch plane to NY, watch movie starring first guy tossed in pool.

Private eye, hardest bitch LA, three gorgeous women. Only real laugh whole goddam trip.

Home sweet home, Ramona into number, strokes me for losing, real pal, so nice want to belt her. Starts cooking like back in Havana. Ask her if trying to kill golden goose, answers have to keep strength up, answer back feed that BS to brother Carlos, biggest leech U.S.A. Snaps at me, always pick on brother, can't help if got bad back. Got bad head, Ramona, bang, off to races. Much better, she winds up crying, kids watching show, love our fights. Tell them do some goddam homework, they grin each other, walk upstairs. Take firm hold of self, tell her okay, turn off waterfall, let's go out. Jump into Mercedes, drive to Miracle Mile, Manhasset, spend fortune, ten dresses, shoes, underwear, Navajo necklace, smiling like Carlos when slip him two hundred. That mile some miracle. Drive home, make her doubly happy, make that the triple. More f'ing this weekend than Secretariat with full stud book.

Back in saddle Aqueduct, win long, win short, win. Pass two million mark, but still not happy, still don't have Derby horse, start to get that sinking heart never get one. Hy lands Northern Dancer nag for Wood, Stickum, real disappointment till now. Trainer, owner figure Dega magic turn him around. Forget to inform Stickum. In contention to head of stretch, flat tire, says hell with this, dead last. Dega players deliver expert opinion. Dega delivers back. Picked up TV, every smartass every channel delivers lecture on obligation to public. Deliver back in interview, papers love it, back-page headlines. Hy says please shut flapping face, tell him f you too, head for sweat box, Rafael . . .

Just as feared, knew, Wineglo wins Bluegrass. By two and a half, no contest. Goes to Derby favorite, Ben Gotch up. Fat Bat, Cal Jones up, second choice, almost g.d. conspiracy. Scoliosis back home, so is Dega. Okay, ride like hell, win, so long Kentucky, see you next year. Hy forgives me, says great adjustment kid, he's right, and so get my reward, must be moral there: just as accept fate, terrific news—Wineglo blows Derby! Correction, Ben Gotch blows it, horrible trip. 17th heaven. Not even in money, 18th heaven. Fat Bat wins it, and if can't take Cal Jones, still makes my day. Hy jumping out of Polo suit: Call Lester Pawkins, inform him available, tell him no way. Mr. P. class act, loyal even to lousy jock, sit tight, trainers different story. Nursed on mustard, especially Tim Seelen, just hang around phone . . .

Call comes in three days. No way it won't. Tim first, then Mr. Pawkins. Would I take Wineglo for Preakness? Smile into phone, take sweet time. Do it for you, Mr. Pawkins. Hy watching, listening, shaking head. Pablo, you taught me something. He's right, buy him dinner.

Fly down Baltimore. Mr. Pawkins sees me, sheds ten years. Even Tim almost human. Wineglo Wineglo. If had wings be angel. In spite of bad trip, came out of Derby sound and happy. Gallop him on Thursday, sing pretty, but let him know boss is back. Gets message, runs like oiled satin. Inform Mr. Pawkins he's ready, I'm ready, both ready. Takes off another five years. Lovely man. Call Laurie Willston Silver Spring, tell her buy some champagne, *Piper,* keep ready, man is back. Drive to motel, need quiet night.

Walk into lobby, fatguy jumps up, surprise, surprise. Rafael. Whathehell you doing here? Wishing my old friend *buena fortuna.* Thank you Rafe, but no beer tonight, need my beauty rest. Sure, sure, shakes my hand, says go get em tiger, turns, turns back, oh you got a minute? Okay yeah a minute, only a minute, but no beer. Grin, promise kid.

Walk to room, sit, he don't look so good, face red and blotchy, maybe switched to cheap wine, reach for wallet, peel off hundred, hold it out. Shakes his head. Go on, take it, Wineglo win it easy, gift to old supportive friend. Hy likes that word, supportive. Keeps on shaking his head, have to admit pleased, dumb proud bastard.

Listen, he says fast and jerky, don't win.

Stare, open mouth, close, open. Did I hear what I heard?

Don't win, Paul.

Face goes hot, keep voice down. Soft, low: This horse can't miss, Rafe.

Eyes stop shifting gears, voice levels off. You got the hands, Paulie, you can do it.

Don't answer, not yet, maybe he exits while he can. Sits there, not going anywhere. Hy once told me: In this world anything can happen. Think of that, finally say it: Rafael, you asking me to pull my horse?

I'm asking you not to kill him to win.

You asking me to pull him?

Don't be so damn technical.

I like to be technical. Are you?

Okay, if you wanna put it that way, okay yes.

Oh Jesus, Rafe, ohjesuschrist.

Get up, turn on TV. Stare at picture, picture stares back, turn it off. Look at my old friend. Who's into you, Rafe?

Never mind that.

You dumb sonuvabitch, you ask *me* to pull and tell me not to mind who's pulling *you?*

Yeah, that's what I'm tellin you. Listen, Pablo, I got a chance to make a big score, pick up my broad and move to Connecticut.

What's wrong with 114th Street?

Ah Paulie, don't give me that shit, not the kid from Great Neck.

Can't believe this, can't believe this . . .

You'll do it, won't you kid?

Do not believe this . . .

Believe it baby.

Look at my old friend who hates el Barrio. How much they dangle?

You mean how much is my score?

Yes.

You come in second, I collect 40 big ones.

And they make 10 million, you dumb sonuvabitch.

Shrug. That's their lookout, I get mine.

You sure?

I'm sure.

How hard they leaning, Rafe?

I tolyou, never mind that, it's a free country, I'm doin it on my own free will.

Very democratic.

That's right, Pablo. Hundred grand for you kid.

Stare at blank TV. Don't look, but tell him, I didn't hear you, Rafe. He says, we go back a long ways baby. I didn't hear you, go back to New York, tell your boys I'm stupid, tell them Mr. Pawkins my illegitimate father and can't screw him, tell them anything, but get the hell out of here.

Gets up, very calm, very cool, very collected, holds out hand. I shake my head. Says sure Pablo, anything you want babe, shrugs, walks out.

Do thousand goddam push-ups before get some goddam sleep.

Preakness. Wineglo ready, Dega ready, odds ready, 2–1 along with Fat Bat. Outside hole, Fat Bat inside. Break good, Bat breaks great, zooms to three-length lead, holds most of it to head of stretch. Show Wineglo whip, grunt. He fires, pulls Bat back. Tough, so is Cal Jones, whacking his horse like hates him. Slow, sure, comes back, tail, withers, head, we're Affirmed and Alydar. Head to head, nose to nose, the wire. Wineglo turns into Alydar, we lose by that nose.

Mr. Pawkins real pro, ran a fine race Pablo, don't blame yourself.

Never blame myself, but fact is fact, we lose. Expect worst from Tim, but must have got his orders from boss: Nice race, Paul, horse came out of it sound, we go for Belmont. Shake Cal Jones' hand, ran great, he did, but we'll be back, maybe different ending. Be my guest, he says, love those comebacks; he can't say thank you?

Call Laurie Willston, tell her forget champagne, sorry can't make it, see you next year, hang up, get into car, drive back motel, check out fast, catch shuttle NY, take taxi to 114th and Third.

Rafael happy as baby colt discovering legs, acts like just made Yankees. Belly out to here. Gives me his special friend hug, says I knew you'd do it baby.

I didn't do a thing, my horse lost.

Sure Paulie . . . Breaks out some Molson, his happy beer. Tell him not drinking tonight.

Okay. Pulls cigar box out of table drawer, opens it, bills with rubber bands, lousy private eye movie. For you, Paulie.

Shove it, Rafael.

Smiles, nods, slips box into drawer, glances into bedroom, his woman watching TV, slugs some beer.

One more time, he says; my old best friend.

The Belmont?

You got it, another 100 g's for Dega.

And 40 for you?

Hey 45 baby.

Asshole, get out *now,* Rafe.

Why?

Don't you *comprende*—understand—*any*thing? I should have turned you in for the Preakness.

Sure, just do it natural, last one was perfect.

Spin so fast get dizzy, slam out, walk downtown, through park, beg somebody try number on me, break his back, one cat approaches near Central Park West, stops, examines, walks past whistling. Get home 3 A.M. Ramona waiting up. Tell her gethehell to bed *now,* don't say a goddam thing about losing. About face, upstairs, not one word. Sit in kitchen till dawn over Great Neck. Finally get up, walk to john. Take one of her goddam sleeping pills.

Aqueduct winds up, move over Belmont. Head crazy, body sane, keep winning, nothing stops that, nothing. But head keeps working, says same thing, over, over, over: Friend does this to me, friend, *best* friend, to me, to me . . . Think I go nuts if think it one more time, think it one more time, therefore must make move, if Dega goes nuts, no longer Dega. Impossible idea.

Go to stewards. Don't mention Preakness, lay out entire Belmont deal. They take it in. Pros. Solemn, sit chilly, Oh Rafe why you ever mess with these boys? Thank you very much Pablo, we'll handle it, that's all, that's enough. Go out and win three.

Story breaks next day, no chance it won't, this not the minors, this the big time baby. Plainclothes boys move in 114th and Third, knock nice and polite, then kick door in, every piece ready. Nobody but his woman. Mr. Laguna? Don't see him all week. Care if we look around? Why I care? They look, tear it apart, put it back together, he's gone all right. Plainclothes boys walk the neighborhood, very proper, very polite. Everybody clams, but they pick up a word here, a look there, bye-bye baby.

Catch up with him Oneonta, his Triple A moment of glory. Picture in cuffs hits every paper NY State. Ramona cloud nine. Knew he was good-for-nothing, saw it in his eyes. Tell her do not want to discuss it, now, *ever.* Okay, still no-good bum.

No-good bum don't give them a thing. Says took a chance and lost, story of every gambler. Correction, says one thing: should have known Pablo Dega 100% honest man. No-good bum don't say a word about Preakness, if he does I'm dead, even though turned it down, must report every nibble. Only talks Belmont, this n-g bum, don't even hint who's into him. Maybe they hit him if he does, but don't think that's the reason. Rafael a man, takes fall like a man. Okay friend, I send your woman money, pay the rent, look out for her, but I never talk to you long as I live.

Honest jock goes back to work. Round of applause first time out. Loses on chalk, booed all way to jocks' room. Back among friends.

Ramona so nice can hardly stand it. Tell her please go back to pain in the ass, face crinkles, never satisfied. Walk outside, circle my property. Shit, maybe she's right, story my life, never satisfied, more I get, more I want, 11 million this year, 15 next. Just the money? No, just *more.* Jump into Caddy, drive to 114th and Third. Nobody on street touch Caddy of Dega. His woman lets me in. Sit in kitchen, drink beer, she sits in bedroom, watches TV. Stay three hours. When drive home all relaxed, beats goddam sleeping pill.

Next morning easy workout backstretch, Wineglo old sweet self. Sing nice as reward, walk him toward barn, hear my name, soft and low. Look to rail, almost fall off, catch self, walk him over. It's Ginny, tall, smooth, calm Ginny. Hop off Wineglo, turn him over to exercise boy, duck under rail.

Whathehell you doing here, Ginny?

Came up to give you some support.

I look around . . . Very nice of you baby, but don't need support.

Calm smile . . . Pablo, are you getting support from Ramona?

In a way . . . Yes . . . No . . .

No man is an island, Pablo.

Don't want to be an island, just a jock.

Calm smile, again . . . Staying at Garden City Hotel through Belmont. Pablo, I know what you've been going through.

Now my turn, calm smile . . . Nobody but Dega knows that, Ginny.

The Garden City Hotel, Paul.

Shake my unsupported head . . . Ginny, you know my rule: Never do it on my own front lawn.

Rules are made to be broken, Paul. Are you happy with Ramona?

Whothehell knows?

Is she happy with you?

She better be. Ginny, go back to Florida. Please. Riding Calder middle of June, see you then.

Thank you, Pablo.

Meaning what?

Meaning thank you . . . Paul, if Ramona ever walks you know where I am.

Almost laugh, don't . . . Ginny, Ramona never walk, I'm her meal ticket.

Paul, if *you* ever walk you know where I am.

Have to give her my A-number-one stare, can't believe she talks like this, not with all her smarts and my training; finally have to spell it out: Ginny, you know damn well my religion forbids divorce.

Thinks about that, hard, face crinkles but this one never cries. All right, she says, I want to do some shopping in New York, but I'll be gone tomorrow, won't even stay for the race.

See you in June, I tell her as she walks away studying the grass.

Keep shaking my head. Head taking some beating this week. Look at classy, retreating frame, need this like horse with game leg. And Jewish broads supposed to be so smart.

Getting itchy, island fever. Inform Hy need something out of town, say Pennsylvania Derby Keystone end of May. Aye aye Cap'n. Lands Wotaguy, picturebook colt with one problem: specializes running just out of money. Tell Hy to mind store, have to solo, call Holly Carstairs, six-foot waitress Atlantic City, met her March after Cotillion. Take off in Mercedes, detour AC on way down, kick, coax, shove Wotaguy into show money, detour AC way back. Ready now, take on whole goddam world, including Belmont, Fat Bat, Cal Jones, odds.

Wineglo ships up fine, so does Mr. Pawkins. Tells me this horse given his life new meaning, true gift his age, you understand that Paul? Sure I understand, my hands, my head, my savvy *my* gift, why not a horse? Tell him do my best for you, Mr. Pawkins, answers haven't slightest doubt you will, my father never say that three million years. Even Tim very decent, give him high marks, has brought horse to this race lovely condition. Coat shines like Simoniz job, filled out, alert, strong. *Ready.* Work him myself: full of smooth juice, idles like my Mercedes. Tell Hymie, Hymie, can't win this horse, ship me back to Panama.

Come into race 3–1, good-looking odds. Fat Bat 8–5 to cop triple crown, makes sense unless you sit where I sit, atop lots of horse. Belmont packed, should be, 80,000, Ramona, Olga, Lorenzo guests Mr. Pawkins, Ginny home Bal Harbor, everything in place.

Move into gate quiet, easy, number six hole, eight-horse field. Fat Bat has rail, rail been gold today and Cal Jones dying prove west coast jocks for real, okay, be my guest. In gate use terrific will power, switch off waterfall of sound, silence, all is silence . . . CLANG, here we go baby.

Break good, 3rd, but take him back, out of trouble, tuck him in, close to rail. Up ahead Bat out fast, maybe too fast, this race good distance of ground, mile and a half, maybe too fast, maybe . .

Lay 5th for a mile, shake wrists, move him to outside, begin to pick up horses, Fat Bat starts to come back. Head of stretch and we're 2nd, resembles Preakness but got some room now, this is real race. Reach back, rap Wineglo once, twice, mean it, knows I mean it. Afterburners go off, *zooooom.* Catch Fat Bat, but he's tough, so is Cal, once again saddle to saddle, nose to nose. I'm hand-riding, so is he, don't hear the slash, smart move, no wasted motion, he's a pro. So is Dega and this his turf. Go full quarter like that, a team, stride for stride, thrust for thrust, bob for bob, this is it, this is racing. Hit 16th pole still dead even, they don't give, we don't give, field somewhere back there, so long, goodbye. Whole world empty except for Bat, Cal, Wineglo, Dega, no crowd, just us. Four hands lifting, pushing, nursing, pulling out that inch, reason we're here, the rest back there. Wire twelve strides away when feel it, the inch, two, a nose, a head, can't relax, more, more, my gift, God do this for nothing!

The end of silence. A *pistol* shot. Rafael's boys? Here? Can't be, too smart. Feel the sag, Christ know that sound now, heard it once before, Arlington, but not my horse . . . More sag, front left leg, the wire, half out of saddle, the wire, reach over, hold up his head, dead game, he's dead game. Hits wire on three legs, crumples, I'm out of saddle.

Can see it all so clear, slo-mo, just like whole world sees it, now, tonight, over and over, same as Rafe sees it in joint: Wineglo down, I'm sailing into space, like lazy cloud, roll over in air, slow, easy, Lorenzo love that, Fat Bat flows past, but the field pounding toward me, all in beautiful slo-mo. Start to float down now, will hit somewhere between neck and right shoulder, Wineglo gone, know it, please inject him fast, feel so bad for Mr. Pawkins, did I push too hard, too far? No, don't think it, don't feel it, no, my job, no . . . Track coming up to meet me, question is where? Cervical, dorsal, clavicle, head? My first time, so what, I win goddammit Rafe, I win. If I make it, tell Hy get off Calvin Klein ass, start working Travers Saratoga, maybe Scoliosis ready, earn your goddam money, here we come baby, oh please pray for me Ramona . . .

KID MACARTHUR

STEPHANIE VAUGHN

Stephanie Vaughn was born in Millersburg, Ohio, and grew up in Ohio, Oklahoma, Texas, New York, Italy, and the Philippine Islands. She was educated at Ohio State University, University of Iowa, and Stanford University. She lives in Ithaca, New York. This is her second appearance in the O. Henry Prize Story collections.

I grew up in the Army. About the only kind of dove I ever saw was a dead dove resting small-boned upon a dinner plate. Even though we were Protestants and Bible readers, no one regarded the dove sentimentally as a symbol of peace—the bird who had flown back to Noah carrying the olive branch, as if to say, "The land is green again, come back to the land." When I was thirteen, my family moved to Fort Sill, Oklahoma, only a few weeks before the dove-hunting season opened. My father, who liked to tinker with guns on weekends, sat down at the dining-room table one Saturday and unwrapped a metal device called the Lombreglia Self-Loader. The Self-Loader was a crimping mechanism that enabled a person to assemble shotgun ammunition at home. "Save Money and Earn Pleasure," the box label said. "For the Self-Reliant Sportsman Who Wants to Do the Job Right!"

"If you can learn to handle this," my father said, "you can load my shells for me when the hunting season arrives." He was addressing my brother, MacArthur, who was ten years old. We pulled up chairs to the table, while my mother and grandmother remained near the light of the kitchen door. My father delivered a little lecture on the percussive action of the firing pin as he set out the rest of the loading equipment —empty red cartridges, cardboard wads, brass caps, a bowl of gunpowder, and several bowls of lead shot. He spoke in his officer's briefing-room voice—a voice that seemed to say, "This will be a difficult mission, soldier, but I know you are up to the mark." MacArthur seemed to grow taller listening to that voice, his spine perfectly erect as he helped align the equipment in the center of the table. My father finished the lecture by explaining that the smallest-size shot was best for dove or quail, the medium size was best for duck or rabbit, and the largest size was best for goose or wild turkey.

"And which size shot is best for humans?" my grandmother said. She did not disapprove of guns, but she could rarely pass up a chance to say something sharp to my father. My grandmother was a member of the W.C.T.U., and he was conducting this lesson in between sips of a Scotch-and-soda.

"It depends," my father said. "It depends on whether you want to eat the person afterward."

"Well, ha, ha," my grandmother said.

"It is a lot of work trying to prize small shot out of a large body," my father said.

"Very funny," my grandmother said.

My father turned to MacArthur and grew serious. "Never forget that a gun is always loaded."

MacArthur nodded.

"And what else?" my father said to MacArthur.

"Never point a gun at someone unless you mean to kill him," MacArthur said.

"Excuse me," my mother said, moving near the table. "Are you sure all of this is quite safe?" Her hands wavered above the bowl of gunpowder.

"That's right," my grandmother said. "Couldn't something blow up here?"

My father and MacArthur seemed to have been hoping for this question. They led us outside for a demonstration, MacArthur following behind my father with the bowl of powder and a box of matches. "Gunpowder is not like gasoline in a tank," my father said. He tipped a line of powder onto the sidewalk.

"It's not like wheat in a silo, either," MacArthur said, handing the matches to my father.

"Everybody stand back," my father said as he touched a match to the powder. It flared up with a hiss and gave off a stream of pungent smoke.

We watched the white smoke curl into the branches of our pecan tree, and then my grandmother said, "Well, it surely is a pleasure to learn that the house can burn down without blowing up."

Even my father laughed. On the way back into the house, he grew magnanimous and said to me, "You can learn to load shells, too, you know."

"No, thanks," I said. "My destiny is with the baton." I was practicing to be a majorette. It was the white tasselled boots I was after, and the pink lipstick. Years later, a woman friend, seeing a snapshot of me in the white braided costume, a sort of paramilitary outfit with ruffles, said, "What a waste of your youth, what a corruption of your womanhood." Today, when I contemplate my wasted youth and corrupted womanhood, I recall that when I left high school I went to college. When MacArthur left high school, he went to war.

It is nine years after the gunpowder lesson, and I am a graduate student teaching a section of freshman composition at a large university. On a bright June day, at the end of the school year, one of my students, a Vietnam veteran, offers to give me a present of a human ear. We are walking under a long row of trees after the last class of the term and moving into the dark, brilliant shadows of the trees, then again into the swimming light of the afternoon. We are two weeks short of the solstice, and the sun has never seemed so bright. The student slides his book bag from his shoulder and says, "I would like to give you a present for the end of the course."

Ahead of us, the plane trees are so uniformly spaced, so beautifully arched that they form a green arcaded cloister along the stone walk. A soft, easing wind passes through the boughs with the sound of falling water. "Don't get me wrong," he says. "But I'd like to give you an ear."

Did he know that I came from a military family? Did he know that I had a nineteen-year-old brother in Vietnam? Did he know that my sense of the war derived largely from the color snapshots MacArthur had sent of happy young men posed before the Army's largest movable artillery weapon, their boots heavy with red dust, the jungle rising like a green temple behind them? There were two things MacArthur asked me to send him during his thirteen-month tour—marinated artichoke hearts and Rolling Stones tapes. The only artichoke hearts I could find came in glass jars and were not permitted in the Army's mailbags. The first Stones tapes I sent were washed away in a monsoon flood. I sent more tapes. These were stolen by an old man who wanted to sell them on the black market. I sent more Stones tapes. These MacArthur gave to a wounded boy who was being airlifted to a hospital in Tokyo.

It has been said that the war in Vietnam was so fully photographed that it was the one war we learned the truth about. Which truth did we learn, and who learned it? One of the most famous pictures to come out of the war was the videotape of the South Vietnam chief of police firing a bullet into the head of a prisoner, a man who stood before the chief in shorts and a loose plaid shirt. He looked the chief in the eye, looked with fear and no hope, and was still looking with fear and no hope in that moment when he was already dead but had not yet fallen like a rag into the Saigon street. There were other memorable pictures like that. There were also ones like the picture of the blond, blue-eyed soldier, his head wrapped becomingly in a narrow bandage ("Just a flesh wound, sir"), reaching toward the camera as if to summon help for his wounded comrade. This photograph, with its depiction of handsome, capable white middle-class good will, was so popular that it appeared in every major American news source and has been republished many times since, whenever a news agency wants to do a story on the Vietnam era.

That picture always reminds me of my student, a man in his late twenties who had served three tours of duty in Vietnam and was being put through college by the Army so that he could return to active duty as an officer—the student who stood before me pulling a canvas sack from his book bag on that dazzling June day at the end of my first year as a teacher.

"Don't get me wrong," the student said. "But I would like to give you an ear."

"What would you want to do that for?"

"I want to give you a present. I want to give you something for the end of the course." He withdrew his hand from the sack and opened it, palm up.

You probably have heard about the ears they brought back with them from Vietnam. You may have heard how the ears were carried in pouches or worn like necklaces, the lobes perforated so that they could be threaded on a leather thong. You may have heard that the ears looked like dried fruit, or like seashells, or like leaves curling beneath an oak tree. The mind will often make a metaphor when it cannot make anything else.

A human ear, though, still looks like a human ear. It is only after you have stared at it for a long while, at its curving ridges and shallow basins, that you begin to see: here is the dry bed of a wide river valley, here is the tiny village, the bright paddy, the water buffalo. Here is the world so green you could taste that greenness even from an altitude of ten thousand feet in a jet bomber.

As the student and I looked at each other in the sunlight, two young women strolling along the walk separated in order to pass us—parted like river water moving around an island. They were laughing and did not notice what the student held in his hand. "So," said one of the women, "my mother calls me back to say they had to put the poor dog to sleep, and you know what she says?" The student and I turned to hear what the mother had said. "She says, 'And you know, Anita, that dog's mind was still good. He wasn't even senile.' "

When the student turned back to me, he was smiling. "What a world," he said. He extended his hand.

"Thank you," I said. "But I do not want that present."

We had begun to move again. I was walking slowly, trying to show with my easy pace that I was not afraid. Perhaps he was angry with me for something I had said in class. Perhaps he was on drugs.

"It's O.K.," he said. "I have lots more."

"Really," I said. "No, but thank you."

"If you don't want this one, I can give you a better one." He reached into the bag again.

"How can you tell which is which?" I said calmly, as if I were inquiring about fishing lures or nuts and bolts or types of flower seed.

"I can tell," he said. "I've got this one memorized. This one's a girl." The girl, he told me, was thirteen. At first, the men in his outfit had taken pity on her and given her food and cigarettes. Then they learned that she was the one who planted mines around their encampment in the night.

It took us a long time to cross the campus and shake hands and say good-bye. Two days later, the student left a bottle of vodka on my desk while I was out. Apparently he had been sincere in wanting to give me a present. I never saw the student again. I did not see another war souvenir of that kind until after my brother returned from Vietnam.

The autumn we lived at Fort Sill, our family ate five hundred doves. There was a fifty-day dove season, a ten-dove limit each day. Every night, my mother brought the birds to the table in a different guise. They were baked and braised and broiled. They were basted and stuffed, olive-oiled and gravied. But there were too many of them, each tiny and heart-shaped, the breastbone prominent in outline even under a sauce. Finally, a platter of doves was set before us and MacArthur said, "I am now helping myself to a tuna casserole. There is cheese in this casserole, and some cracker crumbs." He passed the platter to me. "And what are you having, Gemma?"

"I'm having jumbo shrimps," I said. "And some lemon."

In this way, the platter moved around the table. My mother was having lamb. My grandmother was having pork chops. My father hesitated before he took the meat fork. All his life, he had been shooting game for the dinner table. He believed he was teaching his family a lesson in economy and his son a lesson in wilderness survival. No one had ever made a joke about these meals. He looked at MacArthur. Although my father had never said it, MacArthur was exactly the kind of son he had hoped to have—tall and good-natured, smart and obedient, a boy who could hit a bull's-eye on a paper target with his .22 rifle. "All right," my father said at last. "I'm having a steak."

However, after dinner he said, "If you want to play a game, let's play a real game. Let's play twenty questions." He took a pen from his pocket and flattened a paper napkin to use as a scorecard. He looked at MacArthur. "I am thinking of something. What is it?" We were all going to play this game, but my father's look implied that MacArthur was the principal opponent.

MacArthur tried to assume the gamesman's bland expression. "Is it animal?" he said.

My father appeared to think for a while. He mused at the candles. He considered the ceiling. This was part of the game, trying to throw the opponents off the trail. "Yes, it is animal."

"Is it a toad?" my grandmother said.

"No, no," MacArthur said. "It's too soon to ask that."

"It is certainly not a toad," my father said. He made a great show of entering a mark against us on the napkin. This was another part of the game, trying to rattle the opponents by gloating.

"Is it bigger than a breadbox?" my mother said.

"Yes."

"Is it bigger than a car?" I said.

"Yes."

"Is it bigger than a house?" MacArthur said.

"Yes."

"Is it the Eiffel Tower?" my grandmother said.

Again my father used exaggerated motions to record the mark. MacArthur dropped his head into his arms. This was an unmanly response. "Settle down," my father said. "Think."

"Can't we play some other game?" my grandmother said. "This game is never any fun."

"We are not trying to have fun," my father said. "We are trying to use our minds."

So the game went, until we had used up our twenty no answers, and my father revealed the thing he had been thinking of. The thing was "the rocket's red glare"—the light from exploded gunpowder. Gunpowder, if you analyzed its ingredients, was actually animal, vegetable, *and* mineral—providing you agreed that the carbon component could be derived from animal sources. He poured a drink and leaned back to tell us a story. The first time he had played the game he was a soldier on a ship going to England. The ship was in one of the largest convoys ever to cross the Atlantic during the Second World War. The sea was rough. German submarines were nearby. Some men got seasick, and everyone was nervous. They began to play games, and they played one game of twenty questions for two days. That was the game whose answer was "the rocket's red glare." My father had thought that one up.

That was as close as he ever came to telling us a war story. He had gone from England to Normandy Beach and later to the Battle of the Bulge, but when he remembered the war for us he remembered brave, high-spirited men not yet under attack. When he had finished speaking, he looked at his glass of Scotch as the true drinker will. He looked at it as if it were a crystal ball.

The spring following the season in which we ate whole generations of doves, MacArthur acquired two live chicks. A Woolworth's in the town near the post was giving chicks away to the first hundred customers in the door the Saturday before Palm Sunday. MacArthur was the first customer through the door and also the fifty-seventh. He named the chicks Harold and Georgette. He made big plans for Harold and Georgette. He was going to teach them how to count. He was going to teach them how to walk a tightrope made of string and ride a chicken-sized Ferris wheel.

A week later, Harold and Georgette were eaten by our cat while we were at church. The chicks had been living in an open cardboard box on top of the refrigerator. No one imagined that a cat as fat and slothful as Al Bear would hurl himself that high to get an extra meal.

Looking at the few pale feathers left in the box, MacArthur said, "He ate them whole. He even ate the beaks."

"Poor chicks," my mother said.

"They were making an awful lot of noise up there," my grandmother said. "They should have kept those beaks shut."

Everyone looked to see if MacArthur was crying. In our family, people believed that getting through a hardship intact was its own reward. "This is nothing to be upset about," my father said. "This is the way nature works." It was in the natural order of things for cats to eat birds, he told us. Even some birds ate other birds. Some animals ate cats. Everything we ate had once been alive. Wasn't a steak part of a steer? MacArthur looked away just long enough to roll his eyes at me. My father began to gesture and to project his voice. Now he was lecturing on the principles of Darwinian selection. He used the phrase "nature red in tooth and claw." He seemed to like that phrase, and used it again. The third time he said "nature red in tooth and claw," Al Bear walked up behind him and threw up on the floor, all the little bird parts of Harold and Georgette still recognizable on the linoleum.

MacArthur never became a hunter of birds. By the time he turned twelve, and was given a shotgun for his birthday, we were stationed in Italy. The Italians, always a poor people, would shoot a bird out of a tree or blast one on the ground to get a meal. They had gone through entire species of game birds this way and were now working on the German songbirds that flew south for the winter. Thus, the misfortunes of the Italian economy allowed my brother to turn from real birds to imitation ones. Soon after his birthday, he was taken to the skeet range at Camp Darby, where he was permitted to shoot fifty rounds at black-and-yellow discs, called pigeons. Fifty recoils of a large gun are a lot for a boy, even one big for his age, like MacArthur. By the time he got home that day, there were bruises beginning to bloom across his shoulder.

"Maybe he should wait until he's older," my mother said.

"What ever happened to the all-American sports?" my grandmother said. "Couldn't he learn to throw or kick something?"

Months later, when we all drove into the post to see him shoot in his first tournament, MacArthur kept saying, "See Kid MacArthur forget to load the gun. Watch fake birds fall whole to the earth." "Kid MacArthur" was what he called himself when something went wrong. He did not like the general whose name he bore. He did not admire him, as my parents did, for being the man who said, "I shall return." MacArthur was not one of those ordinary names, like John or Joan, which you could look up in my grandmother's Dictionary of Christian Appellations. MacArthur was a name my brother had to research. General MacArthur, he decided, had talked a big game but then allowed his entire air force to be bombed on the ground the day after Pearl Harbor. General MacArthur had sent his troops into Bataan but had not sent along the trucks that carried food for the battalions. The general had fled to Australia, uttering his famous words, leaving his men to perish in the Death March.

"You'll be fine if you don't look out any windows," my father said. "Looking out the window" was his expression for allowing the mind to wander.

"I'm pulling down all the shades on my windows," MacArthur said. "I'm battening all the hatches in my head."

Something overtook MacArthur when the tournament got under way and he finally stepped onto the range, the only boy among the shooters. The bones of his face grew prominent. His eyes became opaque, like the eyes of a man who can keep a secret. By the second time around the stations, he was third among the five shooters. No one spoke, except a man named Mr. Dimple, who was an engineer working for the American government in Italy, and the only civilian on the skeet range.

"That gosh-damned sun," Mr. Dimple said. "Those gosh-damned trees." It was a hot, bright day, and the angle of the sun made it difficult to see the discs as they sailed in front of a pine forest at the back of the range.

"Maybe we need a fence in front of those trees," Mr. Dimple said. After his next two shots, he said, "Darned if the wind didn't get to those birds before I did." It was clear that Mr. Dimple was disgracing himself before the cream of the American Army. When he spoke, the other men looked at the grass. The women, seated behind the semicircular range, looked at each other. Their eyes seemed to say, "Our men are not going to complain about any trees. Our men are not going to complain about the wind or the sun."

"I'm not wearing the right sunglasses," Mr. Dimple said.

MacArthur stepped up to the station just in front of the viewing area and called for the pigeons. "Pull!" Swinging to his right, he aimed just ahead of the flying, spinning disc. He pulled the first trigger and began the swing back to his left to get the second sailing bird before it touched the ground. The first bird exploded in a star of fragments and fell to the earth with the sound of raining gravel. The second bird fell untouched and landed on the ground with a *clack* as it struck another unexploded bird. Perhaps because his swing back had seemed so sure, so exactly timed, MacArthur could not believe he had missed. He shook his head as he stepped away from the station.

My father looked over at him and said within hearing of everyone on the range, "Whenever you step back from that peg, you step back the same way, hit or miss. You do not shake your head."

Mr. Dimple put his hand on his hip and sighed at his gun. Colonel Ridgewood and Major Solman looked away.

"Do you understand?"

MacArthur did understand. He was embarrassed. "Yes, sir," he said. As the group moved to the next station, the other men nodded at my father and gave MacArthur friendly punches on the arm. He was not going to grow up to be a Mr. Dimple.

The next year, MacArthur won a place on the championship team my father took to Naples. For years, my father liked to tell about MacArthur's first day on the range. "He was black-and-blue all over," my father said. "But he never spoke a word of complaint."

Two years later, we returned to the States to live on a post on Governors Island, which was in the middle of New York Harbor and so close to the Statue of Liberty that we could see her torchlight from our bedroom windows. It was on Governors Island that my father received a letter from the government which seemed to imply that MacArthur might not be an American citizen, because he had been born in the Philippines. He was not quite a foreigner, either, because his parents had been born in Ohio.

"He's a juvenile delinquent, is what he is," my grandmother said one day when my father was trying to explain the citizenship difficulty. She had slipped into MacArthur's room and found a cache of cigarette lighters. "Where does a fourteen-year-old boy get enough money to buy these things?" she said. "What does he do with them, anyway?"

"He doesn't smoke," I said, although I knew that with my father the health issue would not be the central one.

My mother beheld the lighters with great sadness. "I'll have a talk with him tonight."

"No one will speak to him yet," my father said. He was troubled because the evidence of MacArthur's criminality had been gathered in a kind of illegal search and seizure.

"Does this mean that MacArthur can never become President of the United States?" I said. In our family, we had been taught that if children were scrupulously honest, and also rose from their seats when strangers entered the room, and said "Yes, sir" and "No, sir" at the appropriate moments, and then went on to get a college education, they could grow up to be anything, including President of the United States. Even a woman could be President, if she kept her record clean and also went to college.

No one smiled at my joke.

The document my father held seemed to suggest that even though MacArthur was the son of patriots, someone somewhere might question the quality of his citizenship. It was a great blow to learn that he might be a thief as well as a quasi foreigner.

The document was a letter from the Judge Advocate of the post advising that foreign-born children be interviewed by the Department of Naturalization and Immigration. It also advised that they attend a ceremony in which they would raise their right hands, like ordinary immigrants, and renounce any residual loyalty to the countries of their births. It did not "require" that they do these things but it did "strongly recommend" that they do so. We never learned why the government made its strong recommendation, but there was something in the language of the letter which allowed one to think that foreign birth was like a genetic defect that could be surgically altered—it was like an extra brain that could be lopped off. (A Communist brain! A Socialist brain! The brain that would tell the hand to raise the gun against American democracy.)

"What were you doing in his chest of drawers?" my father said.

"I was dusting," my grandmother said.

"You were dusting the contents of a brown sack?"

"This would never have happened in Ohio," my grandmother said. "If we lived in Ohio, he would already be a citizen and would not have to hang around that neighborhood after school."

"In this house, we do not take other people's possessions without asking."

"That's the point." My grandmother picked up a lighter with each hand. "These *are* other people's possessions."

It was dark when I slipped out to intercept MacArthur. At night, it was always a surprise to ascend the slope of the post golf course and come upon a vision of New York City standing above the harbor, the lights of Wall Street rising like fire into the sky, all the glory and fearfulness of the city casting its spangled image back across the water to our becalmed and languorous island. If you looked away from the light of the city, you looked back into the darkness of the last three centuries, across roofs of brick buildings built by the British and the Dutch. The post was a Colonial retreat, an administrative headquarters, where soldiers strolled to work under the boughs of hardwood trees, and the trumpetings of the recorded bugle drifted through the leaves like a mist. It was a green, antique island, giving its last year of service to the United States Army.

My grandmother never boarded the ferry for Manhattan without believing that her life or, at the very least, the quality of her character was in peril. She did not like New Yorkers. They were grim and anxious. They had bad teeth. They did not live in a place where parents told their children that if they bit into an apple and found a worm, they would know that they were just getting a little extra protein.

"About how many do you think she took?" MacArthur said to me.

"She took about exactly all of them."

His face went slack. He still did not have that implacable expression that was supposed to help you through any crisis. "I was going to hock those on Monday to get some more cash for Christmas."

"By Monday, you will be restricted to quarters. By Monday, you will be calling your friends to tell them you can't go to any movies or parties over the holidays." I handed him a lighter. "I don't think they've got them counted," I said. The others were still lying on the dining table.

He was grateful for that lighter. "Thanks," he said. "This is the best one."

"How about a light?" I said. I opened a pack of my father's cigarettes and took one out.

He snapped open the lighter and ignited it so deftly that the whole movement looked like a magic trick. "This is what we learn to do at P.S. 104," he said.

Neither of us smoked, but we inflicted the cigarette upon ourselves with relish, exhaling fiercely into the raw night air. "I'm not asking where you got them, of course," I said.

He smiled. "I won almost every one of them throwing dice and playing cards. At lunch everybody goes out to steal, and after school everybody plays for the loot. Remember me? Kid Competition. I'm good at games."

"That's a story you could probably tell them," I said.

He ground the cigarette out under his foot. "Look at me," he said. "I'm littering Army property." Then he said, "I did steal a couple of them. Either you steal, and you're one of the guys, or you don't steal, and you're a sleazo and everybody wants to fight."

He was very tall by then. The bones close to his skin—his wrist bones, knees, shoulder bones—looked as though they had been borrowed from a piece of farm machinery. If you were as big as he was and also the new kid at school, someone would always want to fight you. We had started walking and were now on the dark side of Governors Island, standing by the seawall that looked toward the small lights of Brooklyn. The wind was blowing at our backs from the west, bringing the sharp, oily smell from the New Jersey refineries, but we could also smell the salt and fish taste of the ocean, and for a moment I could imagine us far away from every city and every Army post and every rural town we had ever known. He leaned across the railing of the seawall and looked tired. He had posed for himself an even more demanding ideal than the family had, and he was humiliated to perceive himself as a thief.

"Look," I said. "Just tell them you bought a couple of lighters with your lunch money to get the stake for the gambling." He nodded toward the water without conviction. "Don't ruin Christmas for yourself."

"O.K., I won't."

The next day he volunteered the truth to my father and was not only restricted to quarters but also made to go uptown to meet the victims of the crimes. My father wore his uniform, with the brass artilleryman's insignia, two cannons crossed under a missile. MacArthur wore the puffy green jacket and the green hat that had inspired his friends to call him the Jolly Green Giant. They were a gift from my mother and grandmother, so he had to wear them. They made him look like a lumbering asparagus stalk, a huge vegetable king, who could be spotted on any subway platform or down any length of city blocks. At each store, he removed his green hat and made a speech of apology, then returned one or several of the lighters. Since the lighters were now used, he also paid for them out of his Christmas-shopping money. It hurt him to be the one who had nothing to give on Christmas morning. And at school he was an outcast.

"I am now Kid Scum," he said. "The Jolly Green Creep."

He got a Certificate of Citizenship, though, and when he entered the Army, four years later, he went in as a real American.

On MacArthur's last day of leave before he left for Vietnam, we drove him to the Cleveland airport and then stood like potted palms behind the plate-glass window of the terminal building. My father had retired from the Army by then, and the family had returned to Ohio.

"He ought to love the heat," my grandmother said. "He was born in the heat."

"He's a smart soldier," my father said. "It's the smart men who are most likely to get through any war." My father had always believed in smartness as other people believe in amulets.

The plane began to move, and we strained to find MacArthur's face in one of the small windows. "There he is," my mother said. "I see his hand in the window."

A woman standing next to her said, "No, that's our son. See how big that hand is?"

The woman's husband said, "Our son was a linebacker at Ohio State. He weighs two hundred and sixty-five pounds."

"He's a good boy," the woman said, and we all nodded, as if it were obvious that physical size could be a measure of a person's character.

After we left the freeway and drove south to the fertile, rolling land of the Killbuck Valley, which had never produced a war protester, my grandmother said, "I believe in Vietnam." She emphasized the word "believe," as if Vietnam were a denomination of the Christian faith. In the nineteen-fifties, she had been a member of something called the Ground Observer Corps. Members of the Corps scanned the skies with binoculars, looking for Russian aircraft. At that time, she lived in a small Ohio town whose major industries were a bus-seat factory and an egg-noodle plant. Twice a month, she stood on the roof of the high school to keep these vital industries safe.

"I believe in luck," I said. "I believe the Jolly Green Giant's luck will get him through. Remember how he always won at bingo?"

"We took care of the Japs and the Jerries," my grandmother said. "We held off the pinkos in Korea."

"I do not think that any pinkos are planning to invade the United States," I said.

"You've got a lot to learn," my mother said. "They're already here."

"When you get back to school, I do not want to hear that you are marching in those protests," my father said.

I was already marching, but that was a secret. "Isn't this the place where we notice the grass?" I said.

When my father was still in the Army, we spent all of his leave time going back to the Killbuck Valley. As we crossed the state line and drew closer to the valley where the Killbuck River ran and all of our relatives lived, my father would say, "Doesn't anyone notice that the grass is getting greener?" We used to say, "Naw, this grass looks like any other grass." We made a joke of the grass, but we all did love the look of that land. On some level, the grasses of the Killbuck Valley, the clover, timothy, alfalfa, the corn, wheat, and oats, the dense woods of the hills, the freshwater springs, and the shivering streams—all of this was connected with the necessity of a standing Army. It was as if my father had said, "This is what we will fight for."

MacArthur had been out of the Army for a year, and his life seemed defined by negatives—no job, no college, no telephone, no meat. He lived alone in a rented farmhouse deep in the Killbuck Valley, about twenty miles from the town where the family had settled.

"He comes every other Sunday and all he eats is the salad or the string-beans," my grandmother said to me. The soul of our family life always hovered over the dinner table, where we renewed the bond of our kinship over game and steaks and chops and meat loaf. My parents and grandmother perceived MacArthur's new diet both as a disease and as a mark of failing character. When they went to visit, they took along a roast or a ten-pound bag of hamburger.

"See what you can find out," my mother said. I was home for Christmas week and on my way out to see him. "Talk to him. See if he has any plans."

He did not have any plans. What he had was a souvenir of the war just like the one my student had tried to give me on that June day under the trees. This one was tucked into a small padded envelope lying on the kitchen table. The envelope made me curious, and I kept reaching out to finger the ragged edges of brown paper as we drank a pot of tea. MacArthur, sitting on the kitchen counter because there was only one chair, finally said, "Go ahead. Look." I opened the envelope and looked. There was a moment then when the winter sun was like heavy metal in the room, like something that could achieve critical mass if a question mark sparked the air. For some reason, I thought of the young woman reporting what her mother had said about the dead dog—"And you know, that dog's mind was still good. He wasn't even senile." I thought of what I had wanted to say to my student that day: "I didn't think that something like this could look exactly like itself so much later and so far away."

"That's not mine," MacArthur said. "That belongs to Dixon." His face was as flat as pond ice, and I saw that at last he had achieved the gamesman's implacable expression. Even in the long curves of his body there was something which said that nothing could startle or move him.

"Who's Dixon?" I said.

"Oh, you know who he is. My friend the space cadet. The one in the V.A. hospital."

"The one from Oklahoma." Now I remembered Dixon from the snapshots. He was the one who glued chicken feathers to his helmet.

"This is his idea of a great Christmas present," MacArthur said.

His eyes were so still and wide I could see the gold flecks in them. He looked away, looked down at his legs dangling from the counter, and I suddenly felt the solitariness of that rented farmhouse in the Killbuck Valley, the hills and fields hardened under snow, the vegetable garden rutted with ice. When I stood up to touch his arm, he did not move or speak. He seemed to have escaped from me in an evaporation of heat. Even in my imagination, I could not go where he had gone. All

I knew was that somewhere in the jungle had been a boy named Dixon, a boy from Oklahoma, who had grown up on land just like the land my father used to hunt while MacArthur trailed behind with bright-red boxes of homemade ammunition. But now Dixon was a nut who sent ears through the mail, and MacArthur was unemployed and living alone in the country.

Suddenly the ear was back in the envelope Dixon had sent it in, and MacArthur was saying, "I'm sorry, but I don't have much around here you'd like to eat."

Later, we stood out back where the garden was and looked at the corn stubble and broken vines. MacArthur paced the rows and said, "These are my snap beans. These are my pumpkins." He proceeded past carrots, beets, onions, turnips, cabbages, and summer squash, looking at each old furrow with a stalwart affection, as if the plants he named would bloom in snow when they heard him speak.

"They asked me to find out what you plan for the future," I said.

"Oh, great." He kicked a hump of snow. "Did you ever notice how with the family your life is always a prospective event? 'When you're a little older, when you grow up, when you get old just like me'?" He relaxed again and dropped an arm across my shoulders. "I'm just a carpenter now. Let me show you my lights." I thought he meant lamps, since most of his rooms were empty except for secondhand lamps standing in corners. He was restoring the house for its owner, to work off the rent. In the front room, he said, "Now we are going to play a game. Tell me what you see."

"I see an old iron floor lamp."

"No, tell me about the light. What kind of light do you see?" The walls were freshly painted white, but the sun had moved around the house, so the room was growing dark.

"Eggshell light?" I said.

He made a great show of entering an imaginary mark on an imaginary napkin in his hand. "Nooooo," he said. "It is certainly not eggshell light."

Then I understood, and I laughed. "Is it animal light?"

"Settle down, now. Use your head."

"Is it vegetable light?"

He surveyed the room, its greens, and blue-greens and ochres, the pale colors of a northern room at the end of the day. "Yes, I think you could call this vegetable light. Maybe *eggplant* light." He laughed and wadded up the imaginary napkin.

We moved through the house then, making up ridiculous names for the light we saw. We found moose light, and hippopotamus light, and potato-chip light. We found a violet light we named after our cousin Neilon's purple car, and an orange light we called Aunt Sheila's Hair, and a silver light we called Uncle Dave, after the silver dollars he used to send us on our birthdays. We returned to the kitchen, with its wide reach of western windows, and saw the red light of the sunset splayed across the cabinets. "Oh, yes," MacArthur said. "And here we have another light. Here we have a light just like the light of the rocket's red glare."

The sun had dropped below the tree line when he went to turn on his lamps, and I put on my coat. "Well, I have to go," I said. "I'll keep writing. I'll come see you the next time I'm back."

He walked me to the car, holding my arm as I slipped over the pebbly snow. We stopped to look at the western sky, now furrowed with that fierce red you see at that time of year when there are ice crystals in the air. All the things nearby had become brilliant black silhouettes—the stand of trees to our right, the boarded-up barn, the spiky fragments of the garden. The sky grew fiercer and gave off a light I could not name.

"The shortest day of the year," MacArthur said. He reached into his jacket and withdrew the brown envelope. "Take this," he said.

He held it out, and this time, because he was my brother, I said, "All right," and took it. I hugged him and got in the car. I knew he was not going to be home for Christmas. "You're going all the way to Oklahoma to see Dixon, aren't you?"

He had already started back to the house and had to turn to face me with his surprise.

"Remember me?" I said. "I'm the Kid's sister. I'll think of something to tell them at home."

"Thanks," he said.

When I got to the bottom of the lane, I stopped the car to wave. He had come back through the house and was standing on the dark porch, legs evenly spaced, like a soldier at ease, the gold light of his house swooning in every window. Before I drove off, I slipped the envelope under the front seat with the road maps, thinking that someday I would remove it and decide what to do.

It was still there five years later, when I sold the car. During those five years, my father, always a weekend drinker, began to drink during the week. My grandmother broke her hip in a fall. My mother, a quiet woman, was now helped through her quiet by Valium. MacArthur finished restoring his rooms and moved to another farmhouse, in a different county. Finally, he took a job as a cook—a breakfast cook, doing mostly eggs and pancakes—and in this way continued to be a person without plans.

The boy I sold the car to was just eighteen years old and wanted to go West to California. He was tall, like my brother, and happy to be managing his own life at last. The cuffs of his plaid flannel shirt had shrunk past his wrists, and, seeing his large wrist bones exposed to the cold bright air, I liked him immediately.

"Are you sure you're charging me enough for this?" Leaning under the hood, he looked like a construction crane. "This is one of the best engines Ford ever made," he said. "Whooee!"

"Believe me. I'm charging you a good price."

He wanted to celebrate the purchase and buy me a drink. "I bet this old Betsy has some stories to tell." He winked at me. He could not believe his good luck, and he was flirting. The cold spring air seemed to take the shape of a promise, but then there was still the problem of the envelope under the front seat. In five years, I had removed it several times. I had thought of bureau drawers and safe-deposit boxes. I had even thought of getting Dixon's address and sending it back. Again and again, I slid it under the seat once more unopened.

"Come on," the boy said. "Let's have a drink and tell some stories."

"Really, I can't," I said. "I have to go somewhere." I didn't want to get to know him. I had meant to retrieve the envelope before I turned over the car, but, standing on the curb, signing the pink slip, I discovered it would be easier just to leave it there.

"Hey," the boy said. "Look what you did. You made a sheep."

"What?" I said.

"You made a sheep with your breath. Hey—there, you did it again." Now I tried to see what he had seen in the frosty air, but it was gone. He gave me the money, we shook hands, and he got in the car. "Not many people can make a whole sheep," he said. He turned the key. "Most folks just puff out a part of a sheep."

"Wait," I said.

He put the car back in neutral and leaned out the window. "You change your mind? You hop in and I'll take you to Mr. Mike's Rock-and-Roll Heaven."

"No," I said. "I have to tell you something. There's something I didn't tell you about the car."

He stopped smiling, because he must have thought I hadn't given him a good price after all—that there was a crack in the engine block or a dogleg in the frame.

"Well, what the heck is it? Just lay me out then. The last car I had broke down on me in three weeks." He was remorseful now and disappointed in both of us.

I paused a long time. "I just think I should tell you that this car takes premium gas."

He was happy again. "Shoot, I knew that," he said. He put the car back into gear.

"You be careful," I said. "You have a good trip."

He gave me the thumbs-up sign and edged away from the curb, looking both ways, in case there was traffic.

I liked that boy. I wanted him to get safely to California and find a good life and fall in love and father a large brood of cheerful people who would try to give you too much for a used car and would always wear their shirt-sleeves too short. I watched him drive away and around the corner. I started back to the house but then turned to look at the cloud of exhaust that hung in the air. I wanted to see what figure it made. I wanted to see if it would be a sheep or a part of a sheep or a person or something else, and what I saw instead, before it unfurled into the maple trees, was a thin banner of pale smoke.

MASTER RACE

JOYCE CAROL OATES

Joyce Carol Oates is the author most recently of *Marya: A Life* (Dutton). Her stories have been included in several previous volumes of the O. Henry Awards. She lives in Princeton, New Jersey, where she teaches at the university and helps edit *The Ontario Review.*

Why would you want to hurt me—?

Why hurt another person—?

Though the incident happens abruptly, and the worst of it, in a manner of speaking, is finished within sixty seconds, Cecilia is to remember it in slow motion: the arm pinioning her deftly beneath the chin, the clumsy staggering struggle on the sidewalk, her assailant dragging her into a narrow alleyway, pummelling and punching and tearing angrily at her clothes . . . and the rest of it. No warning, no one to blame (she thinks instantly) except herself, for hadn't Philip and the Americans at the Consulate cautioned her against. . . . She makes an effort, confused and feeble, to protect herself, pulling at the man's arm, using her elbows, squirming, turning from side to side. Stop, please, no, you don't want to do this, *please*—so Cecilia would say in her reasonable soft-toned voice except for the fact that she can't breathe and her attacker is warning her to keep her mouth shut or he'll rip off her head. Yes the accent is American, low and throaty, South Carolina, perhaps, Georgia—yes she catches a glimpse of dark skin, long fingers, and blunt square trimmed fingernails, the palm of the hand lighter, almost pale.

Afterward Cecilia will recall the footsteps hurrying close behind her and her body's shrewd instinct to steel itself against attack, while a more mature—detached—rational—"intelligent"—part of her dismissed the reaction as unnecessary. She is not the sort of woman to succumb to fear, or even to take herself, as a woman, very seriously—not Cecilia Heath.

Nor is she the sort of woman—she has always supposed—who need fear sexual attack: her vision of herself is hazy and unreliable, but she has always assumed that men find her no more attractive than she finds herself.

Now she has been dragged somewhere, her smart linen jacket has been ripped partway off, her skirt lifted—she is being slapped, shaken, cursed, warned—her assailant appears to be both frightened of her and very angry, wildly angry. She doesn't see his face. She doesn't want to see his face. Her body goes limp with terror, she will discover that her clothes are soaked in perspiration, though still, *still,* that amazed stubborn voice of hers, that relentlessly civil voice, is trying to plead, to reason—*Please,* you don't really want to do this, there must be some mistake—

The man holds her from behind, panting and grunting; awkwardly, and angrily, he jams himself against her buttocks, once, twice, three times; then releases her as if in disgust, thrusts her away, gives her a hard blow to the side of her head; and it's over. Cecilia is sprawled gracelessly on the ground, her nose dripping blood, her breath coming in shudders.

Her assailant is gone as abruptly, and very nearly as invisibly, as he appeared. She hears his footsteps, or feels their vibration, but she can't move to look around. "Oh but *why. . . ?*" Cecilia whispers. "Why at this time in my. . . ."

Fortunately, she thinks, she hasn't been badly injured; perhaps she hasn't been injured at all. Fortunately she is not far from the Hotel Zur Birke, three blocks away in fact; and Philip will probably not be waiting for her; and no one has witnessed her humiliation; and no one need know. (Though, surely, humiliation is too extreme a word, too melodramatic?—Cecilia Heath does not consider herself a melodramatic woman. Her instinct is simply to withdraw from trouble and attention. In any case she has not been humiliated, she has been ill-used—the result of bad judgment on her side.)

She gets to her feet shakily, carefully. She dreads someone approaching, a belated witness to the encounter, someone who will discover her in this vulnerable exposed state: an American woman, an American woman who speaks very little German, not a tourist precisely, well, yes, perhaps she would be considered a tourist, with some professional connections, her case would be reported not only to the Mainz police but to the United States Consulate and to the United States Army since her assailant (she knows, she cannot *not* know) was an American serviceman. . . . One of the hundreds, or are there thousands, of American servicemen stationed nearby. . . .

"Oh why did you do it, *why,*" Cecilia says half-sobbing, "I meant only to be friendly. . . ."

Her right ear is ringing, blood seems to be dripping down the front of her English silk blouse, she's dazed, her heart racing, of course she isn't seriously injured; the assault would not be designated rape; the man hadn't even torn off her underwear, hadn't troubled.

Nor had he taken her purse, Cecilia sees, relieved. It is lying where she dropped it, papers and guidebook spilling out, her wallet safe inside, her passport safe . . . so there is no need to report the embarrassing incident at all.

At this time—early summer of 1983—Cecilia Heath is traveling in Europe with a senior colleague from the Peekskill Foundation for Independent Research in the Arts, Sciences, and the Humanities, a specialist in European history named Philip Schoen. Philip is fifty-three, almost twenty years older than Cecilia; he claims to be in love with her though he doesn't (in Cecilia's opinion) know her very well. He is also married—has been married, as he says, "most of his life—not unhappily." Why does he imagine himself in love with Cecilia Heath?—she can't quite bring herself to inquire.

In the past fifteen years, since the publication of his enormous book *The Invention of Chaos: Europe at War in the Twentieth Century,* Philip Schoen has acquired a fairly controversial, but generally high, reputation in his field. Cecilia has been present when fellow historians and academicians have been introduced to Philip, she has noted their mode of address, a commingling of gravity and caution, deferential courtesy, some belligerence. She has noted how Philip shakes their hands—colleagues', strangers'—as if the ceremony were something to be gotten over with as quickly as possible. Do men squeeze one another's fingers as they do ours, Cecilia has often wondered. Do they dare. . . ?

Though Philip Schoen avidly sought fame of a sort, as a young scholar, by his own confession "fame" now depresses him. Perhaps it is the mere sound of his name, *Schoen* having taken on qualities of an impersonal nature in recent years, since he was awarded a Pulitzer Prize, a Rockefeller grant, a position as Distinguished Senior Fellow at the Peekskill Foundation. . . . He jokes nervously that his rewards are "too much, too soon," while his wife would have it that they are "too little, too late."

A tall, spare, self-conscious man who carries himself with an almost military bearing, Philip Schoen is given to jokes of a brittle nervous sort which Cecilia cannot always interpret. (Her own humor tends to be warm, slanted, teasing—not the sort to make people laugh loudly. She has always remembered her mother and grandmother murmuring together, in some semi-public place like the lobby of a theater, about a fast-talking young woman close by who was making a small gathering of men laugh uproariously at her wit: *vulgar,* to have that effect upon others.) Philip is impressed by what he calls Cecilia's anachronistic qualities, her sweetness and patience and intelligent good sense; he really fell in love with her (or so he claims—it makes a charming anecdote) when she wrote a formal thank you note after a large dinner party given by the Schoens: the first note of its kind they had ever received in Peekskill, he said. ("Do you mean that nobody else here writes thank you notes?" Cecilia asked, embarrassed. "Not even the *women. . . ?")* Half-reproachfully Philip told her she was the most defined person of his acquaintance. She made everyone else seem, by contrast, improvised.

Cecilia has known Philip Schoen only since the previous September but she has been a witness, in that brief period of time, to a mysterious alteration in his personality and appearance. His manner is melancholy, edgy, obsessive; his skin exudes an air of clamminess; the whites of his eyes are faintly discolored, like old ivory, but the irises are dark, damply bright, with a hint of mirthful despair. By degrees he has acquired a subtle ravaged look that rather suits him; his sense of humor has become unexpected, abrasive, inspired. If asked by his colleagues what he is working on at the present time he sometimes says, "You don't *really* want to know": meaning that doing professional work in the history of Europe, or, by extension, in history of any sort, is a taxing enterprise. Also, he has confided in Cecilia that it's an unsettling predicament to find oneself posthumous while still alive—to know that one's scholarly reputation, like one's personality, is set; that the future can be no more than an arduous and joyless fulfillment of past expectations. Failure is a distinct possibility, of course, but not success: he *is* a success.

"But why call yourself 'posthumous'?—I don't understand," Cecilia said.

"Perhaps one day you will," he said.

In late March he dropped by unexpectedly at Cecilia's rented duplex and asked her rather awkwardly if she would like to accompany him on a three-week trip to Europe. He was being sent by the Foundation to interview prospective Fellows for one of the chairs in history—men in France, Belgium, Sweden, Finland, and Germany; and he had the privilege of bringing along an assistant of sorts, a junior colleague. Was she free? Would she come? Not as an assistant of course but as a colleague?

—a friend? "It would mean so much to me," he said, his voice faltering.

They looked at each other in mutual dismay. For weeks Philip had been seeking her out, telephoning her, encountering her by accident in town, for weeks he had been watching her with an unmistakable air of suppressed elation, but Cecilia had chosen not to see; after all he was a married man, the father of two college-age children. . . . Now he had made himself supremely vulnerable: his damp dark eyes snatched at her in a sort of drowning panic. "Of course I can't accompany you," Cecilia heard her soft cool voice explain, but, aloud, she could bring herself to say only: "Yes, thank you, it's very kind of you to ask, yes I suppose I would like to go . . . but as an assistant after all, if you don't mind."

He seized her hands in his and kissed her, breathless and trembling as any young suitor. Did it matter that he was nineteen years older than she, that his rank at the Foundation was so much superior to hers, that his breath smelled sweetly of alcohol. . . ? Or that he was married, and might very well break Cecilia's heart. . . ?

On the flight to Frankfurt Philip tells her about his family background in a low, tense, neutral voice, as if he were confessing something shameful.

His paternal grandparents emigrated from the Rhine Valley near Wiesbaden in the early 1900s, settling first in Pennsylvania, and then in northern Wisconsin: they were dairy farmers, prosperous, Lutheran, clannish, supremely German. Until approximately the late thirties. Until such time as it was no longer politic in the United States, or even safe, to proclaim the natural superiority of the Homeland and the inevitable inferiority of other nations, races, religions.

"The Germans really are a master race," Philip says, "—even when they—or do I mean we?—pretend humility."

Though he has visited Germany many times for professional purposes he has never, oddly, sought out his distant relatives. Perhaps in fact he has none; that part of Germany suffered terrible devastation in the final year of the war. Yes he had relatives in the German army, yes he had an uncle, a much-honored bomber pilot who flew hundreds of successful missions before being shot down over Cologne. . . . "As late as the fifties I had to contend with a good deal of family legend, stealthy German boasting," Philip says. "Of course if hard pressed my father and uncles *would* admit that Hitler was a madman, the Reich was doomed, the entire mythopoetics of German-ness was untenable. . . ."

He believes he knows the German soul perfectly, he says, but by way of his scholarly investigations and interviews primarily: not (or so he hopes) by way of blood. Historical record is all that one can finally trust, not intuition, not promptings of the spirit; a people is its actions, not its ideals; we are (to paraphrase William James) what we cause others to experience.

He breaks off suddenly as if the subject has become distasteful. He tells Cecilia, laughing, that there is nothing more disagreeable than a self-loathing German.

"But do you loathe yourself?" Cecilia asks doubtfully. "And why do you think of yourself as German rather than American. . . ?"

Philip takes her hand, strokes the long slender fingers. His gesture is sudden, surreptitious, though no one is seated in the third airliner seat and in any case no one knows them. He says lightly: "My wife would tell you that the secret of my being is self-loathing—by which she means my German-ness."

A symposium on contemporary philosophical trends was held that spring at the Peekskill Foundation. No aesthetician participated; no specialists in metaphysics or ethics. There were linguists, logicians, mathematicians, a topologist, a semiotician, and others—all men—who resisted classification. The chairman of the conference began by stating, evidently without irony, that since all viable philosophical positions were represented it was not unreasonable to expect that certain key problems might finally be solved. "Only in the presence of my colleagues would I confess to such optimism," the gentleman said, drawing forth appreciative laughter.

The sessions Cecilia attended, however, were consumed in disjointed attempts to define the "problems" at hand. Equations were scrawled on the blackboard, linguistic analyses were presented, the philosophers spoke ingeniously, aggressively, sometimes incomprehensibly, but so far as Cecilia could judge the primary terms were never agreed upon; each speaker wanted to wipe the slate clean and begin again. One particularly belligerent philosopher made the point that the habit of "bifurcated" thinking, the "hominine polarity of ego vis-à-vis non-ego," was responsible for the muddled communication. Which is to say, the custom of thinking in antitheses; the acquired (and civilization-determined) custom of perceiving the world in terms of opposites; the curse, as he phrased it, of being "egoed." Hence civilized man is doomed to make distinctions between himself and others: mind and body: up and down: hot and cold: good and evil: mine/ours and yours/theirs: male and female. . . . The list went on for some time, including such problematic opposites as vocalic and consonantal, reticular and homogenous, violable and inviolable, but Cecilia drifted into a dream thinking of "male" and "female" as acquired habits of thinking. *Acquired habits of thinking. . . ?*

But why, Cecilia wonders, holding a handkerchief to her bleeding nose—why hurt another person?

Cecilia and Philip, in Mainz, in Germany, are no longer quite so companionable. In fact they are beginning to have small misunderstandings, not quite disagreements, like any traveling couple, like lovers married or unmarried.

Cecilia speaks very little German, which gives her a kind of schoolgirl innocence, a perpetual tourist's air of surprise and interest and appreciation. Philip's German is fluent and aggressive, as if he half expects to be misunderstood; he responds with annoyance if asked where he is from. Though he had enjoyed himself previously—especially in Paris and Stockholm—he now seems distracted, edgy, quick to be offended. The clerk at the Hotel Zur Birke, for instance, was brusque with him and Cecilia before he realized who they were and who had made their reservations, whereupon he turned apologetic, smiling, fawning, begging their apologies. ("The very essence of the German personality," Philip muttered to Cecilia, "—either at your throat or at your feet.") His eye for local detail seems to be focussed upon the blatantly vulgar—American pop music blaring from a radio in the hotel's breakfast room, "medieval" souvenirs of stamped tin, graffiti in lurid orange spray-paint on walls, doors, construction fences (much of it in English: KILL, FUCK, NUKE, PRAY) which Philip photographs with a tireless grim pleasure. The enormous tenth-century Romanesque cathedral which Cecilia finds fascinating, if rather damp and oppressive, Philip dismisses as old Teutonic *kitsch,* preserved solely for German and American tourists; the Mainz Hilton he finds a monument to imperialist vulgarity, a happy confluence of German and American ideals of fantasy, efficiency, sheer bulk; even old St. Stephen's Church, partly restored after having been bombed, offends him with its stylish Chagall stained glass windows . . . the blue so very pretty, so achingly pretty, like a Disney-heaven.

Cecilia is surprised at his tone, and begins to challenge him. Why say such things when he doesn't really mean them, or when they can't be all he means?—why such hostility? "I have the caricaturist's eye, I suppose," Philip admits, "—of looking for truths where no one else cares to look."

But Philip is beginning to find fault with Cecilia as well. His objections are ambiguous, likely to be expressed half-seriously, chidingly. . . . Frankly, he says, she puzzles him when she isn't exacting enough by ordinary American standards; when she's overly tolerant; quick to excuse and forgive. In the hotel's newspaper and tobacco shop, for instance, Cecilia returned a few German coins to a clerk who had, in ringing up her purchase, accidentally undercharged her by about sixty cents; and the man—heavy, bald, bulbous-nosed—became inexplicably angry with Cecilia and spoke harshly to her in German, in front of several other customers. Whatever he said hadn't included the word *Danke,* certainly. "And you think the incident is amusing?" Philip says irritably. "How can you take such an attitude?"

"I'm in a foreign country, after all," Cecilia says. "I expect things to seem foreign."

Walking in Mainz on their first evening, trying to relax after the strain of the Frankfurt airport, Cecilia and Philip find themselves in a slightly derelict section of town, across from the railroad station, by the Hammer Hotel, where a number of black American soldiers are milling about in various stages of sobriety. They are touchingly young, Cecilia thinks—nineteen, twenty years old, hardly more than boys. And self-consciously rowdy, defiant, loutish, *black,* as if challenging respectable German pedestrians to take note of them.

One of them, laughing loudly, tries to grab hold of a Binding Bier sign affixed to the hotel's veranda roof, but falls heavily to the street. A driver in a Volkswagen van sounds his horn angrily as he passes and for a minute or two there is a good deal of shouting and fist-waving among the soldiers.

"Strange to see them here," Cecilia says, staring.

"Yes. Unfortunate too," Philip says.

They are stationed at a nearby army base, Philip explains, probably employed in guarding one of the United States military installations. It might even be a nuclear weapons site, he isn't certain.

Cecilia has been reading about recent anti-war and anti-United States demonstrations in Germany, in the *Herald Tribune.* The Green Party is planning an ambitious fall offensive—the hostility to the American military is increasing all the time. She feels sorry for these soldiers, she says, so far from home, so young. . . . They must feel totally confused and demoralized, like soldiers in Vietnam. And so many of them are black.

"Yes. It's unfortunate," Philip says, urging her along. "But the situation isn't at all analogous to Vietnam."

A heavy-set black soldier is staggering about in the street, clowning for his buddies and two very blond girls, German teenagers perhaps, who are whistling and applauding him. Cecilia slows, watching them. She feels an odd prick of guilt—or is it a confused sort of compatriotism, complicity? The soldiers are here, stationed in West Germany, thousands of miles from home, only because they are in the service of their country; protecting, in a manner of speaking, private citizens like Cecilia Heath and Philip Schoen. It is a sobering reflection to think that, if necessary, the men would die in that service. . . .

When they are some distance away, headed back toward the Neue Mainzerstr. and a more congenial part of town, Philip says: "We're only about one hundred miles from the East German border, don't forget. It's easy to forget, in a place like Mainz."

"What do you mean?"

"I mean that our soldiers are political hostages of a sort, under the protection of the United States military. Their presence isn't very agreeable to anyone but it is necessary."

" 'Hostages'. . . ?"

"The fact that there are thousands of American soldiers in West Germany makes it less likely that the Soviets will attack: it's as simple as that."

Cecilia draws away slightly to look at her companion. She cannot determine whether Philip is speaking ironically, or with a certain measure of passion. Since coming to Germany he hasn't seemed quite himself . . . not quite the man she believes she knows. The edge of antagonism in his voice has the curious effect of provoking her to an uncharacteristic naivete. "But is a Soviet invasion a real possibility?" she asks. "Isn't it all exaggerated, as the anti-arms people say?"

"For Christ's sake, Cecilia, nothing is exaggerated *here,*" Philip says. "Don't you know where you are?"

But still the matter does not rest. Their odd disjointed conversation, their discussion-on-the-edge-of-quarreling, continues even at dinner. Cecilia supposes it is pointless of her to question Philip Schoen on such issues, her knowledge is haphazard and blurred, much of it, in truth, garnered from the *Herald Tribune* of recent days; but she cannot forget the black soldiers, their foolish conspicuous behavior, their air of . . . wanting to be seen, noted. If Cecilia Heath does not take note of them, who will? Yes, she says, the situation resembles Vietnam in certain ways: an army consisting of many impoverished blacks, very young ill-educated men, men who probably know little about why they are where they are, or even, precisely, where they are. In a way it's a tragic situation.

Philip laughs irritably. He says that, in his opinion, the "tragedy" is Germany's. He feels sorrier for the Mainz citizens than for the United States soldiers. In recent years the soldiers have caused a good deal of trouble in Germany: drunk and disorderly behavior, drug-dealing to young Germans (even school children), assaults, vandalism, even rape and robbery. Maybe even murder, for all he knew. Such things were hushed up. As for the blacks. . . . "The Germans ignore them completely," Philip says. "They aren't sentimental about certain things, as we are. They don't assume virtues when they don't have them."

Seeing her startled expression Philip says that he isn't a racist—she shouldn't think *that*—but he likes to challenge liberal pieties; he wouldn't respect himself as a scholar and an historian otherwise. It is his role as a professional to challenge, for instance, the media's image of such countries as Poland, Czechoslovakia, Hungary. How innocent are they, historically—objectively? What are their records concerning the treatment of Jews and other minorities, and neighboring countries—("provided the neighboring countries are weaker")? Fed by a sentimentalist public media, how many Americans know anything at all about Poland's terrifying history of anti-Semitism—or of Hungary's belligerence against Rumania—or of the cruelty of the Czechs toward any number of defenseless minorities? One might in fact argue that Poland provoked Germany into the invasion of 1939, for instance, by way of her intransigence in the early 1920s—insisting upon mythical rights against the Germans, and invading German territory by force; invading Lithuania as well, and the Ukraine, and even Russia—in a grotesque attempt to consolidate a little empire. Did anyone in America know? Did anyone want to know? Truth isn't very popular these days.

If the Germans became outlaws, Philip says, who could prove that, following the catastrophic Treaty of Versailles, they were not forced into an outlaw mentality: which is to say—outside, beyond, *beneath* the law? Perhaps Hitler was no more than the Scourge of God.

Cecilia protests faintly, scarcely knowing what to say. Her field of training is art history, particularly nineteenth-century American art; it is probably insulting to Philip for her to attempt to argue with him. Quoting statistics, referring to treaties, invasions, acts of parliament, acts of duplicity and vengeance of which Cecilia, frankly, has never heard ("to understand Hitler's Reich, and by extension present-day Germany, you have to understand Bismarck's 'siege mentality' of the 1880s"), Philip makes Cecilia appear to be something of a fool. What has triggered this episode? Merely the sight of those eight or ten black soldiers by the Hammer Hotel? Cecilia is so upset she drinks several glasses of wine quickly, fighting the impulse to tell Philip that she doesn't care for his facts, his precious History, if they contradict what she wants to believe.

Finally she makes the point that not all Germans are racially prejudiced, as he'd said ("Now Cecilia of course I didn't say *that")*—what of the two young German girls who were with the soldiers by the hotel? They all appeared to be getting on very well together.

Philip shifts uneasily in his seat—they are sitting now in a dim, smoke-hazy cocktail lounge in the Mainzer Hof, as a way of postponing the awkwardness of returning to their own hotel and their separate rooms—and makes an effort to smile at Cecilia, as if to soften his words: "Those 'girls,' Cecilia, were obviously prostitutes. No other German women would go anywhere near those men, I assure you."

It throws you back upon yourself, the starveling little core of yourself —so a friend of Cecilia's once told her, lying in a hospital bed, having been nearly killed in an automobile accident. He meant the suddenness of violence; its eerie physicality; the fact that, as creatures with spiritual pretensions, we do after all inhabit bodies.

It throws you back upon yourself, the starveling little core of yourself. The aloneness.

Cecilia thinks of her assailant, who was not quite visible to her, but irrevocably real. Oh yes real enough—convincing in *his* physicality. She will never know his name, his age, his background; whether he is married; has children; is in fact considered a "nice guy" when not aroused to sexual rage. (He had been drinking too, Cecilia recalls the odor of beer, his hot panting breath, the smell of him.) She will never know whether he felt any legitimate pleasure in performing his furtive act upon her, or any remorse afterward. Whether in fact he even remembered what he'd done, afterward. Did men remember such things?

The German prostitutes were so young, no more than seventeen or eighteen, surely. And so blond, so pretty. Cecilia sees them vividly in her mind's eye, she notes their blue jeans, their absurd high heels, their tight-fitting jersey blouses, their unzipped satin jackets—one crimson, the other lemon yellow. She notes their glowing faces, their red mouths, the drunken teetering in the street, the clapping of hands (had the black soldier's antics genuinely amused them, or was their response merely part of the transaction?), the streaming blond hair. *The starveling little core of yourself,* Cecilia thinks. *The aloneness.*

The evidence Cecilia Heath will not provide, either to Philip Schoen or to the authorites: while Philip spent the afternoon at the Johannes Gutenberg University, speaking with graduate students in the American Studies Department, Cecilia, grateful to be alone, spent the time in the Mainz Museum (paintings by Nolde, Otto Dix, Otto Moll which she admired enormously), in the Gutenberg Museum (a sombre, rather penitential sort of shrine, but extremely interesting), and in a noisy pub on the Kaiserstr. where, believing herself friendly and well-intentioned, she struck up a conversation of sorts with six or seven black soldiers.

It's true that such cheery gregarious behavior is foreign to Cecilia Heath. She is usually shy with strangers; even with acquaintances; she spends an insomniac night before giving a public lecture, or meeting with her university classes for the first time; someone once advised her —not meaning to be unkind—that she might see a psychotherapist to help her with her "phobia." Yet for some reason, here in Mainz, liberated for a long sunny afternoon from Philip, she must have thought it would be . . . charitable, magnanimous . . . the sort of thing one of her maiden aunts might do in such circumstances: *How are you, where are you from, how long have you been stationed in Mainz, when will you be going back home, do the peace demonstrations worry you, is it difficult being in Germany or do you find it . . . challenging? The German people are basically friendly to Americans, aren't they?*

(Cecilia takes on, not quite consciously, the voice and manner of her Aunt Edie, of St. Joachim, Pennsylvania: the woman's air of feckless Christian generosity, her frank smiling solicitude. In the early fifties this remarkable woman had helped to organize a Planned Parenthood clinic in St. Joachim, had endured a good deal of abuse, even threats against her life; but she'd remained faithful to her task. Even after the clinic was burned down she hadn't given up.)

So it happens that Cecilia Heath talks with the soldiers for perhaps fifteen, twenty minutes. Cecilia in her dove-gray linen blazer, her white silk English blouse, her gabardine skirt, her smart Italian sandals. Cecilia carrying a leather bag over her shoulder, a little breathless, shyly aggressive, damp-eyed, her hair windblown, a fading red streaked with silver. (She wonders afterward how old she seemed to them, how odd, how "attractive." They were so taken by surprise they hadn't even time to glance at one another, to exchange appraising looks.) She introduces herself, she shakes their hands, she makes her cheery inquiries, she can well imagine Philip Schoen's disapproval; but of course Philip need not know of the episode.

Harold is the most courteous, calling her Ma'am repeatedly, smiling broadly, giving her childlike answers as if reciting for a school teacher (he's from New York City yeh he likes the Army okay yeh he likes

Germany okay there's lots of places worse yeh he's going home for Christmas furlough yeh ma'am it sure is a long way off), Bo is the youngest, short and spunky, ebony-skinned, brash (No ma'am them Germans demonstratin an shootin off their mouths don't worry *him*—howcome she's askin, do they worry *her)*, Cash, or "Kesh," asks excitedly if she is a newspaper reporter and would she maybe be taking their pictures. . . ? They talk at the same time, interrupting one another, showing off for Cecilia and for anyone in the pub who happens to be listening; they make loud comments about Mainz, about the Germans, about the food, the beer (they insist upon buying Cecilia a tankard of beer though it was her intention to treat them to a round); but two others whose names she hasn't quite caught—Arnie, Ernie?—Shelton? —regard her with sullen expressions. Their faces are black fists, clenched. Their lives appear clenched as well, not to be pried open by a white woman whose only claim to them is that she and they share American citizenship . . . in a manner of speaking.

Cash half-teases her that she must be a reporter, else why would she be bothering with *them*, and Cecilia, flushed, laughingly denies it. "Do I look like a reporter?" she says. And afterward wonders why she made that particular remark.

For an art historian she doesn't always *see* clearly enough; she isn't exacting; in fact she can be "perplexingly blind"—so Philip has said, critically, kindly; so Philip has been saying since their arrival in Germany. For a critic of some reputation she isn't sufficiently . . . critical. After all, to be sentimental about foreign places and people simply because they are foreign is a sign of either condescension or ignorance. It can even be (so Philip hinted delicately) a sign of inverted bigotry.

Again and again Cecilia will tell herself that she wasn't condescending to the soldiers, she isn't that sort of person, in fact she feels a confused warm empathy with nearly everyone she meets . . . but of course her intentions might be misunderstood. Her empathy itself might be angrily rejected.

Yet is there any reason, any incontrovertible reason, to believe that her invisible assailant was actually one of the men in the pub. . . ? There is no proof, no evidence. The soft gravelly Southern accent might have belonged to any number of Americans stationed in Germany. And of course she didn't see the face. Hearing the running footsteps—feeling the acceleration of her heart—she had not wished to turn her head.

It takes her approximately ten painful minutes—walking stiffly, her arms close against her sides—to get to the Hotel Zur Birke. Only on the busier street do people glance at her, frowning, disapproving, wondering at her disheveled hair and clothes; but Cecilia looks straight ahead, inviting no one's solicitude.

(Yet it is a nightmare occasion—Cecilia Heath alone and exposed, making her way across a public square, along a public street, being observed, judged, pitied. A dream of childhood and early girlhood, poor Cecilia the object of strangers' stares, in a city she does not know, perhaps even a foreign city. . . . How ironic for it to be coming true when she is an adult woman of thirty-four and her life is so fully her own. . . .)

Fortunately there is an inconspicuous side entrance to the hotel, and a back stairway, so that Cecilia is spared the indignity of the central foyer and the single slow-moving elevator. On the stairway landing she sees her reflection in an ornamental coppery shield: sickly-pale angular face, pinched eyes, linen jacket torn and soiled, signs of a recent nosebleed. The sight unnerves her though it should not be surprising.

She will deal with the situation efficiently enough: she will soak herself in a hot bath, prepare to forget. There is a dinner that evening at eight hosted by a German literary group and Cecilia doesn't intend to miss it.

Her hotel room is on the third floor, near the rear of the building; Philip's is close by. While she is fitting her key in the lock, however, Philip suddenly appears—he must have been waiting for her. He says at once in a frightened astonished voice: "What has happened to you? Good God—"

Cecilia refuses to face him. She tells him that nothing has happened: she had an accident: she fell down a flight of stairs, five or six steps maybe, nothing serious: nothing for him to be alarmed about.

"But Cecilia, your face, your clothes—is that *blood?* What happened?"

He touches her and she shrinks away, still not looking at him.

Now follows an odd disjoined scene in the corridor outside Cecilia's room, which she is to recall, afterward, only in fragments.

Philip seems to know that something fairly serious has happened to her but he cannot quite think what to do, what to say. He keeps asking her excitedly what *exactly* happened, where did she fall, was it out on the street, were there witnesses, did anyone help her, how badly is she hurt, should he call the downstairs desk and get a doctor, should he call the Consulate and cancel their plans for the evening. . . . Cecilia, turned away, half-sobbing, ashamed, insists that she hasn't been injured, it was only a foolish accident, a misstep, a fall, she banged her head and one knee, tore her jacket, her nose started bleeding, she has only herself to blame . . . won't he please believe her?

Philip takes hold of Cecilia's shoulders but she wrenches sharply away, ducking her head. He doesn't repeat the gesture and she thinks, *He's afraid of me.* For some seconds they stand close together, not touching. Each is breathing audibly.

He *should* call a doctor, Philip says hesitantly. She might have a sprain, a concussion. . . .

No, Cecilia insists. She *hasn't* been injured, she *isn't* upset, won't he please let her go inside her room?

But he should cancel their plans for the evening, at least, Philip says. He had better call the Consulate. . . .

No, says Cecilia, that isn't necessary. If she doesn't feel up to going out by eight o'clock he must go alone, certainly there's no need to cancel his evening, the dinner after all is primarily in his honor and not hers.

But he couldn't do that, he couldn't leave her. . . .

Yes, please, oh yes, Cecilia says, trying to calm herself, she isn't at all injured, she's only a little shaken, if she can be alone for a while . . . if she can relax in a hot bath. . . . Please won't he believe her? Won't he leave her alone?

Cecilia has managed to unlock her door. Philip, reprimanded, rebuffed, doesn't try to follow her inside the darkened room. He stands in the doorway, staring, so visibly distraught that Cecilia can't bear to look at him. *He knows,* she thinks. *That's why he's so afraid.*

As Cecilia is about to close the door he says, again, in a faltering voice, that he'll be happy to cancel their plans for the evening if she wants him to. He doesn't want to go to the dinner alone, he'd only be thinking of her, *is* she all right . . . really?

"Yes," Cecilia says, her face now streaked with tears. "Yes. Of course. *Yes.* Thank you for asking."

As she is undressing the telephone rings. It is Philip, agitated, rather more aggressive. Where exactly did she fall?—did someone push her? —was her wallet taken?—why did she stay out so long, alone?—*it was one of those soldiers, wasn't it*—

Cecilia quietly hangs up. The phone doesn't ring again.

In her bath she lies with her head flung back and her eyes shut tight, tight. It is her head that aches, that buzzes, the other parts of her body are numbed and distant. Her buttocks are not sore—they have no sensation at all.

She imagines her mother, her mother's sisters, even her father, her family's neighbors, gathered to sit in judgment on her. Whispering among themselves that Cecilia Heath should not be traveling with a man not her husband . . . a man who is another woman's husband . . . even if they are not lovers. Especially if they are not lovers.

It isn't like Cecilia. It *isn't* Cecilia.

She recalls her first gynecological examination at the age of eighteen, the sudden piercing pain, the surprise of it, the uncontrolled hysterical laughter that had turned to sobs . . . and hadn't she done something absurd, dislodging one of her feet from the metal spur, kicking out wildly at the doctor? . . . angering him so that he'd said something mean and out of character: *You had better grow up, fast.*

And so she did.

But perhaps she did not. . . ?

In the other room the telephone is ringing. But the sound is faint and distant and not at all threatening.

A long time ago, a decade ago, Cecilia Heath was in love and more or less engaged, but nothing had come of it; nothing comes of so many things, if you have patience.

She keeps her eyes shut tight so that she needn't see the soldiers' expressions, the grinning flash of teeth, the faint oily sheen of dark, dark skin; she wills herself not to hear again that command, *Shut up, keep your mouth shut,* low and throaty, she had supposed it a Southern accent but in truth it might be any Negro accent at all, New York City, Baltimore, Washington, South Carolina, Georgia, hadn't Bo said he was from Atlanta, and what of Arnie, or Shelton, who had stared at her with such hatred, *Keep your mouth shut or I'll rip off your head.*

She sees no face, no features; she can identify no one; she has nothing to report. Philip is quite mistaken—her wallet wasn't touched. Her passport wasn't touched. Consequently it would be pointless to report the incident to the authorities, pointless and embarrassing to all concerned, the Mainz police, the United States Consulate, the United States Military Police, pointless and embarrassing, a matter of deep shame to both her and Philip. She has Philip Schoen to think of as well as herself. *Keep your mouth shut or. . . .*

She has scrubbed away all evidence of her attacker. Semen, sperm. Perspiration. She has discarded her stained underwear, she will never again wear the linen skirt and jacket, the expensive silk blouse is ruined past recovery, far simpler to fold everything up carefully and throw it away. (She recalls as if from a distance of years her girlish vanity, her excitement, when she bought these clothes for the trip; for her honeymoon fling with Philip Schoen *who claimed to be in love with her.)* No evidence, nothing remains. A few bruises. That ringing in her head, in her right ear. Impossible to press criminal charges against a person whose face you have not seen and whose voice you did not clearly hear, impossible to press charges against such impersonal anger, such sexual rage.

Your feelings are wounded, aren't they. Not your flesh.

You liked the soldiers and wanted to think . . . yes, badly wanted to think . . . they liked you.

Though doomed, the evening begins successfully.

There are nine of them around the table—Cecilia, and Philip, and an information officer from the Consulate named Margot (a German-born American woman, Cecilia's age), and six Germans (five men, one woman) who are writers, and/or are involved in American studies at the University. To disguise her sickly pallor and the discoloration on the right side of her face Cecilia applied pancake make-up hurriedly purchased in the hotel's drugstore—Cecilia, who never wears make-up, who has always thought the practice barbaric—and the result is surprisingly good, judging from the others' responses. (Philip has said very little. Philip is going to say very little to her throughout the evening.)

Yes, the German gentlemen behave gallantly to Cecilia, even rather flirtatiously. Perhaps they sense her new, raw vulnerability—perhaps there is something appealing about her porcelain face, her moist red lips. August who is a philologist and lover of poetry, Hans who teaches English, Heinrich who has translated Melville, Whitman, Emily Dickinson . . . and fiery young Rudolph who will shortly publish his first novel . . . and even the most distinguished member of the German contingent, the white-haired professor of American history Dr. Fritz Eisenach . . . all appear to be quite taken with Miss Heath of the Peekskill Foundation. Dr. Eisenach addresses her so that all the table can hear, querying her on nineteenth-century American art, in which he claims an interest of many years—for such "supreme" figures as George Fuller and John La Farge. As it happens Cecilia is the author of a monograph on Fuller, published when she was still in graduate school in New Haven; and her main project at Peekskill is to do a study of La Farge whom she has long considered an important painter . . . indeed, it is Cecilia Heath's professional goal to raise La Farge from his respectable obscurity and establish him as a major American artist. So her replies delight Dr. Eisenach, and for some heady minutes Cecilia finds herself the center of attention.

Philip smiles in her direction, sucking at his pipe, saying nothing.

When asked about La Farge he professes innocence: he intends to wait, he says, for Cecilia's book.

They talk variously of American art, German art, the journals of nineteenth-century German travelers in North America, the history of Wagner's *Ring* in America, the mingled histories of American and German transcendentalism in its many permutations and disguises . . . they spend a good deal of time on the menu . . . the Germans' intention being to treat their guests to a fully German dinner, a representative German dinner, yet not the sort too readily available back in the States. (Cecilia is to sample, with varying degrees of appetite, such delicacies as Räucheraal—smoked eel; Gänseleber-Pastete—goose liver paté; Ochsenschwanzuppe—oxtail soup; Rheinsalm—Rhine salmon; Schweineleber and Schweinhirn—pork liver, pork brains; Hasen—hare; and any number of wines and desserts.) The food is hearty and tasty, the Germans speak English fluently, the conversation rarely flags, Cecilia feels herself borne along by the very current of her hosts' sociability, hearing her own frequent laughter, glimpsing her reflection in a bay window opposite. (The dinner is being held in a private dining room in a restaurant on the Bahnhofplatz, candlelit, charmingly decorated with oaken beams, paintings of the Rhine Valley, a massive stone fireplace piled high with white birch logs. The atmosphere is warm, gracious, convivial, a little loud. Cecilia wonders how she and the others appear to passers-by who happen to glance inside: very like old friends, probably, even relatives, men and women who are extremely close. She wonders too how Philip and she appear to their hosts. They are lovers, surely? But lovers who have traveled together for years, lovers who know each other's secrets, who have forgiven much, whose courtesy toward each other has become second nature. . . . Called Frau Schoen by the German woman, at the beginning of the evening, Cecilia felt obliged to correct her; and wondered if Philip overheard. Frau Schoen, she might have added, is back home in Peekskill, New York.)

The talk shifts to politics, the films of the late Fassbinder, an organization in Frankfurt for refugees from the East, pacific and ecological and vegetarian movements among the young. . . . Philip and Cecilia will be flying from Frankfurt to West Berlin on the following afternoon, they are leaving the Federal Republic of Germany, consequently tonight's celebration has an additional symbolic value. Yes they have enjoyed their brief stay in Mainz very much. Yes they hope to return again someday soon. And next time—so August Bürger insists—they must stay longer, two weeks at least.

Cecilia and Philip glance at each other, smiling, compliant, pretending to be flattered. Cecilia is reminded of the way Philip and his wife Virginia glanced at each other from time to time in their home—how effortless it is, to put on a mutual front, to deceive observers. There is even a kind of pleasure in it.

By degrees the dining room becomes over-warm, the conversation too intense. Cecilia would like to return to her hotel room but cannot bring herself to move. Her head aches again, her breasts are sore. Had her assailant pummelled them? . . . she can't recall. Philip and Professor Eisenach and the shrill-voiced Rudolph are discussing the Green Party, and the international peace movement, and the hoax of the Hitler diary ("a disgraceful episode," the Professor says, shaking his jowls, "brilliantly hilarious," says young Rudolph), and Aryan mythology, and the manufacture of Nazi memorabilia in the German Democratic Republic, for export to the West. (This too is disgraceful, and cynical, says the Professor; but Rudolph insists that it is justified—if idiots in the F. R. G. want to buy such trash, and kindred idiots in the United States, why not sell it to them? "Such arrangements are only good business," Rudolph says.) They discuss the ironies of the new dream of German unity ("a dream acknowledged only in the West," says Hans), and the hunger of all people for national heroes . . . for something truly *transcendent* in which to believe. . . .

("So long as the 'transcendent' is also good business," Rudolph cannot help quipping, a bad little boy at his elders' table.)

Cecilia drifts off into a dream and finds herself thinking of her mother, but her mother is dead . . . and of her father . . . but, dear God, her father is dead also: they died within eighteen months of each other, during the confused time of Cecilia's "engagement." When she rouses herself to attention the atmosphere has quickened considerably. Hans is speaking passionately, his forehead oily with perspiration; August is speaking, laying a hand, hard, on Rudolph's arm, to keep him from interrupting; Professor Eisenach warns sternly of the "Fascistoid" left; the German woman Frau Lütz reminds them, should they require reminding, that the students of the 1920s were far more anti-Semitic than their teachers and parents—as, she believes, Dr. Schoen himself discussed in his excellent book.

Philip graciously accepts the woman's praise. He surprises his listeners, Cecilia included, by rather contemptuously dismissing the peace movement: after all, he lived through the sixties in the United States, he'd been teaching at Harvard at the time, he'd had quite enough of "youthful idealism."

Rudolph begins to speak loudly, excitedly, waving a forefinger. It isn't clear to Cecilia—part of his speech is in German—if he is attacking Philip or siding with him. Perhaps he is attacking the red-faced Eisenach? Rudolph's sympathy with socialism, he says, is such that he has come to the conclusion that the "forced de-Nazification" of Germany by the United States was an act of imperialist aggression; so too, the "forced democratization" of Germany. He believes in a Left that is pitiless and unforgiving of its enemies—especially its German enemies. He believes in a Left that proudly embraces German destiny. As for History, he says with majestic scorn, spittle on his lips and his eyes wickedly bright—History has no memory, no existence. If he had his way he would ban all books written before 1949 . . . which is to say, six years before his own birth.

Philip laughs and regards him with a look of affectionate contempt. "No German born in 1955 can be taken seriously," he says.

Everyone at the table bursts into laughter except Cecilia and Rudolph, who sit silent.

Belatedly, Margot from the Consulate tries to change the subject. Did Philip and Cecilia visit St. Stephen's Church, did they see the famous Chagall window?—but Philip ignores her. He and Rudolph are staring at each other, clearly attracted by each other's insolence. So very German, thinks Cecilia, feeling a wave of faintness. It is an old story that has nothing to do with her.

It is late, nearing midnight. Coffee and brandy are served. Chocolates wrapped in tinfoil. Too many people are smoking, why has no one opened a window. . . ? Frau Lütz who teaches English and American literature at the University asks the Americans their opinions of "Black Marxist street poetry"; the smiling gat-toothed Heinrich asks about "revisionist gay" readings of Whitman and Hart Crane. Again the subject of Fassbinder is raised, arousing much controversy; and does Werner Herzog ("the far greater artist," says August) have a following in the States; and is there sympathy for Heinrich Böll, his attitude toward disarmament, his involvement in the blockade of the American military base at Mutlangen. . . ? In the midst of the discussion Rudolph says languidly that he himself would not wish the enemies of Germany destroyed; for as the aphorism has it, our enemy is by tradition our savior, in preventing us from superficiality. At this August bursts into angry laughter and tells the Americans to pay no attention to Rudolph, who is drunk, knows nothing of what he says, and has never visited the East in any case.

"How dare you speak of my private business!—you know nothing of my private business!" Rudolph says in a fierce whisper.

It is no longer clear to Cecilia what the men are arguing about, if indeed they are arguing. It seems that Rudolph is only courting Philip, in his brash childish manner. . . . In the flickering candlelight he looks disconcertingly young; his face is long and lean and feral, his eyes hooded, his lips fleshy. Stylized wings of hair frame his bony forehead, stiff as if lacquered. The *enfant terrible* of the Mainz circle, petted, over-praised, spoiled, he has nonetheless a charming air of self-mockery. (Unfortunate, Cecilia thinks, that he isn't qualified to be a Fellow at the Peekskill Foundation—he and Philip would certainly liven things up there. But it is Dr. August Bürger, the philologist-poet with the impressive credentials, whom Philip has been interviewing in Mainz.) Now Rudolph and Philip are speaking animatedly together, for the benefit of the entire table, of the folly of German submersion in "European civilization"—that phantasm which had no existence, could never have had any existence, since Europe is by nature many Europes, nation-groups, language- and dialect-groups, clamoring for autonomy but, for the most part, fated to be slave states. Slave states!—Does Cecilia hear correctly? Or is she simply exhausted, depressed? The expression arouses a good deal of comment on all sides, but Philip and young Rudolph pay no heed.

Hans, sighing, draws a large white handkerchief out of his coat pocket and wipes his gleaming face and says in an aside to Cecilia: "I am teaching four courses each term, Fraülein Heath, elementary and intermediate and advanced English, and am not given to idle speculation, but what of the new Pershing II rockets, Fraülein, which your country is so generous as to wish to store with us? Germany has become a land-mine, Fraülein, in payment for its sins. Do you agree? Are you informed? The Soviets boast that they will destroy us how many times, and the Americans are to retaliate by destroying them how many times. Forty, sixty, one hundred, five hundred? Yes, Fraülein," he says, showing his teeth in a broad damp smile, "it is only a joke, no offense is meant, we have here not the privilege of offense after all. For Rudolph and his comrades the destruction of Germany is perhaps no loss, as for your President Reagan also, just payment for our sins. Please, Fraülein, on the eve of your departure from Mainz, do not take offense—I am but making jokes printed in the newspapers every day, a commonplace."

Cecilia, flushed, slightly light-headed, would say that she favors peace and disarmament, she doesn't favor war, or even the stockpiling of weapons; but so banal a statement might provoke mocking laughter. Even now Rudolph is laughing with a hearty brutality at something Philip has said, a reference perhaps to the Schoen who flew a bomber for the German Air Force, or is there another Schoen, a Nazi major, about whom Cecilia has yet to hear. . . . Professor Eisenach makes a passionate drunken speech, his eyes damp and his voice trembling, in Wilhelmian Germany and yet again in the 1930s the Church freely acquiesced to the State, and did the *intelligentsia* protest? Not at all. Never. A disgraceful history of abnegation, a disgraceful history of. . . . There must be worship, and gods, and devils, and sacrifice; when there are untroubled times it is the peace of apathy and impotence, young men and women indistinguishable from one another in hair style, costume, behavior . . . it is all *a waiting for the end.* The others listen to the Professor's rambling speech with barely concealed impatience. Then August brings up the subject of the East, addressing the Americans (but Philip especially): Does their country feel sorry for the East Germans?—is their special sympathy for the East Germans? If so they are fools and must be better informed, for the East Germans went from Hitler to Stalin with ease—"*It is all the same to them! The same!*" At this Rudolph stammers in protest; and August accuses him of being a traitor and a fool; and Philip, sucking on his pipe, expelling a thin gray cloud of aromatic smoke, assures the table that he himself feels no sympathy for the East Germans, his sympathy is solely for the West Germans, amnesiac for so many years, and made to be on perpetual trial in the world's eyes . . . made to feel shame for being German. Indeed, words like "shame" and "guilt" strike the ear, Philip says, as distinctly hypocritical. Is German "shame" indigenous, for instance, or a matter of import? And "guilt". . . ?

Several of the Germans propose a toast to Philip, in German, but Professor Eisenach demands to know if Dr. Schoen is mocking them? What can such sympathy mean?

"But Professor, we are foolish to question sympathy, from any quarter!" Frau Lütz says chidingly.

"You carried it off quite well," Philip tells Cecilia quietly on their way back to the Hotel Zur Birke. His voice is just perceptibly slurred; there is a slight drag to his heels. But clearly he is in high spirits—a good deal of his soul has been restored.

Cecilia doesn't ask what he means. She says, "And so did you."

But Philip, keyed up, nervous, isn't ready to end the day, the long festive celebratory evening. He finds his hotel room depressing, as he has said several times, would Cecilia care to have a final drink, a nightcap, at that Rathskeller up the street. . . ? Philip is pale, smiling, aging around the eyes, a wifeless husband, a lover without a beloved, clearly deserving of female sympathy. But Cecilia is suffused with a sense of irony as if her very flesh might laugh; Cecilia draws unobtrusively away. They have not touched since that awkward meeting in the hotel corridor—they have hardly dared look at each other all evening. Cecilia understands that it falls to her to assuage this man's guilt for thinking her despoiled by denying the very premise for such thinking, she understands that he is eager as a small child to be assuaged, eager to believe whatever she tells him; but she does not intend to tell him anything.

They are standing in front of the Hotel Zur Birke, a solitary tourist couple, apparently indecisive about what to do next. It is late, past midnight, the wind has picked up, clearly Mainz is not Frankfurt or Berlin in terms of its nightlife, why not give up, why not simply go to bed? But Philip doesn't want to go to bed alone. Philip seems to be frightened of being alone. He detains Cecilia, asking what she thought of the Germans at dinner. Wasn't it all supremely revealing? The casual remarks as well as the political—? That quintessential Germanness he'd find amusing if it weren't so terrifying—the secret gloating pride in their blood, in their race—in sin, guilt, history, whatever they choose to call it—

Cecilia surprises him by laughing, laughing almost heartily, as she slips past him and enters the hotel.

There, in her room on the third floor, she falls asleep almost at once, as soon as she turns out the light and finds a comfortable position in her bed. She will not be accompanying Philip to West Berlin the next day—she will make her own arrangements at the Frankfurt Airport to fly back home. It should not be very difficult, she thinks; even informing Philip about her decision should not be very difficult. She supposes he will understand.

He will never have to touch me again, she thinks.

Released, profoundly relieved, she sinks through diaphanous layers of sleep, aware of herself sinking, drifting downward, her physical weight dissolved. She sees a creek out of her childhood—the St. Joachim—she smells the wet, newly mowed grass in the cemetery where both her parents are buried—she hears her Aunt Edie's voice raised in welcome: Cecilia, a child of eight or nine, shyly poking her head into her aunt's kitchen, standing on the rear porch, holding the screen door open. It is summer but quite windy. Raindrops the size of golf balls are pelting the roof. A river has overflowed its banks, a lake has overflowed, the very light is strange, pale and glowering, a sunken city is rising slowly to the surface, a city of spires, towers, old battlements, partly in ruins, blackened by fire . . . and now a cathedral of massive dimensions, its highest tower partly crumbled, its edifice stark and grim . . . and now a cobblestone street, puddled with bright water that strikes the eye like flame . . . Cecilia, alone, is half-running along the empty street, she is both relieved that it is empty and on the brink of terror, for what if she is lost?—Yet she cannot be lost since she seems to know where she is headed, hurrying forward as if in full possession of her senses, looking neither to the left nor the right. She is barefoot, only partly dressed. She is breathless with fear. No matter, she seems to know where she is going, behind her footsteps suddenly sound, close behind her, overtaking her, but she does not intend to turn her head.

MAGAZINES CONSULTED

Action/Image, 266 12th Street, Apartment 12, Brooklyn, N.Y. 11215
The Agni Review, P.O. Box 229, Cambridge, Mass. 02238
Amazing Science Fiction Stories, P.O. Box 110, Lake Geneva, Wisc. 53147
Antaeus, Ecco Press, 1 West 30th Street, New York, N.Y. 10001
Anthology Magazine, Box 1100, Brooklyn, Mich. 49230
Antietam Review, 33 West Washington Street, Hagerstown, Md. 21740
The Antioch Review, P.O. Box 148, Yellow Springs, Ohio 45387
The Apalachee Quarterly, P.O. Box 20106, Tallahassee, Fla. 32304
Arizona Quarterly, University of Arizona, Tucson, Ariz. 85721
Ascent, Department of English, University of Illinois, Urbana, Ill. 61801
Asimov's Science Fiction Magazine, Davis Publications, 380 Lexington Avenue, New York, N.Y. 10017
The Atlantic, 8 Arlington Street, Boston, Mass. 02116
Beacon, 51 Fairmont Street, Cambridge, Mass. 02139
Black Ice, 571 Howell Avenue, Cincinnati, Ohio 45220
Black Maria, P.O. Box 25187, Chicago, Ill. 60625-0187
The Black Warrior Review, P.O. Box 2936, University, Ala. 34586
The Bloomsbury Review, 2933 Wyandot Street, Denver, Colo. 80211
Boston Review, 991 Massachusetts Avenue, Cambridge, Mass. 02138
California Quarterly, 100 Sproul Hall, University of California, Davis, Cal. 95616
Canadian Fiction Magazine, P.O. Box 46422, Station G, Vancouver, B.C., Canada V6R 4G7
Carolina Quarterly, Greenlaw Hall 066-A, University of North Carolina, Chapel Hill, N.C. 27514
The Chariton Review, The Division of Language and Literature, Northeast Missouri State University, Kirksville, Mo. 63501
Chicago Review, 970 East 58th Street, Box C, University of Chicago, Chicago, Ill. 60637
Christopher Street Magazine, 249 Broadway, New York, N.Y. 10007
Cimarron Review, Oklahoma State University, Stillwater, Okla. 74074
Clockwatch Review, 737 Penbrook Way, Hartland, Wisc. 53021
Colorado Review, Department of English, Colorado State University, Fort Collins, Colo. 80523

Confrontation, Department of English, C. W. Post of Long Island University, Greenvale, N.Y. 11548

Cosmopolitan, 224 West 57th Street, New York, N.Y. 10019

Denver Quarterly, Department of English, University of Denver, Denver, Colo. 80210

Descant, Department of English, Texas Christian University, Fort Worth, Tex. 76129

The Echo, P.O. Box 40, Media Center, Huntsville, Tex. 77340

Epoch, 254 Goldwyn Smith Hall, Cornell University, Ithaca, N.Y. 14853

Esquire, 2 Park Avenue, New York, N.Y. 10016

Fiction, Department of English, The City College of New York, New York, N.Y. 10031

Fiction 84, Exile Press, P.O. Box 1768, Novato, Cal. 94948

Fiction International, Department of English, St. Lawrence University, Canton, N.Y. 13617

Fiction Network, P.O. Box 5651, San Francisco, Cal. 94101

The Fiddlehead, The Observatory, University of New Brunswick, P.O. Box 4400, Fredericton, N.B., Canada E3B 5A3

Five Fingers Review, 100 Valencia Street, Suite #303, San Francisco, Cal. 94103

Forum, Ball State University, Muncie, Ind. 47306

Four Quarters, La Salle College, Philadelphia, Pa. 19141

FM. Five, P.O. Box 882108, San Francisco, Cal. 94188

Gargoyle, P.O. Box 3567, Washington, D.C. 20007

Gentlemen's Quarterly, 350 Madison Avenue, New York, N.Y. 10017

The Georgia Review, University of Georgia, Athens, Ga. 30602

The Glens Falls Review, The Loft, 42 Sherman Avenue, Glens Falls, N.Y. 12801

Grain, Box 1154, Regina, Saskatchewan, Canada S4P 3B4

Grand Street, 50 Riverside Drive, New York, N.Y. 10024

Gray's Sporting Journal, 205 Willow Street, P.O. Box 2549, South Hamilton, Mass. 01982

Great River Review, 211 West 7th, Wirona, Minn. 55987

The Greensboro Review, University of North Carolina, Greensboro, N.C. 27412

Guest Editor, 179 Duane Street, New York, N.Y. 10013

Harper's Magazine, 2 Park Avenue, New York, N.Y. 10016

Hawaii Review, Hemenway Hall, University of Hawaii, Honolulu, Hawaii 96822

The Hudson Review, 65 East 55th Street, New York, N.Y. 10022

In Writing, The Publications Board, Stanford University, Stanford, Cal. 94305

Indiana Review, 316 North Jordan Avenue, Bloomington, Ind. 47405

Iowa Review, EPB 453, University of Iowa, Iowa City, Iowa 52240

Kansas Quarterly, Department of English, Kansas State University, Manhattan, Kans. 66506

The Kenyon Review, Kenyon College, Gambier, Ohio 43022

Ladies' Home Journal, 641 Lexington Avenue, New York, N.Y. 10022

The Literary Review, Fairleigh Dickinson University, Teaneck, N.J. 07666

Mademoiselle, 350 Madison Avenue, New York, N.Y. 10017

The Magazine of Fantasy and Science Fiction, Box 56, Cornwall, Conn. 06753

Magical Blend, P.O. Box 11303, San Francisco, Cal. 94010

Malahat Review, University of Victoria, Victoria, B.C., Canada

The Massachusetts Review, Memorial Hall, University of Massachusetts, Amherst, Mass. 01002

McCall's, 230 Park Avenue, New York, N.Y. 10017

Memphis State Review, Department of English, Memphis State University, Memphis, Tenn. 38152

Michigan Quarterly Review, 3032 Rackham Building, University of Michigan, Ann Arbor, Mich. 48109

Mid-American Review, 106 Hanna Hall, Bowling Green State University, Bowling Green, Ohio 43403

Midstream, 515 Park Avenue, New York, N.Y. 10022

The Missouri Review, Department of English, 231 Arts and Sciences, University of Missouri, Columbia, Mo. 65211

Mother Jones, 607 Market Street, San Francisco, Cal. 94105

MSS, State University of New York at Binghamton, Binghamton, N.Y. 13901

The Nantucket Review, P.O. Box 1234, Nantucket, Mass. 02554

New Directions, 80 Eighth Avenue, New York, N.Y. 10011

New England Review and Breadloaf Quarterly, Box 179, Hanover, N.H. 03755

New Letters, University of Missouri–Kansas City, Kansas City, Mo. 64110

New Mexico Humanities Review, The Editors, Box A, New Mexico Tech., Socorro, N.M. 57801

The New Renaissance, 9 Heath Road, Arlington, Mass. 02174

The New Yorker, 25 West 43rd, New York, N.Y. 10036

The North American Review, University of Northern Iowa, 1222 West 27th Street, Cedar Falls, Iowa 50613
Northwest Review, 129 French Hall, University of Oregon, Eugene, Ore. 97403
The Ohio Review, Ellis Hall, Ohio University, Athens, Ohio 45701
Omni, 909 Third Avenue, New York, N.Y. 10022
The Ontario Review, 9 Honey Brook Drive, Princeton, N.J. 08540
Other Voices, 820 Ridge Road, Highland Park, Ill. 60035
Outerbridge, English Department, The College of Staten Island, 715 Ocean Terrace Staten Island, N.Y. 10301
The Paris Review, 541 East 72 Street, New York, N.Y. 10021
The Partisan Review, 128 Bay State Road, Boston, Mass. 02215/552 Fifth Avenue, New York, N.Y. 10036
The Pennsylvania Review, University of Pittsburgh, Department of English, 526 C.L., Pittsburgh, Penn. 15260
Phylon, 223 Chestnut Street, S.W., Atlanta, Ga. 30314
Playboy, 919 North Michigan Avenue, Chicago, Ill. 60611
Playgirl, 3420 Ocean Park Boulevard, Suite 3000, Santa Monica, Cal. 90405
Ploughshares, Box 529, Cambridge, Mass. 02139
Prairie Schooner, Andrews Hall, University of Nebraska, Lincoln, Nebr. 68588
Quarterly West, 312 Olpin Union, University of Utah, Salt Lake City, Utah 84112
Raritan, 165 College Avenue, New Brunswick, N.J. 08903
Reconstructionist, Church Road and Greenwood Avenue, Wyncote, Penn. 19095
Redbook, 230 Park Avenue, New York, N.Y. 10017
River City Review, P.O. Box 34275, Louisville, Ken. 40232
Salamagundi, Skidmore College, Saratoga Springs, N.Y. 12866
San Francisco Focus, 500 8th Street, San Francisco, Cal. 94103
San Francisco Review of Books, P.O. Box 33-0090, San Francisco, Cal. 94133
The Seneca Review, P.O. Box 115, Hobart and William Smith College, Geneva, N.Y. 14456
Sequoia, Storke Student Publications Building, Stanford, Cal. 94305
Seventeen, 850 Third Avenue, New York, N.Y. 10022
The Sewanee Review, University of the South, Sewanee, Tenn. 37375
Sinister Wisdom, P.O. Box 1023, Rockland, Maine 04841
Shenandoah: The Washington and Lee University Review, Box 722, Lexington, Va. 24450

The South Carolina Review, Department of English, Clemson University, Clemson, S.C. 29631
South Dakota Review, Box 111, University Exchange, Vermillion, S.D. 57069
Southern Humanities Review, Auburn University, Auburn, Ala. 36830
The Southern Review, Drawer D, University Station, Baton Rouge, La. 70803
Southwest Review, Southern Methodist University Press, Dallas, Tex. 75275
The Spirit That Moves Us, P.O. Box 1585, Iowa City, Iowa 52244
Stories, 14 Beacon Street, Boston, Mass. 02108
Story Quarterly, P.O. Box 1416, Northbrook, Ill. 60062
St. Anthony Messenger, 1615 Republic Street, Cincinnati, Ohio 45210-1298
The Texas Review, English Dept., Sam Houston University, Huntsville, Tex. 77341
13th Moon, Box 309 Cathedral Station, New York, N.Y. 10025
This World, San Francisco Chronicle, 901 Mission Street, San Francisco, Cal. 94103
The Threepenny Review, P.O. Box 335, Berkeley, Cal. 94701
TriQuarterly, 1735 Benson Avenue, Evanston, Ill. 60201
Twilight Zone, 800 Second Avenue, New York, N.Y. 10017
Twin Cities, 7834 East Bush Lake Road, Minneapolis, Minn. 55435
University of Windsor Review, Department of English, University of Windsor, Windsor, Ont., Canada N9B 3P4
U.S. Catholic, 221 West Madison Street, Chicago, Ill. 60606
Vanity Fair, 350 Madison Avenue, New York, N.Y. 10017
The Virginia Quarterly Review, University of Virginia, 1 West Range, Charlottesville, Va. 22903
Vogue, 350 Madison Avenue, New York, N.Y. 10017
Washington Review, Box 50132, Washington, D.C. 20004
Webster Review, Webster College, Webster Groves, Mo. 63119
West Coast Review, Simon Fraser University, Burnaby, B.C., Canada V5A 1S6
Western Humanities Review, Building 41, University of Utah, Salt Lake City, Utah 84112
Wind, RFD Route 1, Box 809, Pikeville, Ky. 41501
Woman's Day, 1515 Broadway, New York, N.Y. 10036
Writer's Forum, University of Colorado, Colorado Springs, Colo. 80907

Yale Review, 250 Church Street, 1902A Yale Station, New Haven, Conn. 06520
Yankee, Dublin, N.H. 03444
Zyzzyva, 55 Sutter Street, Suite 400, San Francisco, Cal. 94104

Printed in the United States
by Baker & Taylor Publisher Services